"**S**ocially deemed as an outcast, a loner, a weirdo and a rebellion of many common sorts. Ryan Vinci takes this novel and dives into the dark gaping butthole of art and pain, reality and mystery, lust and love . . . And he pushes extremely far beyond the line of just what is measured as politically correct. This book is a strong toxic concoction of foul words and strangely poetic insight seen through the perverted eyes of a very controversial and misunderstood man. Spoken through tainted heart and absolute comedic rage, he opens up on his most passionate pleasures, unspeakable vices and grimy thoughts, and lets us vastly explore his poisoned mind in ways we didn't know possible. Let me be the first to say it . . . This novel is not for everyone . . . but then again— neither is he."

— Riot Wallace.

This is a work of fiction. Any similarity between the characters and situations within its pages and places or persons, living or dead, is unintentional and coincidental. This is purely a work of dogmatic and opinionated humor and entertainment . . . Enjoy the ride . . .

PUBLISHING HOUSE OF

CAPSIZING BRYAN ENTERTAINMENT

SEX, DRUGS & IMAGINATION.
Copyright © 2016
By Ryan Vinci.

www.capsizingbryan.bigcartel.com

Sexdrugsimagination@gmail.com

Instagram.com/Capsizingbryan

Book design: by Ryan Vinci

Cover design: by Matt (The Stilts Man) Parsons

Contact: Matt Parsons @ www.stiltsdesigns.com

Edited by: Tiana Bowling

Revised by: Sean Thomas

ISBN: 978-0-9988600-2-2

SEX, DRUGS & IMAGINATION

A LOVE STORY . . .

WRITTEN BY

RYAN VINCI

Dedicated to STM.

"It's only after we've lost everything that we're free to do anything . . ."
                                    — Tyler Durden. Fight Club. 1999

INTRODUCTION:

"Fuck what you believe in, what you stand for, what you think you know or understand. This moment is what's real, right now, this very moment . . . And you will never get this chance again."

T he day was a Sunday, the air was thick and the temperature outside was cold and moist. I found myself walking alone through a silent park. This was not unusual for me, however, on this particular day, I did come across something very out of the ordinary . . . Or should I say someone . . . As I turned the corner at one of my favorite trees that overhung the walkway causing a deep and dark shade consumed path of travel, I saw a man lying by himself with a bottle of Sailor Jerry next to him. He was not dead, just very incoherent. Profoundly drunk, if you will. His breathing was heavy, his eyes ran damp with tears and his words rang strong with passion. I made my way over to him in calmness not to scare the man and cause a violent interaction, but with just enough grace for him to know I was there. He laid unaccompanied on the grass, soaked in urine, crying and chatting with himself.

"I fucked up. I'm very sorry things got so out of control. I fucked up big time." The man repeated to himself a handful of times.

Sorrow cracked in his voice, and pain settled in his lonely presence. This was no common man; I could clearly see that, which made me intrigued. Compelled and confused, actually.

I walked into his eyesight and stood over him, blocking what little light that would shine on his face from the dense branches above as they shifted in the wind, completely devouring him in darkness at certain moments. He drunkenly picked his head up and looked at me . . .

"Do you know who I am?" The man asked me.

"I have no clue who you are, sir. I'm sorry." I said back to him.

"AHHH . . . Don't be sorry, why should you know who I am?" He replied in a heartbroken sting.

"Should I know who you are, mister?" I asked.

He rose like a broken winged bird from his grave of insolence, faced me with a fierce smirk and stared at me for a calm twenty five seconds . . .

"I, I am Ryan Vinci. I am the one that no one talks about, but all wish to love. I am the one who sucked this city dry of every bit of beauty it had and came in the face of the angels that built it. I am the one with the cock, the heart, but mostly the fucking cock. I am the one who begs for death, but gets life instead. I am the reason we all must believe." He spat at his highest volume while flailing about in his piss soaked jeans.

All before he spun around and collapsed right back down to the ground and showered himself in throw up. And that was the day I met . . . Ryan Vinci.

Desperation is not your only peer.
Live in the moment without fear.

I helped him back up from his puke pile and walked him over to the nearest park bench, sat him down and took his bottle of booze.

"What seems to be the trouble, young man?" I asked him.

X

"It's over, Bob . . . It's all fucking over." Ryan responded.

"My name is not Bob." I attempted to say . . .
But before I could, he began to speak again.

"You see, Bob, I had it all. I had everything I ever wanted."

"Then how did you lose it?" I asked.
Ryan pulled a smoke from his pocket, lit it up, took a long drawn out drag and exhaled with force.

"Because I wasn't the person I was said to be." Ryan replied.

"What's your story, Ryan?" I cornered him with a question.
He looked over at me, then at the bottle of liquor in my hand, then back to me, and once more back to the booze. I handed him back the bottle and watched him gulp down the last of the liquor and toss the bottle into the open and empty park.

"My story, Bob . . . My story is a tale which could only be written in a storybook, one that only the Devil himself would enjoy." Ryan said.
It was then, at that very moment, that I knew I was sent here to help this man, care for this man, love this man, and hopefully save this man. I felt, for the very first time in my plot on earth, that this was my purpose.

I could go on and tell you that this man did get the help he needed, the love he obviously deserved, but then I would be lying. Then I would be watering down the story to boost the mindfulness of the audience that happy endings actually do come true. And honestly, I just can't do that. Not because I'm against lying and I stand tall on a white horse of honesty. I lie everyday. But instead of me serving you thousands of words of bullshit and lies, I will get down to the brass truth, for the mere detail that the story must be told in all its purity . . . Ryan died that night. He found himself overly enthralled with too much booze, pussy and drugs, and could no longer go on. However, that being said, the doctors say he didn't die of consumption . . . In fact, he didn't come anywhere close to dying of an overdose caused by the exercise of drug and alcohol abuse. Plainly stated, he died of a broken heart. His body literally followed his hearts need to stop beating, and slowly just shut down. His world went black and no more light would ever come through again . . .

Forget this man,
For this man will always be,
Forgotten.

Lucky for me, for us, and hopefully for the world, I spent the last thirteen hours of Ryan's life listening to his story and writing down every word, as he wanted his story told. And before he took his last breath and his eyes shut forever, he asked me to remind the world of this . . .

"Life is a traumatic act, and none of us are getting out alive."

— Ryan Vinci.

CHAPTER ONE:

"Without our shame, we have no pride, without our hate, we have no love, without our tears, we have no smile."

W hen I finally woke from my drunken blurred somber, I realized I was on the floor, lying on my back with spew clogging my throat and blocking my airways. My eyes struggled to open from this empty black vision that had consumed my sight. I fought to regain my consciousness and release the puke that had flooded my lungs. I turned over to my side and let loose the chocking vomit onto the ground. For a few long and daunting minutes, I laid on the rug gasping for air. I was overwhelmed with a splitting headache. I had vomit on my face, arms, chest, hair and clothing. My thoughts were vacant as I strained my mind for an answer. Expressionless, aphonic and hopeless—I was formally lost, more than I ever thought possible. I had a damp feeling around my penis—I took a look down to my pants . . . Only to learn I had pissed in them. Next to me laid a squandered bottle of liquor and the last cigarette I ever thought I would smoke. It was burnt out from the hard impact. I was wholeheartedly misplaced and longing for a decent conclusion.

How could I have failed at something so idiotic as suicide? What went wrong? This was not the plan, not the plan at all. I must've fucked up? I couldn't formulate any more reasonable deliberations and forced myself up from the polluted pile of puke to which I was self-possessed. I staggered to my feet, walked over to my desk chair and took a comforting seat. Ironically the seat I chose conveniently faced a mirror. And the reflection that I saw was utterly repulsive, to say the least. My grown self with throw up covering my upper body and sitting in a puddle of my own urine. Just the joyous fucking sight I wanted to see after an unsuccessfully finishing act of depression and despair.

I slowly sipped on water, searching my minds knowledge for an answer why? Staring at the worthless and ego-shattering representation of my own self was an eye opener. The produced image of vulnerability I looked upon was downright pathetic and wretched. I asked myself many questions as I sat and gazed into this mirror of insignificant manifestation. What in fact was I actually trying to accomplish with this act of self-centered behavior? Did I really believe that this ending of life was going to get back the only woman I've ever loved? And even if she did come back, what would she think of me now? When my tombstone is placed upon this green-grassed earth; what would I be remembered for? What would I stand for? What was my legacy? FUCK! Did I even have a legacy to leave behind? The only real papered legacy I have is the ability to ingest mass amounts of alcohol, smoke tons of pot, swallow some questionable pills, get strangers to sleep with me, and every once in awhile lay some clever words down on a page in the hopes of impressing my unsatisfied insides. Was there anything to prove my mortal existence?

For almost an hour I sat in my chair asking deep and painful questions to hopefully justify this failed suicide attempt. Wide-awake and shaken, I longed for significance, a reason, or a purpose. I really had nothing that defined me or set me apart from the rest of the world. A feeling that didn't sit well with me at all. Through my many narcissistic choices I managed to lose the most beautiful love of my life, been fired from more jobs than I've ever quit, lost all hope in writing, and most importantly—I forgot what was real . . .

"I'm sorry, Bob . . . I think I might have confused you. In order for you to truly understand and comprehend this story, we are going to have to rewind to the very beginning, back to where it all started. Starting with the actions, the words and the experiences that have led me to this point. Allow me to restart this tale for pure clarity."

My Chaotic Childhood.

"This is no longer what you think is valid and true. This is merely your imagination playing a game with your sense of reality . . . Let's get lost together!"

As a growing child I want to say I was happy, or at least somewhat remotely happy given the turmoil and disorder that surrounded my family. My mother had three children and all of them were boys. I was the youngest of three. When my mother was twenty-two she had her first child; and when she reached the age of twenty-five, she had already given birth to three little boys, which is not an easy burden for any person to hold. For a great portion of our lives my family was socially poverty stricken. We didn't have too much, but we didn't need too much to be happy, we always pulled through as a family. My mother worked her ass off to give us kids the best life she could provide through the means and resources she had available to her; day in and day out. And surprisingly, she did it with a smile on her face.

My mother is one of the most wonderful people I've ever had the pleasure to know. She is honest, caring, sweet, loving, hard working, unselfishly genuine, and the best mother a kid could ever ask for. My mother was wrongfully sucking into a world of unreserved pandemonium, a long exercise of drug use, and suffered both mental and physical abuse from a man that once called himself, her 'Husband.' My mother made sure to always give us kids an abundance of love. Nurtured us in a motherly way and tried her very best to steer us clear from the hard lessons of right and wrong. As a young mother, life for her was anything but easy. She had three little men to raise, not to mention a violent, drug-addicted husband that refused to give her the freedom that she deserved. Unfortunately, struggling seemed to be the only function that ever worked out in her favor. And no matter how hard she tried to break free, she always got forced into a position of degradation and contempt.

My father, 'Fulton,' married my mother when they were both very young, around the age of nineteen I believe. They were always partiers, drinkers, drug enthusiasts and night owls. However, that type of lifestyle cannot consist after having three children. A set of values my mother was willing to abide by (most of the time) just never a set of terms Fulton ever chose to live by. You see . . . My father, Fulton, is a special breed of piece-a-shit. He's a liar, con artist, drug addict, thief, cheater, an abusive alcoholic, a manipulator, and just a down-right cock-sucking asshole! For many years he put my family through hell just to satisfy his own self-centered needs. Never once did he ever stop and apologize for his selfish habits or own up to his many destructive ways. He always kept moving forward in a downward spiral of bullshit, lies and deceit, till he finally slammed face first at rock bottom.

My two brothers, 'Travis' and 'Floyd,' are both older than me, and are uniquely different in every aspect. Growing up, we were not always close as children. We fought and battled much like many brothers do, but always understood we would stand by each other until the end. My eldest brother, Travis, is a very artistic individual. He's calm, he has a genuine care for the ones he loves; and he's just a delight to be around. Travis just always seemed to find himself at the wrong place at the right time. As a youth he chose to surround himself with people who didn't have much value or quality for life. And as you would think he found himself in the world of partying and drugs at a very young age. Travis' father took off when he was a baby, and Fulton took on the responsibility of raising Travis as his own son. However, Fulton would use that information to satisfy his own need for power and control over my mother; and would constantly beat and abuse Travis to spite my mother. Fulton would then turn around and smoke pot with Travis and try to persuade him into believing that the beatings were somehow justified and necessary.

My other brother, Floyd, is the middle child. He is a very different breed all together. He always had a strong sense of anger stemming from the many years of feeling unloved and forgotten as the mild child (which from what I've read, is a common trait for a middle sibling to feel) Floyd is ultimately a great person, don't get me wrong in any sense. He cares deeply about his family, he is a Goddamn ace at everything he does, he has a slightly off sense of humor that I love, and will go through any amount of pain required to protect the ones he loves.

I on the other hand, was always quiet as a child. Not silent, just watched my words very carefully. I found simplicity in the many dark and deep caverns of my imagination, creating fantasies and alternate realities to avoid the one I actually lived in. I also paid very close attention as kid. I watched how people talked, walked, their body language, facial expressions, voice tones, always studying and analyzing. I found comfort and relaxation in my own head.

Growing up, Floyd and I were persistently at each other's throats, fighting, battling and driving my mother fucking crazy. We attempted to pass the blame on each other, but always fell short, and in the end we both took the ass whooping together. As you could imagine, the beatings were always brutal. But there was one type in particular that will forever resonate in my brain. Fulton would sit us side by side, take the head of Floyd and myself, put one hand on each side of us, just on the ear. And with a swift and forceful slam, smack our heads together, ear-to-ear! Five sometimes six hits in a row, reassuring his need for control and supremacy. The deafening sound that would come from that powerful act was downright sight changing. Our eyes went blurry for minutes and our ears would ring for days on end. The lumps that would remain on our heads are indescribable. And that's just to name one event. To give you a list of the many methods Fulton would use to beat us would be a daunting task. One I don't wish to divulge in. However, just to give you a vivid example, I once saw Fulton run into our bedroom naked and drag my brother Floyd to the middle of the street where he beat the shit out of him for ten minutes or so, all while his dick was swinging around, not giving a shit who saw him. A rare breed of piece-of-shit Fulton was!!

There was one common emotion we all shared in my household . . . FEAR! We lived a day-to-day basis with it weighing us down. We were all very aware it wasn't right or vindicated, but none of us had the power to change it or resolve the problem. We just accepted our state of affairs for what it was, and attempted to find some sense of peace in this disorganized and frenzied world we lived in. A good term I feel that described it clearly would be, 'Walking on Egg Shells.' Cliché, I know. However, everyday, before we did or said anything, the first thought that crossed our minds was, "I hope this doesn't get back to Fulton." Even if what you were about to do or say wasn't even remotely close to being wrong. Fulton would make you the victim, the weak, the puppet. He had a sadistic technique of manipulating his way inside your head and making you fear him. He got off by watching others live in his shadow of terror. Somehow he forced his way into the driver's seat of your mind and refused to leave. This was our daily reality and we could either fight it or accept it. No other choices. The credence of fear begins to break you down as a person, just as it did for all of us in one way or another. We all had different coping mechanisms to help us through this time.

Floyd would wile' out and get violent, break shit, curse at my mother, beat the shit out of me, threaten my mother with suicide, and live in relentless anger. I felt for the kid, as we all did. But, as I've said before, we were all powerless. Nothing we could do or say could break us free from these chains of trepidation and panic. We had no choice but to surrender to the terms of our life, as shitty and downright ruthless as they may have been.

My oldest brother, Travis, would seek shelter with his many dubious friends. Hide behind drugs, alcohol and partying to avoid the truth. I don't blame him either. At this particular point in life, had I understood the effects of alcohol and drugs, maybe I would've given into the mind numbing powers of them also. He was always distant as a child. I think at times he felt as if he was the family outcast. So running from any confrontation or problem was a pleasant option for him. Why face something head on, when you can get fucked up with your friends and never have to feel something real? We've all been guilty of that same assessment at some particular point in time.

I coped by losing myself in play, fantasy, daydreams, detaching my mind from what was real. Living in a fool's paradise, if you will. I never confronted my true emotions, thoughts or feelings. Running and running, as fast as I could to get away from my veracity, all while building an angry lion that was boiling inside me and waiting for the moment to be released.

The unending torture, threats, abuse and mind games my mother had to endure was mentally numbing for me as a child. I have always been a momma's boy. And have always found console in the presence of a woman, especially a great woman like my mom. Having to sit helpless and watch her go through such a traumatic and harrowing time was killing me as a kid. I wanted nothing more than to be physically strong enough to protect her from this unexplainable anguish she unfortunately was victim to. However, that being said, I must vocalize this point. My mother is a GODDAMN FIGHTER! She scratched, clawed and bit her way till the cold and bitter end. Never giving up and becoming one of the self-victimizing sleepwalkers that most people become when commanded to suffer such a challenging time. She just kept on fighting through. Knowing and believing that there would be a sunny day at the end of all the bullshit; and sure enough that day finally did come, not for a quite awhile. But nonetheless, the brighter day eventually came . . .

CHAPTER TWO:
Innocence Lost Is Anger Gained.

"I drink to quiet the voices."

— Matty P.

Around the age of ten, I underwent an experience that I wouldn't wish upon even my biggest enemy. Before we get in to it, let me explain a little more about myself. As I was growing up and getting older, I began to realize that my thoughts were changing, developing in variously different manners and were certainly more divergent than the people in my same age group. I was exposed to evil, abuse, heartache and neglect for many years. And all that exposure at a young age caused me to become cold, numb, callous and unreachable by my true emotions. Even at this young age I knew a little more about the real world than I led people to believe. I knew the act of sex and pleasure, I hadn't practiced it, (not including masturbation) but I at least knew what it was, the meaning of it that is. I understood that not everything in this world is full of beauty and splendor. I began to see the world for what it truly is. A caliginous, sad and anguished land filled with disappointment, regret and disgrace. Not this dazzling place full of only good people

21

and glorious times which most children in my age group believed. I understand now as an adult, that a kid at my age should have never been required to see all the things I did to formulate such thoughts, but I can't change the past, what is done is done. I've accepted the reality of the situation and moved on long ago. However, these new and increasing thoughts were relevant in my mind and I couldn't solve them, nor did I really know where to start if I wanted to. I just ran with my dark thoughts and buried myself deep inside my imagination to help me maintain my sanity . . .

My two brothers and I adventured to the local movie theater to watch the latest blockbuster at the time. The title of the film slips my mind at the moment, nor is it important. My two brothers brought two girls with them, which at the time; they were all young and all looking to hook up. No blame is passed there. I understand, take a girl to the movies, make-out for two hours and leave the theater with a sense of satisfaction. Cool! I get it. The seat I ended up getting stuck in was close to the end of the isle, I would say three of four seats from the stairs, then a spare seat between me and my brother, Floyd, and his date to the right of me, and another spare seat between them and my eldest brother and his date. They wanted their space so they could get frisky with each other. Keep in mind. We were all very young, I was ten at the time, which makes Floyd twelve and Travis roughly fourteen. Any real knowledge of the true dangers out in this world was practically nonexistent. We've all been through some shit at this point in life, but still naive to the pure evil that lurked in arms reach.

As the theater lights went dark and the previews came onscreen, I sat patiently, silent and content. Not a care in the world, just awaiting the film to display itself. In the waiting process, an older man entered the theater and walked up the stairs to my isle. To a certain extent, I paid attention to this man. The film, which I had purchased a ticket for, was still not on the screen, so I had some time to kill. 'People watching' is always a pleasant option to pass the time. I just remember thinking to myself. "Please don't sit next to me. I want to stretch out."

His eyes leisurely scanned the theater, searching for something. He was gazing upon all the empty seats, looking up and down the rows. What was it that he was looking for? At that time I had no idea. But, I was harshly about to learn . . . His final decision was to walk up the isle that I had been sitting. He made his way past the three or four open seats to my left and plopped down in the chair directly aside me. I use the word plopped because that was the piercing noise that came out when he lazily took the seat next to me. It was uninhibited seating, very sloppy, strident, led me to believe he may have been intoxicated. As he sat in his seat, he fidgeted in his chair, moving side to side, almost as if he was uncomfortable. Then . . . With a quick and errorless move, he threw his large jacket over his right arm, nearly half of his jacket ending up landing over my left leg and partially over my lap. My eyes squinted in his direction. I wondered to myself. "Kind of a dick move, give me some fucking space." He chose not to acknowledge my stare or presence at all, which I found rather odd. How could a person be so selfishly involved in his own world that he doesn't realize his jacket just ended up halfway into the chair next to him? I was a young child so I avoided confrontation most of the time, not to cause a scene or get in trouble. I just stopped over analyzing the situation and kindly scooted my leg to the right. I was trying to get it out from under his jacket, or at least give it a nudge so maybe he would realize it was no longer in his private space. The music began to rise in volume as the movie was now about to be presented. I remained quite, innocent, excited to see the new film. I didn't think too much about my uncomfortable circumstance.

Just after the film was displayed on the large screen ahead and silence had falling over the theater, the man to my left began to once again squirm in his chair. His hands began to explore underneath his jacket. I could feel the warmth of his hand as it very slowly started to make its way in my direction. My attention was immediately drawn toward his jacket. I was looking for a movement, a minor shuffle, something that could validate his movement was not just a figment of my imagination, anything to justify this creepy man with a wandering hand. My eyes moved from the screen to his jacket, screen to jacket, again and again. Analyzing and examining the situation, I sat alone and determined to find an answer.

"What was going on?" I silently asked myself.

About twenty minutes in to the start of the movie I felt his hand make its way over the handrail that separated our seats, and very slowly and softly he placed his hand onto my leg. He was calm about it, not to ruffle the jacket and draw any attention to him. I had a brief thought of fault pass through my head. "Was it me that was sitting too close?" I asked myself. He began to stroke my leg up and down, soft and slow, back and fourth. I began to sense something was wrong, so without hesitation I slid my left leg closer to my right leg and his hand fell off and bumped my chair. He straightened up his act for a brief couple of minutes. Now with my leg further in distance. He began to fiddle in his seat once more, readjusting his jacket and slowly gliding closer to me. At this point in time, I didn't dwell on it longer than I had to. I thought in my head. "Maybe a mistake, maybe he thought he was stroking his leg."

He calmly regained his jacket and attempted to gather more coverage over my leg, gradually inching his body my way. His hand was now getting more aggressive; his patience's were beginning to wear thin. Almost to say he was getting desperate. He now moved his hand more quickly to my leg. And with a grabbing touch, took a firm hold on my leg, stroking my leg up and down, harder and a bit faster, reaching higher up my leg and getting closer to my penis, up and down, up and down. I had a rush of anxiety take over my mind and my body temperature spiked to an all time high. I began to sweat and shake as his hand moved its way up and down my leg, finally after gathering a trifling bit of courage, I let out a slight jump, nothing too much to alert the attention of others, but hopefully enough to warn him that I am aware of what's happening. I rapidly moved my leg out of his grasp, looked over at my brother Floyd, who was buried face deep, tongue involved with his date.

"Floyd, we need to move seats." I whispered.

The whispers fell upon deaf ears. Once again I attempted to gather his attention. A little bit louder this time.

"Floyd, we need to move seats." I said with more volume.

He stopped his make-out session for a quick second, looked over to me.

"You're fine, relax." Floyd replied.

He was vastly unaware of the circumstances I was dealing with, had he of known, his reply would have not been so nonchalantly muttered. He went back to thrusting his dates face with his tongue and I was once again . . . Alone with this creepy fuck!

The man was now sitting upright, calm and unconcerned, however, vaguely bewildered. I think he could sense the inevitability of his actions and chose to reframe, but only for an instant. I drew my attention back to the screen, as did the man. Seconds felt like hours, and sure enough . . . His hand was wandered back into my lap. But this time reached for my penis. He took a rough hold of my dick with perverted hostility and careless thoughts. I had no choice but to react at this point. I hastily shoved off his hand, stood up and bolted to the right for my brothers. I pushed my way past them causing a brief scene. They got up in a hurry and followed me down the stairs. We stopped just shy of the exit and my brothers asked what was wrong. I resentfully struggled to find the right words to express my discomfort.

"That guy was fucking touching me!" I said to them.

"What guy? What do you mean touching you?" They asked.

They all glanced up to our previous seats; the theater was too dark to distinguish the look of the man.

"He was trying to touch my dick." I responded in a sharp frenzy.

The whole group became overwhelmed with shock and fear. We didn't want to get in trouble because we knew what the consequences would be if Fulton heard we caused an issue. We three boys were vastly lost of a proper resolution to the situation.

"What do you want to do?" Travis asked me.

"Let's just sit somewhere else." I reluctantly answered.

We slowly made our way to the fourth row back from the front of the theater. Except this time I was sandwiched in the middle of everyone, untouchable, unobtainable. They were protecting me. Even though I'm sure they were just as scared as I was, as any fucking child would be in this type of condition. The girls they had with them were also terrified. My oldest brother, Travis, kept his eyes fixed to the top of theater where we once sat, looking for a feeble movement, a face, any form of danger . . .

With a surprise and fright to us all, the man had made his way down the other stairwell of the theater and across the front of the screen. He snuck his way up from the front of the theater and sat two rows ahead of us. I turned to Travis, whose eyes were still scanning the back of the theater.

"That's him! That's him, right there." I spoke to Travis.

Travis' head whips around and his attention was brought up front. The man sat up front, looking forward for a couple long and frightening minutes. Then, the old-creepy-fuck waited for our attention to no longer be directed toward him. However, that was not going to happen. This old man highly underestimated the bond of us brothers. As much as my brothers and I would fight with each other growing up, we still all looked out for one another. This cock-sucking sicko didn't anticipate such a close brotherhood and he got cocky and arrogant.

He didn't wait more than five minutes till he turned around and gave me a piercing stare. His face was aged, damaged, covered in stress lines. He had dark brown hair with silver streaks, and the look in his eyes was evil, wicked and sinister. You could sense the careless abandon pouring out from his presence. He stared at me for three maybe four minutes, not backing down or fixating his eyes on any other person in my group. Travis, Floyd, and the two girls all stared back at him, attempting to make him acknowledge their existence. But this sick fuck didn't flinch, never even broke a sweat. He just continued gawking at me with a blank and twisted eye.

Travis took it upon himself to find a resolution to our current situation and making the right judgment call. He looked at all of us kids.

"Let's get the fuck out of here!" Travis said.

We all stood up together and headed for the door in a hurry, franticly looking over our shoulders until we finally made it far away from that theater and to a safe hold. Travis made a phone call to our mother, explained the existing turmoil we were in. And minutes later I was home. When I arrived home, my mother and grandmother both tried there hardest to get me to stop crying, but the damage was done. Tears flowed from my eyes as I struggled to find the right words to describe to them what happened. They explained to me the evil that is out in this world, the importance of being responsible and understanding the right time to say something. With their long talks and the love they gave, I did eventually move on. It took months, but nevertheless, I did, in conclusion advance. And I thank and love them everyday for that. Without their care, who knows what would have happened to me? Although, in retrospect, I had no choice but to move on, as shitty and nauseating as it was to live through those forty-five minutes of humiliation. After all was said and done, I was still part of a bigger problem in my own household. Fulton still lingered around, waiting his turn to spit out some contradicting and puzzling, sanctimonious bullshit from his cocaine clenched jaw.

When Fulton eventually caught wind of the story, two weeks later that is (being as how he was never a prominent individual in our family) his attendance was always absorbed with running from drug den to strip club to fulfill his own selfish needs. But, when he did hear about the episode, he of course had to put in his two hoity-toity cents. This was always ranging from variously different peeks of emotions depending on the existing drug and high of choice he was on at that particularly moment. I remember it as clear as it was yesterday. He sat me down; we stared at one another, eye to eye. He smelt of Vodka and had terrible cocaine breath. You would think, with his constant drug and alcohol consumption, that he would be a bit more creative and articulate. Instead, he looked me in the eye, without an ounce of concern or care . . .

"Where do you feel you went wrong?" Fulton puked out this fucking question.

I didn't respond. **FUCK!** I couldn't respond. I was paralyzed by his question. The words to that question should've never been directed in my corner for answer in the first place. How this heartless experience, was somehow remotely my fault, was absolutely baffling to me. I remember thinking this exact thought to myself, as I looked him in the eye. "How the fuck are you so calm and collective after hearing about the cruelty which just took place on your own son? Why are you not up in arms, searching the world for this man and bringing end to his worthless life?"

At this point in life, I was very conscious of what murder was (via books, video games, television, film, et cetera) of course, I didn't know of the harsh penalty which comes after murder, or how to even perform the physical art of it. But I knew what it meant to end a life. They no longer would be a part of this world. And at the age of ten . . . I was ok with that! I saw no wrong in that. And still see no wrong in the death of that man. If I was to tell you that not a day has gone by that I don't wish total harm, complete pain, and extreme, EXTREME SUFFERING on that man. I would be lying. I don't feel another kid should have to endure the agony I did, just so the police can possibly catch him, put him through our exceptionally flawed justice system, watch him serve six-months in jail, and be out on the streets preying on the young once again.

"I ask you, Bob . . . WHERE THE FUCK IS THE TRUE JUSTICE IN THAT? NONEXISTENT, THAT'S WHERE!"

CHAPTER THREE:

My Three Years of Clarity.

"Teach a person a lesson in blood and I promise you that lesson will never be forgotten"

Not too long after that dramatic and vivid living nightmare I so unjustly had to be a victim to. The violence, fighting, alcohol and drug use continued in my household. Fulton was burning his candle from both ends and the conclusion to his madness was near. He knew it, my mother knew it, and to a certain extent, we all knew it. He had burned every bridge he ever stepped fucking foot on. He owed money all around town, had enemies everywhere he went. There was no more proverbial home for him anymore. He drank, snorted, smoked and fucked everything this town had to offer him. He had turned my mother against him through his steady cheating, domestic violence and lies. I found myself less and less concerned about his wellbeing and health. He felt the edge of the plank, so to speak; and it was sink or swim time. So . . . In true Fulton fashion, he did what he always does. He manipulated my brother Floyd, into a road trip with promises of a better life, streets paved in gold, blue skies and perky tittys. And they embarked on a cross-country road trip to the great state of Florida (I say with pure irony) I can still remember it as brilliantly as my first erection.

The bright yellow moving truck pulled up to our two-story apartment. We lived on the second floor, corner unit. I sat in the window gazing out. Fulton didn't climb up the stairs. He was not welcome in our home, my mother made that exclusively clear. She was already losing one son to his con-artistry; she wasn't about to lose anymore. Nor did anyone care to see him off if he did come up the stairs. I watched out the window as he had this shit eating grin on his face in the street. He was always an arrogant prick! My mother gave Floyd the most heartfelt, endearing and loving hug that you can give a person, with tears in her eyes and pain consuming her soul; she had to watch as her second born son left to be with his father. It was a dreadful time for her, and all of us for that matter. Travis was nowhere to be found at this moment, just as most times. He had no concerns to see Fulton off. And for good reason, all Travis ever got from Fulton was regret, abuse, neglect and hate. I don't blame him. My mother and I sat and watched Floyd jump into the moving truck and drive away into the distance. She must've cried for two weeks after that. She would catch herself breaking down while performing the most trivial human acts like making food for us or walking to her car. The pain she must've felt can't be described by anyone. All I knew for sure was, I was tired of watching her cry because of the torment this man that once called himself her husband, put her through. It was fucking heartbreaking.

After the burn of this catastrophic event moderately faded (as much as it possibly could) we all felt a weight lifted from our shoulders. And it was very freeing. We could all finally breathe. The household found happiness again, bittersweet happiness, but nevertheless, a slight form of happiness. We found our smiles again. We didn't have to live day in and day out in dread. The tension weakened and we all regained our composure, if only for a moment. My mother and I were getting seemingly close again and that feeling was inexpressible. We were having fun again, being free, enjoying the company of each other and the good times we had with one another. No longer did we feel like victims of our circumstance. As the days slid off the calendar, the damage slowly began to repair itself. Not necessarily repair, but at least the pain had settled down some. And we were once again, a 'Family.' My mother still had the task of two children to raise and nurture. And she was still working nonstop, always striving toward the greater good for her family, herself, and our overall security. It was a simpler time. A lot less aggression is a great definition. The chains of control and power were no longer our only friend; we all had freedom, and it felt absolutely marvelous.

She found well-deserved comfort in the arms of another man. One who loved and adored us kids. He was always kind and honest with my mother. Which I'm sure was a refreshing change for her. I was now let out into this world to be a kid again. And that I found so damn gratis, maybe a little too much, because no matter what the occasion . . . I somehow always found myself in trouble. I was a smart mouthed little shit with my teachers, a skateboard wielding punk with no regard for the law or authority. But, it was just what kids in my age group did at that time. We didn't mean any harm, just wanted to ruffle a few feathers, run from a couple cops, break a few windows and enjoy this uncomplicated time. Marijuana was the drug of choice in the circle of friends that I ran with. However, I never chose to experiment with pot until I was much older. We would sneak a beer or two from time to time, but it wasn't about getting fucked up at that point in growth; it was just about having some reckless fun. We would ditch a class or two, laugh at fat people, stupid mindless shit that kids do. Everything in life, may I say it? Was fucking perfect! When I speak of 'My Three Years of Clarity.' I mean just that. The time my family had to gather our thoughts, get back to ground zero and be victimless from the nonstop, unremitting tragedy and anarchy which consumed us for so many years, was

33

completely and utterly fucking beautiful. I understand I may be straining the same point twice. But I can't stress enough the liberation and humbling feeling we all shared.

Around the age of thirteen, my middle brother Floyd had returned back from Florida. With stories of his own anguish, and I'm sure some psychological damage that he refused to tell anyone. Nevertheless, this story I am telling you, isn't about him. His time spent in Florida with Fulton, is his and his alone. We lived out our time as a wholesome and happy family. We all smiled when giving the chance, laughed when we felt comfortable. And showed love to one another when the time presented itself. We were never perfect. No fucking family is, but we had each other and that was all we needed to survive. More than I can say for the multimillion-dollar empire families out there. We never needed money to be happy. Don't get me wrong money does help. However, money was not the main focus of our family's happiness. We stood by one another trough thick and thin. We did then and we do now. Consider that my first ostentatious, pretentious and brazen statement of why my family is better than yours. Ha-ha-ha . . . Sorry . . . I had to laugh at that . . .

Just before my closely approaching fourteenth birthday, Fulton invited my two brothers and me out to Florida to visit him for Christmas. He wanted to prove to us kids, my mother doubts (and I still believe to this day) his own magnified ego, how faultless and mature he had become as an adult. My mother deliberated the thought for a week or so, going through every possible scenario and every reason why and how it could go wrong. Which, I must say, I don't blame her. Fuck! Giving the unconditional hell this abusive con artist put her through; wouldn't you question his entire shit covered word? Fulton stood for nothing, fell for anything, ruined and deceived everyone. What would you do? But, as reluctant as she was, she agreed to let us fly over for a week to spend Christmas with our so-called 'Father.' She felt a bit of sympathy for the poor bastard. As I think we all did from time to time. Even though that was merely because of his manipulating, influencing and self-satisfying ways he would trick you into feeling empathy for him. Which was all fucking bullshit if you ask me? She knew in her heart, and in her mind, this wasn't a good idea. As many warnings and red flags she could've told us to look out for. There was nothing, and I mean enormously fucking <u>nothing</u> in this world, that would've prepared me for the desolation and wreckage that was about to ensue . . .

Give a dog from the street,
Just one treat,
Watch him eat,
Then, he'll go for your feet.
Once you fall to the floor,
He'll bite you sore.
You'd better be smart,
Because next is your heart.

CHAPTER FOUR:
My Christmas Trip with Fulton.

"Where the fuck do I begin? That question is exclusively and wholly directed toward my inner soul, or at least what's left of my cold, dark and black soul. With a cigarette burning in the ashtray to my left, a stiff Sailor Jerry and Coke poured to my right, my fingers struggle to find the words to tell this story . . . Let us fucking start!"

W hen my two brothers and I traversed to the state of Florida, I was already on edge. My experiences and encounters at this point in life had left me frustrated, meaningless, angry, and more importantly my sense of this professed 'Home,' was lost in the abyss. As pleasant and calm as I found myself living with my mother in a civilized channel of peace and tranquility, I still longed for more. I was a young, easily influenced and a tremendously brain-washable child. I had no inner strength. Not mind, body or soul. My lack of confidence left me out in the open, heart on the sleeve type of person, to give it a proper definition. I unfortunately needed what every child at my convincible age desired. I needed a Father. One to protect me, teach me how to shave, love me after I lose my first fight, and support me during my first breakup.

"Cry for help much?"

"Fuck you, Bob! Just listen—"

The week we all spent together in Florida was seemingly genuine and real, it was almost to say, 'fucking normal.' At that very moment in time, we all had a father. Fulton, for the first time, in a very long time, had his head on straight. He was respectful, caring, and sensible. We didn't feel scared. The dark cloud of fear that followed us for so many years had dissipated. The sun beat upon our arms and the blazing flame of distress was no longer blinding. We were a generated family, and I must say . . . It felt fucking great. He was present in the period that we all shared together. The outrageous moments of him flying off the wall in cocaine induced hostility was sidelined, put to rest if only for a fleeting moment. Fulton treated us all very well for that coming week. He followed suit in the fatherly duties of entertaining us, having concern for our wellbeing, embracing in our interests and caring for our opinion. It was magic. Granted it was nothing more than a well-purposed, methodically thought-out act. A melodramatic show of gratis behavior, but who were we to question the real difference . . . Or should I say whom the fuck was I to know the difference? He took us to all different places of enjoyment in Florida. We went go carting, paint balling, fed the gators, did some fishing, and raced little remote control cars. We did more in that short trip than I think Fulton's ever done with us kids throughout our whole lives. All this loving and fun, 'Fatherly Compound' performance I was witnessing, was really starting to get to me from the inside. Something was changing inside me, and I was looking for an opportunity to embrace that change.

That week past with the blink of an eye, as many moments do when things seem to be indisputably real and fun, and before you knew it the day of our flight home had promptly approached. We all sat in the bedroom of his house tending to the chore of packing our suitcases for the long trip home. Well . . . Two of us three children loaded a bag for flight. I chose, with every fiber of my being to stay, to create, and to live out a new life in Florida. Without a courtesy phone call back to my mother in California about the recent change in development, we four sat in the airport of Daytona Florida. My two brothers attempted the best they could to hide their real feelings of doubt and shame in my choice of lifestyle modification. They would slip in comments when they got a quick and brief opportunity.

"Are you sure you want to do this?" They would ask me.

"Yes, I know what I'm doing." I shortly answered.

And to state the record! I really did trust the words that so stylishly and candidly fell from my tongue.

The plane that I should've been on took off without a hitch. And just as I have felt alone in so many different occurrences in my life, I was now wholeheartedly, outright, enthusiastically and undisputedly, 'FUCKING ALONE!' Stuck in an inconceivable prison to deal with my selfish choices, ready to accept my punishment and face the consequences that were mine to take. The cost of my perplexing and unfathomable decision was about to unfold itself before my very eyes in a way I never knew imaginable . . .

Leave me behind to find my ace,
For this is my place.
I don't ask for help,
Nor will I ever yelp.
Love down,
Sad frown,
Hate pound,
And me found.

CHAPTER FIVE:

My Year with Fulton: Part One.

"The intoxicating Sailor Jerry Rum has hit its sweet spot as the cigarettes have begun to collect in the ashtray. The preparatory words are starting to blur as they fall upon the bright-lit screen ahead. Love me till the end of time."

On the very quiet and staggeringly unanswerable ride back from the airport with Fulton, to this new land which I was to call 'My Home,' and the new adventures that I was going to claim as my own, we didn't say but two words to each other. The bleakness was our comfort, our friend, and solely our demise. Fulton stopped at a liquor store on the trip back home and purchased a container of orange juice and three single shot plastic bottles of cheap Vodka. He proceeded to empty out just enough liquid from the orange juice and filled the rest with Vodka. As we drove down the long and empty highways of Florida, I felt a sense of resentment. I think he had a feeling that the party was over, the fat lady has sung her last note and this was now his reality. Reduced to taking care of this snotty-nosed bastard he calls his son. The tension was thick, the air outside was hot and humid, the Vodka was Black-woman-strong and the feelings from both parties were vastly scrambled. I was very

SEX, DRUGS & IMAGINATION

observant as a young child, I paid attention; it's fucking free for God sakes! I didn't need a Ph.D. to feel the mourning in the car. His party had finally died. You would probably feel the same sorrow also if your nonstop party lifestyle just got cock-slapped to death by an imposing little shithead. Nevertheless, the realism of the situation was relevant. "No going back now." I think is the deliberation that both minds in the car commonly shared. I wanted nothing more than to have a real father, and the understanding of his needs were still unclear to me.

The minute we arrived to his house my mother had already called six maybe seven times, leaving annoyed and confused voicemails. My brothers snuck in a phone call at the airport before their flight took off and they had alerted her of the new dynamic of circumstances. She was angry—Go figure? I don't blame her . . . Fulton was just as overwhelmed with the new found information as she was. He tried his best to explain to her that this was not his choice; he was not playing some game of manipulation to win the heart of the youngest child. This was my choice, my idea, purely my decision. But, he somehow (surprisingly) fell short with the right words to express that point. Which was not like him at all, that son of a bitch could sell ice to an Eskimo. He could sweet-talk even the tightest-assed Jew into running to the bank to give him a loan. After a long and tedious conversation, with the phone being past back and fourth between Fulton and I, she was forced to deal with the situation the best she could. I wasn't leavening, she wasn't clear of my motives (nor was I at the time) all I did know was; I was there to see what my Father had to prove to me as a man, and I wasn't leaving there till I got my Goddamn answer, whatever that conclusion may be. The response my mother was looking for wasn't uncovered during our chat and she had no choice but to accept the nature of the beast, as world changing as it may've been.

The next morning of our new adventure was blurry and indistinct. I was a fresh-faced child with more to lose than I ever thought. I had the world at my fingertips, the wind behind my sails, and many lessons to learn. What was a drug addicted father to do? He really had no fucking clue. What a shocker? So, the baffled motherfucker proceeded with this . . .

"Do you want to go to school?" Fulton asked.
I contemplated that sentence for several minutes. Just the sheer fact alone that a parent would actually present that question to a young child, and not to ruin the ending but (I was never really a big follower or advocate in the whole school system to begin with) so his question was disreputable to me beyond belief.

"I would rather not." I answered.

"Ok. Well, I have to enroll you or else your mother will kill me." He quickly answered, without much concern in my overall education.

And just like that, without haste we were on the road to search for a fitting school. The school of choosing was of my selection and I picked it because I thought it looked cool, however, knew wholeheartedly, I had no real intentions of ever attending this establishment. This was merely a kind act to silence my mother's doubts of Fulton's parenting skills. We walked in, enrolled, had the formal teacher, parent, student introduction and we were on our way. The school didn't start for a couple days, which left us with plenty of time on our hands to get into some trouble. Fulton was waist deep in his recent con-artistry business of his current fixation. And at that point in time, was an auto body shop just on the outskirts of town. I rather enjoyed going to these shady business deals, it was much fun for a kid of my age. I felt a sense of power, looking up upon my dad, watching him talk, act, walk with confidence and pride, controlling the conversation and making these people believe that they were making the right choice. It was thrilling; and wouldn't you know it. The deal closed right on time and just a few short days after the lease was signed, doors were opened and the place was ready for business.

Around the same time of opening the business doors was my first day of the bloody eighth grade. I dreaded the day actually coming to fruition. But here it was and I had to attend. I took a hold of my backpack and made my way to the bus stop. I had no friends (seeing as how I was hanging out with nothing but adults since I decided to stay) so the feeling was a bit lonely at the stop. All the kids were chatting with each other about some stupid bullshit that happened over the past break and I was never the wiser. I was the pungent outcast at the bus stop. And for some reason it didn't bother me. This whole school shit was beyond me. I had a small sense of fear but it didn't stop me from boarding that bus once it finally arrived. As we pulled up to my new and exciting school, I was a bit careless. Anything that could happen today would never break me down or even compare to the things I've already gone through. I knew in my head I was mentally stronger than most of my class put together; so I approached it as nothing more than another obstacle in my battle of life. Didn't mean shit to me. A very bad way to approach school, and my overall education for that matter, but who was I to know any better?

I attended my classes as instructed and before you knew it the lunch bell had rung out and the entire school found themselves sitting in the cafeteria. I was the new kid, which in most cases means the unappealing dipshit-loser sitting alone in the corner. However, in this small, Podunk, backwards-ass, country school of Florida, I was the main fucking attraction. I found myself surround by a fleet of cute girls, a couple cool male friends, and the conversation was amusing, fresh and electrifying. I'll never forget this day. A small, fragile, timid little boy walks up to my table to tell me a little secret his friends had bestowed upon him. I must add; I was strangely tall, very pale, and a sickly thin looking teenager. I had acne on my face and thick curly hair atop my head, an Afro to be more precise. I was not a sight to be seen by any

44

means. But, I walked with swagger, I owned it, it was who I was and I didn't mind. That was my image and I didn't care much at all. He butts in on our conversation and points over to his two buddies, two 'Insane Clown Posse' looking faggots.

"Hey, my friends wanted me to tell you that Halloween is over and you should take off the mask. Ha-ha-ha." This little dick strangler says to me.

My table stops in stun! They were beside themselves as they awaited my clever answer. This was my moment to prove myself and I had to step up. So, I kindly responded the best way I knew how, in true California-fashion, with some Los Angeles anger and bravado.

"Go tell your friends that I fucked both their mothers' anally!" I said to the little fucker.

That little shithead walked away and perfectly whispered to his two buddies my foul answer verbatim. They all looked over to my table with a snarling face of disrespect and ill repute. Honestly... With the look those kids gave me, you would've thought I had just fucked their mothers' anally or something.

"I will admit to you, Bob, because I feel like we're getting to know each other. I was scared shitless, but it was important I held my ground and didn't show my true fear. I didn't want to show any signs of weakness in front of my new and easily replaceable friends that I was in fact — An overall pussy!"

"Of course."

After the last bell had rung out and school was vacated, I RAN my fucking ass to the bus stop, jumped on that bus and went home.

When I arrived home, I told Fulton I didn't want to go to school anymore. School in itself as an entity was stupid; they couldn't teach me anything I couldn't learn on my own, I was ready to be a man. Any fucking excuse I could come up with and pull out of my book of lies to never have to go back to that school and probably get the most savage assbeating I legitimately deserved for my polluted and ill-mannered words. And just as easy as that, I didn't have to attend another day of eighth grade while I resided Florida. I laugh it off now because chances are those fucking assholes became drug addicts, probably overdosed once or twice, and they're either locked up in jail for some heinous crime committed on the innocent, or dead by now. That seemed to be all that decrepit state would breed. A whole state constantly producing nothing but fuckups, scumbags, degenerates and hate-monger's, at least from my own perspective, but who am I to judge. But, if not, I wish them the best. HA! No I don't. Fuck 'em for trying to bitch me out.

In hindsight, I should've returned back to school and took the asswhooping I was rightfully going to be awarded like a man. Over the next several months I was going to suffer through a much more unpleasant time of utter confusion that the friendly beating of my ass would have been a fair punishment compared to the real pain and metal perplexity I was about to undergo. But, I digress —

After I dropped out of the eighth grade, Fulton invited me to join him side by side as his 'Right Hand Man' in his recent shady, warped, distorted and most likely highly profitable (for the moment) exhibition of a self-styled business scheme. I benevolently agreed, seeing as how I really didn't have any other future plans or aspirations holding me back now. I took a firm hold of the rains in my current position of power (or so I thought was power) and I held on with dear FUCKING life. I was at the mercy, the will and ultimately the demolishing of this choosing of fate that I was so eager to execute. Prove my worth as a man, my loyalty, feel the absolute supremacy of a King. There I stood, head high, feet planted solid on the ground, and there was . . ."No fucking turning back now." I had to accept the blood which ran fat and grave through my veins, acknowledge what I was as an existence, a person, a man; beyond the restrains of civilization, beyond law, and most importantly; beyond death. We headed off to work to instruct his employees to the day-to-day activities of the business. A business that he had no fucking clue how to run, but— 'Fake It Till You

Make It,' was his business model. He had what I like to call today, 'A Good Support System,' even if all of them were drug addicts and dealers.

Fulton's main body man at the shop was 'Jeff.' He was a short, toothless, chain-smoking and scratchy voiced, dirty Floridian. Jeff was married to a woman named 'Karma.' She was a vibrant woman, full of knowledge and wit beyond belief. She was not the prettiest sight by any means, but she was very sweet and always made sure to comfort my mind even in the most disheveled situations. Jeff and Karma lived in a mobile home out in the sticks of Florida. They were both the sole business partners of the body shop. And ironically, were also Fulton's coke dealers. There was another man who worked in the shop named 'Rooney.' He was a twenty something Iranian man with only nine fingers and was a master at welding. He was a kind soul, he always seemed to have genuine care for my wellbeing and I gathered that respect from day one. Rooney was always straightforward with me; he never hid behind some bogus facade like most of the other enigmatic characters I met. He was honest and good hearted. I don't think he was cognizant of the darker sides of the business. Rooney mostly kept away from all the partying, the drugs and the bullshit. I spent most of my days out in the shop with Rooney. He would teach me how to take apart cars, weld, sand, bodywork, motor swaps and anything in between. He was a very knowledgeable individual.

Fulton was married at the time (to his second wife) a woman named 'Amber.' She was a very pushy bitch, just a downright forceful person. She always insisted that I call her mom. I never did refer to her as mom for two reasons.

One: I already had a loving a caring mother and I didn't need another.

Two: I just wanted to be a dick to her.

Amber had two fatherless sons of her own. The first-born was 'Dennis.' He was a late twenty's ginger kid with absolutely no loyalty to anyone or anything. Dennis would throw anybody under the bus to save his worthless ass. Amber's other son was an early twenty's autistic man-child named 'Derrick.' He was an interesting character to say the least. Derrick was utterly fascinated with tits. He always wanted a pair of his own. Derrick would strap on a bra, blow up balloons and stuff them in tight. He had some kind of weird fixation about men with hooters. On the other hand, He was by far the smartest person I think I've ever met. He was a wiz with numbers, words, spatial perspective, computers and anything else that involved mental brilliancy. It was absolutely impressive to watch him figure out any technical problem. Derrick couldn't shoot a basketball or ride a bike to save his life, but he didn't need to, the kid had his amazing and unique brain.

Every other day Fulton would take me to a house that was about forty-five minutes from where we lived. A man named 'Dane' owned the house. No matter the time of day or night we went to Dane's house, there was always three more people that were there; 'Johnny, Sabrina and Kevin.' I'm not sure if they lived there or just happened to always be there while I was around. They were all fittingly normal folks, they paid me attention, fed me when I was hungry (didn't reframe from cursing or making racist comments in my presence) but nevertheless, a seemingly decent group of human beings. For several months we would visit Dane's house. Fulton and the other four adults would dip away to a room in the back of the house for hours on end while I was left out in the living room playing with the cat that roamed around the joint. Ten sometimes twelve hours they would lock themselves in the back of the house. I was a lot smarter than I led on; and was well aware they were doing cocaine and most likely tag-teaming Sabrina back there. But, I didn't give a shit. It beat going to bed early just so I would have to wake early for another insignificant day spent in school. Till six or seven in the morning we would stay at Dane's. Most of the time I would crash out on the couch and Fulton would wake me when he was done snorting lines and it was time to leave.

When we finally did arrive at home, Amber was irate to say the least. Just as this nonstop party lifestyle of Fulton's had wore thin on my mothers' patience's; it was beginning to have the same bitter effect on Amber's. They would have brutal arguments over his whereabouts, the people he was associating himself with, and not to mention the fact he was keeping a young and easily impressionable teenager out till the morning twilight. Four a couple hours they would fight, yell, slam doors, break windows, the whole nine yards. It was the same ole' mayhem I was accustomed to, just in a different state with different faces. Amber would always feel the need to grill me on our whereabouts, but I never gave her the satisfaction. I would lie and tell her we stayed at the shop, dozed off, lost track of time, just as Fulton would coach me to say hours before hand. After their extensive arguing, they would fuck loudly in their bedroom like captive apes in a wildlife gangbang for about an hour or so. With piercing howls, vigorous slapping, madly placed smacks of pleasure and pain; and then Futon would pass his ass out on the couch in the living room till about three or four in the afternoon the next day. He would sleep off his cocaine comedown and reboot for another round of madness and havoc. I would hit the Florida beach to surf all day and release my tension. It was a seemingly simple time (to a certain extent) if you can deal with the arguing and drug abuse by the people that were (apparently) in charge of your safety and welfare. But, there was a storm coming — And we all could feel it.

Pleasant trees and double D's.
She had a porn star bum and drank Catholic rum.

"Well, Bob. Now with most of the bosky cast described. I guess there's nothing left to do but pour up another cocktail, light a smoke, throw on a Pink Floyd album and skip to the track 'Welcome to the Machine.'

49

Let's dive right into the deep end of this cesspool and hope we don't resurface with five eyeballs and three dicks."

"Very lovely, Ryan."

"You know you love it, Bob."

"I'm getting real tired of your wrong name shit, Ryan." I said to him as I watched him just devilishly giggle and take another sip of booze.

CHAPTER SIX, SIX, SIX:
My Year with Fulton: Part Two.

"I don't worship the Devil, I just don't believe in God."

One particular night Fulton and Amber decided to have the family over for dinner. Derrick and I already lived in the house so it wasn't too hard for us to attend. Dennis, Amber's first born son (the soulless ginger) also showed up for this out-of-character dinner thrown in celebration. I wasn't too aware of what the occasion was; I just really enjoyed free food so I didn't mind getting out of my room to eat. We all sat around the dinner table, laughing, joking and smiling—playing happy little fucking family, if you will. It was late in the evening when Fulton and Amber decided to enlighten us on this reason for gathering, and they informed us that Amber was three months pregnant and they were going to be having another boy. It was a joyous time for the family. We celebrated the conception of a new member to this defective crew of individuals and enjoyed our time together. It was nice, calm, relaxing and true. But, as I've learned too many times before this, Fulton is never one to accept things for just what they are. Whether they are good or bad, he is never satisfied with a still life. That bores a person like him. He was never a "live in the moment" of jollification type of guy. He must always strive for confusion. And just as I predicted . . . A couple short weeks after our dinner of merriment, the old Fulton was back to his shady ways.

His intense drug use was worsening and it was happening racecar fast. He was no longer in control of the ability to hide it. I saw it, Amber saw it—everybody fucking saw it. He would come out from his many frequent bathroom breaks throughout the day with a nice little white ring around his nose. The atrocious fighting between him and his wife was swelling. They were going at each other's throats everyday. We were getting thrown out and let back into that house more times than I can count. The end was slowly imminent and there was no stopping this freight train from colliding with its fate.

On this specific night I am recalling; Fulton and Amber had a heated fight that lasted hours. Broken glass lined the floor, punched in walls, slammed doors and angry words exchanged from both parties. It was about money, drug use, staying out all night with a child, running a business he let her have no part in. It was vile. He got banished to stay in my room on the bottom bunk. She didn't want to see him. And I'll be honest; I didn't have a fucking choice but to let him sleep in my room. For a couple weeks we shared a room. Then, on one specific night, all Fulton's bridge burring and backstabbing came to our doorstep and there was entirely NO BACKING DOWN!

The night was late, two or three A.M. I was asleep on the top bunk and Fulton was on the bottom. He was wide-awake in a strung out cocaine daze, just like most nights for him. That was when the loud piercing sound of shattering glass echoed through the house . . . We had a **MOTHA-FUCKIN' INTRUDER!** Fulton sprung out of bed in a coke-frenzy. I was awakened by the loud sound of the crushing glass and the shaking from Futon's swift and rigid jump out of bed. Fulton didn't hesitate; he took off running down the stairs to discover the source of the sound. I was a mere step behind. Amber came running out from her room on the bottom story. Amber and I watched Fulton run into the garage and grab a giant fishhook that he had bolted to the end of a long stick. He took a solid clench of his huge meat hook-looking, home-built contraption, and scrambled out the front door. He was in hot pursuit of a black male. Amber and I stayed in the house, called the police and frantically awaited their arrival.

The next thirty minutes felt like an eternity. When the police finally did arrive, Fulton was walking up the street from a heavily vegetated Florida forest. He was covered from head to toe in blood and he had been stabbed three times in the midsection with a small pock-etknife. His shirt was ripped to shreds; he was shaken and distraught. But, he still had an affirmative grip on his hook. The cops that arrived at the scene (to the surprise and astonishment of both Amber and I) were actually Fulton's friends. He had this unique way of befriending anyone and everyone. The cops, the criminals, old, young and everybody else in between . . . It didn't matter what social category you fell under, he would always find a way to befriend you.

The police had apprehended the black male just a short mile away. He was beaten, broken, bloody and fish-hooked through his body and shoulder, with chunks of flesh missing from different parts of his body. He was in real bad shape and had to be hospitalized for three weeks. They filed a report, asked some questions, and then went along their merry way. I was fucking mysti-fied to say the least. I couldn't believe it. I get skate-boarding tickets in my hometown, yet some how this fucking guy hooks another human being and gets no punishment or penalty at all. Fucking amazing! Never-theless, after this definitive and bloody happening went down; it dramatically shifted things in the household. A transfer I really didn't see coming. Fulton and Amber took a tight grasp on this Mafioso mindset. They began to talk about protecting this family and covering our tracks, preserving our bloodline and getting ahead of the competition.

"Just some weird fucking shit, man."

"Sounds like it."

This newly found gangster persona, which they had adopted, was enormously way out of my league, my understanding, my wheelhouse and my perceptive reason. Yeah, I've been in a fistfight or two in my life, but the talk of murder, betrayal, time to 'Stand Up and Fight to Protect This Family Talk,' was overwhelmingly outrageous. I was caught in the descending spin of this crashing plane and I had no Goddamn parachute. Of course, at any minute I could've phoned home to my mother and kindly asked her to extract me from this ridiculous situation. But, I had two significantly persistent thoughts in my brain.

One: I was fucking mortified of what my mother would say at this point, seeing as how I have already missed over half a year of school. I was hanging out at drug dens till the morning hours. My fourteenth birthday had come and passed. I really should've known the difference between right and wrong. Also, why the hell didn't I make this phone call months ago when shit began to spiral out of my control?

Two: The choice to stay in Florida was mine and mine alone. And frankly, between you and me, I wanted to see this experience to the end. I've always been a sucker for adventure, and this little escapade, I clearly knew was one I may never get the chance to live through again. So, my conclusion was. "Might as well remain and see how this story ends." Despite the dangers I was being subjected to. I was intrigued by delusion.

Fulton took it upon himself to do some investigating and track down the nature of this intruder. He called every last one of his dubious contacts and finally managed to gather the correct information. Turns out that Dane, the man's house I would spend all night at while Fulton and his four friends would lock themselves in the bedroom and do blow and from what I assume (gangbang Sabrina) was upset about a certain drug debt that Fulton never paid up for. Dane sent over some street thug with noting to lose and even less to gain, to nicely send a message to Fulton by breaking in and rattling the cage a bit in the hopes of collecting his debt. But, little did he anticipate or predict—if you push an almost thirty year, strung-out junkie to the breaking point, THE FUCKING WAR IS ON!

Fulton and Amber started plotting, planning and purposing a technique to strike back. And the time for retaliation was upon us. I was consumed and eaten alive by this lawless mobster lifestyle. It was fucking exhilarating. Granted, I should've never been there in the first place, but nevertheless, that's neither here nor there. I was there, I was now involved (to a point) and I was going to watch this shit explode in front of my eyes, one way or another. Fulton and Amber set out to send back a responsive message of their own. The next coming days the house was on lockdown. Nobody came or went without permission. Fulton slept in the downstairs living room with an arsenal of weapons around him, keeping watch, protecting, snorting lines and drinking for days. He was to defend this family and nobody was going to stop him. A week or so had passed and no trouble has been brought to our forefront. And the time had come to send a message of vengeance back.

Fulton invited an unconventional 'Friend' of his over to the house. A twenty-something, stocky black man with a shaved head, time in prison and nothing to lose. The gang-banger type, with prison ink, pants sagging low, dropping the N-bomb even around the company of us white folks. Where the fuck he ever met this notorious clown was far beyond the grasp of my intelligence. Nor did I ever want to know the real truth of their friendship or meeting. I stayed out of this situation the best I could. I just watched from a safe distance. Fulton, Amber and this black fellow whose name was 'Stagg,' conspired and schemed in the kitchen for many nights and their whispers were hard to make-out as I intrudingly listened from my upstairs bedroom. I couldn't actually decipher the real particulars or details of the plan, just knew some shit was going down! A few days went by with Stagg continuously coming and going, arranging and machinating with Fulton and Amber. And wouldn't you know it, the stage was set and the time was upon us. Their plot was going to be fulfilled.

The night was late, around midnight or so. I gazed from my window in perplexing anticipation as I watched Fulton and Stagg climb into Fulton's Corvette and vanish into the darkness. I was unaware of the plan (any fucking plan at that) but I was curious to discover it. Three days slugged by and Fulton never returned home. Amber kept quieting my doubts and worries by telling me "Everything was going to be ok." But, I didn't know what to believe or even whom to trust. This situation had fallen far beyond my control and I was scared and horrified, but I played it cool. My fear was not to be shown to anyone. And just as gradually as those three days crept by, on day number four, Fulton walked through the door. I am aware now from the beauty of television and film that Fulton was laying low to keep the heat, the fuzz or the bacon off his trail, but at that moment I assumed the worst.

Fulton entered our house with cock in hand and not a Goddamn worry in the world. He was calm, collective, and just as arrogant as always, and from what I could tell, remotely sober. He first took Amber into their master bedroom where they proceeded to fuck like noisy wild animals for hours. Then he made his way upstairs to my bedside where I was laying and watching television. He had me turn off the TV so he could explain what he had to do to protect this family. He kept the facts vague and empty, however, explained to me that we were safe and wouldn't have any more problems or issues . . . Or so he foolishly thought!

Weeks went by very gently. The disarray had subsided and trouble was out of our realm. Fulton was home most of the days; the house was no longer on lockdown. I spent most of my days surfing and playing video games. It was calm for a quick moment—That was until the truth of his actions hit the front page of the local newspaper and the police came knocking on the front door. There it was: Broadcasted on the front page.

LOCAL MAN BURNS DOWN HOME OF DRUG DEALER!

Fulton was arrested as the main suspect of arson to a local home. The same drug den that just a few short weeks prior, I spent so many sleepless nights playing with the cat and watching the sun rise. Stagg, his black accomplice was nowhere to be found in Florida. He got the fuck out of dodge before shit hit the 'Proverbial Fan.' The police detained Fulton for about five days as we all hung in suspense awaited the outcome at my house; time was becoming our enemy. I contemplated calling my mother and telling her the whole story and asking for my removal from this situation. Amber was getting closer to giving birth to her third child. And to be honest, none of us in the household knew what to do without Fulton around. That's not because he's some bright guiding light that we can't formulate our own plan of action without him. No, no, no! It's because the cocksucker would manipulate his way inside your head and make you feel as if life can't move forward without him. Fucking prick! But, I'm digressing again . . .

Before we could speculate the worst—Fulton was somehow released with no charges. They claimed they didn't have enough evidence to convict him. Again, fucking amazing how he always seems to skate by with a slap on the wrist when it came to criminal activity. Fulton arrived home and once again he and Amber darted to the bedroom to mate like screaming chimpanzees. Mind you, she was now borderline ready to pop with that child inside her, which in my opinion is pretty fucking nasty. Poor kid, he's in there getting cock-poked on the top of his head for hours at a time; can't be a pleasant feeling. Nevertheless . . . That's beside the point. We were all back together again and striving to be an 'Ordinary Family.' The next coming months were quiet around the home front . . . Too quiet . . .

The birth of Fulton's fourth son (or third legitimate son) was now the ultimate veracity of our situation. We all enjoyed our time together, loving, caring and tending to the new member of our twisted little Mob style family. Well . . . Some of us did. Fulton was getting restless with this basic, grounded, may I say it, boring lifestyle. Nothing was ever good enough for this man. So, in true Fulton-fucking-fashion, he had to find a way to complicate things once again. The drug use continued and he started to formulate these obscure and highly schizophrenic thoughts that we were no longer safe. He embedded fear into the hearts and minds of us all. Manipulated the family into his dark and twisted self-destructive fantasyland, and Jesus Christ! We all believed him. Fulton began having these thoughts that Stagg was going to turn him in and the whole 'Perfect Little Family' we had, with the pretty house on the beach and the business in the city, would finally meet its ruins and go up in flames (no pun intended) We were all eating out of the palm of his hand and the bastard knew it. He made a selfish declaration and ran this fucking choice into the ground.

The night was getting late, around eleven or so. I was in my room watching television. The new baby was sound asleep and the moment of deliberation was upon us. I heard two sets of footsteps climbing the stairs and swiftly making their way to my bedroom door. There was a knock—

"Come in." I answered.

The door was opened and I was presented with Fulton and Amber. They asked me to shut off the television. I was curious of what in the fuck this could possibly be about. I sat up, preceded to turn off the tube and gather my attention to them. They had their wannabe mafia faces on, seriousness covered their grins, and I could sense a bomb was about to explode.

"Ryan, you want to protect this family, don't you?" Fulton and Amber articulately asked me.

I had to take a second to think about this as they deeply stared at me awaiting my retort.

"Yeah, of course." I hesitantly replied.

"Good." Fulton served back. "We need you to do a huge favor to protect this family." Fulton finished.

"What's that?" I responded.

Fulton took a breath, fixated his eyes on me tight, watching, probing and waiting to see my true inner strength as a man . . .

"—We need you to kill Stagg." Fulton grimly asked me.

SMACK!

I felt a freezing cold chill run down my spine (as cliché as that sounds) and I was implausibly speechless for seconds as they cold bloodedly peered at me. I could feel the icy stares from them both. It was painstakingly bone chilling in the room. My body began to shake beyond my control.

"N . . . N . . . N . . . N . . . No!" I timidly stuttered back.

Amber quickly and heartlessly chimed in.

"I told you he wasn't ready! He's not strong enough!" Amber said.

With a cracked upset tone in her voice as if I just foiled the bitches' master plan.

They started to argue with one another over the current state of events. Back and fourth the fighting persisted. Fulton was adamant with his point that I would never be suspected. Amber was strong with her point that she should have the honors of the kill to stand up for this family. She was unwavering in the fact that she was ready for such an unholy duty. I sat in unlimited consternation and shock. The room was beginning to spin, the sound of their voices slowly started to fade out and my vision was being consumed by a bright white light of fear. I wanted nothing more but to cry and run home, run five thousand miles back to my mother's arms. However, I didn't want to show any form of weakness. If they just asked a fourteen year old to commit a murder, what would they do to me if I ran and snitched? So, I sat there, observing as they came to a final conclusion to the task that was just laid out before me. The conversation lasted about ten minutes; the longest ten minutes I have ever experienced. Then, they came to a resolve. They both looked at me with piercing eyes, dry expressions and empty minds.

"Ok, you won't have to do anything you're not ready for." Fulton explained.

They rubbed my head, said goodnight and exited the room. The door shut behind them and I was left alone, astounded, dazed and throbbing in soreness. My mind ran wild with delusion and inclusive regret. "What the fuck am I involved in?" I kept repetitively asking myself.

I curled my little body into the tightest fetal position I could ever physically execute. I had sweaty palms, tears pouring from my eyes and snot gushing from my nose. I laid in that placement and cried myself all through the night till the sun had risen the next coming morning. I was now wholeheartedly, sincerely, the most passionately ALONE I have ever felt before. I knew if I was going to make it out of this state alive, I had to evolve, I had to adapt, and I had to do it fast. I had to watch my own back, my own ass and my own existence. At that abundantly fearless yet comprehensively hopeless moment, I transformed from a boy to a man. I was no longer scared of death, of punishment, or any form of this so-called 'God or Satan,' we all must fear. It was an instant of self-clarity. If I wanted to see my entire life out to the end, I was to trust nobody. Not Fulton, not Amber, not the baby, not the autistic man-child in the other room, not a fucking soul! This was purely a battle to stay alive and primarily to survive. This was now my battle; it was personal. And I intended to win this combat. It was time to fight, with guns blazing and positively no fear in my heart, my mind, or care for my physical wellbeing. I wasn't leaving this world till foam was flowing from my mouth. You were about to see a man get mean, a child advance to a different spectrum, a conscious brain fall as far as thoroughly and unremittingly possible from the almighty Grace of righteousness.

CHAPTER SEVEN:
My Year with Fulton: Part Three.

"If I cared about what you thought I would forever remain silent. I speak to shock, entertain, offend and pass truth."

— The Sailor Jerry has hit the spot again.

T he next week to come not a single person in my fucking household brought forward any attention about the night which I was egotistically and uncaringly stressed with a burden that I never thought I had the pure strength and impressive power to ever hold on my own. My posture as a human had changed. I stood tall and mighty. My mindset drastically fluctuated and my beliefs in Godliness or overall holy safety were nowhere to be found. And to state the record, were not going to be my salvation. The task of my protecting my own ass was only mine to achieve. God was not going to help me. Fuck him and fuck everyone was my attitude. I've never been a religious person and I never will be. I had no choice but to live out my days in this walking nightmare and cope with the consequences however I saw fitting and chose appropriate. The drug use of Fulton was stoutly mounting and my concern for him, Amber, the baby, any person in this Godforsaken state was swiftly dwindling. Just as wholesome and playful as the story once was when it first began, was no longer the same viewpoint. The tides had shifted, the moods have changed, and the unrelenting marital fighting would not stop. They couldn't find common ground to save their worthless lives and just like that . . . Once again Fulton and I were banished from the house. We jumped into his Corvette and hit the open road once again.

Except, this time when we sat beside each other in the car, the feeling was significantly different from just a few short months back when I made the verdict to stay in this circumstance. Back when I felt resented and unwanted. Now I was the one with the judging eye, this show was now under my puppet fingers and I wasn't passing the responsibility of puppet master to anyone. Not until I went to my 'Real Home.' I was wiser, stronger, faster, younger and more agile than him and anyone else who stood in my way of getting back to my mother's love. He was becoming transparent, lucid. I could practically see the bullshit collecting inside of him. I was sitting next to a man, with a pending arson case, no regard for his own life, no care for my wellbeing, and it was clear to me. It wasn't father and son anymore. It was man on man. Dog eat dog shit! Only the strong will survive. Darwinism baby! We took shelter out in the sticks of Florida with Jeff and Karma. They accepted us with open arms, why wouldn't they? Fulton was a coke addict and they sold coke. It was the perfect business model. I on the other hand was closed hearted, isolated and self-controlled. I knew I couldn't trust anyone now. My only feat to accomplish was getting home safe. Besides the obvious answer of me calling my mother and admitting defeat. No, no, no! That would've been too easy. I said before I'm a sucker when it comes to adventure and I was going to see this shit through until the cold and bitter end. Or I'm just a complete dumbfuck that doesn't know the right time to step away from a situation that I'm not really too much invested in? One or the other I'm sure is true. It was a Goddamn war, one that I was going to succeed in! As the nights flew by in the middle of bumfucked nowhere, and the days jetted by at the body shop, Fulton was devising a plan to strike back at Amber. And the ending to his shitty story was slowly writing its final chapters.

On one particular night, out of an idiotic fit of heavily coke induced paranoia and rage; Fulton took off in the dead of night to get his revenge. I was sound asleep that night but was quickly awakened by the sound of his Corvette barreling out. Fulton at this point had been up for days. I lost count of the correct number, but I think it was four maybe five days straight he was up snorting blow, chain smoking, pounding liquor and fucking anything that crossed his destructive path. He was determined to get his self-justified vengeance anyway he could; no matter the consequence or the people it would affect and endanger in the end. He drove over to Amber's house that night with a tall, white young male (A man that perfectly fits the description of my exact look and stature) and Fulton and this anonymous man decided to boost Amber's car in the middle of the night and drive the fucking vehicle into a tree in an infuriated path of cocaine inhibited annihilation. I'm not really sure how he thought this event was going to play out. All I can say is; he had to have at least one second of sober realization during this crime, just a moment of clarity, something, anything, however . . . Apparently fucking not! He really is this fucking stupid and ignorant. Not only did he steal the car with no gloves on, covering the steering wheel in his fingerprints. He crashed the fucking car into a tree at the auto body shop that he owned, leaving the car there over night, with his blood on the inside from smashing his head against the windshield during impact. What a fucking dumbshit!

The next day the cops showed up to Jeff and Karma's house, just as we all knew they would. And like clockwork, Fulton found himself back in jail. Now for the second time since I've been under his accountability. Fulton and I had now become a liability and dilemma to Jeff and Karma (seeing as how they sold drugs) so, I was pressed out from their house while Fulton was locked up and driven to my grandmother's house where I would reside till the release of Fulton. My grandmother did the best she could with the means she had available to take care of me. She was old, brittle, nervous and easily scared. I stayed with her for a couple days till Fulton resurfaced once again from jail, and when he got out... He came out in a fury of wrath.

His friend Johnny dropped him off to my grandmother's house, and he had already snorted astronomical amounts of cocaine on the trip home. When he showed up he was desperately strung out, entirely unreachable by what was real or by who was real. The true form of long term drug induced psychosis was now our reality. He lost it, in every sense, every structure and issue. He rapidly started talking nonsense, slurry his words, twitching of the eyes and limbs. He locked himself in the bathroom with nothing more than a pair of hair clippers, his bag of coke, some alcohol and went to town. The stint lasted roughly thirty maybe forty minutes. It was both revealing and shocking to my grandmother and I. She and I were both mutually scared. However, we didn't want to call the cops. That's all he needed was to get locked up a few short hours after he was released. My grandmother had me call Johnny, the man who had just dropped him off, and nicely asked for his help. I kindly and effectively asked him if he could double back. Shit has hit the fan and it was far out of our control. He returned promptly to help us. Johnny knocked on the bathroom door and spoke with Fulton through the closed door. It was hard to make out the intoxicated words that he was saying from behind the door, just stutters and mumbles. It took another twenty minutes for Fulton to open the door.

But when that door did open . . . Fulton had shaved seventy percent of his hair. He looked like a cancer patience that had just undergone a few treatments of chemotherapy. His hair was a disaster. One side completely bald, the other side fully consumed with hair, with patches still hanging on for dear life (It was actually a bit funny) I laughed hysterically on the inside, making sure not to show my humor outwardly. I wasn't going to push the addict over the edge, nevertheless, pretty fucking ridiculous. Johnny helped him shave the rest of his existing hair, cleaned him up, walked him to the couch and laid him down. After we saw Fulton take his last cocaine eye twitch and pass out, Johnny left into the night. I took a spot on the couch with Fulton (under the wonderful impression that he was asleep for awhile) I attempted to calm my racing heartbeat and fluttering mind to hopefully get some rest. However, as luck would have it . . . Fulton woke up. He rose in a frantic hurry. He was lost, confused, was unaware of how the fuck he got here. That was when I heard him ramble out one of the most entertaining sentences I've ever heard.

"Where the fuck is I? And where the fuck is my hair?" Fulton spoke aloud.

I, being the strong and self-preserving child that I was, answered his questions of puzzlement and disorder. I attempted to talk him down in the dead of night, around four A.M. or so, however, he was still externally isolated. He took another twenty or thirty minutes to gather his bearings. Then, with a dense and rapid slap of realism, he was sucked back inside his body and found the ground beneath his feet once again. He looked in the mirror at his new distasteful image. And he was dumbfounded, speechless, and just as thunderstruck as I was. He found his center again (or whatever center he ever had) and Fulton walked over to the couch with me, took a seat, relaxed and drank some water as we talked with each other. And for the first time in a very long time, he was actually being honest for a short-lived second.

"I lost fucking control." He said to me.

"No shit, Sherlock." I silently muttered under my breath.

He was fading, dozing off, slipping into a drug addict's worst nightmare . . .

'THE HORRIFIC COMEDOWN!'

Although, he had one more burst of energy left in him, and he jumped up with all his coke fueled might, placed his body over mine, put his hands over my arms knowing he was stronger than me, held me down and proceeded.

"Are you upset with me because I got high?" Fulton asked.

I answered wisely and conservatively. Not to aggravate the drug addict into any more uncalled-for behavior.

"No, it's fine. Let's just go to sleep." I replied.

"I broke down, I got high. I smoked some pot and I lost it." Fulton added.

"I don't know if you know anything about a pot smoker, Bob-o'? I know more now than I did then, seeing as how I'm a frequent smoker as an older individual. However, I knew enough about weed back then also. I had many friends that did it, brothers that did it. And I knew that a pot smoker never smokes a joint and gets bizarrely violent and inaccessible. The most you do is smoke some weed, get hungry, get happy, get tired and go to sleep. That's about it. They shouldn't even put weed in the class of a drug. It's fucking harmless. Trust me. That's just a public declaration. But, let's get back to it—"

Fulton was lying to protect his own ass, just as he's done many times before this, and as I saw his eyes getting very heavy and his grip on my arms becoming tremendously weak. He fell down to his side on the couch and drifted into a cocaine coma, one that he would not wake up from for about two and half days. He just slept on the couch mumbling to himself and every once in awhile getting up to poop.

"Cocaine is a helluva drug!"

When Fulton finally did rise from his comedown, he looked like shit, smelt worse and felt even more brainless. He couldn't for the life of him put the pieces back together of this scattered puzzle that was the last three days of his existence. He didn't take too much time trying to reconstruct his demolished glasshouse of a life. He grabbed a baseball cap, threw it over his shiny dome and we headed off to work with his new haircut front and center. However, it wasn't nearly enough coverage to hide his glossy, ultra white, reflective baldhead. He looked fucking dimwitted and foolish. And there was no way to cover up his blunder. He couldn't smooth talk his way out of this one like he did for some many other mistakes before. Fucking asshole deserved to be the dipshit in the room for once!

When we arrived at work, most of the shop had already heard of his little episode and prepared some jokes of amusement. They all made light of his ridiculous appearance, ridiculing him on his uncomfortable state of current public manifestation. He was the butt of the joke. And I truly believe that began to drive Fulton mad. He was never before put in the corner of humiliation. And he was not going to start now! As idiotic and unintelligent as he felt, no words or comments, and certainly no mockery was going to stop him from returning to the center of attention that he was accustomed to.

The next coming two weeks or so were passing by hastily and affectively. Time was no longer a standard of mine—it was not my friend, my enemy, my acquaintance or foe. I had only a few important things on my mind. Staying alive, steering far away from trouble and getting home safe. A certain day in question came about and everybody was at the shop. The day was bright, weather was beautiful and times were good.

"I say the day in question, Bobby-boy, because at this point, I had seen, heard and lived through so much shit, that the days began to devour themselves. As much as I wanted to cope and decipher the months of despondence I was wrongly forced to suffer through. I didn't have a moment to myself to figure out this maze of despair. I just trucked along with everyone else, never looking back, never apologizing, never taking an ounce of responsibility, blame or care for what has unfolded."

I was no longer sitting in the room as a child surround by a group of drug addicted adults. No, no, fucking no! I was placed in a room full of drug addicts as an adult, my own man, a thought evoking person of my own existence, if you will. I didn't give two shits for any of these people. I had no care to listen to their advising suggestions. I was now an observer of a diabolical scheme and design—one that I intended to win and defeat all these feeble minds that sat before me.

All the males and some of the women would hang out after hours once the shop doors had closed. They all drank, cursed, kissed, indulged in more bathroom breaks than any normal person ever should (snorting cocaine) and on this particular night I'm recalling. Two police cars pulled up to the front of the body shop . . . And the wild hamster frenzy was fucking on! Every adult jumped up, began to pull out sacks of cocaine from all pockets and orifices of their bodies, flushing them down the toilet, splashing water on their faces, downing mouthwash, correcting their image and outward appearance for the bacon.

KNOCK, KNOCK, KNOCK!

The cops were at the door. All the adults continued to sit, stand around, converse with one another and played it cool, a dazzling coy to protect their own asses. The counterfeit scene play they exercised was brilliant, charming, endearing. They were all fucking marvelous in their own right. I think all drug-addicts are born actors. Fulton opened the door and the police were exposed to a sight of five men, three females and one child. They slowly stepped in without a kind gesture of invite or inquiry. They leisurely scanned the room. Every person in that room had a rap sheet longer than the declaration of independence (everybody except me) and they went through the room, asking pressing question and "Investigating," if you will. The beautiful veneer of a simple and uncomplicated gathering of friends was outstandingly executed perfectly by these people. The wool was pulled right over the eyes of the police. The cops made their rounds through the room from person to person, asking questions and judging the responses they got. All answers from these adults were kept short and to the point, and the conclusion of there visit was to be presented. They had to arrest Fulton yet again, suspicion of arson and grand theft auto. The two crimes that he was already locked up for, and released without enough evidence to convict. If you ask me, smells like something's fishy here? They slapped the cuffs on him and walked him to the patty wagon. One of the officers approached me.

"Are you going to be safe if we take your father in for questioning?" He asked.
I already had my retort set in mind before the matter was brought to doorstep.

"I'll be fine." I answered as I pointed at Jeff and Karma. "I will stay with them." I responded.

"Ok, suit yourself." The cop replied.
We all peered out the window as the police car drove away and Fulton was locked up once more (now for the third time since my arriving here) and for those of you not paying attention . . . I believed the police were baiting an elaborate and complex trap, and I was finally starting to see some daylight coming through the dark clouds.

CHAPTER EIGHT:

My Year with Fulton: Part Four.

"If I didn't have anger, I wouldn't have any emotions at all."

T hree or four days after that incident, Fulton was finally released from jail. I had been taking refuge at Jeff and Karma's for the time being, much to their reluctant acceptance. Silent and abandoned, I didn't feel any sense of optimism or sanguinity anymore. I think at this point in a child's life, they're supposed to feel as if the world is at their fingertips, their expression, and their adolescent belief. However, the only feeling I was expressing was: "Please, kill me now. Take me away from this wretchedness, this misery, this woe."

I was gloomy, unsympathetic and soon to be doomed to fail. Or so Fulton thought. I had been collecting my defense, my salvation, my rescue and my Goddamn freedom. I was razor sharp, clever, prepared and energized to clash. When he was set free from the prison of his own demise, he had made a few friends. Or should I say, "Prison Friends." I am not the smartest person in the world, never claimed to be and never will be. That being said, I know just enough to keep me out of the penitentiary, just as I knew when I was fourteen. Any connections you make while you're locked up for a crime, is nothing more than a bogus, phony, untrustworthy and highly disreputable 'Connection.' Not be trusted, never to be seen again, a passing face, nothing more. Just like a fart, claim it for a second, have a chuckle and carry on with your life. Don't ever look back. Nevertheless, Fulton was true to his convictions that these two fellows were as legit as blowjobs and apple pie. The crimes in which these two men were originally locked up for were not clear to me then, nor did I really care. But, after spending two minutes in a room with these men, I could sense something was amiss.

About a week after Fulton's independence was granted to him from the legal system, these two men surfaced at the body shop to have a conversation with my dear ole' cock sucker father. They headed off into the open field behind the shop and talked for nearly an hour or so. I paid attention to the conversation the best I could while trying to accomplish my duties as a child/slave rat of the shop. The words that they exchanged were unclear to me. They were roughly three hundred yards or more away from the shop. I could vaguely see them, all I could make out was their humanly silhouettes. However, was nowhere near close enough to conceive an actual voice. After Fulton ended his conversation with his 'Prison Friends,' the two men jumped into their busted, kaput ass ride and drove off into the expanse.

Not even two short hours later, five police cars pulled up to the shop. Each car had two officers inside. Ten cops exited their cars and stormed the gates. The police handcuffed Fulton, and with vigor and assertiveness threw his dumbass in the back of the cop car. They ransacked the shop, going through every bank statement, quote, estimate, names of employees, addresses, accounts, customers, any piece of information they could get their hands on, confiscating and seizing it all. I sat on the couch, quietly examining and observing the ruble as they overturned every desk and drawer in the office. I was once again speechless, sitting in alarm and anxiety. I bit my tongue and watched with intrigue, awaiting the outcome of their intrusive entry. I didn't know what they were looking for or why they arrested Fulton at this point, just silently waited for my answer.

Then, I got my answer. The chief leading the investigation entered the room. He looked over to me with a judging and intense eye. He approached the seat that I was assertively planted on, and asked me to stand. I did so, not to find myself in any form of trouble or nuisance. He then asked me to turn around and put my hands behind my back (which I found rather odd) but I did as he asked. He then proceeded to read me my 'Miranda rights.'

"You have the right to remain silent. Anything you say can and will be used against you in a court of law. You have the right to an attorney. If you cannot afford an attorney, one will be provided for you. Do you understand the rights I have just read to you?" He asked.

"Yes, I understand." I replied.

"Good. You are being arrested for the suspicion of arson to a home, grand theft auto, and the conspiracy of murder for hire." The chief replied.

"—Wait, Ryan? Murder for hire?" I asked as Ryan sat on my couch spewing his vast recollection of his childhood.

"It was something along those lines, Bobby-D. Jesus Christ! I was fourteen! Give me a fucking break. My memory is a little fuzzy. I can't verbosely recall the concrete words."

"Sorry. Go on, please."

The chief handcuffed me and walked me out to his personal undercover cop car. I will say this, because FUCK THAT COP! He was nowhere near gentle, meek or docile with the muscle of walk. It was hurried, slapdash and antagonistic. Fuck, I get it. I, at that very existing point in time, was "considered a criminal," but shit! Have a little common courtesy and decency for the protection and security of a minor. Is that too much to ask?

I was detained, driven to the police station where I sat my young ass in a holding cell for almost two and a half days. Granted, all the police officers in the jail were very kind to me. They made sure I never went hungry, cold, uncomfortable or disturbed. I thank them from the bottom of my heart for that. They treated me as a human being and not a merciless criminal. And that was absolutely class of them. I was set free and driven back to my grandmother's house where I was told by the cops.

"You are no longer allowed to leave the sate of Florida. You are a suspect of an investigation and your rights have been suspended until you are cleared as innocent." The police officer said.

WELL FUCK! . . .

I found myself in quite a predicament. All I wanted to do was fucking cry, cry and cry for Goddamn days. However, this was neither the time nor the place. "You must stay strong, Ryan." Those were the transitory words I kept repeating to myself, to help keep my sanity and my perception. Show any sidestep of weakness now and spend the rest of your days in a prison of your own fault of speaking or acting wrongly. Like I said before, this shit was a war, one that I was going to prevail as champion, and finish in complete guiltlessness. I was not here to prove I wasn't Fulton's associate or accomplices. I was here to confirm the fact that I was an innocent child, whom in the first place should've never been subjected to this indignation in the first place.

I was put on trial for my own everlasting spotless innocence. Criminally charged for the crimes of 'First Degree Arson, Grand Theft Auto, and The Conspiracy of Hire to Kill.' Three life changing criminal charges that most people live their whole long and beautiful lives without ever having to experience; yet, there I was, at age fourteen, with three pending charges against my sovereignty (and I was to state the oblivious) petrified beyond measure. I wanted to get out of this one alive, safe, and of course innocent and childlike. This meant I had to word my defense wisely, prudently, soundly and judiciously. Make my flawless claim to the 'No Understanding' of the acts that I have seen or heard. Play the coy card, and get the fuck out with my balls in tack. I really did think it was going to be that easy. Why? I don't fucking know why? I just thought in my cranium, my intellect, my body and courage. "There is absolutely no way in hell, Fulton would sell out his own son to protect his ass." And I did trust that shit. To a certain extent, that is. At least about eighty percent of that I essentially believed in. I still had a twenty percent chance of hesitation and query. Nevertheless, in a sense, the numbers were high in my favor for a win, and I thought to myself. "You might see your way out of this one anyhow."

My mother in outlying California, five thousand far, far miles away (which at that time seemed so distant) had caught wind of my legal trials of rampancy, freedom and unpolluted self-determination. She of course, had no choice but to chime in, seeing as how she was justifiably entitled to that honor, being my mother, my guider, my only caring and sober parent. She wanted to tell me her thoughts on the recent exposure of tribulations that I was involved in. She was pissed the fuck off, to say the least. We had a greatly comprehensive and incredibly angry phone conversation of why I didn't call months ago during the first arrest of Fulton. We talked on the phone for a couple hours and I got her up to speed on the recent activities that have taken place. The current conditions of lockdown I was in with the state of Florida, and all the details in between. She booked me a plane ticket while we were on the phone with each other, and had some insightful words to say.

"You go to that trial, you tell the truth and you get out of this shit. Then, you get your fucking ass in the car I send, you get your fucking ass on that plane and you get your fucking ass home!" Mother madly spewed.

"Yes, mother." I sacredly replied.

We hung up the phone and that night zipped by ever so quickly. Before I knew it, the morning had come and day one of this bullshit, lie-consuming trial that I was mistakenly and wrongly implicated in, was upon us.

The police showed up to my grandmother's house at seven A.M. sharp. I was dressed to impress and thrill. I was handcuffed, walked outside and situated in the back seat of the squad car. On the long drive to the courthouse, my palms were sweating, my heart was racing, my asshole was puckered up nice and tight, and my mind was clear. I had to prove my innocence and noninvolvement in these relevant crimes. It was time to smile, use the right words, talk with respect and dignity, and make sure not to walk my stupid ass into the flames of my own despair.

The Story of Kat and Drake: Part One.

Ravaged and pleased they sat in the silent dark

With nothing but pain and loss in their heart

If only a breath was wishing so shy

Failing to say that they longed for a cry

Forgetting the past and striving for cheer

Finding only despair and an abundance of fear

Alone in the meadow with sun as a glare

They sat in the wind and enjoyed a long stare

Love was troubled and they had lost their desire

Sex was an escape and the situation grew dire

Hope was restored when they found a bright light

Through a painful event they learned they had fight

It was time for this world to see their glory

Listen your ears and hear their brave story

She endured the long nights collecting his shame

Rightfully so, she adopted his name...

To Be Continued...

CHAPTER NINE:

My Year with Fulton: Part Five.

"Laugh as often as you get the chance. Cry when you feel hurt. Fuck as much as possible and never forget what is real."

Day one: (Insert) Law & Order sound.

The police car pulled up to the front of the courthouse and the war was on! Both officers exited the car, opened my door, got me out, grabbed me by my feeble handcuffed wrists and walked me through the courtroom doors where we were going to have ourselves a good ole' fashioned showdown of the minds! Tombstone was about to explode with gunfire.

Fulton was dressed in a bright orange jumpsuit, which was very suiting for the cocksucker. He was sitting at his desk of defense beside his lawyer. The two officers kindly removed my handcuffs and sat me down behind the railing, just shy of twenty feet from Fulton. The courtroom was dead silent; nobody moved, looked around or did a thing. I sat in suspense and curiosity. The Bailiff entered and addressed the courtroom.

"All rise for the Honorable Judge Rhinestone presiding." He said.

Everybody in the courtroom did as they were instructed. The Judge entered, walked to his chair of ruling and took a seat.

"Please be seated. Bailiff, which is our first case" Judge Rhinestone asked.

The whole room collective sat at once. The sound of such an event is overwhelming. Everybody collapsing down together, it quickly gathers your attention and tightens up your body. On the way down to our seats, Fulton placed both his arms on the rests of his chair and did a half-turn back to where I was sitting. We looked at each other, eyeing one another intensely—affirmatively. Then . . . Fulton gave me an overconfident, smug, ego-driven and suspicious wink. A wink between two people (when they are not flirty) is a symbolizing sign of trust, a confirmation of nobility. Made me think for a brief second? "What does this mean?" What I came up with was this; without any words said to one another, he was deliberately speaking to me, and he was saying; "Don't worry son, I got this shit under control. You're going to be alright." It was a comforting moment. I felt a sense of relieve, it was a bit late, but nonetheless, a nice split second of ease. Then . . . The bailiff proceeds to read the details of the first case on the docket, OUR GODDAMN CASE, to the court.

"Your Honor, our first case is, Fulton and Ryan Vinci, vs. the United States of America."

When I heard my name getting called in the case explanation, my mouth went dry, my throat began to tighten, my heart started to beat faster than a racecar in the red. "I am really fucking involved in this shit! I can't fucking believe this!" Were the words that were pounding against the inside of my confused brain?

This was real, this was happening, and there was nothing I could do about it. As much as I wanted to run the fuck out of that courtroom, I didn't want to get shot and killed over this dumbshit. I was once again forced into an awkward and desperate arrangement that I never wanted to be put in. I felt like I was getting raped. Well—The best I can image getting raped would feel. The courtroom went about their opening act of explaining the evidence and the material of the case; describing the crimes that both Fulton and I were getting charged with, and the punishments to those crimes, if we were both actually convicted guilty. It was fucking brutal to sit there and hear these allegations against my own name. I was dumbfounded and numb, speechless and anxious. And just when I felt hopeless and pitiful . . .

"The prosecution may call its first witness." The Judge said.

The Prosecuting Attorney stands from his chair, arrogant and brash.

"The prosecution calls Ryan Vinci to the stand." He said.

SLAP! There it was! My name was said in the same sentence as prosecution. I was eager to state my defense, even though I was appropriately and completely scared shitless. I rose from my seat and slothfully made my way to the bench.

"Place your left hand on the bible, raise your right hand, and repeat after me. I swear to tell the truth, the whole truth, and nothing but the truth, so help me God." The Bailiff said to me.

I carefully listened to his instructing words and did just as I was asked, word for word, beat for beat, not too find myself in any more trouble than I already have. I repeated all the words he asked of me, and then was told to take a seat at the bench. I did so. With the risk of using a boring and redundant cliché, my heart was racing a million miles a minute. I can't describe fully enough the anguish I felt at that bench. I was as ready as I ever could've been to state my claim of innocent youthful naive and judicious understanding to this case against my freedom.

"Were you involved in the crimes which are being charged against you?" Judge Rhinestone asked me.

"No." I quickly retorted.

The Judge then turned his attention to the prosecuting attorney.

"Does the prosecution have any evidence binding Ryan to the crimes that he is being charged with?" The Judge asked.

"Yes, your Honor. We have a recorded conversation of Fulton and another mans voice talking with our two informants. In the recording we can clearly hear Fulton attempted to put a contract on the head of Dennis, which is Amber's first born son, and Fulton's stepson." The prosecuting attorney said.

The courtroom takes a sigh of intrigue. All the heads in the courtroom begin to look around, eyes widened and expressions bleak. The room sat in shock as the plot began to thicken. It was at that moment, I was once again slapped across my face with a punch of realism. I always knew Fulton had some strong hatred toward Dennis, but I never thought it was enough to put a hit out on him. I quickly racked my brain as I sat on the witness stand, searching for an answer to this riddle. I formulated as many reasons as I could, slightly losing focus of the more important task at hand of defending my own innocence.

"Can you please play the tape for the courtroom to hear?" The Judge asked

"Yes, your Honor." The DA responds.

As the DA stood to play the tape, I continued to dig my brain for a logical reason why Fulton would want Dennis dead. The best explanation I could gather was— Amber only had two sons that were not Fulton's. One was an autistic man-child so far gone from the actual truth and reality of the situation that he was no threat to Fulton. Dennis on the other hand, was the only generally rational and somewhat sane child that Amber had. Not to mention the fact that Dennis was a disloyal traitor. He would abandon ship the minute the boat took on even an ounce of water. And that type of treacherous stance led Fulton to believe that Dennis would be the only liability to bringing his case of incorruptibility and unrefined self-righteousness to the truthful ground of chastisement.

The DA got to the center of the courtroom where a table sat with a tape player on top. I was vastly unaware of what was on the tape. I just had an uneasy feeling that what ever was on it, probably wasn't going to be any good. Everything else has been fucked up since I decided to stay with my dear old dad, why would this tape be any different? Before the DA hit play, he looked over at me.

"Is there anything you would like to say before this tape is played?" He asked.

His question fell upon my deaf ears because I was still stuck inside my own head, thinking, deliberating, and searching for an answer of what the fuck could be on this tape. I was hoping, pleading and (praying even) that whatever is on it, does not involve me.

"Ryan, is there anything you would like to say before this tape is played?" The DA asked louder to gather my attention.

I was strongly whipped back into my body. I took a deep breath and a dry swallow.

"Nope. Play the tape." I calmly replied.

He hit the play button . . . And what I heard was highly disturbing, but, also somewhat entertaining and funny. On the recorded conversation we could unmistakably hear Fulton hiring his two "Prison Friends" (he swore were legitimate) to kill Dennis and dispose of the body, all for a certain price, and also including a few suggestions of where the best places are to discard of his body. FUCK! They had all the evidence they needed to prosecute.

"Do you know anything about this, Ryan?" The DA asked me.

"Not a clue. I don't know who those men are." I shakily replied.

"You were not present during this conversation?" The DA hastily asked.

"I was not. I was in the shop working." I responded.

"Do you have any witness's to confirm that you were 'in fact' working during this conversation?" The DA replied.

"I do. The man's name is Rooney. I was working with him all day while my father was talking with these men." I said in slight apprehension.

"Ok. If need be, we will have to call Rooney to the stand to verify your noninvolvement with this conversation." He retorted. "The prosecution rests for now, your Honor." He then finished.

"Does the defense have anything to add to his statement?" The Judge asked.

Fulton's lawyer stood from his chair.

"Yes, your Honor." He said.

He then educated Fulton to stand from his seat and describe his perception of the situation. Fulton produced from his chair as swaggeringly pompous and egotistical as ever. He looked at me — then looked to the Judge — then back to me — then back to the Judge. He was smirking, had a sense of ruin in his eyes. As Fulton spoke, we all listened in tense anticipation. The entire courtroom heard the words that seemed to fall so unproblematic from his smug tongue.

"Your Honor—" Fulton took a deep breath . . . "Ryan was present every step of the way." He then unmorally finished his bogus proclamation.

Like God's giant cock slapping you across your soft face and knocking you to the ground!

I was dizzy after I heard his retort. My heart sank to the bottom of my stomach. I think it might've jumped out of my asshole and ran out the courtroom doors, I'm not quite sure. All I did know was, I was astonished, stupefied, bemused, and to be truthful and rash, not surprised in the fucking least. He was trying to sell out his own son to save his own ass, just to guarantee the fact he wouldn't have to spend his prison term alone. The day just kept on getting worse. I think this is where some of my anger issues began to build. "So much for your fucking wink, huh pops?" was my first thought.

"OBJECTION!" Fulton's lawyer shouts at the top of his lungs. "My client is clearly unmistaken of the true clarity of the story. I wish to be granted a recess till the following morning?" He followed his outburst with.

I, at that very point in time had no choice but to crack a very inappropriate smile. It was really inconvenient and badly timed, I will admit that, but it was merely to help me preserve my own sanity. The Judge caught it out of the corner of his eye and looked over at me.

"Is something funny, son?" He asked in bitter tongue.

"No, nothing is funny." I replied.

"Then why are you smiling?" Judge Rhinestone asked me.

I point directly at Fulton.

"I'm smiling because I was not involved in this shit at all and he fucking knows it!" I yelled at my highest volume.

The courtroom takes a wheezing breath, eyes widened and assholes furrowed. The Judge slams his little hammer of declaration down on its plate.

"Order!" He proclaims. "You will not use that kind of language in my courtroom!" He says.

"I'm sorry, your Honor. This is funny to me because I was not involved in this stuff at all." I finish my statement with those expressions.

Emphasizing on the word stuff so visibly obvious that everyone in that courtroom knew I really meant shit! Judge Rhinestone throws his hammer down to its plate once again, resorting order to his only form of superiority and dominance. He probably had a small and shriveled, pathetic excuse for a cock. The courtroom was quickly taken back under his command.

"This courtroom is released for the day and will reside tomorrow morning at eight A.M." He proclaims in anger.

I think I might've upset him. The entire courtroom stands from their seats and makes haste for the door. The deputies quickly take Fulton far away from me. His lawyer approaches me and invades my personal bubble. He asks me to join him in his office to have a cherished and intimate conversation of truth. The door to his office closes and I was asked to take a seat.

"I would rather stand." I self-importantly respond.

He then proceeds to sit half-assed on his desk while we converse.

"Were you, or were you not involved in the charges you are facing?" He challenges me with this question.

"Fuck no I wasn't involved!" I impatiently and crossly answer.

I was fucking enraged to say the least. There was no hiding my true nature of emotions.

"Ok. I believe you. But if you want to get out of this you have to listen to me and listen well." He said.

"What do I need to do?" I rapidly react.

He then preceded to whisper in my ear . . . Just wait, you will know the whispers soon enough—Then he leaned back up . . .

"Tomorrow, when you arrive, I will do all the talking. You only have to answer yes or no to my questions. I will ensure that Fulton stays silent. All you need to do is keep your answers short and to the point like I just told you." He explains.

"I will do what you told me." I ruefully answer.

"Good. Go home, get some sleep and be ready for tomorrow."

Once again I was handcuffed and walked out of the courthouse by two police officers like I was fucking 'Hannibal Lecter' or some shit, placed in the back seat of a squad car and driven down the long stretch of Florida highway to my grandmother's house. I was un-cuffed and informed not to leave, move or talk to anyone about the case. I knew my boundaries and I was going to abide by each one of them. My grandma had many pressing and vital questions of just how severe the case against Fulton was, and the charges he was now facing. She also was slightly concerned for my security and welfare also. However, she was always strong on Fulton's side. Fulton was one of her four children, and she would stand by that mans side till the bitter and burning end. I kept her informed the most I legally could. Not to unravel or decode this case in any shape or form, and end up destroying, dismantling or demolishing my own train of liberty. We both stayed up late that night, talking almost till the next rapidly arising morning . . . And just as familiar and common as we were to this particular awakening; the cops were KNOCKING at the door again.

They threw the handcuffs over my delicate young wrists and I found myself once more in the back seat of a police squad car. They drove me down the wide, extensive stretch of Florida highway, to the punctually sooner, rather than the yearningly later, immediately approaching courthouse. My door was swung open and I was asked to exit the vehicle.

"What doesn't kill us will only make us stronger."

CHAPTER TEN:

My Year with Fulton: Part Six, Six, Six.

"Jesse James was an outlaw and Wyatt Earp was a policeman, and there was one thing they both had in common. They were both as dignitary and as individually different as they chose to be."

Day two: (Insert) Guns N' Roses. Sweet Child O' Mine.

This shit was going to be Rock Star epically unfolding before my eyes. And I was the badass, cold-blooded, lead guitarist. I was fucking 'Slash,' man. Everything was as fresh as a bright blue sky and I was about to be taken away to that special place where I would probably breakdown and cry.

The two officers walked me into the courtroom and I was once again presented with the luminous and graphic illustration of Fulton in his bright, ever so decent orange fitting jumpsuit. He didn't even attempt in the art of looking me in the eye. Not even a meaningless gaze, a kind gesture of appearance or a representation of my perseverance through this whole confusing and fucked up situation. He had chosen to involuntarily, unconsciously and instinctively stare ahead. He was animalized and demoralized, perverting his attention to the entering Judge Rhinestone. What ever the words his lawyer had said to him had finally found their way to the core of his black, frozen, hollow and empty soul. Or what was left of his buttfucked soul. He had been diminished, compressed, his ever so cockstrong and indestructible ego was found reduced and defective. He was a complete and different person altogether. To be honest (with a slight moment of care) it was a bit heartbreaking and corrupt to see him this way. So much for being an iron willed King! He folded faster than an untested poker player or a fragile dog out in the wild hunting for its meal of the day.

Nevertheless, it wasn't the time for sympathy, worry or compassion now. I was still part of a heavily collapsing and inevitable grave ending card house. I had to stay watchful and strapping. I was not going to be found as a victim to this hastily failing game of charades. The Bailiff took his place in the center of the courtroom and entered the Honorable Judge Rhinestone. The room was tense and thick with curiosity. Today was the day the defense was to rest its case. And I was hoping, on tenterhooks, even praying if you will (as much as a Godless believer can) that I got out of this shit unharmed and without my beautiful tight young asshole violently gang raped in jail. The Judge took his seat and ordered the room to sit. It was dead silent in the courtroom. You couldn't slip a fart out to save your life. Everyone sat with fascinating ruse. Fulton's lawyer was called on first. He stood and cleverly offered up his piece of truth.

"My client, Fulton, pleads guilty to the count of first degree arson, grand thief auto and hire for murder. His son, Ryan Vinci, pleads not guilty to the charges against him. He was nothing more than an innocent bystander and was merely a victim of circumstance." His lawyer stated.

Goddamn that shit sounded so fucking amazing to hear. The words not guilty have <u>never</u> felt so good to hear.

"Does Ryan Vinci, have anything to share with the court about his purposed innocence?" The Judge asked. Fulton's lawyer looked at me.

"Yes, your Honor. He would like to state his claim of disannulment to the crimes charged against him." He said.

"Please approach the bench young man, this time, without the profane language please." Judge Rhinestone said to me.

I got up from my seat and walked to the Bailiff where I was swore under oath in the court of law and asked to take a seat at the bench. My armpits were sopping in nervous sweat and my throat was fixed. It was time to speak.

"I, Ryan Vinci, state for the record, that I had absolutely no involvement in the charges being tested against my name. I was asleep during all this criminal activity and I have no knowledge, nor any recollection of the events which I am being charged for." I said to the court. And those were the words which Fulton's lawyer coached me to say the day prior in his secret whispers. And I must say. The Oscar for best actor of the year goes to . . . Drum roll please . . . Ryan Motha-Fuckin' Vinci! I was reciting the words he told me to speak ever so smoothly and festively. I was fucking flawless and perfect. It was the brightest day of my acting career.

"Alright. The court will take an hour recess and the jury will come to a final verdict." The Judge informed the court as he slammed his hammer down.

The sound of that mallet being slammed down made my heart jump in uncomplicated fright because I knew the time of decision was now here, and I had no choice but to wait for my resolve.

Two officers took Fulton away to a holding cell in the courtroom; he didn't look in my direction at all, not even a slight glimpse. The two cops that drove me here approached me, asked to stand, turn around and put my hands behind my back. The cold metal handcuffs were slapped on my wrists and I was placed in another holding cell. It was a light grey bricked, unkind and empty room. Nothing more than a metal bench and an assailing camera pointed at the bench and staring upon you with an esteemed and judging eye. That hour of my life was by far the most deliberately slow moving hour ever. I was forced to sit in seclusion, with nothing but my own thoughts and remembrance. If a person was going to break, crack or fold, this was the time. I couldn't stop sweating and I wished for just a cold glass of water to ease my dry throat.

Click! Clack! The door to my tank, my cage, was being unlocked from the other side. The door opened and the fresh crisp air wisped in. It felt amazing. I was walked into the courtroom and placed standing side by side with Fulton. I was un-cuffed and stood strong, tall, ready to accept the conviction and implore of either innocent or guilty. Fulton was still cuffed, locked down in his chains of justified conduct. I was no more than five feet from him. Neither one of us acknowledged each other, just stood looking forward and waited for the Judge to speak.

"Has the jury reached a decision?" The Judge asked. The jury spokesman stood.

"Yes, your Honor, we have. We the jury, find Fulton, guilty on the count of first degree arson, grand theft auto, and hire for murder." The spokesman said.

"Why the hell did Fulton get to go first?" Was my Goddamn thought? The anticipation was killing me. I couldn't stop sweating profusely. "Read my fucking outcome already!" I yelled inside my head.

"And we the jury, find Ryan Vinci, not guilty on all charges and dismiss him as an unintelligent minor with no insight of the crimes against him." The jury spokesman said.

Even though he pretty much blatantly called me stupid to my own damn face by using the word unintelligent (which was a dick move) I wasn't about to step out of line and say something dim to ruin this wonderful moment. I was now free to go and that shit was undyingly fucking awesome! The officers quickly walked Fulton far away from my sight and into his new life of nasty prison food, and freezing cold, cock infested showers.

DON'T DROP THE SOAP DOUCHBAG!

CHAPTER ELEVEN:

Grand Finale of The Fucked Fulton Story.

"I didn't ask to be such an animal . . . I just never figured out the difference until it was all too late."

Day three: (Insert) Temple of the Dog. Say Hello to Heaven.

T here I was, cleared and released for freedom and liberation. The world was now my oyster. My plane ticket was booked, a luxurious town car which my mother spent 'assloads' (yes, a technical term) of money on, was coming in the next ever so hastily approaching morning to drive me to the airport and send me on my way to harmony and serenity. I had but only one more colossal hurdle to jump in my story of desperation and heaviness of heart before I was to depart. I had to go to the prison and see Fulton one last time. I knew as decisively and realistically sound as possible, this was not going to be an effortless or easy feat by any measure. But, an act I was obliged, yet grateful, to see through until the tart and depthless end.

My grandmother drove to the prison (with a police escort of course) because grandma was very elderly.

And with all due respect, couldn't drive for fucking shit. The drive was slower than thickly moving molasses. We pulled into the parking lot of the prison, wide-eyed, both emotionally encircled and struggling for words to in fact speak. The camera at the visiting prison door scanned our bodies, checking for peril or threat. The loud buzzing sound of the alarm went off to open the door and we were cleared for access. The door was harshly swung open and there stood an officer. He checked grandma's bag, her body and coattails. He then checked my pockets, socks, shoes, and all and any hidden crevasses. No threats were detected and we were moved along to the holding cell. We were trapped behind a wall of glass with nothing but a phone and two chairs in which to seat our bottoms. Grandma and I sat on our seats of legitimacy while we awaited the graceful arrival of Fulton.

Grandma and I waited forty-two long and ever so pressing minutes till Fulton was unfolded before our eyes. An officer walked him in with both his hands cuffed in front of him. He was in his flamboyant and vivid orange jumpsuit. He took a seat at the chair which he was granted and quickly touched the glass. Before he even held the phone to his ear, he put his hand tense against the glass. Like a pit bull locked in a cage, a tiger tranquilized in discipline or an inmate in solitude. It was downright sad and credence destroying. As much anger and pure hate I had towards Fulton. He was still my father, my seed. And there was nothing that could ever alter that fact. It was so fucking hard and remorseful to see Fulton locked behind this window of compliance and surrendering regret. I had no other choice but to breakdown and cry. My eyes started to water faster than a teenage girl at a 'Twilight' screening, my mouth started to salivate more than a fat kid at an all you can eat buffet, my words began to slur faster than a drunk in police custody and my nose was beginning to run rivers bigger than 'Ozzy' at a free cocaine giveaway. That being said, no disrespect to Ozzy at all. That motherfucker is a God in my world. I have grown up on his words and love him till the day we meet in The Seats of Hell. I wanted to use Lindsay Lohan as a reference, but that twisted, valueless, stupid cokehead bitch doesn't deserve my writing. You're welcome I used your name for a pithy trice . . . But I'm way off point—

I couldn't stand to see him behind this glass, locked away in a prison of uncertainty and clout. I felt a rapid sense of blame and guilt. Here he was, my own father, trapped, sheltered and spellbound behind this glass fence of penal complex. As he picked up the phone to talk, my grandmother snatched the other end of the listening phone ever so bustled and with rushed apathetic obey. We only had twenty minutes of conversation time. He knew that, I knew that, grandmother knew that. So it was time to manage his words as prudently and shrewdly as possible.

"Ma, can you please hand the phone to Ryan?" He asked my grandma.

She did as she was asked. I took a compact grip of that grubby, villainous, spit-covered phone and listened to the last face to face words my biological father would ever articulate to me. I was a bit inquisitive and prying to his everlasting echo.

"Son, I want you to know, I'm not mad at you. I'm sorry things had to turn out this way. It is up to you to protect this family and be the 'King.' I will see you once I get out."

That was the last words (still till this day) I ever saw him verbalize in person.

I couldn't contain my perpendicular distress anymore. I slammed the phone down and ran out of that the room as a gutless coward. His backhanded confession of guilt was as far from the valid responsibility of truth that it ever could've been. And I was forced to give up, reside and overlook him forever. All I wanted was for him to take liability for his actions. JUST ONCE! However, he was too stubborn in his own innocence to grant me even that small and insignificant favor. "How in the fuck are you not mad at me? What in the fuck did I ever do to land you in this place? Besides of course tell the truth, the whole truth and nothing but the truth, so help me God?" That was the only question that was in my head.

I sat outside waiting in the parking lot, alone and crying, until the time of visitation was up and my grandmother came walking out through the prison doors. She was upset with me, perturbed with my selfish and childlike acts of running away from my own so-called 'father.' She didn't know the real truth, never has and never will. All I can say is. "God Rest Her Naive Soul."

She will never have to be a victim to his web of deceiving, bamboozled, idiotically self-centered lies. After many prolonged and exhausting years of abuse and fraudulence, she thankfully died to rest in peace from this unchained and aggressive life her own son had enforced her to suffer through. I love, miss and will always have the utmost respect for my grandma. I wish her nothing but peace and stillness in her grave of rest. However, that poor woman had to stand by one of the most psychotic individuals I have ever known. That moment in time will forever remain as one of the most nightmarishly accounts I was ever blessed with the opportunity to witness with my own two eyes. I am awakened at night with that vivid and colorful scene being played out. It's just tragic. Nevertheless, I was now a whole, complete, one hundred percent free MOTHER FUCKER!!

Cue the music: Moby. Flower.

God Fucking Dammit, that shit felt so great. Words can't describe clearly enough the feeling that was in my stomach, my soul, my mind and my body. It was fucking epic. I had my swagger back. I was picked up the next following morning in a spotless town car, chauffeured to the airport like I was 'Donald Trump,' escorted to my seat on the plane by a sweet, pretty little number of a flight attendant. I took a firm place on my window spot and I was FINALLY ready to go home! Both reassured and relieved by the utter fact, that it was time to be a kid again. The captain started the loud jet propelled motors and we took off into the open sky. Free and clear!

On the flight home, I was hooked up with some headphones from the same pretty little thing that walked me to my seat. I sat my chair back, threw them bad boys on and watched the in-flight movie with great attention and respect. I can't remember the name of the film. It was starring 'John Travolta' as a congressman running for presidency who has to overcome a sex scandal . . .

"—Wait! Primary Colors. That's the name of the film, great movie. Check it out sometime, Bob."

The reason why I mention this film is; this particular experience is the true power of how the universe works. An ironic event if you will. One that was both earth shattering, and entirely fucking bona fide in my life. It was a moment of complete disbelief in God, or maybe belief. I don't really know? I don't think I'll ever be able to figure out the true makings of this spiritual decipher. Allow me to explain for your confusion . . .

Fulton and I would eat at Cracker Barrel from time to time. After our meal we would sit out front on the wooden rocking chairs they had for sale. Fulton would have his after meal cigarette and he would always sing the same song to me.

"You are my sunshine, my only sunshine, you make happy when skies are grey. You know the song I'm talking about."

The reason why I bring this up is because, as I sat on that airplane, mystified and focused to that film as if it was the last cinematic adventure I would ever see. There was a part in the movie that John Travolta's character, 'Governor Jack Stanton,' sings that song to another person. It was at that instant . . . I fucking lost it! I started to cry, laugh, scream and joke. Snot was running from my nose and I didn't give a shit. I don't think the people sitting next to me appreciated it none, but fuck 'em, that's what I say. The hot little flight attendant that sat me came to check on the racket coming from my chair.

"Ryan, are you ok?" She asked me with worry and concern in her gorgeous voice.

I looked that beautiful, young woman in the eye and repeated the following, very deafeningly, verbatim.

"I am better than ok . . . I just hate this fucking song!" I shouted.

The two people next to me were taken aback, shocked at my foul language and volume control, or lack thereof.

"Alright, can you please keep your voice down though? There are others on the airplane." She asked me.

"Yeah. Sorry." I said to her.

She went about her business with the other passengers. I then, unrelentingly, loudly and periodically cried the entire five-hour plane ride home. Not out of sadness, sorrow, guilt, or missing my father. OH FUCKS NO! I cried out of pure, inclusive, total, uninhibited joy and content.

"I was no longer a victim."

CHAPTER TWELVE:

Salvaging My Teen Years.

"If you lose your sense of direction, love will always be your compass home."

I was back at home with my loving and endearing mother, times were great and life was beautiful. There was nothing that could harm me anymore. I rode bikes with my friends, hated high school (much like every kid) stayed up too late, farted and laughed about it, ate entirely way too much candy and chocolate and loved every untainted and profound second of it. I was an extremely ugly kid when I hit my pubescent years. Tall, skinny, pale, had an Afro atop my head and acne plagued my white face. However, none of that mattered to me. I was just happy to be home.

As averagely normal and seemingly straight-laced I was to the public, I still had the burden of my past events weighing on my mind. And the repressed memories were only fueling my already ravenous lion, to the point where that lion was starting to eat me alive. I couldn't help but hear such trivial, unimportant measures at school—much like this example:

"Oh my God! Can you believe Jimmy called Tiffany fat?"

That type of stupid, brainless, ignorant mined dribble (the typical high school norm if you will) which always drove me nuts, would always make me think to myself. "You kids don't even know what true pain is." I went to high school in Valencia, California. What kind of pain did those kids have? They were all loaded with cash. What? Did your Daddy's black card get declined at Abercrombie and Fitch? Go fuck yourself! Clearly I had anger issues. I didn't think I was better than anyone by any means, I still don't and I never will. I just had absolutely no need, or want for that matter, to surround myself with these immature people, talking about the latest phone on the market or some party that got raided—or what ever the topic of the month was. So, on the third week of my eleventh grade year, I went to my mother and told her (not so much asked) more stated a claim of my own independence.

"Mom, I really don't like my high school. I can't deal with the dumb conversations and acts that happen there. I am going to enroll in a charter school, which is very sound educationally, and finish out my time out there." I declared to her.

"Alright." She replied.

The next week I was enrolled in a new and exciting form of school. I was given books and packets, told to read, follow and answer all the questions in the books and packets. Come in twice a week, for an hour at a time, and take the testing required to gage my knowledge. Perfect. I had my own car, a friend at my new school. We picked the same days and timeframes, rode together, and knocked out three, sometimes four tests at a time. And we both were starting to gain lead over all the kids in our age group. For a person like myself, a self taught writer, and just an all-around hands on learner, this was the ideal setup for me. It freed up time for me to ride my dirt bike and have fun. And the best part was. I wasn't forced to sit and listen to incoherent, senseless recollections of normal high school life and activities. "One of my better decisions in life." Ha-ha. I laugh at that because

I've done some really stupid shit in my day. Making good choices was not an acquired taste of mine until I grew up a bit. To be completely honest, I still do make some very questionable choices. But we'll get there soon enough . . .

Just before my happily impending seventeenth birthday, I was alerted with a dreaded phone call. One that I never wished to get; a play of events I never wanted to deal with again.

Fulton had been released from Prison and sentenced to ten years of probation in the state of Florida. He wasn't to leave the state of Florida or the country, ordered not to indulge in drug activity or associate himself with any dubious or shady characters. So, in true and pure, arrogant and narcissistic Fulton-fashion, the cocksucker skips town a week after his granting of freedom and makes his way west to the beautiful, sunny state of California. As I listened to his voice over the phone, I had a painful engulf of fear and terror. I felt the same feelings that I had repressed for two years now. My strong and unyielding self worth that I've been building since I got back to my mother's arms was literally shriveling in front of me. I began to have flashbacks of that cold and hard seat at the witness stand, fighting for my own freedom and hearing my name being called with the word prosecution next to it. The frosty metal handcuffs around my wrists holding me down like a dog in a kennel. The back seat of the police squad cars, the holding cells, the trial, the visitation room, it was all rushing back and rapidly crippling me to my knees. "No fucking way this shit is happening again?" I thought to myself as he egotistically spoke on the other end of the phone.

My palms and armpits began to pour with sweat, my throat was tightening and my body was going numb. I didn't want to, I couldn't, and I refused to believe this was real. That this man showing back up in my life, was in fact tangible legitimacy. He had taken asylum in a city just a short thirty-minute drive from my home. I had no words to express the point clear and definite enough to him, that I had no fucking intentions to see him at all (or ever again for that matter) I just sat quietly, listening as he asked for my embrace. I didn't know how to retort to his stipulation. I froze in shock and panic.

"Ok, I will try and make it down there this week." I said to him.
Knowing damn well there was no way in Hell I was going to see him.

I was angry, irritated, pissed off and my pain and aguish were both too strong for me to forgive his actions and grant this piece-of-shit the pleasure of a face-to-face conversation. Fuck you and the white horse you road in on! That's what I say.

The short nine-month endeavor of him taking hidden residency in some ghetto California City, on the run from 'Johnny Law,' escaping his real punishment and prosecution, was vastly never ending. I didn't know how, nor had the power to accept this bitter fact of accuracy. In the time it takes for a baby to take shape and be given life, this douchebag was in my state, my home, and my very world. It was fucking pathetic . . . I was pathetic! Not having the strength to tell him to kick rocks and go climb back under the rotten bag of shit from which he crawled. It was sad. However, a super storm was brewing and he was going to find his ass right in the eye of the storm.

For the longest nine months of my life this current little act or charade of his went on and on as I sat in tension and disbelief. My brothers didn't have the same unchained anger and hatred that I held towards Fulton. Plus, they were both into the partying scene. So, they would go down and hang out with him a few times a week, smoke pot, drink some beers, watch Fulton snort coke, God only knows what else. They would ask me every time if I wanted to partake in the festivities. I always made up a fictitious and fabricated bullshit excuse of why I was too busy and took off running far, far away from that jackass and his cocaine nonsense.

Fulton would make a phone call to me once a week to ask why I haven't come to see him. I back stepped the question each time, always digging my own grave, hiding from saying the actual and real words I wanted to speak. "Because you're a fucking asshole and I never want to see you again!" That's what I was longing to say, but didn't possess the bona fide courage to ever speak . . . Not yet at least . . .

After about eight and a half months of me dodging his calls and invites to hangout, he gave me a friendly phone call. He had pressing questions and concerns of my whereabouts. He was pushing me to the breaking point, his voice was aggressive and abusing, and his true self was showing through the cloudy haze of falsehood and manipulation. And his world was about to crash down before his cock sucking eyes.

I FUCKING SNAPPED!!

"I HAVE NOT COME TO SEE YOU, BECAUSE YOU ARE A PIECE OF SHIT, MOTHER FUCKER! I HATE EVERYTHING ABOUT YOU! I HATE HOW YOU TALK, I HATE HOW YOU LOOK, AND I HATE HOW YOU SMELL. I HATE WHAT YOU STAND FOR, I HATE WHAT YOU BELIEVE IN, I HATE WHAT YOU PUT ME THROUGH AND I HATE HOW YOU'VE HURT THIS FAMILY...BUT, MOSTLY, I PURELY JUST HATE YOU! I DO NOT WANT TO SEE YOU, SPEAK TO YOU, OR EVER HEAR ABOUT YOU AGAIN! YOU ARE THE BIGGEST ASSHOLE, PIECE OF SHIT, COCK SUCKING, MOTHER FUCKER I'VE EVER MET! YOU CARE ONLY ABOUT YOURSELF, YOU SHIT ON EVERYTHING AND YOU BELIEVE IN NOTHING! YOU'RE A DRUG ADDICT, A LIAR AND A CHEATER. YOU'RE ABUSIVE AND YOU HURT EVERYONE THAT CROSSES YOUR SELF ABSORBED PATH! I HAVEN'T SEEN YOU BECAUSE FRANKLY, YOU ARE DEAD TO ME! YOU ARE NOTHING BUT A SHITTY STORY THAT I ONCE HAD TO LIVE THROUGH! I LIE TO PEOPLE WHEN THEY ASK ME ABOUT YOU. I TELL THEM YOU DIED BEFORE I WAS BORN! I HOPE, WISH AND PRAY NOTHING BUT THE VERY WORST FOR YOU! I PRAY THAT YOU HAVE

THE MOST PAINFUL DEATH POSSIBLE! WHEN YOU DO FINALLY DIE... I'M GOING TO COME TO YOUR FUNERAL AND PISS ALL OVER YOUR GRAVE, YOU PIECE OF SHIT, MOTHER FUCKER! NOW HAVE A GREAT DAY!"

I smashed my phone on the ground, shattering it into pieces. That was literally, the last time I ever spoke to my so-called 'father.' The ever so clearly and abundantly fucked soul of Fulton was now nothing more than a bad memory, just a terrible nightmare. Fuck him and everything he stands for. Die Slow Mother Fucker! Die Slow!

"Goddamn that felt good! I need a beer. You need a beer, Bob?"

"Sure, I'll take one after that, Ryan."

Shattered is my dreams,
Together is my reality.
Love may be broken, as it seems,
But persistent is my lethality.

About a month later, his copiously offended ex-wife in Florida, Amber, caught wind of his actual location, called the Florida police and sent them down to pick him up. Fulton, being the one-step ahead of everyone, self-centered, self-loathing, narcissistic and arrogant prick that he is; picked up shop and jumped ship just before he could get apprehended. I was greatly happy he had left the state. However, was still frightened that he will resurface like he always does. And bring a tornado of garbage, filth, pain and damage with him. Much like he always did.

My grandfather shares the same undying distaste for the man as I do. And we started playing a game. We called it 'Tracking Fulton.'

"Ok, it wasn't really a game. But for the sake of entertainment, I spiced it up a little bit to get a rise out of you, Bobby-boy. We did however do this . . ."

Every week or two we would log on to the Internet and Goggle his name. Searching dozens of criminal sites, digging for the mug shot and rap sheet we were probing for. This went on for almost a year. The only mug shot and criminal report we could find was his in Florida, and the case was still open, which meant he hadn't been chopped down off his tree house of deception and muck. And then . . . The most glorious, celebrated, superbly liberating thing happened . . .

His mug shot finally appeared on the Internet and Fulton had been caught in Texas. The cock sucker set up a liquor store, gotten married again (to his third wife) and he was playing the whole nourishing father figure, churchgoer, decent human being card. Just another one of his many cleverly thought out con-artistry grand performances. Turns out he got arrested by the local police in Texas for selling alcohol and cigarettes to minors out the back of the liquor store. When they investigated his name, they exposed all his lies, crimes and all the methodically fabricated sham he was running from. He played his cards very well though. Almost a year he managed to flee from the 'Bacon Brigade.' Nevertheless, there was only so long he could run from the great and powerful bitch that is 'Karmic Justice!'

Fulton used to have a saying that he loved to spit from his polluted mouth. By far one of the most idiotic, contradicting, pointless and flawed sayings I've ever heard.

"You can't change the stripes on a tiger." He would always say.

Let me explain what it meant to him when he used to coolly and calmly spat it from his cocaine-clenched jaw.

"That no matter what you do in life. No matter how good of a person you are, and try to lead a normal and fulfilling life, you can never be a bad guy. Why? Because you are born well, good and pure at heart. There for the act of evil is not in your bloodstream. And, no matter if you are the filthiest, dirtiest and downright most disgusting of bad guys. You can never be a wholesome and reformed person. Good is not in your nature, you will always be bad, so why try to pretend to be something you

111

cannot be? By character, outlook, personality, temperament, physics, laws of nature and what ever else binds us to our one and only form of existence. We can only be what we are born as and nothing else. If you're good, than you can only be good. If you're evil, than you'll always be evil until the end of time; never changing, never altering and most importantly, never evolving to a different state of life and belief."

In short: "You can't teach a tiger to hunt for vegetables, just as you can't teach a bird to read a book."

Ergo: "You can't change the stripes on a tiger."
The skills, mindset, disposition and eager to hunt which that tiger is born with, is all the tiger can ever be, nothing more, nothing less.

This to me is the biggest line of bullshit, absurdity, dispute, backwards-assed piece of theory, and complete lack of education that I've ever heard. Let me explain why . . .

A tiger is a creature of instinct, a hunter by nature. However, a tiger is a survivor by trait, a trait resulting from the tiger's very long bloodline. You don't get a long bloodline like the tiger's history by not learning how to evolve and adapt. Of course, the tiger would like to eat a fat and ripe antelope for dinner. But, in times of need and starvation the tiger will settle with a smaller prey; a sick, defenseless cub which has fallen off the trail of the stronger animals. Through the many years of a tiger's life they are forced to settle with what is available and existing to the pride rather than what is satisfying. Why you ask? To survive the day and strive for a better tomorrow; however, the tiger knows that in order for their pride to hunt tomorrow, they must eat today. They must stick together, gain knowledge, evolve and strengthen their fight; but most importantly . . . They must change.

Through my many years of breaking this down, deciphering—picking it apart—dissecting and exploring this phrase. I have come up with an interpretation of my own.

"Would you like to hear it, Bob? Trick question. You don't have a choice." Ryan laughed at his own stupid joke before continuing. "If you think a creature, whether it be an animal or human, can not change, progress, develop, acclimatize and grow. Become smarter, faster and stronger—also expand in knowledge and awareness. Then you my friend . . . You are the prey. Welcome to the jungle!"

Fulton was finally arrested in Texas and was sentenced to eight years in prison. He finally got some of what he fucking DESERVES!

SEXUAL INTERMISSION CHAPTER:

The Losing of my Sweet Virginity.

"Excuse me for being honest, truthful, daring or openly realistic. If you think this is hard to read, try fuckin' an elephant with a tick dick."

— Lil' Wayne.

"The story, which I am undoubtedly going to tell you, Bob, is neither relevant nor important to the finishing upshot to my tale of attempted suicide, heartache and vexation. But, is funny, and will remain till my last hour and my last vanishing breathe, categorically fucking comical. Shut up! Enjoy this shit and laugh, that is all I ask."

"With an opening like that, how can I not, Ryan?"

When I was a saccharine and tender sixteen years old, I was living with my mom in her condo, in an ultra-clicky and very pompous city of Valencia, California. My two brothers' were also staying there for a bit. My eldest brother, Travis, had called over three girls from a distant city.

"You do the math, my friend. There are three boys in my family circle, so a girl for each one of us."

115

"Yeah. I got that. No need for an explanation, you condescending prick." I replied back to Ryan with a sarcastic tone.

"Just checking your math skills, Bobzilla."

Travis came rushing in from outside, where he was on his phone call of convincing awareness and demonstrative eagerness. I was sitting on the recliner of the living room, watching television, stuck in my familiar comfort zone like most nights. My other bother, Floyd, was tight on his position on the couch watching the same brain numbing television that I was fixed to. My brother Travis rushed through the door, with tainted promises of ladies on their way over. He was excited and overwhelmed with pure joy. He said a charming form of words to me, which I never and still don't think I'll ever have the pleasure to hear again.

"Ryan, get your ass up, take a shower, the girls are on their way. Don't look so depressed. We're gonna fuck these girls tonight, be happy." Travis said.

I had no other option but to chuckle. I have jacked off, masturbated, self pleasured, or stimulated my gentiles till the last ending cum (what ever you want to call it) so many Goddamn times at this point in my life, that I knew my own cock better than I knew how to brush my teeth or tie my shoes. I was still a virgin, but had watched countless hours of pornographic films. I felt I was prepared to do some screwing, only if the moment was awaken of course.

The girls arrived without a hitch. Three young, experimental and decently attractive ladies, not super models by any means, but what the fuck did I care? I was sixteen. I would've banged a tailpipe if you told me it felt well. All six of us hung out in the living room at my mother's condo, which, at that time was also Travis' bedroom. He would sleep on the pullout couch at night. The condo was small, had three bedrooms, my mother occupied the master bedroom, Floyd had another room, and I had the other, up the stairs, just off the entrance way. We all sat around that living room, talking, laughing and getting to know one another. I was shy, coy and a bit timid, which meant I kept my ass planted on the recliner. The hours of the night slid off the clock as we all had fun, and the time of playing the game of 'Pick a Mate,' had finally rose.

Floyd took one of the girls to his bedroom, the door closed, and he had pulled his card. Travis and I were now in the living room with the other two girls. I was distant from the conversation, sitting on my recliner of caution. Travis and one of the other girls were hitting it off, flirty, touching, laughing and it was obvious and clear to everyone, they were ending up together. The other girl was talking to me the best she could, attempted to break me from my bashful shell. She then got up, walked over to me, and took an affirmative seat on my lap.

"Well, looks like I get you. You want to show me your room?" She said to me.

"Umm . . . Ok." I watchfully replied.

I was excited but scared at the same time. The most sex I've had was with my right hand. We got up from the recliner, walked upstairs to my dark red painted room with black spray painted logos on the walls, and we were now alone; just her and I. My heart was racing, my palms were sweating, but I was curious to see what the outcome of this situation was to be. We sat on the bed, tongue tied and awkward.

"What do you want to do?" She asked me.

"I don't know." I apprehensively responded.

"Do you have condoms?" She then questioned.

Which . . . You bet your ass I did, every kid at sixteen stockpiles condoms in the hopes they will use them, but normally they just end up getting wasted through a lonely jerking session of thy old cock.

"Grab your condoms, turn the lights off and let's start." She said to me.

I wasn't going to try and overanalyze what that statement meant. I jumped off my bed, hit the lights, grabbed my infinite string of condoms and hopped back on my bed in enthusiasm.

We started to kiss, touch and play. She was leading the act, at first, and it was nice. We were making progress, but I think it was very lucid that I was unmistakably inexperienced. We were slowly undressing, kissing and feeling on each other. My style was sloppy, misguided and unproven. Then, she stopped the kissing, pulled away and looked at me. "What happened, did I break it?" I quickly thought to myself.

"Are you a virgin?" She asked me.

My desperate secret had been revealed, and I was forced to lie, not to look stupid in these current circumstances.

"No, I've had sex before, lots of sex." I poorly worded my reply.

"Ok, then prove it." She said to me.

A challenge was presented, to prove my bravery and my worth as a cock wielding man. All right, it was game time. I've seen enough porn. I could figure this shit out. Like I said before, I'm a hands-on learner.

I rolled her over and took full control. I got us both completely naked, and I then proceed to fuck, bang, hump, pound and fornicate that girl, 'Lionel Richie Style,' All Night Long (All Night) it was fucking adventurous and epic. We were doing every position in the book, there was limbs being thrown every which way around my bedroom. I was licking parts of another human being I never knew were there, tasting strange fluids I never knew existed. I was cumming every thirty minutes. I was burning through my stack of condoms, but I didn't give two shits, this was awesome. It was an all night screw fest. I had a small twin bed that was pushed up against the wall, and I would fuck her missionary, cowgirl, rabbitstyle and doggystyle. She asked me to pull her hair and slam her head against the wall. Consider it done. Thunk, thunk, thunk, was the sound of her head being whacked against the cold, hard wall as I pulverized her from behind.

We would flip, rotate and change positions every time I would bust a nut. When it came down to the new condom switch, she would lay me on the bed and suck me off for a bit, teasing me, playing with my cock, then she would slip another condom on and ask for more. I slapped her ass, ripped her hair back, pressed her head down and pounded, fucked, slammed, screwed, banged, porked and humped that girl till the next rising morning. Without any form of exaggeration, embellishment or ornamentation, I must've came ten times that night, throwing my cum filled condoms on the floor and reaching for another—all while getting blowjobs, handjobs, my nutsack licked and learning how to eat pussy. I was playing the difficult game of finding the G-spot, the clit and doing some asshole tickling, a very informative, educational and enlightening event to say the least. It was a wild and extremely memorable night. One, which will forever linger as fully and completely fucking entertaining to me, just as it was for me on the night it all . . . Went down.

"If you know what I mean?"

"Oh . . . I got your childish joke, Ryan."

"You're no fun, Bob."

"Just finish your damn story."

The next morning we all woke. I had a smile on my face and a feeling in my cock that was ever so mind blowing. I just had one of the best times of my life, and it was at that moment, I thought to myself. "Oh yeah. I can definitely do that for the rest of my life." She and I got out of bed, headed downstairs where the other four were already awake and sitting. The morning was a little awkward, but Travis broke the tension up real fast.

"So, we have to go do something for a friend. You girls are gonna have to take off." He said to them.

"That's cool. We have to get home anyways." One of the girls answered.

We walked the girls to their car, said our goodbyes, and sent them bitches on their way. They drove away into the distance, never for me to see that girl ever again.

My two brothers' wanted to get some well-needed breakfast, and they told me to change out of my sleepwear and let's head to the local diner. I went up to my bedroom, cock firm and comfortably impressed with my performance last night. I went through my wardrobe and pulled out a dark pair of jeans; put them on, no underwear of course. I was hanging like a 'Rock Star' now. Grabbed my black, very tight-fitting, 'Guns N' Roses' T-shirt, put that bad boy on and we headed off to get some food and talk about our audacious nights. Just shy of visiting a hooker for my first time, this was the most 'Rock N' Roll,' bad boy, ego-changing, and self-esteem altering experiences of my life. And I don't ever regret the outcome of that event.

"On a side note, Bob. I still own that same 'Guns N' Roses' T-shirt to this day, and still squeeze my considerably larger frame into it from time to time. Just as a nostalgic flashback of the simpler times that were."

"There's an image I didn't need. Thanks for that nightmare inducing thought."

Ryan just laughed as he guzzled down some more liquor.

CHAPTER THIRTEEN:

The House of Animals.

"Don't think of all the things you fear, just be pleased you feel."

T here I was. Young, wise, strong and granted the next eight years of my life to be peaceful and complimentary. I was in this world to cope, survive and conquer. I was now free to make my own choices, my own mistakes, and more importantly . . . Write my own ending. I was unchained from the accustomed doghouse of vindictive fury, torture and abuse. The day was brighter and the nights were crystal clear and luminously beautiful. The death defying game of chicken had unfolded to its cold and shallow end. And I came out victorious. And stronger than I ever knew possible . . . Momentarily that is . . .

Cue the music: Birdy. Shelter

Just where one shitty and decrepit chapter wrote its last stuttered words, another page was turned and it was time to put pen to paper and create something beautiful, something unforgettable. My mother sold her condo and we had both moved into a hugely overpriced house with all the makings of an opulent compound. The house had four bedrooms, a pool, a spa, an outdoor smoking patio that was enclosed by screens and an enormous back-yard, just an all around absolute magnificent home. She and I shared the confines of this overwhelmingly elegant home for about three months or so. She had met a new fellow named 'Dick,' that had the ability to hold her attention and it was nice to see her with a smile on her face. I was quickly getting involved with a young girl named 'Trinity,' that I had met off the lovely Internet fucksite that teenagers used to meet and hook up (otherwise know as MySpace) and I was ever so happy. I was attending high school twice a week and swiftly closing in on graduation. I was still striving for my own independence so I went out and got myself a nice little fulltime job sitting behind the bulletproof glass at a bank, slanging cash and credit for a seemingly fare wage. Life was becoming a moderately self-soothing period.

My two bothers would come up on weekends and we would all sit by the pool and have some fun. My mother was one of those 'Cool Moms' if you will, and would let us all have a couple of drinks by the pool as long as safety was taken into account. Trinity and I were becoming more serious with every passing day, and she was to become my first 'real girlfriend,' even though at seventeen years old, I really didn't know a Goddamn thing about love. But, I went along with the motions of what I thought was a healthy companionship. We were all having a good time and enjoying the company as a slightly misunderstood and highly dysfunction family. Around the center of my seventeenth year of living, my mother came to me with a question that I had been longing for my whole so-called adult life.

"Dick got a job offer in Arizona and we are going to move there. You have a fulltime job and you're basically supporting yourself. You are more than welcome to come with us, or you could stay here, find some roommates and live on your own? You decide, Ryan?" My mother asked.
I didn't contemplate that question for more than a fleeting second before I answered.

"I'll find some roommates and stay. Thanks for the offer, but I will manage, momma." I quickly said back to her.

Who wouldn't want to stay? Get set out into this big and bad world before I was eighteen. Where the fuck do I sign? Most of my life I've struggled for self-government and self-determination. And here I was granted an easy path with absolutely no strings attached. I snatched that forbidden fruit faster than cock-swinging Adam ever could. It was no troublesome task to fill the three empty bedrooms of my new home. All it took was two phone calls and I had found four people that were move-in-ready. My brother Floyd was one of them, along with his girlfriend at the time—they were to share one of the empty rooms. A male friend of ours from high school took the other room and his on and off again fling occupied another. What could go wrong? Five people under the age of 24 all existing beneath one roof with access to a huge pool and stylish spa (not to mention alcohol and drugs) sounds pretty fuckin' safe to me! Sign me up!

I was the youngest of the household, standing loud and proud at seventeen and a half. I had my own truck, my own job, my own rent to cover, my girlfriend, and one of the most satanically possessed cats to ever walk this planet. This cat was a fucking nightmare.

"On the record, Bob. I love animals, sometimes more than people. However, that being said, this cat was the most evil present I've ever purchased for a person. I bought the feline as a gift for Trinity, but lo and behold, her parents didn't want any more pets, which meant the burden of taking care of this little asshole animal was mine. Before you go getting your panties all in a bunch over my inconsiderate tongue towards an innocent animal . . . Let me explain myself."

"Ha-ha-ha. Please, go ahead, Ryan."

"This cat would literally creep in the shadows of my room at night waiting until I was sound asleep, planning his assault, waiting for me to shut my eyes in slumber—Then attack the fuck out of me. He would go for my neck, ears and mouth. The bastard once scratched my eyeball while I was sleeping. MY FUCKING EYEBALL! I couldn't see for almost a month. I fucking hate that cat. But, I digress, let's keep moving . . ."

"Let's." I replied with a giggling tongue.

The first couple of months in the household were going excellent and well. We all settled in as roommates, enjoyed our company and respected our boundaries. We threw more kickass parties than ever imaginable; and the sweet smell of marijuana, alcohol-ridden youngsters, unprotected sex and regret filled the air. Life was simple and free. I was an avid pot smoker at this time (after mom left) and I became an all out stoner. A burnout toker, if you will. I was higher than 'Snoop Dogg' at a 'Kotton Mouth Kings' concert. I started drinking with the older crowd that ran threw the house, and found that the effects of alcohol and weed can really make for an interesting sex life. Trinity would indulge from time to time, creating for an even more difficult and sloppy sexual experience. She was never really a social person at the time, which caused confusion and a slight form of resentment in our relationship. I always wanted to be a part of the parties, and she would rather lockup in my room and watch television. You can see how this could generate an issue. She never wanted to be part of the shenanigans, which meant I couldn't be a part of the tomfoolery. However, I had to form a little system to have my cake and eat it to. Every time I left my room for a cigarette break. I would go to the kitchen where the party mostly was held. Shotgun a few beers, hit a joint and return in a timely fashion so I didn't get in trouble. Get in trouble in my own house that I pay for. Can someone say pussy-whipped? (I sarcastically laugh) Nevertheless, I made the best of my situation.

As the parties started to become a four sometimes five nights a week occurrence, my substance intake began to grow, and needless to say, my performance at work was suffering. However, I didn't really give a fuck. I hated my job so there was no love loss there. I was enjoying my years as a wild and (occasionally) reckless teenager, when Trinity would allow it that is. This time in life was purely epic. Every morning that I would wake up late for work, I had to shake off my hazy marijuana coma, drink some water to settle my hangover, only to walk into my living room and see a scattering of people all around. Couch surfers, vagabonds, drifters, all passed-out, slightly clothed, smelling like shame and disappointment. Goddamn it was Rock-Star Gold. I loved every transitory second of it . . .

But, just as the fun and genuinely uninhibited times were, all good things must come to an end. The pile of bills began to stack so high that they eventually came toppling down. None of us could come up with the money to maintain this 'Charlie Sheen' lifestyle and we got evicted from the property. Kicked to the curb, banished, ejected!

Thanks for coming out . . . NOW GET THE FUCK OUT!!

I boarded up in a city roughly about thirty minutes from my job, in beautiful Burbank, California. I was squatting in my grandparent's garage (my mothers' parents) and was still romantically distracted with Trinity. She lived in the city that I worked, which was convenient. But, this now meant I was a bitter commuter. Waking up at the ass-crack of dawn to battle through loads of traffic to a job I outstandingly hated, only to feel slightly privileged and thankful to work for a careless corporate establishment that had no worth or concern for their employees. Oh-Fucking-Joy! The short thirty minutes between Trinity and I was beginning to wear thin on both our patience's. She refused to drive to my city, not because she was lazy, but she never had money. She didn't work, only attended school, which meant every activity, movie, event or adventurous time had to be funded by my dime only. And that was really starting to piss me off.

I was eighteen years of age now (soon to be nineteen) and I had absolutely nothing to show for it. I found myself over drafted, consumed and buried in debt, and applying for more. Not a good position to be in. I just couldn't do it anymore. I needed to be free once more. I longed for detachment but lacked the confidence or stride to vocalize my words correctly . . . So, I sat around and did what I was told, making sure not to stir the boiling pot.

At this current stage in life my ugly and awkward face was starting to blossom into a somewhat more attractive flower. Therefore my phone was ringing more often than not. Ironically (my best friend now) Levi, was at this time actually, my archenemy. Why you ask? Drum roll please . . . You guessed it . . . All because of a girl. He was dating an equally controlling lady (just as I was) and Levi, constantly assumed I was a threat. We hated each other till the bitter end. We couldn't even be in the same room with out trying to rip each other's throats out. However, Levi had just gotten out of his tainted relationship and him and I ran into each other at a party. We had a well-needed conversation of the misconstrued intentions that he thought I had for his girl. And from that night on he and I were starting to grow as friends, buddies, companions. And soon to be everlasting heterosexual life mates.

On this particular night I am recalling, I was drafted to go to some whack-ass tea party with some of our 'Couple Friends' if you will. You know what I'm talking about. Couples always surround themselves with other couples, never the fun single guy or wild party girl. No!! It's always the boring, lackluster couples of the girls choosing. Kill me now . . . Nevertheless, there I was at this completely uninteresting and even worse, unentertaining tea party with the other couples. One of the kids at this party (or lack thereof party) was holding it at their parents' house. All so we could gather around and sip on some nasty tea and listen to her dad talk current events, inflation prices, political nonsense, earlier times, and some other unless jargon I had no intentions of ever retaining. What kind of lame teenagers hold a tea party in the first place? Pour up the liquor and let's make some bad decisions already.

But, there I was, in one of the most dreary times of my life, listening to her dad go on and on about some dull and unimportant twaddle, all while daydreaming that I was getting wasted and waking up naked in a bizarre place. That was when one of the most significant phones calls from Levi came through. I kindly walked outside to answer my phone and was altered about a raging house party in my hometown of Burbank. One of our buddy's parents was out of town and he had the house to himself for the weekend. The liquor was in abundance, the joints were getting passed around and the ladies were getting wild and crazy. An epic party is how he described it.

"That's my kind of fucking party." I said to Levi.

"Get the group together and get your fucking ass down here, brother!" He shouted back.

We hung up the phone and I went strolling back inside with a shit-eating grin from ear to ear. I was going to free these poor teens from a penitentiary of boredom and monotony. I informed them of the new change in party dynamic and everyone was more than overjoyed . . . Everyone—but Trinity. She for some reason was not onboard. Overboard even. She had absolutely no care to indulge in this act of careless youth and teenage years. Sometimes I felt she was 17 going on 80. All she ever had desire to do was wrap up in a blanket, sit in front of a television and sip on tasteless fluids. She pulled me aside so we could have the dreaded 'Talk.'

"Why are you so excited to go hangout with your friends?" She asked me.

"I want US to go. Not me, US. It's going to be fun, don't worry." I replied.

She then began to cry very generously, and extremely unattractively, asking me pressing questions of my true intentions.

"Why do you want to go so bad? What's your plan? Who am I going to talk to when you're running around doing your thing?" She asked.

She pushed and pushed my limit of understanding until I was backed into a corner and had no other option but to react with a jiffy of anger.

"We're going to drive down there, get wasted, find a room, have some sex and pass the fuck out! I want you to come. I want you there. Stop fighting me on everything. Can't you just once be happy?" I said back to her.

In my defense, that was exactly the same thing we did at her house. We would steal a bottle of liquor from her parents, hide out in her room, watch television and catch a buzz, then have some sex and go to bed. Same fucking thing I wanted to do at the party, just with people our own age to wake up to the next morning all dazed and confused . . . But, that point was lost upon deaf ears and she started to cry even more. I wanted nothing more but for her to be happy, come to the party as my girlfriend, have some drinks, some laughs, and we both head off to do our own thing. That was entirely it. She was adamant in the point that I had ulterior motives; other than the obvious one of getting wasted and forgetting about this inconsiderate life, if only for a quick second. I attempted to reinsure her any motives of my own selfishness were nonexistent and absent. I just wanted to enjoy her company with friends, see her smile, socialize and escape the pressures of life for a short time.

"Unfortunately, Bob, there was a reason we fought so much at this time in life. And not one that I am proud about by any measure, but an episode that hurt us both, and inevitably was the reason we could no longer find peace in our relationship. About three months prior to this phone call about a house party, Trinity and I found ourselves in a predicament that we really didn't know how to understand or even handle. She became pregnant, and we both lost the true intelligence of what to do. We were both kids ourselves. I was only eighteen, and she was only seventeen, and honestly, a child cannot raise another child. It just doesn't make sense. We both knew that, and we both agreed to have an abortion. It was, in fact very hard for us to make this decision, but also very necessary. We didn't have the means, housing or responsibility to raise a child. So together we made our choice and had to live with it. But, I believe as time passed, it began to make Trinity resent me, or resent our relationship. I am not really sure of which. I thought it was something we both wanted, but apparently not as time unfolded. It's not fair for me to sit here and talk for her, because only she can vocalize her true opinion on the matter. I however, can speak from my side. And this event was sad, it was hard, and it was something I still think about. But that being said, it was also the right choice. She and I didn't work well as a couple, and we certainly could not work as parents. I stand by the choice till this day, on the sheer fact alone, that we had no real knowledge of the real world, or where we were heading as working individuals. So bringing a child into this world when were both children ourselves, was a selfish thing to do. And looking back now, I still believe that."

"Wow. I didn't see that coming." I replied in shock. "I think that was the realest you've been this whole time, Ryan?"

"Believe it or not? I do have a soul, Bob."

"I didn't question your soul, maybe just your sincerity towards the world."

"That's understandable . . . Now, that being said, let's get back to this party . . ."

After an hour and a half of us standing outside arguing and disagreeing about my true intentions and wants of this party, the conversation shifted to a needy sense of talk. And I don't, and will never do well with that type of discussion. I'm not badmouthing her, I am just stating that I like a confident person, self-ensured, levelheaded, and this was not that type of conversation we were having.

"I really just wanted to spend the night with just you." Trinity said.

"Honey, we literally hangout every night. We have not had a night apart in twenty-three months. We're always together and secluded. I'm not trying to get away from you, but I'm not going to your house to watch TV again. I won't do it. I'm sorry. Jesus Christ, we're teenagers. Stop taking life so seriously, please? Relax a little bit and have some fun." I finally found my balls and confidentially spoke.

"Fuck you, you stupid asshole. Go to your dumb party with your loser friends." She very immaturely replied.

"Ok. But I want you to know that I want you to come." I kindly said back to hopefully ease her pain.

"Fuck you. This is over between us." She said as she jumped in her car and drove away.

What was I to do? I had never been involved in a 'real break up,' so I was assuming this was a breakup? I jumped in my truck and headed to my hometown of Burbank . . . However, I didn't make it more than three minutes down the freeway when Trinity called me to tell me what a selfish prick I am. She can't believe I would actually go. I don't deserve her. Blah, blah, blah. I won't bore you with all the words. But, to save some face, I did everything for that girl. She was just too stubborn for me. We're friends now, thankfully, but we were just too young to understand what love was. After our thirty minute conversation of her talking 'AT' me and telling me what a terrible person I was, I had arrived at the party and asked her what she wanted to do about us? I didn't want to breakup, but she was being so mean and vindictive, and needless to say I was growing tired with her aggression.

"I hate you and I never want to see you again." Trinity yelled at me then hung up.

All right, that must mean the breakup is over. I took those harsh words as she was over this fling of enjoyment and it was time for us both to do our own thing. I walked inside that house party with authority and right.

It was time to get drunk, smoke pot and forget the rest of the world is around us. I only went there to drink a few beers with my friends and have a flawless and careless night. But when you add a slight sense of anger with a little bit too much alcohol, you get yourself a concoction for some gratuitous and superfluous behavior.

Trinity preceded to text my phone for the next couple hours, telling me how mad she was, calling me an egotistical prick that didn't care for her. She hated everything about me, et cetera. I was being nice, truthful and endearing, telling her that my only intentions were to drink and have fun. Nonetheless, she was strong in her mindset that I was this wildly fornicating rabbit going down there to have intoxicated casual sex with someone else.

"Which, I will be completely honest and sincere with you, Bob. That was not the case at all. That being said, there is only so much verbal abuse one person can take until they fucking snap."

I hit my point of ruin and it was time to express myself. If you're going to call me a feral sex pistol, I might as well live up to the title . . . Let the hunt begin . . . No, no, no. I'm only joking. I wouldn't do that. I have dignity and self-respect . . .

I am the wandering Baboon.
I am the howling Wolf.
I am the unbeaten Lion.
I am the blood of Gods.
Mixed with the intentions of the Demons.

SIKE!!

I got beyond wasted on any booze I could find; I got extremely stoned on copious amounts of weed. And I had myself some drunken, uninhibited, and completely unprotected sex in the bathroom with a tiny, blond, freaky little nymphomaniac, and I don't regret a fucking thing. Thanks, Levi.

"Ha. There is the bit of hypocrisy I was speaking of, Ryan."

"Fuck off, Bob. I was a Goddamn kid. I didn't know what I was running from. I just knew I was on the run."

"Justify it however you want, you're the one who must live with it."

"I was young, dumb and full of cum."

"Sounds like you managed to solve the full of cum problem." I sarcastically replied with a vicious attack at his outlook.

"That's true, I did let that out. But, I was still a fucking idiot kid."

"I would be lying if I said most people hadn't done the same dumbshit as you growing up. It's part of life."

"Thank you, Bob."

"Not a fucking compliment, Ryan!" I attacked once more as he washed down his cigarette smoke with a rush of alcohol.

The Story of Kat and Drake: Part Two.

If only the truth was an easy creation

They hit brave seas to feel a sensation

The trip was a journey of fun and delight

Learn as you may but don't conclude right

The weary ocean is one fickle mistress

In the suns bright rays the moment was lustrous

As they sailed the high waves their story was growing

Trough voyage and strength their love was now flowing

With many cold nights she spent in his arms

His mind was compelled to her many rare charms

With nothing but wind guiding their fate

This trip was becoming anything but second rate

He had a large heart he was longing to share

She accepted his past and proceeded with care

With every long mile and salty sea splash

This love was now real, with no signs of crash...

To be continued...

CHAPTER FOURTEEN:

Officer, I'm Not As Think As You Drunk I Am. To Swear I God . . . What?

"The mind is a terrible thing to waste."

I was now nineteen years of age, single, and had my best friend by my side. My performance (or lack thereof) at the bank job became increasingly too low for them to value me as an employee any longer. Plus I got caught stealing about $1,300 bucks, and they quickly canned my malignant ass after uncovering my dirty little secret of burglary. I didn't give a hoot though. I wasn't born to be a bank teller. Also, I had stopped going to my charter school a few months back, and after receiving a curiosity call from my teacher, asking if I was planning on returning to finish out my final units and earn my diploma. I lied and said I would return, then swiftly put that idea in my rearview and kept on moving and shaking. I decided to drop out of high school and join the real working force. So I did what every guy without a diploma does . . .

I started working an extremely physical construction job with long hours and drastically hard labor. However, I was making roughly around four thousand dollars a month, which was a substantial amount of money for a kid my age. I had boosted an identification card and military I.D. from my eldest brother that said I was twenty-three, which I 'Nicely Barrowed,' with every wholesome intention of giving back. Ha-ha, yeah right! Thanks buddy. I had moved out from my grandparent's garage and in with my middle brother, Floyd, and his girlfriend at the time. The unit we rented was a two-bedroom apartment that was connected to a quadplex style of housing. The building was located in the center of a teardrop shaped concrete jungle looking island. Naturally, we gave our little compound of deviance and delinquency a suiting nickname, and dubbed it, 'The Island.' My rent was only three hundred and fifty dollars a month, which meant I had plenty of extra money for some good ole' fashioned alcohol and substance abuse. And Goddammit! I was going to blow every last dime I had. For a lack of better words, it was time for some mother fuckin' trouble! What better way to stir up some trouble; then with and equally self-destructive individual?

Levi and I began rampaging down a road of negligent and outlandish conduct. We were two young hooligans that were ready to party and fuck shit up! Two careless, hopeless, pot smoking, orgy drinking, and money blowing fools with nothing to lose and even less to gain. What we lacked in common sense and legal reason, we more than exceeded in friendship and loyalty. As we walked this line . . . Excuse me—a more appropriate turn of phrase would be 'stumbled.' As we stumbled down this line of rambunctious and disorderly behavior, we formed a bond, a testimony. An oath if you will. We took an oath to stand by each other's side till the cold and bitter end; and never, and I mean never, let anyone or anything stand in our way of riding this full throttle thrill ride of insubordinate actions and truly mutinous times. At least not until we came skidding up sideways to our graves of rest with a cigarette burning, a bottle of liquor in one hand and a joint in the other, covered in scars and bruises, bank accounts broke and bodies aching in pain as we knocked over the tombstones on the way in screaming out "WHAT THE FUCK JUST HAPPENED! CAN WE RIDE AGAIN?" To quote 'Scarface.' "The World Was Ours."

We were just two dumb youngsters having a gas of a good time doing some very dubious shit. I believe they call that your early twenties? One thing was certain; trust was never an issue with Levi and I. We had nothing but an abundance of trust for one another. Trust in our word, our women, our money, and most importantly our lives. You see . . . We had a saying—no, wait . . . better yet, a way of life. "You are only as good as your word, so a man that doesn't live up to his word. Well he isn't any good, now is he?" We lived by that motto then, and still do till this day. We had a good support system for one another. No matter the place we went, or the amount of people we were around, we always looked out for each other. No fucking questions about it! We possessed the ability to communicate in a crammed party of a hundred people, in an ear splittingly loud nightclub, or a tremendously overcrowded strip club without ever speaking one word. We had looks, a wink, a smirk, or a nod that let one another know, "I see you brother, and I got you. If shit goes down we're getting out of this motherfucker together and safe." It was an oath of safety and reliability. It's not everyday you come across a friendship so profound. Nobody was going to touch us! And no one was ever going to hurt us. We had each other and that was all we needed to survive. We were not afraid to stand side-by-side, stare this cruel world right in its pretty little face and say, "Fuck you world! Give me the best you got! I dare you!"

— Can you say the same for your best friend? —

Both of us were making large amounts of money for our age, and surprisingly we were quickly running out of ideas on just how to blow it fast enough. Don't get me wrong, it's a good problem to have, but nonetheless, still a problem. So we searched, explored and dug for a new spending outlet. And just as one would, if you look for trouble in this world, Goddammit, you'll find it! We developed a passionately intense appetite for strippers. It started to become our 'Go-To-Plan' if the plans for the night fell through. We knew just where we would end up. We spent so much fucking money on these tantalizing, beautiful and enchanting strippers. They should name a college after us, at least a wing for God sakes. But, we'll settle for a dorm. When it came to partying at this age, we were not always wise to say the least. Looking back on it now, maybe we made a few bad choices. Most weekdays after work we would drink all night with friends at 'The Island,' smoke some weed, pop a pill here and there, just plain destroying ourselves till the early morning hours before we had to wake and go shift around work in a dazed and confused flutter. Not a good idea when working around power tools, but what the hell did we know? When weekends would come around . . . That was when the games really began . . .

Every Friday night would start with a bowl session (which is slang for smoking marijuana) shotgun some beers, take some shots, beer bongs, beer pong, take some more shots, smoke some more Mary Jane, and then let the slurring insanity ensue. Levi and I would make a round of phone calls, digging for the best fitting house party, bar or club for the evening. Find something that was interesting enough to catch our drunken attention, grab some beers for the drive (AKA 'Road Sodas') and head out to fuck shit up. Wherever the blurry breeze chose to bring us for that particular night was fine by us. And when we showed up, we did it with force (but more importantly) significantly more alcohol and weed for the entire party. Anytime we entered a house party it was with a handle of liquor and a thirty pack of Bud light each. Not to mention a pocket full of joints for all to enjoy. Nobody wants to be the most intoxicated person at a sober party. Might as well share with everybody so we can all get blackout schnockered and the chaos can justly prevail. That's what we believed. But, I lost my train of thought. Let me get back on track . . .

We would inhabit whatever choosing of drunken activity for awhile, getting more than pleasantly numb and awaiting the inevitable siren of the pigs or the draw of the strip club to catch our fancy. And after one of the two options eventually happened, and trust me, one of the two always did; we would walk back to the truck to play a spectacular game (which I'm almost certain we invented) a game that we rather enjoyed playing. What's the game you ask? Well, allow me to explain. The game is titled "Rock. Paper. Scissors. Who's going to drive?" . . . Which I'm coining by the way . . . However, here is the object of the game. You play a go for the gold game of rock, paper, scissors. One shot, one winner. No best outta three bullshit. This is going for the gold time! Sack up and be a man. Here is the tricky part, you really, really (and I can't stress it enough) really want to win this fucking game, because, and this is very crucial so listen up, the lemon of the game has to perform a certain activity that follows their defeat. And it is far from pleasurable . . . You have to jam your finger down your throat to induce vomiting, not too much to knock you out for the entirety of the night, but just enough to see somewhat legally straight, and that poor bastard had to drive to the strip club. Like I said before, not a game you want to lose.

"And before you think I'm not aware of the jeopardy we put ourselves in, Bob? Please keep your Goddamn fucking opinion to yourself! I am fully aware it's an incredible dangerous game. We were nineteen, Bob, cut us some fucking slack please!"

"I didn't say anything, Ryan."

"You didn't have to, I could feel your damn look alright."

When we would arrive at the 'Furry Pussy Cat,' the vomit-ridden fellow had to wipe the shit off his shirt and get their act together. We would pound some beers in the truck; smoke a joint followed by a cigarette, and head on in for some beautiful naked girls.

As we entered the doors to this fine establishment, our intentions were clearly known. We are here to get our fucking rage on. We were such frequent faces at this particular club that most of the strippers knew us very well and they loved when we arrived. We were kind, respectful and very, very generous with our money. We were the loud, drunk and obnoxious money throwing fools you might see standing up front at your local strip club. Slapping Asses and spending cheese! Unfortunately, the place we frequented most often was a nonalcoholic serving institution. However, we developed a great rapport with the waitresses that worked there. And they would sneak us out some vodka from the strippers to keep us good and liquored up to make sure the dollars kept raining down. I will admit, at times we had moments of eccentric douchebaggrey, but that all goes hand-in-hand with the atmosphere of a strip club. Being young and annoying is part of finding yourself. Or so I believe? Most of the time we were so fall down drunk that we got spotted as easy targets for accumulating funds from, which is fine by me. It's all in good fun. I understand how the game works, and more power to the women who know how to play it.

I can't speak for Levi, but I can say from my own point of view, going to this strip club was much like being home for me. I've always had a fun and appreciative relationship with strippers. I understood them a little better than your everyday woman on the street.

"Not just because I'm only drawn to crazy, drug using, sex addicted maniacs. That's not the case at all."

"No judgment here, Ryan." I laugh as I respond.

I just felt a connection with some of the beautiful women I had the pleasure to meet. I had a fucked up past with my own father, so maybe that contributed to our sense of correlation? I gave them the attention they deserved, looked them in the eye when they spoke (don't get me wrong, I was happy they were naked) but they knew I didn't need to be there. I never had too much of a problem getting laid, and I wasn't some fat, old, lonely chump itching to rub up on some young tail. I just really enjoyed the company of an interesting girl that just so happens to take her clothes off for a living. It's almost to say we trusted each other (as much as someone paying to see another person's snatch can trust) nonetheless, we gave one another mutual respect and attention, and I do wish the very best to all the women I had the pleasure to talk to at that club. It was a fun and extremely adventurous time in our young lives. One I will never take back.

"Plus, I just really love strippers!" Ryan giggles out as he takes a heavy hit of booze.

"Hey, who doesn't, right?"

"That's absolutely fucking correct, Bob!"

As wild and crazy as my life had become at nineteen juvenile and guiltless years of age, it was still a very clear and evident point to make sure I never got too out of hand with the drinking and drugs to end up sharing a jail cell with Fulton. I maintained my overall sanity (the best I could that is) and always made sure to keep it simple. Stay away from the hard stuff and just have some fun. I suffered with depression and anxiety, much like most youth does while going through challenges. However, always knew in the back of my head that everything was going to be ok. "Don't cry over spilt milk," that's what my grandmother always says. For the most part I was happy and content. I felt . . . No . . . I actually believed that I had it all figured out and I was ready for a commitment, a vow or a faithful pledge to another person. I thought I was ready for love. So, naturally I searched and I probed for a compatible partner. And by that, I mean I was fucking, screwing, banging and copulating every female I shared a conversation with.

However, I couldn't seem to find a suiting lover to save my life. It was beginning to transpire as and exhausting and redundant task. I gave up on those hopes of correlation and moved on—which ultimately was probably a good thing in the long run. I was too immature and infantile for a lasting love. I would have probably fucked it up just as I've done with so many other things in my life; and before you know it, I would've ended up destroying the ego of some poor, innocent woman that didn't deserve it. At nineteen, I was a sucker for love (actually I still am) but at that young age I fell in love twice a month, but fell out just as quickly. I just really love women. They are my heart and soul. They speak to a part of me that I can agree with. Women ultimately make me a better person. But I had no luck finding Mrs. Right and I strayed along my path of self-destruction.

Levi, at this particular time of life, fell into a bit of a disagreement with his current living situation. And the concord was made that he would be better off finding shelter on his own terms, and he was banished into the world to fend for himself. He was lost and dumbfounded with the idea of where to go. He had options to stay with his mother, but he longed for his true independence. He wanted to be his own man. A feeling we can all relate with. He saw how much fun and freedom I had, and he chose to seek out that style of independence. Levi refused to admit defeat and move to his mother's. That just wasn't an option for him. He called me up on the night of his exile and enlightened me on the circumstances at hand. I told him to come by my place and we will work it out. We talked and talked for many hours on this subject, working out the details and playing the field of his probability. After much beer consuming and weed smoking hours, it hit me right in my comfortably numb face.

"Why don't you move in here?" I said to him.
Both parties clearly knowing that my apartment was only a two bedrooms. And both bedrooms already have a paying occupant.

"And what? Sleep on the fucking couch?" Levi asked.

"Fuck that! I own a California king, we can share my bed. We'll split the rent." I threw back his way.

"Before I continue Bob, let me first say this. We are (just as we were then) and will forever be, as heterosexual as possible. But, we had a bond and that bond wasn't going to be broken. We were to look out for each other till we both took our final breath. That's what true friendship is. I was not about to let my best friend go one night uncomfortable or challenged. Not while I was alive."

"Very noble of you, Ryan." I replied in a snarky tone.

"Fuck off, Bob."

"You move in here, share my bed, we'll split the rent and we can party all the time. It will be awesome. You can get back on your feet and we can have a great time. What's the worst that could happen? Some people will make some gay jokes; laugh at two men sharing a bed. Who gives a fuck! Fuck 'em. They don't compare to shit." I said to Levi.

He logically thought about it for a couple minutes.

"Fuck it. Let's do it, sounds good to me." Levi answered.

We went to my brother and his girlfriend and laid the new contemporary information upon them. This was the plan of attack and it was to be a 'nongay' and un-weird condition. They both had no problem with it, as they shouldn't. Two grown men sharing a bed, what's so strange about that? Ha-ha-ha. As comical as you may perceive this to be, it was one of the best times of my life. We were always close (and apparently getting a lot closer) but we had a blast bringing girls to our place and trying to explain why there was only one bed in 'Our Room.' Well, how bad do you want to know the answer to that question?

However, we made do. It was a funny time for us both. We made the best out of what the situation was and never had a problem with it. At certain times it really was a ridiculously hilarious event. Both of us would come back from partying all night (one of us smelling like vomit from playing our infamous game) we were both fall down wasted, slowly stumbling into the house, joking and laughing along the way as we attempted to carry one another till we hit the bed to pass out. It was fucking priceless. My brother and his girlfriend shared a wall with us; and they could hear as we drunkenly muddled to our bed. They always had fun screaming out good-natured homosexual slanders at us through the wall, which was very entertaining at our current state of inebriation.

"You homos make it home safe?" They shouted.

"Yeah, we're good." We shouted back.

"Alright. Goodnight." They screamed back.

"Goodnight" Levi and I would shout back.

It was a very short and extraordinary time we both shared a grown man bed for. Levi landed on his feet, given that he's a strong-willed, ultra independent person. He moved out to a place of his own and I moved to another house with my same roommates. However, I was still quietly searching and longing to fall in love. And just as the true nature of the universe works . . . You put something out there. And it's going to come back to you, tenfold.

CHAPTER FIFTEEN:
The Magical Marilyn.

"This is not your Grandmother's vagina stimulating love novel."

T he night was rainy, cold, depressing, and ironically, Valentines Day. I was down 'n out on myself on this particular day, and was in one of my world hating, cynical, kill us all moods that I slip into from time to time. I couldn't consume enough liquor or smoke enough weed to put a smile on my worthless face and the world could see it. I didn't want to see anyone, dance, talk, laugh or drink. I just wanted to be alone in my own despair. Levi was immovable in the idea that we should go out and have some drinks, have some laughs and with a little bit of luck, have some fun. He told me I should be around some happy people and hopefully pull me out of this unpromising funk I was in. I told him the happy people could suck my dick without a condom on while I'm on the john. I felt this shit covered rubbish world had nothing to offer me that could make me feel happy or peaceful. Fuck the world and fuck you for making me go was my mindset. I suffer from severe mood swings. Or should I say, I struggle, the ones who have to deal with me are the ones who suffer. But, Levi was not backing down in his promise to bring me to tranquility.

We jumped in my truck and hit the road to one of our local watering holes. We were both single at the time so we didn't care too much it was Valentines Day. However, we were both also only twenty years of age. This particular place was always crawling with bouncers and security. And being that we were not of legal drinking age, getting into this spot always took a slight bit of finesse and sprite trickery to get in. One of us would enter first with my brothers' stolen I.D. that I had boosted a few months back, and after that person would get in, they would slide the I.D. into a pack of cigarettes and walk to the smoking patio. The other person, who hadn't been allowed access yet, would approach the other and ask to bum a smoke, then in turn they would hand that person the pack of cigarettes with the I.D. in it and they would grab a smoke from the pack as well as the I.D. We would smoke the cigarettes together, pretending we had no fucking clue whom each other were, and then go our separate ways.

Now the person who is still on the outside of the fence, would walk to the doorman, flash the same I.D. that was just used less then ten minutes prior, and hopefully gain entrance. And let me tell you this, out of the couple of hundred times we pulled this little maneuver, not once did we ever get denied. It became a flawless fucking system we were running and we could pull off this scheme in less then seven minutes. We got it down to a science. And the best part about this trick was, the I.D. didn't actually fucking look like either one of us. It was a slight resemblance, but if the bouncers paid even the tiniest bit of attention to the picture, it's perfectly clear that the picture is not either one of us. But, in order to use a fake identification (or another persons' I.D. at that) you have to be confident and walk to the door like you own the motherfucker! Stand up tall, make eye contact; talk to the guy if you have to, anything to make it seem as if he checking your credentials is actually a waste of your time. You can't be scared. But, I'm getting way off track. Let's get back to the story . . .

As we entered the bar, Levi had one goal in mind, get Ryan fucking wasted and attempt to put a smile on his miserable and cheerless face. We headed to the bar and drank countless beers, took a large amount of shots (more than I can tally) had a few cigarettes and watched as the beautiful women danced around. However, nothing was going to make me feel heavenly or idyllic. That was of course . . . Until I laid eyes on 'Marilyn.'

I was standing outside in the moist air with a buddy I hadn't seen in a while. We were both having a smoke and catching up. As I picked my head up to take a hit from my cigarette, I saw her through the glass.
'The Magnificent Marilyn,' the most awe-inspiring female that ever lived. She was dancing atop a speaker, proud, noble, and ever so graceful. She was alluring, statuesque, exquisite and superb. Absolutely fucking astonishing. A breathtaking brunette, standing at a staggering five-foot-eleven from the ground, with a perfectly fitting set of silky smooth legs that could reach the clouds of heaven. She had a glowing complexion and extraordinary features. Marilyn was, with no other words to stress the point properly, the most beautiful woman I've ever seen in my entire black hearted, devoid and infantile life. She was dazzling, wise, charming and remarkably brilliant. My eyes were fixated to her, I couldn't look away, nor did I want to. I was trapped in a paradox of mystification. She was elegant, polished, and utterly fucking perfect! Her seductive beauty had the power to silence a war zone, level a kingdom, and make even the mightiest of Gods treble where they righteously stood.

I resided outside in the desperate rain, chain smoking cigarettes and hating everything I've become. I watched as she danced around with a large charismatic smile on her face, all while laughing with such excellence. I wanted nothing more than to approach her and tell her all the reasons we should be together, except, was at a stubborn loss of words, and my mood was far from lovely. So, I held myself outside, like a coward, a mouse, smoking my life away and dwelling on the thought of my death. I knew as abundant as humanly possible I was not going inside to talk to her. Not a simple introduction or glace of attraction. I was going to linger in my rain-covered hell of loneliness. My friend, whom I stood with, could judge from my lack of conversation that I was no good company at all. He didn't try to talk me out of my short of excitement. He just smoked his cigarette and let me be. I was miserable and unapproachable.

"What a burden I used to be on the world, huh Bob?"

"You sound like you could be hard to be around at times."

"Thanks." Ryan says as he laughs while sipping his stiff drink.

Anyhow, as I settled there, with the fallen rain becoming my only companion, I was found in a widespread skepticism and disbelief. Marilyn had made her way outside for a short cigarette break. I quietly watched her as she walked out—then, I spinelessly hid under the hood of my sweatshirt, not to make eye contact or even a passing flame. Marilyn didn't hesitant to bring my insecurities to a vital reality. She walked right to me, faced me with eagerness and want.

"Why are you standing out here in the rain?" Marilyn angelically asked me.

I had no choice at this moment but to counter with an answer. In a very despairing frenzy, I looked up from my rain soaked hood and was forced to be a man.

"I am not in a good mood tonight and I don't feel like being around people." I answered.

"I understand. Well, I really wanted to introduce myself. I'm Marilyn." She held her hand out as she talked to this sorry soul of a person. (AKA me)

"I'm Ryan, nice to meet you." I said as I shook her hand.

"Stop looking so fucking sorry for yourself and come have fun with me." She followed her introduction with.

"Ok, let me finish my smoke and I will join you." I replied.

"You better. Don't be a coward." She finished her words with.

Then cracked me the most striking and effervescent smile I have ever had the pleasure to see in my murky life. I was hooked. That feeling of heart consuming love rushed over me, and I was a victim to her ravishing will. "How in the world could such a beautiful angel want to talk to such a broken demon like myself?" Was the prolific thought bouncing around inside my head.

I didn't have time to try and translate the meaning of our introduction, nor should I begin to try. All I did know was; if I wanted to see the outcome to this cold and rainy prologue, I had to get inside and talk to her. I threw my cigarette to the floor and made my way back inside to talk with her once more. She was incredible. I gazed upon her as she danced with ease and sophistication. Marilyn grabbed my hand and pulled me onto the dance floor with her, moving and grooving her body against mine. I did the best I could to keep up with her seductive dance style, grinding and hopefully 'Dropping It Like It's Hot' at all the right moments. And . . . Wouldn't you know it? I actually started to smile. A real smile, one of happiness and enjoyment, one I didn't think would find its way to my face on this showery Valentines Day. But, it did, and all because an angel gave me a significant chance.

After about an hour of dancing, Marilyn pulled me outside for another smoke break where she disclosed to me that she was only twenty years old and had to get in with a fake identification card that she had gotten in college, which I found to be both ironic, as well as entertaining. What were the chances that both of us had to endure the same procedure to get drunk? Was it fate, or just a coincidence? Who was I to know? As we both found amusement in our underage adventure at the bar, Marilyn asked me if I was a pot smoker? Which luckily I had brought a pipe and some weed in my truck, and I quickly answered, 'yes.' Without much delay we headed off in the rainy night to take a dry safe refuge in my truck to enjoy a midnight bowl session. We talked about everything from religion to artistic values, politics to music, film to life, love and the never-ending pursuit of happiness. We had an immense amount of common interests and point of views. Hit after hit of the potent marijuana we grew closer and closer until finally the sexual tension could no longer be contained within, and we jumped at each other; kissing, grabbing, foundling and pouring our souls into one of the most intense make-out affairs ever awarded. With nothing but the torrential rain as a sounding milieu, we exchanged tongues of pleasure and charm, wording each slip of dialect with precise brilliance. With wandering hands and steamy windows we found something unique. This was unlike most encounters I've lived through. Most times I find myself in the frequent element of sneaking into a grungy tavern bathroom or place of lonely nakedness for a quick and superficial fuck. However, with Marilyn, I wanted to take my time, make every second fell like a minute and every kiss feel as if our breath was ferociously snatched from our lungs. This was real, this was special, and dare I say it . . . This was love . . .

Just as swiftly as the escalation of this glorious situation grew, the night had come down to its last minutes and the lifeless end of our time together was about to be. We took a dry sanctuary underneath my sweatshirt and I ran her back up the stairs to her friends inside the bar. We exchanged phone numbers, had one last sensational kiss for the road, and went our separate ways into the rainy night.

— The falling rain will be the reason we cry after death. —

The next two days I became giddier than a little schoolgirl at a 'Bieber' concert. I plotted and paced at my house, contemplating what I would say if I did in fact work up the balls to call her. Walking back and fourth, talking to myself, practicing my words in front of the mirror, getting them just right for verbalization. I didn't want to fuck this up, which meant the execution was key, was dire. The night was a Sunday, and I told myself I had finally worked up enough nerve to make the call. This was it; this was the moment of truth. I headed over to Levi's house to consume some beers and take the edge off. Plus he always had the power of putting my over-bearing voice of insecurity to ease.

"Just relax and call her. If she doesn't answer, then you are in the same place as when you started and you'll be just fine, brother." Levi said to me.

"Alright. Here goes nothing." I replied.

I took out my cell phone, slowly dialed her number, and much to my surprise . . . She actually answered.

"Hello." Marilyn's beautiful voice came on the line.

"Hi, this is Ryan. I'm not sure if you remember me, but we met at the bar the other night? We smoked pot in my truck and waited until the rain settled down?" I weakly responded.

"Of course I remember you, silly. What are you up to tonight?" She asked.

"I'm just hanging out at Levis' house. What about you?" I replied.

"I'm doing the same. I'm just having a cocktail at my apartment. Would you like to come by and join me for a drink?" Her mouse like voice asked me.

"Absolutely, I would love to. Text me your address and I'll head on over." I chokingly responded.

"Perfect, I will see you soon." Marilyn replied.

I hung up the phone and awaited her text.

"I won't lie, Bob, I was overwhelmingly nervous she wasn't going to text me, so I chain-smoked and had a couple of shots as I waited for her message.

Levi found it rather funny to see me in such a dumb-founded pose. He chuckled at me and told me to 'fucking relax.' Which was indeed good advice. And with the holi-est of holies, my phone chirped out with a text message. She had sent me a message with her address, asking me to pick up a bottle of Captain Morgan, and the words, "Don't be a flake," written at the end of the message. I was flushed over with happiness at that very moment. I said goodbye to Levi, jumped in my truck, hit the store of liquor to pick up the items for this festivity and followed suit to arriving at Marilyn's place in a timely fashion. She buzzed me in the main door at her complex and I made my way through the long hallways. I was fucking inundated with anxiety, so I opened the bottle and took a couple swigs as I made my way to her unit. I reached her door, took a breath, and knocked . . . This was it . . . This was the moment we've all been waiting for . . .

When the door opened, Marilyn was even more beautiful than I had remembered. She was dressed very casual in an incredibly small pair of shorts, slightly exposing her firm butt cheeks. Her long, stunning, bronzed legs were the first part that caught my eye. As I looked up, she was wearing a very tight fitting tank top that was tensely absorbed to her tastefully defined upper body. Marilyn looked utterly bewitching, smooth, and just downright noteworthy. I was wearing my favorite tight fitting black 'Guns 'N Roses' T-shirt (the one I lost my virginity in) a dark blue pair of jeans with no underwear underneath, and a pair of chucks.

"Wow! You look just wonderful." I said to her.

"Why thank you." She replied with a very cute smile. "Come on in."

I followed her into the apartment and we made our way to the kitchen. We poured ourselves some drinks and walked to the couch. She already had a joint rolled up (my kind of style) and we lit it and comfortably sat back on the couch with the sound of music playing in the background. The song that played was 'Talk Show Host' by 'Radiohead.'

We indulged in the joint and had a couple of drinks while she shuffled through her IPod playing me some of her favorite songs. We both would serve back questions of intrigue to get to know the true and inner makings of one another. We talked for two, maybe three hours that night, all while getting a well endowed buzz and getting very flirtatious with each other. Our hands began to wander and our tongues once again found their way back to each other. We shared a long and endearing kiss, playfully teasing and foundling. Gently touching and provoking our inner sexual desires and bringing our body temperatures up and our minds slowly toward the brink of zealous collapse. After thirty minutes on the couch, with enthralling music playing in the background, and the heat of craving infatuation reaching its limits, Marilyn stood from the couch.

"Want to go to my room?" She asked

"Sure, lead the way." I replied.

Cue the music. Glory Box. Portishead.

She took a firm and magnetic grip of my hand and led me down the hall to her bedroom that was plastered with beautiful paintings that she had artistically performed herself. She laid me down on the bed and climbed over me, slowly kissing and caressing my neck. I ran my hands down her back and butt, feeling every beautiful inch of her body, not to miss any edge of her breathtaking and dramatic frame. As we kissed, I placed my hands on her sides and rolled her over, got on top of her and took over control (a move she was rather pleased with) and began to savor every last trail of her polished olive skin. Marilyn was much taller than most of the female race, so to have a man with the ability to make her feel small, really turned her on. Also, might I ad . . . Got her incredibly wet. I slid my hand into her underwear and began to massage, play, touch and tickle her pussy. Marilyn took her hand and forced it down my pants (quickly learning) I was 'Flying Commando' and took a solidifying grip of my cock and started to stroke it up and down. We both started to moan and sigh in complete pleasure. Teasing and playing, getting our privates ready for intercourse.

We worked our clothes off and I began to kiss her neck, leisurely making my way to her breasts, spending eminence time and respect to them both. Gradually moving down her stomach, licking, kissing and sucking on her beautiful skin as I slowly descended, making my way around her attractive belly button and up the side of her ribcage, making her tighten in joy and satisfaction. Unhurriedly I made my way to her gorgeous pussy. I began to gently and deliberately lick, taste and feel every part of her cunt with my tongue. From the top of her clitoris to the bottom of her vagina, sucking, licking and slurping up her refined juices. She tasted better than the blood of the Gods. I started to play with her pussy lips while I pushed my fingers inside her, feeling the deepest part of her pussy as she was beginning to constrict and shake in gratification and bliss. I stayed down there for forty minutes or so, until I heard her scream my name in not one, but two intense orgasms. Then, slowly, lazily, bit by bit, kiss and taste of her lovely body I generated my way back up to her lips where we shared a thankful kiss from her panting tongue. Her eyes were now wide open and her breath was tremendously short. She was ever so grateful for my emphatically kind gesture of commitment to her downstairs.

"I've never been eaten out like that. You're very good." Marilyn appreciatively said.

"Thank you for letting me adventure every part of your beautiful body." I kindly retorted.

She then grabbed my rock hard cock, opened herself up and she slide my erect dick inside her. I was now on top of her, and when I felt her tight pussy wrap and clinch around my penis, I completely buckled in felicity. The inside of Marilyn was wet, warm and fixed, she felt beyond wonderful and my cock was very happy. She made me feel homesick for a place I've never been before. I started to press inside her, deeper, harder, all while kissing her lips and sucking on her neck. The moans rose in level and the euphoria drenched over us. The speed was increasing and the screams were getting louder, much louder, and even waking her roommate. I fucked her hard, deep and ever so passionately. She was wet, dripping in ecstasy and delight. The smell of sex filled the air. It was a mixture of sweat, heat, infatuation, body fluids, yells and enjoyment. I began to turn her over, grabbing her ass and giving her a few slaps in the process. She was absolutely savoring the slaps, even asked for more. I gave her a couple red mark-leaving hits. The pain was exciting her and getting her pussy soaking wet and her mouth dirty talking.

"Fuck me, Ryan." She shouted.

I spit in the palm of my hand, rubbed it on my cock, and pushed myself deep inside her. Her tone of volume went ever louder as she felt every inch of my cock. I pushed, forced, fucked and slammed away at her enchanting pussy, sopping wet with her juices around my penis, I lost my angry outlook on life and found peace; even if only for a fleeting moment. I took my hand and impressively rubbed it up her back, hard and firm, so she could feel me making my way to her head. I grabbed her hair tight, powerful, and strappingly pulled her hair back. Marilyn loved every second of it, shouting my name and begging me for more. I kept her hair taut in my grasp as I fucked the inside of her for the next twenty minutes, feeling every bit of her canal, slapping her ass with my free hand and asking her if she liked it.

"I fucking love it! Fuck me, Ryan" she screamed at the top of her lungs.

My cock was beginning to squeeze in rapture, clench in amusement, and tighten up. My cum was about to explode and I could no longer hold it within.

"I'm going to cum, where do you want it?" I asked her.

"I want your cum inside me. I want to feel you!" Marilyn voiced out her appeal.

I was seconds away from the verge of inner detonation when I forcefully erupted inside her wet and tense pussy, falling down on to her back and letting out my animal roar! The breathing was heavy, our bodies were covered in sweat and the smiles on our faces were ear to ear. I laid atop her back for a while, kissing her neck and licking around her shoulder blades. It was complete heaven.

"That was amazing. I've never been fucked like that before." Marilyn said to me as I slowly kissed and licked around her neck and upper back.

"What do you mean?" I confusingly replied.

"All my last boyfriends did was look me in the eye and make slow, boring love to me. But you, you just fucked the shit out of me, made me scream and cum. That was something else, Ryan." Marilyn laughed as she indirectly told me of her past lovers.

"Happy I could be of assistance." I jokingly retorted.

We rolled over and we held each other while we talked, kissed, tickled and played with one another. Marilyn had told me that she had gotten cold and was curious if she could wear my shirt, the same black and tight fitting 'Guns 'N Roses' T-shirt that had exposed me to what was going to become one of my biggest life hobbies (sex that is) and without an inkling of hesitation, I wrapped her cold body in my shirt to sleep off our heavy sexual buzz. It was a fucking wonderful night, one that I will never forget no matter how much drugs or alcohol I choose to guzzle. It was more than just sex with us (of course) please . . . don't get me wrong, the sex with her was incredible and mind blowing. Some of the best I've ever had. However, that being said, on Gods lovely Sunday, we had a bond that was growing that night . . . And we both felt it.

The next morning when we arouse, I had Marilyn's tall and flawless casing still comfortably numbed and locked in my arms. Half naked and charmed, I indubitable laid with an angel. I was never so mad to hear the buzz of an alarm clock, as I was that morning. I had the new responsibility of starting a new job and suffering through the first day of work at a record label as a mail clerk (or in layman's terms. A fucking mailman) and she had to sift off to school. A simple task that was both slightly awkward (as you would imagine) but also infinitely hard to separate from one another's grasp of solitude. We wanted nothing more than to spend the day together but were burdened with the stresses of this 'so-called' real life. Marilyn was still cloaked in my T-shirt and leaving her suspended aroma behind. We exited the bed, had a quick and hushed cup of coffee and had to make haste to the everyday jobs that lied ahead. She took off my shirt and handed it back to me; all while asking what time I started work.

"In about twenty minutes I think?" I questionably replied.

"Don't you have to go home to shower and change first?" She confusingly asked.

"No. I want to smell you all day long." I captivatingly retorted.

She was momentarily at a loss of words as she gazed at me, watching me as I slid my jeans over my underwearless legs and threw my T-shirt over my upper body.

"That's pretty fucking 'Rock 'N Roll' of you." She proclaimed.

"It's a record label, what else would they expect?" I answered and questioned.

"That's a very good point. I just assume most people want to show up to the first day of their new job smelling like daisies and dressed to impress." Marilyn replied.

"Fuck it! Life's a journey not a chore. If they don't like it, they can fire my malignant ass. I wasn't born to be a mailman. This is just a temporary roadblock till I reach my calling as a writer." I quickly responded.

"I wish I had your type of balls to strive for my dream." She exclaimed.

"I don't have balls, trust me. I was born without gonads actually, a rare case. Testicular agenesis, I believe they call it. (I Googled it one night when I was bored) I'm just really mad in my convictions. Haven't you heard? — Everybody's mad around here!" I excitingly quoted 'Alice in Wonderland.'

Marilyn softly let out an early morning laugh to my atrocious and nonsensical joke, taking a breath and pause . . .

" . . . You're trouble, aren't you?" She asked.

"Where angels go, trouble follows." I replied.

That's a 1968 reference for you fuckers.

Marilyn flashed a seducing grin, with a contemplating look in her eye, she kissed me goodbye and set me off into this brilliant world of animation and magnetism.

"Have a good day, Ryan." She said after our kiss.

I took a dense and frozen clasp of her stiff torso and pulled her in close for one more kiss. Making it long and affectionate, permanent and unforgettable, exchanging our tongues to be known that this hopefully will not be the last. A 'Real Goodbye Kiss' if you will. I looked Marilyn in the eyes, with nothing but ruin and pain in my soul, and faith for a better tomorrow in my heart, letting her know that she could destroy me with a single glace or phrase. A forfeit of power is a more appropriate term.

"You have yourself a wonderful day also, Miss Marilyn." I replied . . .

> To be young,
> Is to be dim.
> To be wise,
> Is to be forgotten.
> To be both . . .
> Is to be dead.

Marilyn walked me to the door, gave me one more brisk peck for the adventurous road that was set ahead and sent me out the door. Just like that, I headed off to the first day at my new job, with nothing but the taste of what I believe was in fact a real life Goddesses on my tongue, and the found memories of what Heaven would be like for us many dammed souls that chose to act in somewhat normalcy. I jumped in my truck, half buzzed, slightly awake and coherent, I set off. The funny part was, that no one told me during the fucking orientation, that this was a uniformed job (which was never given to me) and boy did I look like the big brown asshole showing up to my first day in a pleasantly wrinkled, female smelling T-shirt, with booze and weed secreting from my pores and my drunken lazy eye wandering. On the first day, I quickly solidified myself as the class clown. Not only did I stink, I was ten minutes late. But, like I said before, I wasn't born to be a fucking mailman. I didn't care about this job, and that was perfectly obvious. However, I endured my first day with nothing but Marilyn in my passing thoughts. No other woman before even held a candle to her magnificence. I was truly blessed with her presence.

The next coming months, Marilyn and I grew eternally close, incorporated and loving. I found myself at a new fork in the road, and, well . . . I really enjoyed it.

"Which is probably hard for you to believe, Bob. Because up until this point in the story, I'm sure I most likely come off as a womanizing douchebag with no sense or purpose. But, to stress a point that is utterly important to my vitality—I really enjoyed the relationship that was growing between us. Goddammit, I just enjoyed being loved. It was new for me. It was wildly uncharted territory I found myself in."

"I can believe it, Ryan." I replied to his statement of self-doubt.

I would go to Hell & Back for her. I loved absolutely everything about her. Marilyn's touch, her smile, her look, her eyes, her body, her mind and her smell. I even loved when she would accidentally let out a burp or fart. She was the concluding end to this disconsolate, shitty, valueless and despairing life of mine. When I fall in love, I fall so fucking hard that Jesus himself feels the shake of the unbreakable smack on the pavement. I loved her. Everything she said, when she would laugh, cry, smile and joke. She was the only thing that mattered to me now. And I was going to shield her through the last wish she ever spoke. She was, and not to exhaust the term . . .

— <u>MY FUCKING EVERYTHING!</u> —

The time we shared together was magical, unspeakable, thrilling and full of happiness and joy. It was direly perfect. I found myself so buried in love that the rest of the world was nonexistent and irrelevant. I cared for nothing but Marilyn. I would die for her, kill for her, and lie for her wellbeing. She was one of the most fascinating and interesting creatures I've ever had the harsh pleasure to meet, and I was going to stand by her till the death of us. The sex between us was time consuming, protracted and miraculous. We had one of the most comfortably sound sexual relationships ever bestowed on this retched earth. We were young, very good looking, ready to explore, and had an eager to make one another cum. The absolute perfect harmony you could ask for in a bedroom environment. We played, fucked, ravaged each other, licked one another from head to toe, sucked, touched, tied up, experimented and had some of the most religion questioning sexual escapades ever unfolded. And we were still hungry for more. We were both firmly content with one another. We had a bond, a union... One that was not going to be broken or tested by anyone or anything, so, we took a look out into this world and were ambitious for a new partner of choice.

Marilyn had a desire for other women (which was enormous for me) seeing as how I had the same vast flavor for women also. This was the most wonderful unification known to man. She felt herself in need of some thrill and she desired the excitement of a three-way . . . and I was just as eager, as eager as she. I was aware not to voice my ecstasy too much and ruin the prospect of this enterprise. I let her do the picking of the woman that we were to share our bed with, benefit and pleasure together. The hunt didn't go on for all that long until Marilyn found a suiting partner for our sexual conquest of sheer gratification. She chose her best friend. Her uncomplicated, unattached and uninvolved girlfriend, 'Sonya Jet.'

Sonya was a young woman, in the same age group as Marilyn and I. Twenty-one stunning and dramatically confused years old, and ready to seek out another form of unpolluted bliss. She stood five foot seven, fine looking, brunette hair with blond streaks and piercing brown eyes. Sonya had a large set of tits on her chest for her smaller size and an equally plump ass. She was in a dead-end, traumatic and momentarily unsettled relationship with some guy from her school. The outcome between her and him was daily changing, one minute she was single, the next, in forever lasting love. She was perfect for our act of chaste sexual and animalistic paradise.

CHAPTER SIXTEEN:
Tremendously Tantalizing Threesome!

"Making love to your woman is the purest art of showing affection and care, without the meaningless and empty words."

"I feel it's suitable for this action that I am going to vividly describe to you Bob, have its own beautifully uncut chapter. Being that this glorious novel is titled "Sex, Drugs & Imagination." Time for some real heated Hollywood sex scene shit. Am I right or am I right, people?"

"You are one weird guy, you know that, Ryan?"

"Oh . . . Boy do I ever."

The night of some uninhibited, open, sexually risky and joyous exploration was finally here, and we were as ready as we ever could've been as a couple. It was late, around midnight. It was cold out, too cold for sexy outfits, but wasn't stopping this gathering from happening. Marilyn and I headed off to Sonya's house for some cocktails and fun before the act was surely about to come into fruition. I'll keep it real, I was nervous, as we all were, but we set the tension at ease by playing a well-known drinking game of my generation called 'Beer

Pong.' A fantastic game when played correctly—and sure to quickly give you a comfortable buzz. We played along all while smoking some pot and having cocktails and cigarettes on the side. None of us were making much eye contact or connection. The anxiety was running high. However, the thought was extremely heavy on the minds of us all.

Sonya had her house to herself; her roommates had left for the weekend, which meant there would be no interruptions to bring this act to its downfall (which I believed added to the stress) but we just kept on drinking and smoking till our bodies became numb and flexible. The 'Beer Pong' was quickly losing its enthusiasm, and the night was nearing three A.M. and we three were growing tired of this game of chicken that we were playing. Dancing around the fact of the real reason for this casual gathering, and Marilyn had reached her peak of comfort. She took a hold of the reins of power, led us both into the bedroom, sat us down like a couple of Catholic school girls about to get punished and spanked (that got you perverts going) and elucidated the rules which were to be followed in this threesome with fierce authority and brute fight, and she didn't skip a fucking beat in her influence. It was brilliant to watch her verbalize the rules, which were as reads.

"You two are not to fuck each other! Sonya, you can suck his dick, lick his body and kiss him, but his cock does not enter you. And Ryan, you can taste her pussy, kiss her, lick her, touch her and spank her, but if your dick goes anywhere near her pussy, we're done! Do you two understand?!" Marilyn proclaimed.

"We understand." Sonya and I replied with a scared sense of hesitation.

"Good. Let's have some fun." Marilyn spoke as she laid us down on the bed.

And with our wandering hands as the starting point, we all began to kiss and touch each other, caressing the bodies in the bed and tasting the saliva of one another. We slowly got naked, exploring our bodies and longing for a scream of passion and pleasure. It was an absolutely freeing experience as we all got down to our butt naked forms, just as we were brought into this life, and started to tickle and finger each other.

I was the selected first to be put on the chopping block of deliberation, to prove my sexual awareness and knowledge of the female erogenous zone (which I found rather sexist) Buy hey, who am I to file a sexual harassment lawsuit in the beginning of a threesome. And I was pushed down between the legs of two very beautiful, incredibly wet, and identically eager to cum playful women. This was my time of justifying confirmation as a sexual partner, and Goddamn! I had force and reason to make these women shout, scream and beg for more.

I first started with my girlfriend, Marilyn, licking and tantalizing her pussy. Playing her every which way to make her shake and jolt in pleasure. Licking in and around her cunt, sucking on her pussy lips and slurping up the juices—then venturing to her pretty tight asshole, and giving it the time and patience's it deserves to not feel left out, all while fingering and stroking Sonya's pussy with my free hand. It was multitasking at its very best. I licked Marilyn from the bottom of her ass, to the top of her cunt, making sure I copiously missed no spots in between. I stimulated her clit, fingered her insides with my two index fingers and tickled her asshole with my pinky. I was there to do a job, and I was to see that job done right till the very end. I made sure to suck, lick and enjoy her pussy till the last bit of cum was rushed into my open and accepting mouth. I wanted to see her scream in enjoyment. That was my only goal. I softly slid my tongue across her clit, down to her pussy, around the insides of her, and drifting down to her ass, licking around it, pressing my tongue inside and making sure to pleasure her. I moved up and down her pussy and ass with my keen mouth. With an untamed tongue, I made sure not to miss any zones in the process. I was sheltered in her juices of cum, loving every last wonderful taste of her. When she came, it was a violent and tremendous episode. She firmly gripped her legs around my head, chocking me of air and turning my expression red. All while I was face deep inside her; and with my pressing tongue and forceful fingers of satisfaction, she yelled my name at her loudest volume.

"Ryan, Ryan, fuck yes, Ryan! Eat my pussy, baby!" Marilyn shouted.

It was a very cock hardening experience as a man. She fiercely came twice. And she was ever so thankful and pleased. She took a strapping grip of my pussy juice soaked chin, pulled my face up, looked me in the eye and spoke.

"Now you go take care of Sonya, baby. Show her what you can do."

A request I was damned sure to accomplish.

I moved my face over to Sonya's pussy. Slowly, gently and affirmatively began to give her the same action of execution. I moved my tongue from the bottom of her beautiful untouched and tense asshole, to her fixed and highly neglected pussy (her on-and off-again boyfriend) was a sucker not to give this woman what she wanted and deserved. She was dripping wet with amusement and pure gluttony. I took the right amount of time needed on her to make sure she would squeal at the top of her lungs in animation. I drove my tongue all around her desperate, underprivileged, and very well needing of a certain attention, beautiful and fine tasting cunt. She was in a sheer approval of my drive of helpful cunnilingus. I moved all around her pussy and ass, licking her thighs and insides, not to miss a spot of her unexplored downstairs. Her pussy began to explode with lovely fluids in my mouth. She was in a paralyzing state of relishing pleasure. Marilyn had made her way to Sonya's mouth and they were now kissing, throwing wandering hands on me and making sure the joy was to be lavishly enjoyed by all parities involved. I licked, sucked, tasted, fingered, lapped her pussy and consumed all the vaginal liquefied substances Sonya had to offer my taste buds, for an unforgettable thirty-five minutes or so. Making sure she felt every soft and rough path of my tongue and each suckle of my wide-open mouth of tang and savor. She ended up cumming three times—and was euphorically content, overjoyed and appreciative. I did a job well done, and I got an honor bound and satisfying pat on the head.

"Thank you so much, Ryan." They both muttered in words of shaking, joyous and ebullient merry.

"Are you ready for us to pleasure you?" They asked me in a sparkling and scintillating dialect.

"Yes, I am." I responded in a buzz of anticipation.
It was now my turn to collect on the same timely and glimmering art of a blowjob and cock raising oral sex that I had just given to their lovable and appealing pussies.

I laid down on Sonya's bed, with my hands at my waist. I was awaiting my two mouthed, two tongued, and two-person blowjob of contentment. They both started with a soft licking from my calves to my cock, each taking a leg and gradually making their may to my balls and dick. They were electrifying and torturing me with devotion . . . And it was fucking working. They would look up at me, right in the eyes, and ask.

"How do you like this?" With ever so sexy and cutely seductive, drawing smiles on their faces.

"I am having the time of my life." I replied.
This was one of the greatest times of my life, and I wasn't about to ruin it with my words of choice. I have a tendency of fucking destroying the best moments with my poorly chosen and very profane words. But this was not going to be one of them times. "Keep it short, keep it simple, to the point, and shut your fucking mouth, Ryan." Was the thought that was rushing through my head. "Don't fuck this up for your cock." I said to myself.

They both softly started to lick my shaft, up and down, sucking on the tip of my penis and teasing me. I was a bit nervous, so I was extremely ticklish. I couldn't contain my tender feeling. They knew what they were doing to me—and they both loved it. They had me right where they wanted me. Marilyn would instruct Sonya on the proper way to suck my cock, just the way I loved it. Sonya would take her sweet time and do just as she was ordered to get me squirming and gyrating. My body would tighten in pleasure. Marilyn would stop for an instant and slide her body up to my face, look me in the eye with the most desirable and flirtatious smirk on her face and ask,

"Do you like that baby?"

"I am in heaven." I answered in fulfilled delight.

"Good. Just lay there and let us take care of you, baby." She eyed me down and spoke.

She returned back to my cock with Sonya, and moved her out of the way. She took a firm grip on my cock and looked Sonya in the eye,

"Let me show you what he likes." Marilyn said.

She put her open mouth around my penis and took the entire cock down to the bottom of her throat, slowly holding it inside her mouth for countless seconds, and then retreating to the tip, licking around my tip and making me quiver in disbelief. Sonya would come to my lips and kiss me while Marilyn performed the most mind-astonishing blowjob ever enjoyed. Sonya would grab my hand and put my fingers inside her pussy, telling me to play with her clitoris and make her scream. I would play and play (the best I could focus) while getting my well deserved head—then, these gorgeous women would switch mouths and change positions. Sonya would go down on me for the next ten minutes or so, all while I would amuse and tease Marilyn's pussy.

Marilyn stopped for a second and slid her face down to Sonya's, whom at the moment, was sucking on my cock. She instructed me to 'open my legs wide.' I did just as I was told, like the good little obedient circus monkey that I was. Marlin put Sonya's lips to my balls and told her to suck them all the way inside her mouth. Sonya listened incredibly well to her orders and did just that. And then Marilyn put her open mouth over my cock and swallowed my whole dick down to the pubic area. I looked down at this moment, in pure and abiding enjoyment. And I witnessed my cock and balls trickily disappear before my eyes, lost in the abyss of two craving, striking and longing to please mouths. I felt like I was a God amongst men at that flash. "This is what heaven must be like." I thought to myself, in the most paralyzing trance of my life. They would take turns swallowing my cock to its very last inch and sucking up my whole sack of testicles at the same time, playing with them as they held them prisoner in their mouths of lust, performing one of the greatest cock magic shows ever conceived. 'The Disappearing Cock and Balls' I call it. Countless minutes this went on for, both taking turns making me twitch and tighten. Marilyn came to my face, gave me an endearing kiss, looked me in the eyes, and spoke—

"I want you to fuck me while I eat out Sonya." She requested engagingly.

"You got it." I answered in eroticized chastity.

Marilyn got on her elbows and knees, buried her face deep inside Sonya's pussy, tonguing her and tasting her flowing juice. I quickly erected to my knees, standing loud and proud behind Marilyn. I slide my cock deep inside Marilyn's tight cunt, reaching the very end of her beautiful pussy. I vigorously fucked Marilyn while she ate Sonya's pussy. All three of us were screaming at our loudest volume in sheer entertainment and immaculate carnality. I pounded away at Marilyn as she made Sonya jolt and shake; the moans went up and up and the heat got hotter and hotter. For the next thirty minutes or so, I moved my cock to the deepest parts of Marilyn's pussy while she put her tongue on the inside of Sonya and we were all in triumph and zest. I let out a piercing yell for my vastly approaching cum.

"I'm going to cum!" I shouted in unbelievable confidence.

"Cum inside of me, baby, please, cum inside me!" Marilyn screamed back at me in appetence.

I pushed my dick to the deepest canal of her pussy and let out the most animalistic and manly roars ever heard as my cock exploded with cum inside her. My body weakened and I buckled on top of Marilyn's back for a pithy instant. I was in the truest form of Nirvana.

Sonya got to my side and pushed me off (not gently nudged) but actually forcefully pushed me out of Marilyn's pussy. I took a spot lying on the bed looking at them both. Sonya then laid Marilyn on her back, opened her legs nice and wide, faced her cunt, looked me in the eyes, and spoke—

"I want to taste your cum." She said while she gave me an eternally lasting smile.

"This is fucking amazing. I can't believe this is still going on." I surprising thought to myself. Sonya then took her mouth, and with every suck, lick, swig and gulp, swallowed every last drop of my discharged semen out of Marilyn's pussy. Not missing a splash or ounce. She worked on Marilyn's insides for the next ten minutes, making her shift and shake in luscious, overjoyed and scrumptious passion. I was rigid on the bed watching, remembering, and forever enshrining this as the greatest moment I've ever drunkenly lived through . . .

He was a cocaine cold cowboy,
Lost in lust and love.
He felt no peace or pleasure,
Only hate and harsh thoughts.
God was an enemy,
And the Devil was a coward.
Burning Bridges,
And escaping execution.
Forgetting the fact of fuck,
He fucked just to fuck.
Unpolished poetry for you polluted and poisoned prisoners,
Beautiful bigotry will be your bilingual bereavement.
Remember your relish,
As solitude is style.

As one would think (after a threesome) with the timeless love of your life and her best friend—there was to always be a consequence. An end result, I guess you can say. Even though, all three of us involved, had a lengthy talk that there was to be no feelings, no intimate or personal connection, no care what so ever—just pure, wholesome and dedicating pleasure to make each other cum. However, that being said . . . Before the event took place, Sonya had confessed to Marilyn and I one night weeks before we all hooked up, that out of all her years of sexual exploration, a man, not her boyfriend, one night stands, or long term ambivalent lovers—have ever made her cum. Not with their cocks, their tongues, their fingers or any sex toy or anal plug available on the market. Not in fuck, sensual lovemaking, or handcuffed oral sex . . . "Challenge Accepted!" I said to myself.

After Marilyn witnessed my tongue and fingers give her three screaming orgasms; she had a fleeting second of doubt about the true intentions of her girlfriend, Sonya. After a week or so, the question was starting to ware heavy on Marilyn's mind. She had no choice but to ask me her straining question.

"Why the fuck has Sonya never came with any other man, but you made her cum three times?" She fiercely stared me in the eye and asked.

I was startled, frightened to say the least, but I stayed strong in my convictions.

"Because I'm good at what I do, baby." I confidently replied . . .

"I must say this, Bob. When I made that statement, there was no undertone of cocky, egotistical or arrogant pitch. I take my time in the bedroom. I make sure to make a woman scream. That was the only point I was trying to stress. I'm proud of that. It's hard to come by these days."

"Ha-ha-ha. I am not really sure how to reply to that, Ryan?"

"Take it as a declaration of good hope, Bob."

"Get back to your story, Ryan . . . Please . . ."

"Alright, you old horn-dog."

... As Marilyn sat and was more than under-amused with my statement, I could see the thoughts running rapid in her mind.

"You are good at what you do, but why the fuck, are you the first guy to ever to make her cum?" She questioned with a touch of anger.

I could see her displease and was not going to take the fall for this shit. I shut my Goddamn mouth with my own thoughts about it and let her figure this one out for her self.

"Ask Sonya." I told her.

"I'm going to." She forcefully shot back.

The next couple days went by, Marilyn was mad at me (for a fault which really was not mine) however it was what it was. She was withholding sex to punish me until she got her fucking answer. We headed over to Sonya's for a night of drinking games, pot smoking and laughs. As the night was coming to a drunken end, Sonya, Marilyn and I, ended up outside and alone, having a smoke break and a friendly chat about life, love and the pursuit of happiness. Marilyn couldn't hold back her inquisition any longer.

"Why was Ryan the only man to ever make you cum?" She determinedly asked Sonya.

"What do you mean?" Sonya confusingly replied.

"You said no guy has ever made you cum. So, why was Ryan the first?" Marilyn fired back.

"Well ... To be honest ... He's just really good at what he does."

Fucking verbatim was Sonya's answer. I couldn't contain my well-deserved delight. I let out a childish giggle and an overzealous smirk. Marilyn promptly saw my cocky and might I ad (rightful smile) and gave me a substantially mean and dangerous look of dreading annoyance.

"Shut the fuck up, Ryan!" She yelled at me.

And I did. I shut my fucking mouth like a good little boy that I was. I got bitched-out by my girl. I'll admit it. I'm not ashamed to say it. I wasn't going to breakup over this stupid and meaningless shit. However ... I laughed my ass all the way to the bank in my head. "Don't ever doubt my skills, baby." I repeated in my head.

"If we could sniff or swallow something that would, for five or six hours each day, abolish our solitude as individuals, atone us with our fellows in a glowing exaltation of affection and make life in all its aspects seem not only worth living, but divinely beautiful and significant, and if this heavenly, world-transfiguring drug were such a kind that we could wake up next morning with a clear head and an undamaged constitution – then, it seems to me, all our problems (and not merely the one small problem of discovering a novel pleasure) would be a wholly solved and earth would become paradise."

— Aldous Huxley

CHAPTER SEVENTEEN:
The Ecstasy Trials.

"Those who are born into rich, pampered, happy and seemingly content situations never find true happiness. They self inflict torment and anguish on themselves in the vague hopes of finding some form of real beauty in life. In order to know what genuine happiness is . . . You first must suffer through years of tremendous and guiltless pain."

As money and fruitfully incredible my relationship with Marilyn was. With our many drunken nights of body numbing sex, our casual threesome experience, our endless love for each other, our very long and marijuana-intoxicated talks of our true existence, with the factual information on the table that there was nothing in this world I wouldn't do to make her happy or protect her . . . She was getting bored, dulled out, growing flaccid with our devoted exploit. She had an exploration, a chase if you will, for more excitement, a further extreme for something much more profound and perpetually eternal. She longed for a meaning, a motive, a belief, and a lasting purpose. There had to be something deeper to the reason why we were here, and she wasn't giving up until she found that answer.

She was a psychology major, absolutely fascinated with the human brain and mental thought (maybe that's why she found an attraction to me) my broken, beat down and insecure ass was the perfect specimen for scrutiny. She questioned everything, positively fucking everything. Every look, body language, eye movement, forms of words, laughs, jokes and activities. It was exhausting at times. As much as she was fixated with the human mind, she was also a spacey stargazer. She dove into the rabbit hole of astrology and never came out. She would bury and consume herself in the understanding of every trivial act of human nature. She would come up with lengthy contradicting thoughts of human reason and contemplation. It was a heavy burden to hold, but one that I loved every second of.

As complicated and unreachable she was at times, she was still the bitter love of my life. She would find herself in these dimensions of what our true reality actually is. And she would have no more sturdy legs to stand on. She would snap into parallel universes of anger and hate, and chose to direct them towards me. Or at me, is better said. Maybe because she knew I would deal with the abuse without walking? Marilyn would get fall-down, blacked-out, incoherently drunk, and find the only suitable outlet to her profound thoughts, the only way she could—insulting and harming my ego and perspective. We would have a night of weighty gorge drinking; mix it in with intense weed smoking and popping painkillers to boot. Top that off with staying up too late . . . And we would have ourselves a fucking meltdown. She would hang in for most of the night, but at one point or another along the way, she would snap and I became the threat in her head. She would offend, curse, piety and show a sense of blasphemy toward my chosen character and stance in life. She was wounding, cutting, and attempting to breakdown my strong spirit. All in the hopes of making herself feel better about her fears of death and demise.

On this particular night, it was nipple hardening cold, raining off and on—and Marilyn was on a widespread role. It was a Goddamn slaughterhouse of my moral fiber. She was swearing, executing, stabbing at my past life and reaching for an exploding resolution . . . One I refused to give to her (not because I'm too tough or manly to cry) Trust me, I cry, but because I've been through too much bullshit in my own life for anyone's words to hurt me. Fun, sex and drunkenness are all I desire. Marilyn got shit-canned wasted, was out of her mind drunk and found herself weak and defenseless. She went for my throat with the intent to kill and spill blood. She was abusive the whole car ride home from the bar, punching me, falling down, slurring her words, and on the verge of passing out in my arms. I carried her to my bed, laid her down, removed her clothes (non-sexually) pulled the blanket over her and left a glass of water for the morning. She was just instants away from fallen asleep when she woke in a frantic daze of perplexity.

"Why do you think you're better than everyone, you fucking asshole?!" She yelled at me while I was undressing for bed.

"I don't think I'm better than anyone. What are you talking about?" I hesitantly replied.

"Yeah you do. You think you're smarter, stronger, faster and better than everyone else. What the fuck do you know? Where do you get off? You're broken. Your dad left you as a kid. Your mom left you to fend for yourself. You don't know anything. You are just broken. Broken, broken, broken. Take that!" She finished her smashed and imaginary argument with as she rolled onto her side and passed the fuck out for the night.
She was snoring, moving around and kicking all night. There was no sign of her waking until the next morning.

I stayed up the entire night writing poetry about what the term 'Broken,' actually meant? I was upset, somewhat hurt, but mostly just angry. Nevertheless, I knew in my head, she was just drunk and wouldn't recall this episode (just as she never remembered) so many others before, and I left the poems I wrote on my desk before I left for work the next morning—out in the open for her to find. She didn't have to rise until noon the next day for school, and I knew she would find the poems. She did of course find them, and called me at work to apologize. However, I didn't want to hear her bullshit excuse for her foul words against my sense of self. She had absolutely no recollection of what she said. She just asked me why I was writing poems on the word 'Broken?' What was it that she had said? The whole nine yards of an angry, blacked-out, careless drunk. Nonetheless, we moved past it, much like we did for all the shit before. And time was moving by once again. I understand how it goes with alcohol. Sometimes we say what we want to say, just word it with a form of phrases that our conscious mind would never essentially put together. 'Drunken truth.' An illness we all suffer from, from time to time.

"Would you like to hear the poem, Bob?"

"Let me guess, trick question, I have no choice?"

"Ha-ha-ha. You're absolutely correct, Bob." Ryan replied as he pulled out a crumbled piece of paper from his pocket.

Broken like the fragile wing of a falling bird,
I have no meaning,
I have no purpose,
I have no future.
A bird, that can't fly,
Is one that cannot hunt.
Therefore they can't survive,
That means they can't ever strive.
Weak is the outcome,
And broken is the feeling.
Let it be known that a healing wing,
Will be the reason you feel a brutal peck in your eye.
Underestimate the challenged bird,
And nothing but pain will lie ahead.

She was falling back into her outlook of boredom and lackluster. And it was time for a change. What better way to improve a substance abusing, marijuana enhanced, and alcohol-consuming relationship then with more DRUGS? But of course! That must be the perfect answer. This is going to work out swimmingly. Our drug of choice, as if the chapter title didn't already give it away . . . Was the beautiful pick of body tingling, thought evoking, spiritual finding, striking and exquisite 'Ecstasy.' We were both no slouch when it came to pill dosages. We would take Vicodin, Percocet, Norcos, Oxycontin, Codeine, and anything else we could get our eager druggie hands on to provoke an elevated sensation. If it would fuck you up, you bet your sweet ass we would swallow it.

Now it was time for a new high, a novel buzz, and a complete original potency . . . On a quick side bar . . . Before we go down this road of drug abuse, let me first say this. If you and your lover want to have a great night, pop a couple of the painkillers that I've listed above and drink some liquor and let the madness ensue. You will both be talkative, joking, free of any insecurities you may have, and horny as a Goddamn rabbit in heat. It's fantastic. Your body goes numb and you can't feel your cock even though its rock hard. She can't feel her pussy but it's dripping wet in lust. You can fuck for hours without one person getting tired of hurting. Try it sometime. It's a great night . . . That being said, let's move on . . .

The mind altering and body tingling 'MDMA' was our pick of drug. Well, her drug of choice. I was merely along for this eye widening, feeling divulging, loathing of a comedown—rollercoaster of a fucking ride! She was part of a sorority at college, the president of the sorority actually.

"That's right! I totally fucked the most prestigious member of a useless organization. Take that all you 'Cool Kids' that made fun of me in high school."

"Ha-ha. Bitter, table of one."

"Fuck you, Bobby-boy."

"Continue your damn story, Ryan."

This meant finding the specific drug we were searching for was no hard task by any means. She knew all the right connections to the strongest, purest and most pleasurable ecstasy on campus. I have a slight additive personality (clearly) however, I come from a family of five, which four of those five members, have fought their own tedious battles with drug addiction. And I knew very undoubtedly in my mind; I was not (under any circumstances) going to be the fifth. I didn't need anything or anyone else but Marilyn herself to make me happy. But, she wanted to live the reckless and young dream of experimenting with drugs. Which meant I was onboard until the crashing and fiery end. Life was too short to care about consequence at this point. 'Live Fast, Die Young and Leave a Good Looking Tattooed Corpse,' was my mindset. With the risk of sounding haughty or conceited, there was no substance in this world that would ever make me forget what was real and vital in life . . . Well? I halfheartedly thought and believed.

Just as easy as not using a condom while fucking a stranger you met at a random bar . . . We hit the campus square for a dose of the finest MDMA this side of the Mississippi. And not much to our surprise, we found the quantity we were probing for. A young fellow had just the precise dosage for just the exact price. We made our relatively costly and greatly shady day-lit drug deal in the university campus of Northridge, California, and rushed off to her apartment for examination and consumption. We were both youthful, impatient to know, and longing for drug endurance. It was time to ingest our future and it was oh-so-butthole-tightening. We sat at her small, feeble, lightly stained dinning room table with two glasses of orange juice (apparently) the acidic consistency of the O.J. makes for a better roll, and we looked each other in the eyes, appropriately placed a pill on each of our tongues (like the 70's) took a sip of the juice . . . And swallowed.

When it comes to the kicking effects of ecstasy, the one thing they warn you not to do (or inform you about the proper way, as if drugs have a fucking handbook) is to never sit around waiting for it to hit you. However, there we were, pending the belongings of our current drug digested. Time was moving by slower than a crippled snail in a race with a severely diagnosed retard. We decided to go out to the balcony, smoke a joint, have a cocktail and enjoy a cigarette; a task which was ever so ordinary and familiar for us. However, this time, was a premise which would prove robustly gifted . . .

The ecstasy hit us both like ten tons of bricks, crashing down on our inner souls and limiting our ability to control the possessions any longer. Our teeth began to grind, our jaws were clinching up, our spit was drying, our thoughts were breathtaking and our hearts were racing. A rush of affectionate, open honesty, abiding touch of feelings and pure surviving euphoria was before us. We could talk about anything, without the gloomily haze of definition heavy on our backs. We couldn't keep our hands off each other, our skin felt like moving gel, the fabric of our clothes felt like soft whispers in a shrill environment. Our eyes both began to saucer up, the blacks of our pupils were taking over the color of our eyes, causing a momentarily deceased look of complexion. We stood in the cold temperature of the world, hugging, holding and caressing each other. Significantly listening to every word we both spoke, acknowledging every sentence, every phrase and every speech. Marilyn could tell me about her fears in God and afterlife, our real place of life, our wisdom of awareness in reality and the energy that will become of us when we pass. I could talk about my past events without a quickening sense of self-defecating retribution or the need to explaining the point of when I fell from the almighty Grace. We became one (In all aspects of the idiom) we thought alike, talked the equivalent and felt the same ideals of existence. Two souls became one on that starry, cold and glowing night. On a balcony in Northridge, California, we both found a form of religion and genuineness. As much as we wanted to (not that we really did) we couldn't stop from being pulled to one anther, drawn almost, holding our bodies tight, squeezing our warmth of life to each other and finding hope in our death. It was one of the most emancipated, free and timeless journeys of my life. For hours we stood outside in that chilly weather, sweating from the drug, talking, chain smoking, openly expressing and vocalizing our thoughts on life itself, our meaning, our function, our understanding and our purpose. We were revealing in such subjects as the foreseeable and predictable lifeless end to our bodies, but never our true energy. Northridge has never been so beautiful. What a night of conversation. The capacity to articulate such feelings was so overwhelming and irresistible to our walls of shelter and hide. It was holiness at its purest form. Tried-&-true. Far from any book or 'So Called Bible' could ever tell us how to be, what to think, the acts we should believe in or the people we should love or hate. This was a revelation unfolding before our eyes and we were the apothecaries sent to deliver this essence.

YESTERDAY IS FALSE HISTORY
AND TOMORROW
IS JUST AN UNWRTTEN MYSTERY

A few short and immeasurably passing hours after this indestructible rushing high of transparency and purity . . . The rough, draining, tiresome and evident Comedown was here at our forefront of unity and strength (that's a 1994 'Bush' reference for you kids) which is a diarrhea covered and just an utterly unpleasant experience. This is for those of you who have never personally had the pleasure of stomaching and tolerating an ecstasy comedown (or any drug comedown for that matter) let me depict and illustrate it the best way I possibly can. Without the individual and personal knowledge of stabling this event in your own astute, I will do the best I can.

It is one of the most gruelingly exhausting, abdominal turning, uncontrollably bowel shifting, sleepless and depressing, complete lack of formulating a pertinent line of verbal communication—and just a desperate act of extreme anxiety and misery. Shy of a better term . . . The worst fucking time you will ever watch the next coming sunrise to. A barrenness, despair ridden, vacancy of real life, hollow belief and empty blank stares of pretermission; in the shortest example I can say, the absolute nastiest time you will ever undergo of meaningless disgust. Think of your worst day ever. Your worst day ever played out in front of your eyes. Walking in on your lover cheating with someone else, your dog getting hit by a speeding car, even your loved one getting murdered by a sadistic killer . . . It doesn't even slightly or significantly compare to what a heavily induced drug comedown feels like (granted that's a basis statement) but nevertheless, it's a life shattering time with nothing but sorrow and self-distain in your heart.

You really wish, hope (some might even say pray) if you believe in that fictional, cocksucking God above, for complete death. Please make it quick, make it absolutely painful, I don't give a fuck, just make it fucking happen. You hate yourself, the world, your dog, the next rising sun, and the certainty of God. You hate the subway sandwich in your hand, the water you drink, the warm shower you take, the cigarette you smoke, the people you see and the shoes on your feet and the clothes on your body. You hate the packed and inclusive world as a whole. Everything is a burden and everyone is an enemy. You vomit, you shit. You then shit while vomiting. You shit some more, and vomit a little more, then, you do it all again, for hours and hours this goes on. You can't eat, barley drink water, you can't talk. Your mouth is dry, as if someone threw sand down your throat while you were sleeping. Your words are bleak, and you wish to leave your body, if only for a fucking second. It is the most wretchedly sorry time of your life. I've had a lot of bad days in my life. But no bad day could ever prepare me for a potent drug comedown. I hope that can paint a vivid picture of the hate and dejection you feel . . .

Marilyn and I had run out of drugs and the comedown was here to stay, state its claim as chief of our emotions and lord of our feelings. For the next long, never-ending, rioting and trashing seventeen painstaking hours of living, we both laid on the couch, very weak, speechless, and suffering through mental and physical sting. We couldn't muster up the inner strength to lift an arm of touch, swallow a meal of fiber or sip a taste of well-needed hydration. We were fucking pathetic. Unattractive, sweaty, cold, our bones were aching, our blood was itching, our thoughts were running wild and we couldn't control any normal human function. One minute we were freezing cold and sweating, the next second our body temperatures would spike to an all time high. It was unbearable and gross. These painful physical symptoms lasted for almost a day after that mind blowing high. The next week of your life, you have strong thoughts of suicide, hate and hurt. One minute you're crying, the next you're in a full-fledged rage. You question everything you've ever been told, said, heard and felt. You think to yourself all day and all night. "Is the world even real?"

As agonizing and distressed as these feelings were, it didn't matter, we were both dramatically hooked. These days of pain and suffering were worth the groundbreaking, mind-altering, body stinging, unlimited and unstoppable high this drug would give us. The way we could communicate, touch each other, fuck and feel on this drug was here to stay . . . And for a good while, too . . . We could help each other through the fucking brain melting comedown and that was all that was important. This was going to be the salvation to our complicated and thrill seeking relationship. We were getting ecstasy dirt cheap, in ample supplies, and Goddamn it, we were going to eat it all. For the next four months or so, we were popping countless pills every weekend. We were going through every Friday and Saturday night with a drug-induced buzz, slipping further from the real problem of our relationship and declining in health. For two days at a time we wouldn't eat or drink any water. We just chain-smoked, drank liquor and popped X. We watched as the sun would rise, set, rise again and set once more, both of us clearly knowing that Sunday night was going to be an utter fucking living nightmare. But we didn't give a shit. We were staying together, being happy, and that was really all that mattered at that point in time. Of course, looking back on it now, the obvious answer to our lover issues should have been a sober, straightforward and honest talk, but fuck that! Why do that when we can get wasted on drugs and still remain together? Great thinking on our parts! DRUGS, DRUGS and more DRUGS . . . And we were trying it all. Pure MDMA, Mollies, Special K (A.K.A. Ketamine) Methamphetamine laced with Heroin, Speed laced with Heroin, all have incredibly different mind changing highs and very low and depressing comedowns. It was self-inflicted human testing at its best. We lost our real sense of life and the reality that came with it, always thinking about the next approaching weekend and the high we were going to submit ourselves to. However, when experimenting with drugs, comes the expensive cost of vastly diverse side effects, and there was one night, which will always lurk in my brain as purely awful, disgusting and fucking hopeless.

We got a bad batch of 'Special K' laced with Speed and suffered a lengthy night of nothing but inclusive pain and sheer toleration. We popped the pills with some orange juice, smoked a joint and relaxed on the couch awaiting the effects to kick in. They did, just as we knew they would. And it was nothing but a thirteen-hour trip of having entirely no inner strength to stand from the couch and compulsively twitching and shaking of every muscle in our bodies. As much as we tried to fight back against these suffering jerks of our motor functions, there was no winning. My eyes, my arms, my legs, neck, fingers, even my ass cheeks were twitching. It was daunting, grueling and pure shit. We couldn't even speak to each other. Our voices would yank in pitching volume from the muscle jolts. Thirteen long and rubbish hours we had to sit on the couch watching each other shake like a patient of epilepsy. It was one very, extremely and wastefully shitty time for both of us.

The inevitable comedown hit us. And for the first time ever, we were thankful to undergo that ache. Just too actually stop twitching uncontrollably was fucking fantastic and refreshing. The comedown lasted another long and revolting ten hours or so—but was the only form of peace we had. After we came back to normality, we called up our drug dealer and demanded a fresh and pleasurable batch. We informed him of the side effects we were forced to suffer through, and he genuinely felt sorrow for us. We were comped four free pills, which he said were sure to set our minds at ease. We loaded up our four pills and headed over to my friends dads house. His pops was out of town and he had a gorgeous pad in the hills of Granada to himself for the next five days. Let the chaos ensue . . .

Everybody at the party was playing beer pong, taking shots, smoking pot and having a great time. Just living the young and reckless dream if only for a night. Marilyn and I waited till about midnight, when we could visually see that the intoxicating effects of alcohol and weed had consumed the other partygoers, making sure their attention would not be focused on the two X poppers that were about to invade this establishment. We snuck off to a bedroom, enthusiastically took two pills each, threw on our bathing suits to jump in the spa and wandered outside. It was time to do some binge drinking and pure self-destruction. Grabbing a bottle of Captain Morgan, a joint and a pack of cigarettes on the way outside, we hopped in the hot tub and began to drink and blaze (which) is a younger generations term for smoking pot—and chain smoked till the wealth of ecstasy had taken over our conscious minds and overtaken our reality . . .
Wait for it . . . BOOM!!

Just as we knew it would, the habiliments of E was now the prominent successor of our drug daze. And it was absolutely fucking stunning. The scolding hot water of the spa was now in a pleasantly dream state of fruition, massaging, caressing and tingling our skin. It was calming our nerves, settling our minds and giving love to our souls. The universe had plans for us that night; deep, beautiful and enriching plans. Our bodies had now been drawn to one another, forcefully pulled and nudged, just like the very first time we ever ingested X, and we ran our hands up and down the backs of each other. Loving, caring and quietly kissing in the dark lit spa, soaking wet and alone, we got our erotic emotions rising and our hearts racing. Smoking one cigarette after another and pulling lavish swigs off the bottle of Captain Morgan we got completely wasted. The batch we got had been laced with Crystal Meth, as well as a copiously strong supply of MDMA, a significantly vigorous blend with a mind blowing high. With the risk of sounding like a total drug addict (not that I give a shit what people think) we loved every fucking second of it. Astonishing, gifted, lovely, freeing, seductive and charming. It was an all time high. That wonderful album of Ecstasy opened doors to my mind, my soul, my heart and my eyes that still haven't closed yet.

For roughly five hours we sat alone in that spa making out, groping our genitals and slowly pulling her bathing suit to the side and slipping my cock inside Marilyn's eager pussy. With every deliberate and momentous push she could feel what it meant to be alive. She moved from facing me, eye to eye with my dick deep inside her, to turning the other way and ripping mouthfuls off the bottle of liquor, lighting a smoke and enjoying every inch of my penis going in and out of her internal core. Godly and provoked, we challenged the word of the almighty to find a center that never once existed in this world we all share. An explosion of cosmos and a deflation of belief, this was once again Heaven. Our tolerance for alcohol was very high due to the Meth in the drug—so we were, without a better term to fully describe it, we were 'Fucking Partying!' We would have long and intense make out sessions, grabbing and fondling one another's privates in the eye of the party, not caring what people thought, judged or concerned. This was hope, this was life and this was real. The night was ours and that was profusely clear to the world. 'In-Fucking-Destructible' was how we felt at that very moment—kissing, laughing, touching, fucking, drinking, smoking and having one of the most untamed and uninhibited nights of our young and irresponsible lives. Never forgotten and never censored, we confronted death.

— SHINE ON YOU CRAZY DIAMOND —

We were both burdened with the extremely heavy thought of the soon, hastily approaching, ass-tightening and nauseating comedown. Which was going to be at our doorstep at any minute, and we both knew we would be helpless once again. This meant it was time for us to retreat home to sit alone in desperation and despair. Relaxing on the couch as this mind fucked feeling of suicide and disbelief rushed over our bodies and it was time to be weak and sorry for the next long and daunting hours of hatred, grief and lasting sadness. As shitty as we felt (when we could gather the strength to formulate a sentence of language) we would talk about how great, saintly, sublime and solely thought invoking the night was . . . A once in a lifetime, breathtaking night that will live in my memory till the end of this cold, shadowy, demented and complicated life of mine—as forever being the most inglorious time I've ever had the pleasure to be bestowed with.

"The next portion of this story, Bob . . . Is still up for discussion and I will let you translate it the way you please."

"Alright, I guess I can do that, Ryan."

With the elements of drug use, come nights of infidelity, disloyalty, and breaks in trust and the testing of ones union that you share with your lover. That's just part of the game, and if you're not willing to accept that, well . . . Then don't do drugs! I like to think of myself as a pretty easygoing guy. It really takes a lot to shake me from my sturdy tree house that I have comfortably barricaded myself in. I let most things slide off my back and move on rather quickly (one might even say quicker than most) however, that being said. One thing I do not, and will not ever tolerate, no matter fucking what (but most notably more important) never actually do to another person . . . Is CHEAT! I find it sickening, ill-mannered, disrespectful, wrong, and just a downright spit in the face of your lover. Cheating is a scum filled act, that of which assholes, sluts, cocksuckers and bitches perform. And a ruthless act you should never put another person through. I would like to believe, that up until this point in my life (through the stories I've shared so far) I could be perceived as a wildly open minded and experimental person. Marilyn wanted to have a threesome, I was onboard (that's a given) she wanted to try some new drugs; I was all in till the unforgiving end. However, the rules of relationships really start to blur with heavy intoxication and boundaries of sexual trance.

Marilyn had a friend (a close girlfriend of hers) that whenever they would get together, would always raise an eyebrow of suspicion from my end. Not because I'm some overprotective and jealous boyfriend. But because this bitch would look you in the eye and tell you how much she respected you; then she'd turn around from your view and shit in your cornflakes and watch you eat it with a giant smile on her face. A dreadfully vindictive cunt (but that's written with anger) nevertheless, everybody knows precisely what I'm talking about. Whether it is male or female, your lover has a friend, right now as you read this, you don't trust as far as you can see them (you probably just got insecure) and they are one shady move away from bringing everything you've worked so hard to understand, love and believe in with your lover— to its rapidly crashing ruin. Well, this girl, who's name is 'Darla,' was exactly that fucked up friend.

Marilyn and Darla had a very hands-on friendship to say the least. Marilyn had disclosed some information to me earlier on in our love endeavor that she and Darla

191

used to hookup from time to time, which, when all is said and done, is completely fucking fine by me. Two beautiful women gettin' it on, is a wonderful sight, and/or story for me to hear. Please do share. I'm into that type of thing. I got no jealously issues. I've measured my cock once or twice, and it will forever beat the length of a vagina. However, I feel that type of action is only suitable if I am aware, and either present or informed of the situation before the fact of sexual exploit takes place.

"That being said, Bob. I will share more of my shattered soul with you, in the hopes of entertainment and peace of mind."

"Please do. It is starting to sound like things are getting juicy." I replied.

"Indeed they are juicy, Bob. Indeed they are."

Marilyn and I were always very incessantly secure. We talked every single day we were not with one another in physical appearance, and when we did see one another, there were enormously no secrets for us to hide from each other. She was more than well aware and informed of my past strip club craving. All the same, once Marilyn and I began to hold the championship title of boyfriend and girlfriend, I didn't attend another titty-bar for the extent of the relationship.

"That is the real truth, Bob, and fuck you if you don't believe me, I don't care."

"Jesus, such hostility, Ryan. I didn't say a word."

"Yeah, but I could see you wanted to."

"Let's hear the juice, Ryan."

Marilyn on the other hand, still had her strapping taste for other women. And Darla was on the menu of her sexual appetite.

Marilyn and I had not talked in two days and some change, which, for us, was surprisingly a long time. We would normally talk at least once a day, a simple hi, hello, how are you doing? However, this time in particular, her cell phone was off and she was not answering her home phone (I will not lie to you, I did not fear the worst) I had known Marilyn for almost a year and a half at this point, and knew she was always a smart and safe girl when it came to partying and I knew everything was under control. "Maybe she is just wrapped up with school work." Was my only thought. When I did hear back from her, her voice was timid, weak, tired and stained with guilt. I could sense something was wrong, I just never assumed the worst. We talked for a good hour on my lunch break while I was at work, and the time for me to return back to my slave responsibilities came to fruition and as the conversation was dwindling down. I had no other choice but to ask her,

"Is everything ok? You seem a little out of it." I questioned.

"Yes, I'm fine." Marilyn replied.

"You sure? You don't sound normal?" I asked with insight to find.

"I need to tell you something." She retorted in a struggled voice.

"What's that?" I eagerly asked; now with concern.

"The other night, Darla came over, and, well . . . We took some ecstasy." She said.

"That's fine. As long as you were safe, you don't need to explain yourself to me." I calmly replied, but was now having thoughts of doubt.

"Something happened." Marilyn threw my way.

"What happened?" I asked with an escalation of volume and anxiety.

"Me and Darla . . . Kinda hooked-up." She resisted in speaking.

"What do you mean kinda hooked-up? What exactly happened?" I questioned.

"Ryan, I don't need to draw it out for you. You're well aware of what I mean. We were high and it was an accident. I'm very sorry." Marilyn sympathetically presented her response.

I, being the cock hard, egotistical (falsely confident) alpha male type that I am—was not going to let such deception, treachery and easy plead for forgiveness go off without a hiccup or backlash. I wanted answers. Goddamn firm and concrete, abundantly descriptive and logical answers. What happened, who did what, and how much did you enjoy it? She was going to tell me every last detail, whether it hurt me or not. Was it worth it? Did you cum? If so, how many times? Who started this escapade of betrayal, and who is to blame? My pressuring and analytically justified questions were going to be answered. I didn't care how uncomfortable they made Marilyn.

My best friend Levi has a saying, one that he has been telling me for many years (since we were eighteen) and despite his good advice—I never listened to (well, I do now) but that's beside the point. I didn't listen to Levi then, and I really should have. "Be careful what you wish for. You will get it." I understand it's a saying that has been past around for many long years now. However, when Levi speaks it, you better listen up. No words spoke in this world ever have any real meaning to your inner soul, until they're projected at you from a person you love and that loves you. And that's the truth.

Marilyn went on for the next hour or so, while I skipped out from work to listen, breakdown, interpret and feel every juicy aspect, detail, element and description of the night she cheated on me, shit on my trust and lied. The night she enjoyed the sweet tongue cunnilingus and finger penetrating orgasms from another person, all while she stabbed me in the back. And needless to say, I was speechless, flabbergasted and beside myself in flustered conduct. I have never been one for melodramatic, exaggerated, gone Hollywood or blood and thunder type of performances . . .

Who am I kidding? I'm a Pisces. I live for the theatrics of heartbroken drama and fantasy. I have no medium. It's either all or nothing! I cannot be happy with the settling outcomes of life. I either want it all or nothing. In my little twisted, dark fairytale world, I can never be fulfilled with what is right and stable. I thrive off confusion, heartbreak, chaos, uncertainty and illusions. I cannot be happy in the middle. If life is going great, my work is wonderful, my boss is unexpectedly nice, my bills are paid on time and my lover is satisfied . . . I must find a way to stir the pot and create a sense of pandemonium to achieve a greater sense of purpose. I either want to be bathing in a pool of pure gold and jewels, on a green lush hillside, in multimillion dollar castle being spoon fed grapes by twelve beautiful, naked and horny ladies, with a garage full of lavish exotic sports cars and have a dog named Zeus that eats diamonds for dinner. Or I want to be a drug addicted, washed-up artist, drowning in the gutter, sucking dick on Santa Monica Boulevard for my next fix, all while forgetting my own name, being plagued with terminal cancer and wishing everyday for the end. There really is no in between for a person like me. But, I'm digressing again. Let's get back on track . . .

After her comprehensive and revealing portrayal of her recent sexual intercourse, we were at a crossroad. Should we split forever or continue down this path? That was the question? Marilyn was sincere in her regret, and assured me it was a one-time thing, never to happen again and she was more than sorry for her stepping out of amalgamation. She told me to come over her house after work so we could talk, fuck, take a tiny, colorful pill of contentment and euphoria—and forget this whole little tremble ever happened.

"I won't lie to you, because I like you, Bob, even though you're a bastard."

"Speak for yourself, Ryan."

"Very cute."

I went over there after work, had some vodka drinks, voiced my very soft, indecisive, irresolute and vacillating opinion on the matter, took a small and vibrate pill of feeling changing powers, got some of the most mind blowing, regretful and supremacy ensuring sex I've ever had. And ultimately forgot about this little tickle in the ball sack of the devil's playground. I am easily distracted by sex and even more effortlessly forgiving when it comes to a beautiful woman. Fucking sue me!

"The question I ask you is, because it was a woman on woman sexually cum-tastic experience. Is it 'Essentially' considered cheating? My mother and I argue about this frequently. I say yes . . . Marilyn betrayed my trust, stepped out and received pleasure without my consent. I believe that is unquestionably measured as what the definition of cheating is, a break in loyalty and faithfulness. However, my mother thinks it doesn't mean shit. It is a woman and she can't perform the same as a man; the penetration level is nowhere near the same as a male to female love adventure. What do you think? Is it cheating, or an innocent, vagina stimulating, meaningless night? Help me with my heavy thoughts."

"You know, Ryan. I think I will lay on that egg for a little and get back to it later."

"Fair enough, Bob . . ."

> Baby, do you understand me now
> Sometimes I feel a little mad.
> But don't you know that no one alive
> Can always be an angel
> When things go wrong I seem to be bad
> But I'm just a soul whose intentions are good
> Oh Lord, please don't let me be misunderstood.

> — The Animals

Marilyn and I resolved our perverse lover issues. I backed down from my true point of reason and discomfort (much as I often do with the ones I love) and we began to find 'us' again. The unmatched, luminous and carcass numbing sex was fully rebooted and restored. We were fucking, screwing and banging twice, sometimes three times a day—and seven days a week at that. The ecstasy was once again flowing like the 'Niagara Falls' on steroids (clearly I had issues with self control and dominance) drunkenly blurring off one heavily persuaded buzz to another, drifting through perception and disorder, time and health, vomit and shit. We were now back to burning the midnight oil just like before (Fucking 'Rock 'N Roll) but that didn't matter, she was my unconditional everything. And I just wanted to be close to her; no terrible prospect or moot circumstance would get in my way from feeling her kiss, her touch, her love and her pussy. As wonderfully amazing and magnificently eye opening the nights of ecstasy abuse were with Marilyn and I, the long talks of life, love and the endless pursuit of happiness. And let's not forget the life changing, religion questioning, sweaty, pleasuring; cum filled and heavenly satisfying fuck sessions we shared together . . . We both knew it was time to step it up. We needed to graduate to the big leagues. And this was as perfect time as any.

What better way to move up in the unstoppable impeding drug game then to surround yourself with numerously more paramount drug users. 109,690 other drug users at that! Where else but the very oversized, exceptionally drug consuming, rave of a fucking spectacle, the 2008 'Electric Daisy Carnival,' located at the one and only, Los Angeles Coliseum.

CHAPTER EIGHTEEN:

Raving Mad Lunacy.

"Love thy woman like the Goddess she is. Without her, profoundly you would never understand the pain you truly hide."

T he quick approaching day of drug abuse, dancing, eardrum deafening music, euphoric worshiping and susceptible touching was finally here. Four of us set out to embark on this journey of craziness with the sheer hopes of felling wildly connected intimacy and parallel. Share some affection and sensitivity with the other strange and adventurous people attending this event. The four glorious warriors, standing lusty and dangerous against the stalwart winds of normality, sanity and valiant reason, prepared themselves to set sail into this world of pure exhilaration and liberating jaunt were; my unbelievably sexy girlfriend, Marilyn, my best friend, Levi. A friend of mine from work, Marcos (A.K.A. 'Mufasa') and excitingly, my delightfully ruined conscious of a earthly creature and abstractedly isolated self, pulled anchor and let the zephyr of truth be our guide till the very end.

Irrefutably, they would never catch the midnight riders ('The Allmand Brothers Band' reference for you suckers) and it was time to ship off. Levi was not real big into trying the drugs we brought. He's never been about the use of anything or any substance to find his happy place, which was fine by us. This was a free for all. No judgments, no peer pressure or pushy force of any kind type of party atmosphere. Do what makes you happy, have a great time and be thankful you're alive, that was the communal mindset of the group. Levi decided to stick with just alcohol and still had the time of his life. Levi not wanting to do the narcotics we had brought actually turned out to mean more drugs for the other three—a blessing and a curse, depending on how you look at it. Honestly, it's more of a blessing if you're a habitual drug taker, however, that's beside the point . . .

We arrived early, around two or so in the afternoon. The event was scheduled to launch at five P.M. and we had to get through security, find a spot on the field of love and get set for a night full of partying and drug educed serenity. The security was a little tough, incredibly authoritarian and a bit on the edgy side. This meant I was forced to take one for the team (for the greater good of the group of course) and ensure we all had an unforgettable night. I put our ecstasy in a long and slender plastic tube, lubed it up with some spit from my mouth, dropped my pants in the car and had to sphincter it up my tight and untouched asshole; not too much pressure to break the tube and rectally ingest two hundred dollars of 'X' and be buzzing my ass off all night (no pun intended) Ha-ha-ha.

"No . . . I didn't have to do that. I got you there, didn't I Bob-inator? You should see your face right now."

"I will be real, I started to believe you. For a quick second I thought you might be a little crazier than I first suspected, Ryan."

All the security and staff knew why these people were there, they didn't care all too much, just don't act a fool and you'll be fine. We put it in a tube at the bottom of Marilyn's purse and hit the line. They didn't actually search or pat anyone down that was going in. Go have a great time kids, knock yourselves out—that was their motto. We got though the long line of security and found ourselves in the outskirts of the Coliseum field. As I looked around the already extremely swarming and growing by every second Coliseum, you could see the excitement on the faces of the patrons. Every person was divvying up the drugs of choice they had brought. It was pure and utter adrenaline pumping bedlam in the venue. The musicians had set up their gear and were starting to spin music for the guests of attendance. Everyone was yelling, screaming, kissing, touching and hugging one another. Some people would stand with signs above their heads, that they took the time and delight to make, which read the words 'Free Hugs.' You would walk right to them, tell them you would love a hug, Lo & Behold, you got a Goddamn hug (by a complete stranger mind you) but, you felt as if you've known them forever. It was a gathering of lovers and luster's.

Everyone made costumes, shirts, dyed their hair and wore festive colors to express their individuality. We were just as excited to see what this superb event had to offer and present. That meant our group was sure to make exquisite costumes of elegant and celebratory colors and designs. The congregation that we walked into, our union, our assemblage, was not going to be the ones that stood out like the cold, dark, selfish souls which we truthfully were. But I am (speaking) outwardly from my bitter, dark colored and tainted point of view at that time of life mind you—we went there to party, have tons of fun and ingest some mind altering dope. All while consciously knowing and understanding the true and realistically unfortunate long term effects this stimulant will eventually root and educe on our sense of awareness in the near future, place of memory and ultimately the longevity of our lives . . .

"I forgot what I was just saying . . . Where was I, Bob?"

"—You were telling me about the side effects connected to ecstasy."

"C'mon, man . . . I'm just joking. Don't tell me I gotcha that easy?"

"You're full of jokes, aren't you, Ryan? Finish the story."

We just wanted to enjoy a night of unapologetic paradise, no influential questions or parental advisory; with no regard for authority and supervision . . . It was time to fucking *RAGE!!*

Marilyn wore a very revealing, ultra sexy, bust showing petite bra and a tiny plaid schoolgirl mini skirt, more than half her ass was out in the open and exposed to the cold air. Essentially, only about ten percent of her body was actually covered by clothing. And I must say, was oh so fucking fine and erotically intriguing by me. I loved showing off her flawless, tight and perfect body to the masses. Just as much as Marilyn loved to broadcast her hard gym work and commitment to keeping her body in shape and her attractive personification. I'm not the jealous type, never have been and never will be. If you're a smoking hot woman with perky tits and a tight ass, don't hide it, show the world your beauty, don't be shy. My mother always told me, "If you got it. Flaunt it." It was never my organizing control to publicize her body the way that was esteemed to my confidence. She was a grown ass woman and had the power to show off her phenomenal body, the way her and only she saw fit to the public eye. "You go girl!" That's what I say. With high heels strapped to her feet, she looked absolutely hypnotizing.

All the women at this dazzling, sexy, cock rising and neon smooth event were dressed in scantily clad, self made items of hardly covering garments. Wearing booty shorts, bras, thongs, and close to nothing of coverage (some even got down to the bare essentials toward the end of the night) but we'll get to that . . .

I made an awesome, warm, funny and fittingly appropriate shirt, which I am still madly proud of today. And I won't lie to you (because I like you sons of bitches) I stole the idea from a sign that I was forced to read during an uncomfortable and (thankfully) very negative visit to the free clinic of STD testing. We all have a past don't judge me. The sign was of a gigantic and humorous smiling face, just the brilliant and absorbent outlined face of a happy person, with the words "Smile It's Contagious,' written below it. An expression that I found ever so decent and suitable for this scene of love, peace, unity and the undying care for thy fellow man. I painted it onto a purple sleeved, white faced, baseball cut T-shirt, put on some eyeliner, A.K.A 'Guy-Liner,' threw on a dark pair of blue jeans with no underwear and was happier than a billionaire blog writer. For some reason I found that shirt more than rather amusing. I actually still do.

Levi spray painted his hair all sorts of wacky colors and wore the brightest, most cheerful insignia he owned and strutted around with bottles of water for the enthusiastic and very thirsty guests, helping and showing pure kindness to all the people in need of hydration. He was a walking fucking hydration-station.

Mufasa wore a tri-colored wig that hung down to his shoulder blades, an intensely highlighted tie-dyed shirt, dark jeans and rolled countless weed filled joints. More joints than you would perceivably smoke at a 'Snoop Dogg' concert, and he wore a huge, vibrate, grateful and happy grin on his face the whole night. We were quite the eclectically hilarious, illicitly miscounted, and a beseechingly beautiful group of misfits and fallouts your two eyes of judging trouble would have the snag to ever see.

We did the appropriate task of dividing the ecstasy—creating many rendezvous points for certain times of the night and making a well needed backup plan if shit was to hit the fan. We all took a note of the current time, bought a cold beer, had a cheers and three of us washed down the tiny colorful pills of fun and blissful joy. It was time for the madness to introduce itself. We walked over to the top of the stairwell and took a Birdseye view of the Coliseum field. And what we saw was utterly amazing. A hundred thousand partygoers, ingenuously flailing around on the centerfield in an endless sea of neon lights, people, marijuana smoke and ear piercing techno music. The thousands of flourishing arms, all were colliding together in a wave of stunning illustration and energetic vibrancy. It was a brilliant sight, jaw dropping and anxiety influencing. Our grins grew ear to ear as we took a look at what was going to be the next six hours of our young and enchanted lives.

We made our way down the long stairwell into the Coliseum and heading out to the open field, awaiting the potent kick of the drugs to ensue and watching as many other strange and adventurous people moved gracefully around us. The music was enormously blaring, the pungent smell of weed was consuming in every direction and this was going to be one helluva night. We slowly shifted through the massive crowd, attempting to get as close as we possibly could to the main stage. Tightly packed in like miniature sardines in a massive tuna can of truth and religious escape, with our shoulders to shoulders, dicks to hips and Asses to cocks, I've never felt so damn claustrophobic in my entire life. Enclosed by the other profusely sweating and highly intoxicated people, all feeling great, talking, chatting and kissing one another, it was an eye-opening experience. We all took placement at a comfortable spot on the large grass field and let the party come to us.

The night sky slowly began to fall over the blue heavens and the 'E' was now starting to kick in . . . And very fucking hard! I was dancing out of control, covered in sweat and worship, talking to complete strangers about how much I loved them, getting my back massaged by other women, watching Marilyn make out with other women—and just purely having the time of my life. We would get approached by strange groups of other heavily smashed people, who would ask us, "Are you rollin'?" This is a term for the intense high you undergo on ecstasy. You get the sense you are rolling through many different hills of emotions and highs, a rollercoaster ride type of feeling, a rush of absolute happiness, unconditional love and total confidence, best describes it. Your body feels every sensation and touch, every stiff wind feels like needles of gel caressing your skin and you see colors in a whole new light.

"Yeah, we're rollin'." We kindly replied.

"Take a seat on the ground. I want to give you a gift." Our new friends asked of us.

All people soaring on MDMA always have some entitled sense that they're giving you something, a gift, a peace offering or a lasting prize for your sheer enjoyment. They mean no harm whatsoever so don't be scared. They just want to see you smile, see you happy and dazzle your five senses for a quick minute. Marilyn and I keenly took a seat on the ground, awaiting their profound gift of happiness. There is a little eye tingling trick the underground-raver community has perfected and they've perfected it well. A strange 'Eyegasm' of some sorts (That's a reference courtesy of 'TheChive' for you youngsters) and it's unbelievably sight moving. They would unload a tampon (stay with me now) take out the string and packing, put IcyHot on the inside and create a whistle-like device. They would ask you to sit, keep your eyes wide open, put the IcyHot packed tampon in their mouths and with a soft and gentle blow, push this cold and tingling air into your eyes. When you are enormously high on 'X,' every normal sense of yours is amplified by a million, without exaggeration, a fucking million. You taste different, hear different, smell different, see different and feel different. Your eyes become the gateway to your soul, the lights start to trace themselves and it's fucking incredible.

When these strange, colorful, baggy pants wearing people would soothingly gust this IcyHot air into our eyes, it blew our goddamn minds. The feeling it gave us was just short of supernatural. I could see other dimensions and universes. My eyes would begin to cry out this liquid that I've never felt before—it was soft, gel like. It wasn't tears. This was something completely unique. I could see the music literally suspended in the air for seconds, and watch as love floated out from my heart. I could visualize the thoughts of other people. My hands would begin to sweat and tighten. My heart raced and my eyes widened. I could taste the nectar of the Gods and hear the words of the departed. It was just a mind blasting, erection rising and totally an inconceivable experience. We would take this gift of offering and be along on our strung-out way to dance, kiss and massage the other bodies that surrounded us.

As we walked through the heavily dense population of drug users, we would get grabbed, groped, touched and told we were loved. We were hugged, rubbed and just plain adored. It made me feel special, like I finally had something to offer this world, a sense of purpose, a reality of concern for another stranger. A feeling I was never too familiar with. I normally hate every one and everything (or at least I did. I've changed) but this was eye opening. It was a pleasant and endearing type of joyous love and peace. I danced all night long, covered in sweat (shirtless at one point) talked to anyone and everyone. We sat on the ground watching, as others would perform light shows for Marilyn and I. This is the art of spinning two bright, neon lights at the end of a jump rope looking mechanism, gaining in speed and size of circles—giving you the visual effect that the lights are quickly becoming one. 'Tracers,' is the proper term the ecstasy community uses to describe it. A vivid and explosive act of space, time and reality—all meeting at once in some new and undiscovered dimension and creating one of the most wildly unexplainable visual effects I've ever seen. Fucking trippy, that's what I say.

For many hours I walked through this fairytale land of make believe and love. I must've gotten touched by ten thousand people, watched as my girlfriend kissed a hundred women, was told how special I was as a person and had IcyHot forced air blown into my eyes. Witnessed countless light shows and ate about five or six pills of 'E.' Watched as countless girls would remove their tops and walk around with their tits out (or should I say stared for a pithy moment) one young girl even removed her bottoms for the night and I saw straight Vag. Bam! Right there, right in my face like a firm slap I saw some random girls' pussy (which was awesome by the way) and this was euphoria at its simplest and purest form. How I never knew about these types of events as a teen is beyond me. But, I was happy I could experience it when I was only twenty-one years of age. It was fixed craziness and unrestrained wild behavior. I believe everybody should attend one rave in his or her youthful day. It is pure adrenaline packed madness put on at your nearest city or venue.

"And remember kids, when a stranger offers you drugs. You say thank you, because drugs are expensive."

"Jesus Christ, Ryan, really great advice. I'm glad you're not a father."

"That makes two of us, Bob!"

The closing time of the event was vastly upon us and we still had to battle with the normally trivial task of getting home (which for a sober person is a cakewalk) however, for a person high on the light altering affects of ecstasy is a tedious and hazardous job in itself.

I was the chosen driver for the night, and come hell or high water, I was determined to get us home safely. We strapped into the vehicle, scuffled through the horrendous traffic at the Coliseum, and were on the road heading home. I was forced to take side streets the whole way from Los Angeles to Burbank, given that my motor functions were a little bit fuzzy. Levi passed out drunk in the back seat, he had been dancing and drinking all night and was not going to make it awake for the ride. Marilyn, Mufasa and I were wide awake, strung-out on 'X' and having the time of our lives. The music was bumping in the car. We were grinding in our seats, laughing, talking and became untamed fist pumping fools the whole ride home. The drive was going by without a hitch. We were all having fun and accepted the terms that this was a dangerous choice of getting home. Nevertheless, we were all in it till the very end . . . That was of course . . .

Until I turned down the very last mile and a half stretch of black paved road that was standing in front of us and getting home safe. A bright lit street which I have driven (without embellishment) a million fucking times, nonetheless, not in this current state of trance which I was under the influence of. The road is a simple, flat, straight and easy street, nothing too challenging about it. Yet under my present form of intoxication was an intense, feral, uphill fight the whole way. Between the sheer lack of water, body exhaustion from all the passionate dancing, the hallucinating effects of the ecstasy and the fact that I'm pretty sure I was still rollin' pretty hard out of my gourd—I was now on 'Mister Toad's Wild Fucking Ride.' There were all kinds of different shit popping up from the manhole covers on the ground, Nazi zombies, ghosts, werewolves, vampires and ghouls. The trees were impressively blowing in the very nonexistent wind—they had arms attached to them, smacking on the floor and deafeningly yelling vulgar statements as I past. The streetlights would literally remove themselves from the ground. They ripped themselves out from the concrete and ran towards me, chasing me, following me in the rearview mirrors. They looked like giant two legged creatures with bright and colorful lights for faces. It was fucking crazy, man. I just stayed in my lane, held my legal speed—white knuckled the fuck outta that steering wheel and kept my eyes wide open and fixed on the road as I past what I sure believed was a demented and wicked style of Disneyland (or if you've ever had to spend a day there with a screaming child) then just Disneyland. And I managed to safely get us all home nice and silent like . . . Thankfully, that is!

The next day and a half to follow, Marilyn, Mufasa and I couldn't eat, couldn't sleep, couldn't talk, feel anything whatsoever, or drink even the slightest bit of water. Our stomachs were wrenched in pain, we were in throbbing soreness and it was clearly written on our faces. All we were able to do was sit on a bench that was placed on my outside patio and smoke an ample supply of pot, trying our damnedest to get back to a minor sense of normal. We watched as the sun rose and the morning birds took flight for their everyday acts of survival. We were restless, angry, sad, hopeless and pathetic. We helped one another out the best we could. Telling stories of the untamed fun we all just experienced. In the hopes to help numb the sorrow of this shit tainted time of life we had to go through. We would take turns packing the bowl with weed and passing it around every thirty minutes or so—the lazy and sloth like affects of some strong marijuana are one of the only things that will help to subside an 'E' comedown. It can help you eat. Well? Sometimes eat, but mostly it's to calm your mind from running fucking wild with the thoughts of desperation and suicide. We smoked more pot than I think I've ever smoked before. Nothing was helping; we had no choice but to wait for the lasting affects to ware off and hopefully get some sleep.

Sanity is boring,
And normality is unless.
Hate is pointless,
And love is overwhelming.
Pain is a gift,
And security is a delusion.
Hold tight kids,
Life gets more complicated.

In better news, the appalling symptoms finally did reside to a place where we could lay our heads on a pillow and get some well deserved sleep, passing out and sleeping for what I think was the next two days. We only got up to puke or shit and then passed back out. And would wake again hours later for some more good old fashioned fecal disposal and vomiting—taking a sip of water, having a cigarette and taking a nibble of food. However, a time I would suffer through again and again to have the memories of the night that changed my life.

Levi, whom did not dabble in the dope pleasure of the night, was the only one who didn't have to endure the long and dreadful side effects. And needless to say, he was cheerful and pleased, had an appetite and more. I met him out on the patio for the sharing of a joint and told him the very entertaining story of the treacherous ride home and all the fable monsters and creatures I was forced to encounter along the way. I meticulously detailed the storybook land I drifted in and out of, and we laughed and joked about the dangers.

"Wow. I'm surprised I didn't wake up from any of the monstrous demons trying to attack the car." Levi said.

"Well, I don't really think there was anything on the road? My mind was playing tricks on me. I was just seeing things." I humorously replied.

"No shit, Ryan! Ghosts and vampires are not real. I was fucking with you. Pull it together, brother." He cordially responded. "That must've been some good shit you took." Levi finished with.

We both shared a well-needed laugh and smoked on a joint talking about what a wild and crazy night that both of us would never forget. Leave it to Levi to justify the existence of the world in one sentence. That's why I love him . . .

CHAPTER NINETEEN:
I Lost My Love And I Lost My Mind.

"Arrogant and ignorant people, who claim they have no heroes, hold no legitimate value in my book of life. We all must look up to a positive cause, a prolific person, or a life-changing event or something much larger than our meaningless, shit-filled carcasses. We must believe in a profound change for the greater good. Otherwise, we will be too busy condescendingly looking down on the world and miss the true and stylish beauty that surrounds us each and every day."

I was now twenty-two years old and I had a life-altering rave under my belt, a mind blowing threesome experience that most people can only dream about (not bragging) just slightly embellishing because it was awesome and highly unexpected—A beautiful girlfriend that I loved and admired with every single blackened beat of my numb heart. I was dating a radically unique, proficiently remarkable and astronomically gorgeous woman that I would venture to the depths of hell and valiantly battle the demons of judgment. Face to face with the 'So Called Cowardly Devil' that we all shall not speak of or dare. And all his diminutive peers, effortlessly manipulated and mischievous spirits. With no fear in my core, fight in my eyes and love in my heart—I would solely die for Marilyn. However, I was finding it very hard to perform the everyday responsibilities as a fucking useless mailman at the record label (as you would imagine) due to the nonstop cigarette smoking, late night partying, over excessive spree drinking and let's not forget the thespian style of handsome prescription narcotic abuse (but most not prescribed) and in addition to the drugs, we both chose to ingest substances in secrecy from one another. 'Closet Druggies,' if you will . . . Without a definition needed, things were really shaping up nicely.

Marilyn and I were going through seven maybe eight bottles of liquor a week, smoking an ounce of weed, ten sometimes fifteen packs of cigarettes and spending every dollar we could scrounge up form couches and car seats on persuasive pills of some sort. Our emotions were on a downward spiral of resentment and distaste towards each other. We would have ephemeral fights of the future, financial circumstances, our very disagreeing stance on marriage and kids—also what we were to become as adults. I had, (still have) an inflexible standpoint when it comes to the terms of marriage and kids. I don't ever want either of them. I bury myself in my writing and I love that. Even so, she on the other hand, wanted to someday have both of these very customary household tasks of living. Which is all gravy, do your thing and live your life (and I'm sure you can see where this is going) but this was really beginning to cause a fucking problem in our love life. I am more of a fly by the seat of my pants, live in the moment—work hard on your true passion and everything will be all right, kind of guy. She on the other hand, was the complete and polar opposite. She was very calculating, planned ahead. She had numerous goals and precise timelines she should've hit them by. She also wanted a family of her own. And I'll be honest with you . . . I hate kids I can't give back to the real parents. If vasectomy was an option at birth, trust me, I would've gotten it. But, that's a conversation for my parents. Nevertheless, this was really becoming an issue for us. These fights would last for the span of a full workday. But come nightfall, we would get incomprehensively fucked up on whatever drugs and alcohol we had at our disposal, have a heavenly night of fantastic sex and fuck; and then never talk of the ever so important controversy which was unforgivable in the day time. A significantly dysfunctional and unhealthy way to go about the day-to-day activities of a love affair (we both knew that) however, it was the road which we chose to mutely walk. And like I mentioned earlier, my routine at work was failing significantly and deteriorating even faster.

We were staying up till four sometimes six in the morning. Overwhelmingly drinking booze and chain-smoking pot like the crops were shriveling up and evaporating forever. Spoiling our selves in the unlimited and profuse supplies of pills, any color, shape and potency would do, just to find a more comfortably numb, physically enduring sense of self-achievement and a much higher principle of life. All while trying not to powerfully fuck the solid groundout that was laid deep beneath us during our many, highly and energetically inebriated and overly aggravated sexual exploits of sanctified emptiness and mad disputing love. I was calling in sick (hung-over and drug comatose sick) seven to nine times a month—and when I actually did show up . . . I was falling asleep at my duties, I was also drinking, smoking weed and popping pills on the job. I was, with no other phrase to better express it, A Goddamn Train-Wreck!

You see, Marilyn worked late nights and went to school North of the afternoon—so staying up late and getting bombed was no real problem for her livelihood. I on the other hand had to get up at seven A.M. sharp. And when you drink all night and practically fall down and pass out drunk until the wee hours. It's a real tough battle to overcome. Needless to say, I didn't linger around for very long at that job. Management got tired of my careless shit and they fired my malevolent ass real fast (one year and a two months later to be exact) and kicked me to the curb to figure out some other form of weekly income. I can't really keep track (due to the alcohol and drugs) but this was the third or fourth time I've been fired from a place of employment at this point . . .

"Ok. You got me, Bob. I remember. It was the fourth."

"You don't sound like a very good employee to me, Ryan."

"Isn't that the fucking truth, Old Man?"

Pointless to declare, this current state of unemployment did not sit too well with Marilyn. She was upset with my absence of money and her ability to hide it was quickly growing nonexistent. I was out in the world fending for my next dollar. I luckily had a fall back place to stay in at my grandparent's garage (which I am forever thankful for) but nonetheless, I needed to step up and shape this shit out like a man. I frantically searched and explored for work, finding it to be a much harder task to accomplish than I ever thought. Two months went by and I found no work available. And that meant I was forced to move back into my grandparent's garage due to the lack of rental funding to survive on my own. I could no longer maintain this rock star lifestyle of partying like 'Nikki Sixx' and fucking like 'Tommy Lee' (which I grew to know and love all too well) and I was falling desperately short at keeping my idol girlfriend happy.

However, before I attempt to try and walkout of my fair share of guilt for the alcoholism, the drug trails and the hard partying routine (I'm no hero) I am well aware of that. And I foremost state that. But let me first say this. I didn't care all that much for the dope or the late night partying. I did it solely because it made her happy. And I would do anything to make her happy. Absolutely fucking anything! I'm not saying I was fully innocent, not even in the least. I enjoyed this washed out lifestyle just as much as she did. It was fun for a moment, much fun in fact. That being said, I was content with just loving her. Everything about her, I loved and cared for her deeply, more than I ever thought possible. But, she couldn't see that without the dizzy haze of some kind of substance. I'm not blaming anyone. We were both just as guilty. I presently knew in my own heart I could walk away from the partying lifestyle at any time. I was not bound to it (but unfortunately) she couldn't walk away just as easy. It's not because she was addicted to drugs, because she never was. And I would never talk ill of my love even if that was the case.

That declared . . . Around the same time of me losing my crappy minimum wage job as a rubbish mailman at a heartless corporate record label, Marilyn had gotten herself a new job as a bottle service girl at an ultra rich, super expensive, boojee and douchebag filled club in Hollywood. Three nights a week she was surrounded by wealthy athletes and actors, young and handsome millionaire assholes, you can say (fuck Hollywood. They can all suck my dick) and it erected a problem of emasculating defense. This was surly a concern of mine, but not once did I vocalize my true feelings. I knew to my dying core that I was an honest and loving person. Not a cheater, not a liar (well) somewhat not a liar—not a thief, and mostly not a Shitbag-Hollywood-Deviant. Plus, because I never give in, I wasn't going to give her the satisfaction of the doubt that her current form of employment was an everyday passing thought of mine (until now of course) so silently I took my enfeebled corner and shut my stupid mouth. She was the overall 'Bread Winner' so to speak, and there wasn't shit I could do about it. She was making heaps of money to dress up like a sexy whore, dancing on the empty laps of arrogant, conceited and ego-fueled wealthy men whom were willing to pay one thousand dollars for a bottle of Grey Goose vodka (which) would essentially cost you forty bucks at the liquor store, just in the hopes of looking cool, important and high ranking. Nope! FUCK OFF! Paying a grand for a bottle of liquor to impress the partiers around you does not make you look cool at all! Not even in the smallest amount. It makes you look like "A COCKSUCKING DOUCHEBAG AND SOULLESS FUCKING IDIOT!"

"Take that, Hollywood dickbags! Ryan Anthony Michael Vinci says you can all fuck yourselves! Money doesn't mean power. Money means you don't understand true beauty, you fucking pieces-of-shit! I'm coming for each and everyone of you! Watch your ass! I'm going to make you all look like the fools that you really are! And 'Jersey Shore,' just you wait . . . Because you're next! Wait your turn, assholes. West to East, you're all on my list."

... HOW'S THAT FOR SOME FUCKING POETRY? ...

Two months had swiftly disappeared off the calendar frame and Marilyn was persistently working her new job of exceedingly utilizing her dazzlingly features to grind on the hard cocks of pompous and cash flush men to make more in one night than I was able to make in a week (sexist? Nope, just jealous) and we were growing incredibly distant. We wouldn't talk for days at a time. Marilyn always said it was because she was busy with her new scandalous job, but I knew something was up. However, much like my timid institution has proven, I didn't say much. I let the time tick and tock. And before I knew it, the drinking was severely rising, the frequent use of drugs was mounting (in her part) and she was no longer satisfied with the pills, the alcohol and the weed abuse. Marilyn had a new form of high on her mind . . . The life-destroying drug of a superficial, insecure and motherless actress . . . 'The China White.' Some good 'ole 'Bouncing Powder,' or better yet, 'Booger Sugar;' and I'm almost certain you already guessed it . . . She wanted some tasty, strong, contemporary cocaine. Coke is one drug I refused (and still fully refuse till this day) to ever indulge in. I watched my father get locked up for his endless use of 'Blow' and I was <u>NOT</u> going to follow in his footsteps and end up next to that cocksucker.

"I know what you're thinking, Mister Bob? A 'Dime Bag' smoking, 'Opiate' popping and booze downing enthusiast with morals, what a fucking anomaly, right?"

"It does seem a bit contradicting. But I'm sure you already know that if you must defend it."

On the contrary, I never wanted anything to do with cocaine. An argument I thought I had made terribly clear to Marilyn many times over. But apparently I didn't stress my revulsion for coke well enough. She was growing tiresome, bored and fatigued with our meaningless relationship. And this was time to either show or fold. Marilyn and I would have extensive fights about her independence, her full-fledged woman outlook on life and control of her drug addiction, including her wanting to do coke. Which I blame entirely on her new job and being surrounded by successful millionaires that do cocaine, and I found myself backed into a corner of manly impoverish. And if we've learned anything by now . . . I don't respond well when backed into a corner.

On this particular night, we got into a heavy battle of self-independence, everyday responsibilities and lifelong goals.

"You don't even know where you're going in life anymore. You say you're a writer but you never write. You speak of all your 'so called' life goals to accomplish, but you never strive for any of them." Marilyn portentously yelled at me.

"I write all the time. Just because I haven't dispassionately sold my work for profit does not make me any less of a writer. I love what I do and I try to do it very well." I argued back.

"I agree. But when do you actually think you'll make money from what you're so obsessive about?" She questioned.

"When I'm willing to share my stories and they're complete. It's not easy, and I refuse to give up my creative control for a paycheck. This business can suck my dick if they think I'll break with my meaningful influence to make a little bit of worthless cash. I don't care about money. It's never been about the money, it's always been about the story." I stodgily roared.

"There you go again with your fathers words coming straight out from your mouth. You got it all figured out, don't you? You're so smart and wise? Just let go already. You have to start somewhere." Marilyn unknowingly started the fire within.

"You don't know a fucking thing about my piece of dick father, so I suggest you keep your fucking mouth shut! You're the one who wants to snort coke, not me!" I angrily responded.

"Please! I'm not a druggie like him. I know he never made an honest dime in his life. And guess what? Now you don't either." She spoke and pushed me to the edge.

"First off, bitch. I pay for everything I own, and also all the fun that I indulge in. Yes, ok. I live rent-free for the time being. But my truck, insurance, cell phone, clothing, meals and all my vices are taking care of by my own dollar. Your parents pay for your car, school, apartment, cell phone, insurance, and pretty much your whole fucking life. You work this meaningless, Hollywood nightclub job only to fund your excessive party behavior and drug use. I've been on my own since I was seventeen. Don't you ever try to compare your situation to mine! You have no fucking idea what I've been through and seen. If you dare to try and challenge me, that will be a war you will not win, trust me!" I bitterly and regretfully replied.

I know now, maybe a little harsh way to phrase my argument, but I had a point to prove and those were the words I used to explain that point. I felt then (just as I feel now) it was a very ignorant dispute for us to be having of why I found it so insulting and inconsiderate for her to use cocaine. Marilyn was strong on the fact that my opinion didn't matter. This was going to happen whether I approved of it or not. For hours this redundant and useless fight went on. I was getting pushed back in my corner of obedience and she was getting angrier about some self-fabricated sense of over controlling attitude I was putting on her. This was an insignificant squabble; one I knew there was no chance for me to win.

So I ran like a dog with his tail between his legs. If I was going to be the one to hold this taxing and complex love-ship together, I had to back down and take my seat at the Goddamn kiddies table. Shut my fucking mouth and do as I was ordered (a trade which is almost impossible for me) but I had to sit back and wait for my time to strike. Which, mind you, is a terrible way to live, still, this was now our true form of life and I was going to come out victorious on this one just as I did with Fulton.

I kept my concerns and worries about her longing worship for cocaine hidden and tucked behind my guilty conscious. I let the weeks fall from the calendar as we continued on our path of careless pill popping, pot smoking and rampage drinking. We would party about six times a week, all through the night till the frigid morning hours. Fucked out of our gourds and not giving a flying fuck who witnessed. I can't ever recall when I was actually sober in that time of life. That's when you know its bad, when you look back on the past five or six months. And think to yourself, "When was the last night I didn't pass out completely fucked out of my skull hammered?" I agree with what you're probably thinking, a harmful and utterly dodgy way to live. I am copiously aware of that. However, this was our fucking sincerity, our candor, and I had to accept this indisputable fact of nature. "Keep my mouth shut and do what you're told, Ryan." That was my frame of mind. For five to six moths this lifestyle took over us. I can't commemorate the tangible time span, seeing as how I was blacked-out hammered, and highly drug induced the whole time. All I did know was—it felt like a fucking eternity. Waking up every morning with an aching hangover, puking, I could barley eat, I couldn't have a rational thought to save my life (and with no surprise to anyone) getting shitfaced once more at night and going through all the steps the following day. A defective way of life, however, this was my life at the time.

Marilyn fell back into her ways of getting fucked up and finding an outlet for her anger by degrading everything about me; starting from my look to my smell, my touch, and even so far as my way of life. An abusive time we both endured with one another; going through the motions of hate and love, upset and soreness, gladness and regret, violence and sex, alcohol to drugs. What a fantastic fucking time of love. Ha-ha. Marilyn had come to the end of a very short rope and was sick of everything I did for her. Every nice compliment, every touch of lovingness, every kind word I spoke and every act of passion, lust and warmth. This was the breaking point and none of us were getting out alive from this shit. Marilyn had hit her rock bottom, she felt the taut noose around her neck, suffocating and gasping for air, she finally concluded . . . Her rock bottom was . . . Well . . . "ME!"

Marilyn and I were attending a routine party in the backhouse of Levi's place. We were all shot-gunning beers, taking shots, blasting music, ripping bong loads, chain-smoking cigarettes and laughing at the nonsense which inelegantly spilled out from our intoxicated mouths. The night was California-cold, so probably around 65-70 degrees, but we had a pit fire raging and plenty of overdrawn bills and wood to burn—A typical Friday night for our group. I could sense something was wrong with Marilyn, she was not being her overly affection drunk self with everyone at the party. She was timid, hushed, standoffish, restrained and contained, completely lacking from the normality of her partying persona. I was conscious of her in the surroundings of this shindig, and could clearly see she was vacant from the vibe of the festivity. I nervously didn't want to spark a squabble if one didn't exist, so I calmly proceeded with caution, treaded lightly.

"Is everything ok, babe? You seem a bit out of it tonight." I fearfully asked.

"No. I think we need to go inside so we can talk." She quickly replied.

We removed ourselves from the party and headed in the backdoor of Levi's house, made our way to the couch and took a regretful seat. I could feel it in my gut that something was wrong, and soon the answer would be presented. My first impulsive thought was that my worst fear has come to fruition. "Shit! She's pregnant." I said to myself. Fearing the absolute worst, I sat on the couch in suspense, awaiting my fate of fatherhood and longing for an escape plan to hit me. She took a long, intense and deep breath; her eyes began to slowly tear up as she gazed at me right in the eyes, digging to the inner pits of my core.

"...We need to breakup. You're no good for me. You party too much, drink too much and don't care about anything. You can't find work, you can't take care of yourself and I can't trust you anymore. I feel you've lost your sense of reality and the end is near for you." Marilyn spoke with mastery and genius.

I was thrown back in my seat, shocked, dumbfounded. And I must add, slightly entertained. I shook my head in total surprise and astonishment. I scratched my head, thought wisely of my next execution.

"Are you fucking kidding me? None of this hollow shit means anything to me. I don't need any of this to be happy. All I need is you. I love you, Marilyn. Why can't you see that?" I pitifully and very gracelessly responded.

"I don't believe you. You're too deep in all this and I'm not going to stay around and watch you kill yourself." She heartlessly replied with authority.

I was restrained, vulnerable, numb and frozen to my seat. I couldn't move, I couldn't speak, and I couldn't do a fucking thing to establish the fact I was really alive. We stared each other in the eyes for about a minute as we both sat in the silence. The hearing in my ears began to go, my eyes fixed tight on her and my temperature started to drop.

"I'm sorry, Ryan. This is goodbye." Marilyn finished with.

She gravely hammered these words in my skull, got up, and walked out the front door to avoid being spotted by the people drinking in the back. And she inconsiderable slammed the door on the way out to prove her point. As if I didn't know what a fucking breakup was?

Throughout our entire relationship, she had never slammed a single door, yet she felt this was the precise time to carry out such a disrespectful act, enforcing her decision and taking her stance. I watched her walk away into the distance. My body was stinging, my eyes were watering, my mouth was running dry and my heart was breaking. I had no inner strength to get up from the couch and chase after her. No articulate words to speak to make her stay, no hope, no light, and no choice but to sit and flounder in my own filth. This was heartbreak at its finest and pungent form. I've been abandoned before (referring to my cock bag father, of course) but that was a whole different breed of throb and hurt. I hated my father for many years before I told him to go fuck himself. He was dead to me before I had the brainpower to tell him.

But this moment, this fleeting second of ache was downright leveling, earth shaking. Hearing her voice speak these words, watching her walk away and drive off. It made me numb, callous, cold, scared and alone. Needless to say, I folded. I hit the dirt with my dick in my hand and I was awaiting the ground to give out from under me so I could be sucked away to hell and burn with the rest of the lost souls. Nails against a chalkboard, teeth fillings chewing on foil, needles injecting your veins with toxins . . . This was the bitter end. The end I never thought would come. Yet here it was and here to stay. I didn't know what to do. Should I call her, chase after her, forget her all together, or try to fuck one of her friends to make her jealous? You can see—I had a real dilemma on my hands. I was desperate, sad, angry, confused, lonely, frightened, caving in and wishing for an easy answer. I really had no way of figuring out the resolution on my own. So I turned to my old and trusty friend that has never let me down . . . ALCOHOL.

I stood my sorry ass up from the couch, wiped my eyes dry, collected my thoughts, grabbed a bottle of

Jameson off the counter and headed out back to rejoin the party. I walked straight to Levi, and he could obviously see something was wrong.

"What's going on? You ok, man? Where's Marilyn?" He asked as he looked around me to the inside of his house looking for her body to appear.

"We just broke up." I calmly replied with remorse in my cracking voice.

He looked at me.

"What? What happened?" Levi asked.

"I don't know? She just said we have to breakup because I drink too much." I painfully responded.

"That's ironic. She is always partying. That's her fucking job." He replied.

"I know. I don't want to talk about it. But if you thought we were doing some drinking before. Now we're really going to get fucked up." I forcefully spoke back.

I then cracked the bottle of Jameson and pulverized an overflowing sip to the dome. Levi just looked at me till I finished my gulp of liquor, awaiting my breakdown or outburst. I wiped my burning mouth, handed him the bottle and asked him to "drink with me?" He grabbed the liquor from my hand and mirrored the same tactical guzzle of booze. He cleaned his mouth and we both decided. "Let's get fucking wasted!"

The rest of the night was a blurry haze of abusive and obnoxious alcohol consumption and weed smoking. No regard, no regrets, no morals or beliefs found—just some good old fashioned blackout drinking. Never looking back or speaking of the current state of affairs, we drank till our bodies hit the spot that we were going to sleep for the night. Better yet, where we were going to pass out drunk . . .

People,
Whether they are real or imagined.
They will hurt you,
Leave you,
Make mistakes and demands.
Never will they understand your heartache,
Nor will they stop to care.
Down a path of self-satisfaction and control,
They will never end till you either bleed or cry.
But a best friend,
A brother in arms,
A man of word and loyalty.
Will hit the solid ground with you,
Stand beside you,
Silent,
Caring,
And forever remaining.

When I did awake the next morning (more like late afternoon) I was still heartbroken, perplexed, alone, longing for her innocent touch and missing her angelic voice. As numb as I was from the over excessive bender I put my body through the night before. As tragically dead as I was inside my head, the overall pain still lingered, it did more than linger. It collapsed heavy atop my soul, my mind, my body and survival. The feeling I felt was something of a suicidal mix tape of a love lost 90's flick. Fallen far from reality and even further from Grace, I had to talk with her. I jumped out of my drunken vapor in an anxious frenzy. I picked up my phone and called her, with no real words to say if she actually did answer—I was going to get my reason. And fuck God in his sweet, tasty ass . . . I got it!

"Hello." She peacefully answered.
As if she didn't fucking know why I was calling, almost as if we broke up a year back?

"I need to know. Why don't you love me anymore?" I quickly and desperately replied.

"Ryan, I still love you. I just can't be with you any-more. I need to be alone, I need space." She spat her counter back in my face.

"Is this because of your new job? Did you meet some-one else? I need the truth. Just tell me?" I retaliated back at her camp.

"No, Ryan. I have not met anyone. I just need to be alone, figure some things out on my own. Be my own person." Marilyn retorted with ease in her dialect.
Even though I heard the words spill from her lips, I could sense something was up. This was not our normal rela-tionship. Something or someone was coming in the mid-dle and I needed to know. I could just feel it. But like a scared and timid little puppy in a kennel of kill, I held my hopeless ground. I didn't want to push the issue and get the answer that I knew was true.

"Ok. Whatever you need, Marilyn. I will be here for you when you find yourself. I love you. I will always love you." I cowardly responded.

"Thank you. I have to go." She said as I heard the click of the phone go silent.

That was that. My first real love (my only real love) was ripped away from me in a blurry, shadowed, baffling daze of drugs and consumption. With many questions unanswered and even more to ask, I was once again . . . ALL ALONE!

CHAPTER TWENTY:
The Animal Inside was Unleashed

"Rock bottom is what I desire."

The next two months we played the awkward square dance of talking every couple of days, meeting up, getting drunk, having an empty and vacant fuck and leaving for our worldly errands at furnish. Once again, a very unhealthy way of life, but I was pleased with the fact I actually got to hold her in my arms, even if it was only for a night of sport fucking. She held tight to this false sense of a protective support system through me. Which I believe helped put her mind at ease from time to time. And together we became the most pathetic couple of true emotion dogging clowns this world has ever seen. It was a worthless, distant and strictly a physical game we were playing, one which had no other outcome but to be entirely disastrous. Just as you might think, the feelings were starting to crumple on top of themselves and there was no more ways to avoid the inevitable end of our caring, loving and forever cherished, so called twisted tight rope relationship. I couldn't bite my tongue any longer. My true emotions were blasting through and it was time for a Goddamn answer. I needed to know the truth; I needed a reason (Fuck! I'll be honest as tears fall from my eyes) I just needed Marilyn. I saw an opportunity to get what I was searching for (in hindsight) probably not the best time for me to act in such a super douche manner, but love will make you do crazy things. And this was the most charmingly blinded I've ever been by love. I am not proud by any means of my certain asshole behavior, which ultimately was the downfall of Marilyn and I. However, I was searching for a resolution.

Marilyn's quickly approaching twenty-second birthday was taking shape and I was still sitting on the side lines of her deformed game of love, patiently waiting to get the chance to be her lover once again. Quietly and weak, I did what she said, answered when she called and shut my mouth when she told me not to speak. I was soft and emasculated. I was a polite little puppy dog, obeying every order with command and contentment. Somebody should've smacked the shit out of me and revoked my man-card for this disgraceful way of life I was subjecting myself to. But I was longing to be her man again, and mostly, I was a sad excuse of an alpha male. Her birthday kicked off without a hitch, I threw her a surprise party, inviting a lot of her friends (even the assholes I couldn't stand to look at without a choke of vomit) I invited some of my close friends (only the one's Marilyn could tolerate) and had a wonderful BBQ to celebrate her next year of life.

Everybody showed up, ate great food, caught an endowed buzz and we headed off to the bowling ally for some drunken tomfoolery. The night was going great with all the friends, however, was going far off the path of my favor. Marilyn was living in her own world, she refused to touch me, kiss me, or show me any sign of affection. Not even a slight indication of acknowledgement that I went out of my way to make her happy. This fucking ridiculous game of playing coy towards me, showing no signs of care for one another had hit its boiling point in my head, and I was forced to react. I went about my night getting shitfaced, pretending we didn't just spend the last two years of our lives together. We all partied, bowled, had a great time, many laughs, and heading off to home to do our own things. If you can't sense the feeling of anger and resentment I was carrying, I have a sensation you'll understand shortly.

The next night her friends were throwing her a party with all of their (alleged) school friends. A group of superficial and meaningless college friends that would look you dead in the eye, say I love you, then the minute you turned away, try and fuck you over. To speak frankly, a significant group of pieces of shit, but hey, what the fuck do I know, right? A true friend loves and cares about everything you stand for and believe in. Real friends are ride-or-die type of people. They genuinely want you to do well in life and actually end up happy. However, this was not that group of people. I had no care for these people, or their assbackwards opinions on life. I had real friends, Marilyn didn't. She always gave everyone the benefit of the doubt, and got fucked over in the end. That being said . . . Lets advance. Her friends had a party set for her and Marilyn asked me to come as her platonic little boy-toy. I of course, agreed with no hesitation, just like the good little bitch that I was. She had my nuts in her purse and everyone knew it. Her friends knew it, my friends knew it, and the damn ice cream man knew it. I was no longer a man. That feeling of emasculation was really starting to get old and fast.

Marilyn and I set out for her birthday party, first starting at her girlfriend, 'Lisa's,' house. It was around two P.M. on a Saturday, and the booze was pulled out and poured to perfection. Tequila was the alcohol of choice, and taking lavish shots was the method to get it down our throats promptly. We must've taken five shots each. All while shot-gunning beers and smoking weed. We were getting fucking wasted and the pace was vastly accelerated. The night was coming into its excellence and we had plans of heading to a frat house for the second portion of Marilyn's birthday. A house party thrown in her honor, with a pool, packed full with all of her friends and tons of substances to go around. Do some shots, take a swim, have some fun. That was the thought on everyone's mind. Well . . . Everybody . . . Except me. I knew damn well what I was going to do (DESTROY) so I called my boy, my protector, my fucking main man, Levi.

"What's up, brother?" I asked him.

"Not shit, just hanging out. What about you?" He returned the question.

"I'm going to this house party with Marilyn and her cock sucking friends. I need you to meet me there and watch over me. Some shit is going down and I would like your help if I need it." I kindly placed this information on his lap.

"You got it, brother. Text me the address and I'll be there shortly." He didn't even skip a beat when answering.

. . . THAT'S A TRUE FUCKING FRIEND! . . .

I sent him a text message with the details of the party and went back to the task at hand of taking tequila shots and pounding beers. I had this feeling of anger in my heart, my core, and my mind. This in turn was making the profuse supply of alcohol have no real affects on me (or so I thought) I had a mission, a purpose for the night, and nothing was going to stand in my way. My boy Levi was early so he gave me a phone call and I gave him directions to meet us at Lisa's house. He did just that and had a few shots, had some laughs and waited for the night to fall over us. He could see right through me (he always can) he saw my anger and he didn't even attempt to try and talk me out of whatever was to become. He knows when I set out to do something; I don't leave until I get that shit done.

We lingered at Lisa's for an hour or so and headed to the frat house party. When we arrived, the place was packed, wall-to-wall partiers, all kinds of different substances and drugs being passed around. They had gotten a cake for Marilyn, a nice simple birthday cake with the words 'Happy Birthday, Marilyn' written on it. They did the whole candle blowing ceremony and sang happy birthday. But now . . . Now it was time to fucking rage! Shots, shots, shots, shots, shots, shots, shots!

Marilyn was introducing me to all her college acquaintances as her 'Friend, Ryan,' which was really beginning to piss me off. But I remember it as clear as yesterday. There was this short, fat, slimly little fuckbag, whom called himself her good friend. I forget the little cocksuckers real name, but for the simplicity of the story, Ill just call him, 'Dick Face.' And yes, precisely because he had a face that resembled a dick, at least in my mind! Marilyn and Dick Face would take shots together, smoke joints and have a grand old time. I wasn't jealous. I just didn't like the little cunt as far as I could see him. He was a shady little bastard (actually) ended up fucking her over in the end, but that's not my story to tell. Fuck 'em both, that's what I say . . . He would intrude his big nose in our business and was really looking to get knocked the fuck out. Marilyn got shitfaced real quick and decided it was time for a dip in the pool. She walked over to me and asked if I would like to join her. We didn't have bathing suits with us, which meant the clothing that covered our bodies was merely our only option. "Of course I'll join you, because I'm a fun fucking guy and I will do whatever it takes to make you happy," was the thought in my mind. I answered with a simple 'yes,' though.

We removed all electronics and belongings from our pockets and were off, jumping into the pool fully clothed and having a great time. We were splashing, kicking, dunking each other and loving it. We were making out, drinking in the pool, having a few smokes of pot, the usual drunken pool time activities. I will admit it was very pleasant for a little while. However, it was short lived because we got cold pretty fast and exited the pool to dry off the best we could. The next thing I know, the slimy little Dick Face approached Marilyn and offered her a fresh pair of clothes to change into, completely skipping over me mind you. An offer she was ever so thankful to get, but not so much me. It was a downright insult and that dense, shitty, feeble little carcass knew what he was doing. Without Marilyn thinking twice about my circumstance, they headed off to his bedroom to modify her situation of dripping wet clothing with a fresh set of coverings. And with the risk of using an already exhausted phrase . . .

. . . I FUCKING LOST IT!! . . .

It was time for everyone to see the true fuming and angry Ryan Anthony Michael Vinci, in all its glory and cockiness. I removed my shirt, threw it to the ground and walked inside that frat house with might and rage. I started picking up every bottle I saw, Vodka, Whiskey, Rum, Wine, Brandy and Beer. Any alcohol in sight was confiscated by my demoralizing hands and vehemently pounded by my sarcastic mouth. I would take dreadfully abundant and firm swigs and move to the next bottle I could find. I was seeing red and there was no one that could stop me. Levi stayed sober (thankfully) following close behind me as I marched like a Nazi soldier through this party on a path of annihilation. He was walking behind me and making sure if some one did step up, he was there to back me up. Not the proudest moment of my life. Nevertheless, it happened. And like I said before—love will make you go batshit crazy. I would walk to different groups of strangers, shirtless and in full rage, grab the bottle from their group, pound a well amount of it and walk away. No conversation, no question of share, absolutely no sense of kindness. I was arrogant, inconsiderate and disrespectful. I was truly lord of the douchebags at that moment. "Fuck you. I'm here to fuck shit up!" Was the blank and indestructible attitude that I was portraying at that moment . . .

I made my way from group to group, yelling out profanities at the top of my lungs, laughing hysterically at nothing, just wholly and entirely wrecking myself. I ended up making my way to the kitchen and found an object that was ever so inviting by my inebriated outlook. A weapon of self-destructive appeal, one might say? A Goddamn rolling pin!

"By the way, Bob, why the fuck does a frat house have a rolling pin? My grandmother has a rolling pin, that's about the only person I've ever met with a fucking rolling pin, but that's neither here nor there. I digress…"

"I honestly would have no idea, Ryan. It was probably around for some erotic game playing."

"Yeah. So the cocaine jacked up frat boys can buttfuck each other with it."

"Jesus, you're crude."

The rolling pin caught my confronting eye and it was time to scare the living shit out of some damn people. I picked that pin up, with a firm grasp and rebellious point of view. I began to slam that fucking rolling pin against my head. Whack! Whack! Whack! Whack! Again and again, harder and harder, the group of twenty or so people drinking in the kitchen wanted nothing to do with this. They quickly got up from their chairs and jammed for the door outside. I had no more audience but I continued to smash the pin against my head. Levi walked up and snatched it from my hand and told me 'to chill the fuck out.'

Marilyn heard about my episode and came to find me with that tiny shit eater, Dick Face, and some other faggot chump they brought with them for protection. And to really put this into perspective, I am six foot four and close to two hundred pounds. Add too much liquor, more deep seeded anger issues than any other human being on this earth (besides my brother) and you got yourselves quite a handful to deal with. She found me with her two cock sucking friends and stoutly commanded, actually ordered me, 'to reframe from such obnoxious behavior or else they will ask me to leave.'

"Oh yeah?! I would love to see one person try to kick me out of here!" I yelled at Marilyn and her bitch little followers. This shit was a war now . . . And like the woman beater 'Chris Brown' once said, "I don't wrestle, I

KNOCK bitches out." Or maybe that was the chick from MTV. Either way, you catch my drift . . .

"Look, man. If you don't calm down, you're going to have to go." That shit sucking little cunt boy, Dick Face said to me.

"Shut the fuck up, you little queer. I will beat you to death with this rolling pin. Don't you ever fucking talk to me! You understand?!" I confidently looked him in the eye and screamed.

Dick Face looked to Marilyn, like a scared little hooker on a free fuck giveaway.

"You know what, Marilyn? Screw this guy! Let's go do some blow in my room." He sadly said to her with no real understanding of the atomic aftermath that sentence held.

Marilyn had hit her limit with trying to hide the fact she wanted some cocaine force fed down her whore nose. She stared at me with this face that pretty much read—Fuck you, asshole, we're done here!

"Fuck you, Ryan. Just go home. I'm going to do some blow." Marilyn said to me as she turned away and headed off.

"Fuck all of you people!" I shouted as Marilyn made her way to Dick Face's room to give up on life . . .

Death only scares those,
Who believe in Heaven and Hell!
If you fear no afterlife,
Almighty,
Damnation,
Or rebirth.
Then you have faith in nothing.
And nothing is what you believe in.
So to be religiously wise of nothing,
You have to know,
Not ask.
But in fact know,
That some day,
You are going to die.
And when you do,
It will not be pleasant.
Bloody,
Painful,
Slow,
Miserable and received.
Challenge a person, who believes in nothing,
And nothing is exactly what he will make you.
Forgotten faster than you were born.
I ass fuck God,
And rape the Devil.
With a smile on my deviant face.

I stood there for a few minutes, unspoken, staring down, building in wrath and mistrust. Levi patiently waited by my side. He wasn't leaving me alone for a second. I looked up to him, face red, plagued with anger and hate.

"I'm sorry, brother."

"Hey, man. You do what you got to do." He greatly worded his response.

He knew just as much as I did the true motive of my apologizing statement was not for what I've already done. Rather for what I was about to do. He set his fists behind me, got ready to take a blow or two and followed close behind. I turned from the kitchen and took off in a fast pace to Dick Face's room, found the right door I was looking for . . . And with a vigorous frenzy, KICKED that motherfucker in! Almost off the hinges! No surprise to me, they were already lining up their coke in anticipation. There were three people in the room, Marilyn, Dick Face and that faggot little friend of theirs. They all started to yell at me, telling me to get out, go the fuck home. Needless to say, Marilyn was overly pissed with my actions.

"Go home, Ryan. I will do whatever the fuck I want to do!" She screamed in my face.

"You don't need to do this shit. It's for worthless cocksuckers! They don't care about you like I do!" I drunkenly yelled.

The rest of the men in the party heard the arguing and they all came a running to the hallway I was in. When they turned the corner, they saw the door was kicked opened and me standing there shirtless and full of valor. And now Levi and I were backed into a corner. The end of the hallway was to our right and the group of men to our left, trapped and surrounded. It was time to either fight or die. Levi had two lighters packed in his fists and ready to break some jaws and shatter some knees. I was as pumped as a steroid addicted bodybuilder at a drug hearing, and these fucking pussies started to put in their meaningless input—trying to 'Doctor Phil' me out of the situation like I gave a shit to hear their words. Not they, nor the cops, nor an army of thirty Nazis were going to stop me from getting the pride and respect I was looking for.

"You need to get the fuck out of here." One asshole said to me.

"Fuck this place, I'm leaving." I replied.
I looked to Marilyn, with a disgusted and sickened face.

"Have fun doing your coke, whore." I poorly worded my reply.

Not right by any means, I know that. However, I was very angry, give me a fucking break. I know I was in the wrong to call her such an evil name.

I pushed our way through the pussy filled pack of 'so called' men, with Levi right on my tail, I made my way to the pool area with this entourage of cowards following us. I grabbed my truck keys, my cell phone, cigarettes and Marilyn's cell phone. Pocketed my supplies and headed out the front entrance—still with this group of gutless cowards following close behind. They remained silent, they could see I was out for blood and I would've eaten that party alive if someone took a swing. We jumped into Levi's car and hit the road. As we drove down the highway in a high rate of speed, I was irate to say the least (but like most tragic situations in my life) I chose to laugh it off. I rolled down the window to the car, took a long, extensive and lasting look at Marilyn's cell phone . . . And I chucked it out the window for fucks fun. I took out my own cell phone from my pocket, took a glace at it . . . And I threw that motherfucker out the window also. I started to laugh hysterically and uncontrollably.

"What's so funny?" Levi asked.

"I just threw Marilyn's phone out the window." I answered.

We both started to share a nice laugh for the next hundred yards or so.

"Guess what else?" I asked him.

"What?" He responded, eagerly awaiting my reply.

"I threw my fucking phone out also." I countered.

. . . SKIIIRRRR!!! . . . He jumped on the breaks and slid his car onto the right hand shoulder of the road.

"Why the fuck would you do that?" He confusingly asked me.

"Fuck it. It's just a phone. Keep driving, I'll get another." I carelessly said to Levi.

He threw his car in gear and we made our way down the highway to our hometown.

The next morning when I arose, I was still very intoxicated. I still had a reckless sense of abandon and I was laughing at the past events that had taken place. I got a ride from Levi over to Marilyn's apartment building where my truck was parked. I buzzed her apartment from the bottom of the building, but she wasn't answering. I waited outside until someone walked out and grabbed the door as they exited. I walked up the stairwell and made my way to Marilyn's door. I knocked—ready to take the lashing and fate that was mine to accept. She opened the door (surprisingly) and she invited me in to sit at her dinning room table as a rebellious child sent to detention. We talked for a couple of hours about my arrogant, aggressive and unreachable conduct. We had our full-fledged breakup conversation and I was sent on my way, asked never to contact her again.

However, before I exited the door, she stopped me to hand me a note, a letter which she had hoped to simply put on the windshield of my truck and never have to see my retched face again (I guess I ruined her diabolical plan) I was still excessively smashed to really care about the letter, but instead thought it was humorous that she wouldn't even give me the benefit of a face-to-face to have a breakup, but rather, she would leave me a note to tell me how absolutely disappointed she was with my actions without ever hearing my side of the story. Childish if you ask me, but then again, you didn't ask me. I walked out of her apartment, the door was closed hastily after my departure, and that was the last time we would see each other in person for quite awhile.

"I promise, Bob, I'm almost done with this story of such impressive douchebaggrey, insolence and hateful charm, but unlike most people, I can admit fully when I'm the bad guy, the asshole, the solely fucked animal garbage that I was. So that's exactly what I'm going to do. I acted like a piece of shit that night. I'll say it first."

"Ryan, if I was going to judge you from this whole tale or throw any form of shade to the person that you are, I would've stopped you long ago in the park. Please, tell me how it all ends."

"Fair enough, Bob."

. . . That being said, I got to the bottom of her apartment complex, left the building and read the permanent letter of confusing breakup knowledge, knowing damn well it probably wasn't nice, and had no choice to have a drunken, ill-mannered laugh and do what I do best in a situation that absolutely hurts and shatters me . . . Be a complete and insensitive tool and rebuttal however I saw fit to make me happy. Was it the best road? No! — Not at all! But it's at least my road so fuck you and fuck her if you don't like it. After reading the letter, I of course felt a rush of sadness, remorse, perplexity, suicide, and mostly regret. How did I lose the greatest person in my life? My love, my woman, my heart, by and large, my fucking everything. I pushed her away and now I must live with that guilt. But, I had to do something to stand up for my cause, even if my cause was an ignorant, self-serving and forever lost cause. I finished the letter, pulled my cigarettes out, lit one, took a couple puffs, then grabbed my lighter and lit the letter on fire at the bottom of her complex. Letting it burn, smolder and turn into ashes at the front entrance. I sent Marilyn's friend, Lisa, a text from the bottom of the apartment complex with a burner phone I had (since Marilyn was phoneless) telling her that she can find Marilyn's letter in a pile of ashes at the bottom entrance, eager she would tell Marilyn (a very typical and thespian response for me) jumped in my truck and left for good. Lisa of course, never replied to my text. Why should she? She didn't want to be any part of my melodramatic bullshit. And that was that. Reap what you sow, if you will. I don't have the letter to this day (seeing as how I burned it) but the words will forever echo in my brain. Allow me reverberate the message. And with the risk of probably getting sued for likeness rights, I still write with no restraint . . .

"Dear Ryan,

What you put me through last night was disgusting, retched, wrong, disrespectful, and downright fucking rude. You acted like an animal, and not only disappointed me, but made yourself look like nothing more than an unintelligent, drunk, violent and misguided man. You made threats to beat one of my friends bloody with a rolling pin. You beat yourself in the kitchen with the same rolling pin, and forcefully kicked a door in, to show that you're the toughest asshole on earth. Good for you, I hope you're happy. What you made my friends witness, made me look bad, but also made the judgment of whom I let into my life look even worse. You made a fool of yourself. You said some things that will never be forgotten. I know now you are not right for me. You're not the person I would ever want to spend my life with. I fear you! So good for you, you win. This is what you wanted, right? For people to fear you? What you did can never be forgiven. This is something that will never leave my mind. I told you I loved you, I wanted to be with you, and I will always love you. But, you couldn't wait till I found myself to come back and be with you. So, I guess what I'm saying is goodbye. I never thought you were capable of such evil, and you talk of how you'll never become your father, but all I saw was his words and attitude coming through your body. So who are you really? Maybe you should seek help, because unfortunately, I can't be that help you need anymore. Time is all I needed, but with the comments you tell my friends and the actions you've portrayed, you've proven that if people don't follow your plan, then they are nothing more than enemies. How can you be merciful if you're controlling? How can you be a loving person, if you're a hateful demon? It doesn't make sense. And for that, I must walk away. I don't feel protected by you, I feel scared. But mostly, I feel sorry, sorry for you. Sorry that you may never find yourself until it's too late. I love you, Ryan, but I can't ever see you again. What you did is inexcusable and mistaken. I hope you find inner peace, faith in something, and meaning for life. If not, I only fear the most horrible. Sorry things had to come to this, but you're the worst thing that has ever happened to me. Please find peace, find love, and find meaning. Overall, just find yourself.

Love always and forever, Marilyn."

Here's the kicker . . . One of the funniest, ironic and most outrageous pieces of information about this story is; as much as Marilyn had asked, requested and demanded for space, freedom and time to figure things out alone. She asked for liberation from my overly domineering push of love and closeness . . . Just two short weeks after Marilyn handed me this letter and watched me drunkenly walk out her door to what the world may hold. I found out from a girlfriend of hers (actually a mutual friend) she had a new boyfriend. A bartender from the new job she was working at the nightclub as a bottle service girl. And also found out, that they were in fact sleeping together before we really cut ties with the title of 'Boyfriend/Girlfriend.' Cheating, if you will . . .

"Looks like I got the answer I was searching for, ehh, Bob?"

"Looks like it!"

To add a little comical and truthful karmic justice to this shitshow of a story . . . About a week after I got the information that Marilyn was now seeing a bartender from her work. Some random, passing traveler was heading down the road which I hurled Marilyn's phone out the window of a speeding car, and a few hundred feet past, my phone also. And Lo & behold, this man actually found my phone on the side of the road and it was still in working order. He was truly a kind soul, so he charged it up, called the last number that was dialed from the phone (which of course was Marilyn) alerted her that he had found a phone on the side of the highway and was asking for an address for which he could deliver the phone. At this point in the chat, she was under the impression that the man had found her phone. So, she called me to tell me that an accidental bystander had found her phone on the side of the highway. She asked me if I knew any reason why her phone would be tossed out on the road, stabbing to implicate me to admitting that I stole her phone and threw it out. But I wasn't breaking. I of course, said I had 'no idea,' lying through my clenching teeth. And she told me that this pleasant man was polite enough to drop it off at her friends' house. I pretended to be happy for her in the attempt to end the conversation as quickly as I possibly could and we hung up. The next day I got a ring from her.

"Hello." I answered.

"Hey. So, apparently the phone this man found was not mine. It was yours." Marilyn replied. "Why was your phone on the side of the road?" She asked.

"Huh? That's weird. It must've fallen out when I left the party and I didn't even notice." I calmly retorted.

"He found it on the side of Topanga Canyon, not on the street of the party. How in the world would your phone end up there?" She asked.

"That's so fucking weird. Maybe one of your shit head friends from the party stole my phone and threw it out the window of a car. I have absolutely no clue how it would get there?" I answered, never skipping a beat. (I'd like to thank the academy.)

"They wouldn't do that, they're all good people. But, anyways, it's in Lisa's mailbox. She said you can pick it up anytime today." Marilyn informed.

No surprise to me at all that she would actually defend her cock sucking friends.

"Cool. Thanks. I'll swing by in a few hours and get it." Without a goodbye, I just hung up.

I went by Lisa's a couple hours later and grabbed my tattered and battered 'Razr' phone (which was the hype of that time) from the mailbox. And actually still hold on to the cherished phone till this day. A karmic token, I call it. That maybe I wasn't such a bad person and didn't deserve the treatment Marilyn was putting me through. Or possibly just some demonic luck, who knows? Either way, I got the phone back. That must stand for something.

CHAPTER TWENTY-ONE:

Heartbreak Hangover.

"You can say you don't give a fuck, but do you really understand what that phrase means?"

"Twenty-two years old (a young twenty-two at that) and I've already been through more bullshit with my dead father (he's not dead yet) but dead to me, and I had to endure more vomiting-educing shit than I ever thought imaginable. I witnessed great pain placed upon my family, myself, and this world through this mans reckless and self-loathing actions. Had vast feelings of abandonment, inadequacy, strained self-worth, and even less care about my own wellbeing. But I honestly believed that frame of mind was over forever—I really did believe that. I told myself I would never feel that way again ever again. And Goddammit, I truly believed that to the bottom of my strong core, Bob."

However, there I was, young, single, hopeless, heartbroken, increasingly desperate, and full of doubt about my mortal life. I was out of my mind gloomy, challenged, angry, sad, nutty, and longing to hold Marilyn once more. I wanted her touch, needed her embrace. To be purely honest, I just fucking needed her in every possible conception of the term. I was suffering from heartbreak, a case of symptoms that could essentially kill you if not diagnosed properly. Every second, minute and hour, of every day, all I could think about was Marilyn, nothing else at all, just her and only her. I missed her till the dead, cold, tar black end of time. She was my absolute everything and I didn't care to go on in life without Marilyn . . .

. . . Cue the music. Lana Del Rey. Off to the Races . . .

This was now a novel fork in road I was inchoately placed at. And truthfully, I didn't have the strength to carry on. Should I live, or should I die? Well . . . Give me an option? Then of course I'm going to take the easy way out and find myself a nice grave to rest in.

Let the binge drinking and drug consuming ensue . . .

I was over it all to say the least. Fuck this world, fuck all you people, and fuck the dogs that bark too early in the morning, fuck traffic, fuck coffee and fuck everything. I was ready to hit rock bottom. SHIT! I was fucking eager to hit that bottom. Give it to me. Give me the pain, the sorrow and the extreme suffering. I didn't care about my outcome, my life, my safety, my health, my job, my future, my friends, my family or anything else that was important. Please bring end to my misery? I would ask this so called 'God' of yours. Fucking take me now or send me on the express train to hell. Just send me somewhere far, far away from this retched earth and the thoughts of Marilyn.

That being said . . . If I may, go off track for just a quick second here? I always found that to be a very comical idiom. 'An express train to hell.' What does that even mean? I hope there is an express train. I would hate to think I've lived all these years drenched in complete sin and utter rebel, to get to the gates of hell, and have to stand in a fucking line to accept my eternal damnation. JESUS CHRIST! I hate standing in line at 'Starbucks,' let alone waiting in a line to be punished for all of eternity. Open the damn gates and let me in! I'm ready. I'm here, aren't I? Obviously something went wrong along the path of my salvation. Open the door and let's get this party started. But I digress . . . Let's get back to it . . .

The time for I to get what was coming to me was here. My punishment, my pain, my prison of loneliness was received with gracious belong. I started working a shitty entry-level courier job for a real estate company. You know the type, a low wage job with disrespectful authority figures and even worse moral standards, just an altogether crap job. However, I didn't make it easy to be taken serious as an employee by any means, that's for sure. I would drink all night long, go home around two A.M. and write and drink until I passed out at my desk. Wake up late, go to work un-showered and reeking like booze, drink Jack Daniels and coffee at work, and get off from my penitentiary style of a work environment . . . And wouldn't you know it . . . do it all again the following night. Seven days a week, for many long months I did this. If you put a pill in my palm, I would eat and digest that pill. It didn't matter if it was purple, white, yellow, orange, red, pink, blue or black. I don't want to hear what high it will give me, nor the side affects, nor any after symptoms or comedown. Give me the fucking pill and I'll eat it. I'll smoke any form of pot, weed or marijuana. It was a very dark period for me (and with the risk of scaring you away) I was enjoying the evilness that was growing inside.

I was constantly on the prowl for some hopeless and insecure woman to shatter and destroy her ego. Give me the gift of a simple conversation and I would manipulate you into bed, fuck you hard all night long, pass out wasted, wake up, kick you out and never call you again. I would tell these women how special they are to me, how much I enjoyed hanging out with them, how mind blowing the sex was . . . Blah, blah, blah . . . Then—just throw them in the trash like yesterdays waste, never to see or hear from me again (not embellishing or proud of these thoughtless actions) merely stating the knowledge so the full story is told correctly. This was my life. It was dark, cold, careless and very, very negligent of other people's feelings. I was in such a heartless and insensitive state of circumstances and it was absolutely disgraceful. All I did know was. The feeling I felt when Marilyn left me, that dire need to be a puppet on her strings of cold blooded resentment towards me, no matter how endearing the act of love I would show her—was a feeling I was never going to feel again. Fuck being vulnerable, exposed and open. It was time to be shut down, closed off, walls taller than the clouds of heaven and thicker than the universes' mass. Reckless, inconsiderate and soundly only about my own personal satisfaction, that was my new mindset. I was selfish, egotistical, arrogant and superior over every delicate female brain that gave me the time of day or a simple look of attraction.

I was fornicating, deflowering, fucking, demoralizing, banging, defiling, ravishing, screwing, pounding, licking, tasting and seducing the very best of them, sometimes one, two, three, even up to five, random women a week. And boy, oh boy . . . I got with them all . . .

Squirters,
Screamers,
Milf's,
Young, fresh faced actresses,
A Goth girl that looked like Marilyn Manson,
Strippers,
Drug addicts,
Sluts,
Whores,
Wholesome beauty queens,
City girls,
Country girls,
Sadomasochistic,
And innocent one-night stands.
Cock sucking perfectionist,
Two girls at once,

Hot girls,
Fat girls,
Smart girls and stupid girls.
Skinny girls,
Married women,
Engaged women,
Cougars,
One woman who was more than twice my age,
Nineteen year olds,
Motionless starfishes,
Tight pussies,
Stretched pussies,
Wet pussies,
Dry pussies,
Pretty pussies and ugly pussies.
AND YES . . . . Stinky pussies.
Nice girls,
Mean girls,
Frantic cock addicts,
Crazy girls,
Scary girls
And every beautiful woman in-between.

I was sleeping with any woman that gave me the smallest amount of concern, all while thinking about no one else but Marilyn (which I'm sure is hard for you to believe) but I wanted to just be with her, taste her, fuck her, protect her and love her. However, she wanted nothing to do with me. So, I just kept fucking the pain away, or at the very least, trying to. Hoping that in one of these meaningless flings, I would find some form of truth to my futile life. To use a phrase a wiser person than me once wrote, 'Drowning in a Sea of Pointless Pussy.' And let me tell you, I was certainly sinking. Between the heavy liquor consumption, drug abuse and woman chasing, I found it very hard to breath at times. To be honest, it was never about the sex. I got with these women because I was insecure and hopeless. I wished that one, maybe one; just one of these women would find something special in me and love me. I was so lost in my own head that I felt causing pain to myself, others, and my life was the only way I was ever going to find someone who saw something beautiful in me. Or so I thought.

Sometimes, I really just wanted to be evil, purposely evil just to ensure my place in hell. I didn't know what to do, I just kept fucking, drinking and using drugs till I found an answer. One thing I will stand by though (whether you like it or not) throughout this extremely dishonest and degrading story of careless dick flinging and shagging . . . I never actually lied to any of these women. All men think you have to lie about your current employment, occupation or stance in financial livelihood to impress a girl to suck on your cock and fuck you. However, I did the complete opposite. One thing I knew from witnessing a liar and manipulator for so many tiresome years of my life was; the more lies you tell, the more story you have to try and salvage when the truth ultimately comes out. And don't get it twisted, it will eventually come out. No lie lives forever. I just told the truth, even if it was sad and desperate.

"I'm a heartbroken, depraved, sorry excuse for an adult living in my grandparent's garage, and a slight alcoholic at that. I'm a drug abuser, a struggling writer, I'm valueless, emotionless, and I'm a very careless person. I'm damaged goods, unfixable, unchangeable, and un-savable. I'm only looking for casual sex, a meaningless fling and nothing more. I don't want to make you happy or content. I don't want to be your boyfriend, husband or your long-term lover . . . I just want to make you scream my name."

Don't get me wrong—as charming and romantically sound as that form of words was spoken. It was still just a numbers game. I had to say it to a hundred women before one of them found it appealing. I developed a nickname in my circle of friends, 'Capsizing Bryan.'

"Why you ask, Bob?"

"Rhetorical question. I know you're going to tell me, Ryan."

" . . . Well, Bob. Because more times than not, I ended up capsizing before reaching the shores of vagina beach."

"Very lovely and poetic once again, Ryan."

I would get too drunk, too offensive, make too many laps around the crowded bar, using the same pickup lines on the same women and not remembering. And eventually, failure would be my only outcome. I've been slapped, kicked in the dick, had drinks thrown at me, laughed at, spit on, almost jumped by a group of homophobic cowboys (don't ask) eighty-sixed, puked on, and blamed for marital treachery. However, I never lost my determined endurance for getting laid. This shit was a sport to me, a chess game. A persevering challenge if you will, one that I never lost. When Capsizing Bryan hit the town, expect nothing but pure, unpredictable and quickly escalating entertainment. That's what got me off.

My current form of employment was tremendously failing and failing hard. I couldn't hold a conversation with a family member to save my black drained life. I was having sex with random women and waking up in a dazed confusion with no recollection of her name, or even a meeting at that. I was drinking in the morning hours at work, calling in sick, ditching work all together, popping countless pills and smoking more cigarettes than humanly possible; just a full on train wreck. Nonetheless, I loved every second of this grave ending lifestyle. I knew I was slowly killing myself with the mass alcohol and drug intake . . .

. . . But at least I was dying! . . .

The Story of Kat and Drake: Part Three.

Through many nights of drunken stumbles

And countless words spoke in slurred mumbles

He never thought love was an option

He lived in self-destruction with no real caution

Nothing but violence and utter corruption

That was when he had the most beautiful disruption

He went from a soldier to becoming a king

She gave him her heart and he gave her a ring

With the heavens above approving in delight

They were now burning from the tender ignite

Stuck in the night and watching the storm

She no longer could find the right words to form

She looked him in the eyes with tears of hunger

He looked back at her and only saw blunder

Mistakes were made as they thought they had won

Only to learn, they've just begun.

To Be Continued...

CHAPTER TWENTY-TWO:
The Whacky & Wild Adventures of Capsizing Bryan

"We're all going to die. What do you want to stand for?"

The cynicism and depression was strongly growing inside me, or should I say inside of Ryan, and I found myself less and less concerned about being myself, and more thrilled and accepting of being Capsizing Bryan. Becoming the full-blown train wreck I knew I could always be. My alter ego was taking over my true reality and now I was purely here to stun, excite and entertain. Safety was purely an illusion. Ryan Vinci was solitarily in his murky and shattered mind, longing for Marilyn and wishing for the end. But Capsizing Bryan was free, perverted, amusing and stimulating. Always trying to push the limits of the meaningless things he would do. Also, Capsizing Bryan was quickly tallying up in the number of weird, random and sexually questionable women he would sleep with—fucking and fornicating just to get a rise of soothing laugher out of my friends. I don't blame them at all. This was drastically my path of choosing, and I knew this just as much as everyone else knew it. The elevation of conversations about the idiotic things

I would do and say to people was keeping me alive . . Well—At least for the time being . . .

I finally had an engaging audience and I fucking loved it. When a story was brought up about my dubious behavior, I felt a slight moment of peace. I hoped, wished and prayed to this imagery 'God' you all call your savior that hopefully Marilyn would hear about my current indiscretions, and maybe, just maybe, rethink her leaving me. How in the fuck I ever designed these twisted and stubborn thought of reason was beyond me? And still is to this day. I think I just wanted to hurt her the way she hurt me. I was going to leave her stranded on the side of the unpromising and hopeless road, just as she had left me; lying out there, alone, cold and waiting for the reaper to sweep me up. My ego-enhancing, attention seeking, train of fucked up thought, came up with a phrase to keep it all in line. "Finally, it was my time to amuse." And amuse I sure did . . .

The weight of Capsizing Bryan was growing, building, and quickly taking over my true self. Nevertheless, it was a load that I could hold, accomplish and fully carry out. I found myself at the bottom of an empty liquor bottle every night, my breathing was beginning to get pressingly heavy from the lung abusing cigarette intake, and my fantasy for the high of any drug was stuck in full throttle. The more I drank, meant the more I would smoke, in turn, the more drugs I was willing to ingest.

"A seamlessly good game plan, right, Bob?"

"I think I will save my questions for the very end, Ryan."

All my perfectly executed partygoer behavior would lead to nights for me to convey and coddle in my infantile actions. This did actually get me the laughter and attention I desired. However, the problem with that was, after all the laughter stopped and the attention was gone, I was now stuck with the women of choice. And each time, I was alone in my room, naked, straddling some young (or old) innocent (somewhat) woman of the night. And I had to muster up the old cock for a night of meaningless sex and pleasure, and make sure not to disappoint this woman of the night, and possibly shatter my building reputation. When you give up control of your mind, and begin to watch someone operate through your body, you have to learn a few rules.

1. It doesn't mean anything if you can't feel anything. So stay as numb as you can.

2. Never back down in the face of a beautiful and drunken woman. Fuck her right.

3. No turning back.

"Fuck it, have some great casual phenomenon of uninhibited sex, an unimportant fuck of pleasure and cum, then wake for the morning hours with a story to tell."

That was how Capsizing Bryan chose to approach it. I was merely along for the ride. Every couple of nights I found myself crawling into bed with another random woman, all with diverse tasting pussies and tightness of feeling, fucking and screwing until I couldn't feel anything at all, always waking in the day hours with a dazed and confused sense of reality, and looking to the side of me and asking; "Who in the fuck is this girl? And what happened last night?" A question I asked myself all too many times. "Looks like Capsizing Bryan did it again." I said to myself. I started to go on 7, 8, 12, sometimes even 16 day benders of drinking and drug abuse, finding nothing but the empty arms of a stranger to call home for a couple hours, and truly losing track of all the time that had passed by. When I finally took a few days to let myself to sober up (moderately enough) after these extensive intoxication sprees, I would ask myself. "So, when does self preservation come into play? When do I know I've had enough?" Which is not a good question for a person to ask when all they believe is, that this is just fun.

After you forget the amount of party favors your body is essentially ingesting, you run the risk of permanent damage, or even worse, overdose. And that little fact, I was very aware of, but the concern for my wellbeing was quickly fading as I was steadily getting faded. Not yet suicidal, but my care for life was on a downward spiral—And fast . . . As the new persona of Capsizing Bryan took over, my thoughts of future, life long salvation, or financial security, were thrown powerfully out the window. I really didn't have a game plan, a backup plan, or any plan for that matter. Drink, fuck, smoke, puke, repeat. That was as deep as my thinking was going. After getting written up countless times for calling in sick as a courier at the real estate company, stealing money from the petty cash drawer, and performing my duties on the job under the influence of alcohol, they were forced to press action . . .

. . . YOU'RE FIRED! . . .

This was now number six throughout my life. Six places of employment all decided I was too much of a dipshit to perform even the simplest task of the day-to-day activities of an institution of work, and shit me out of their company bowels faster than a lactose intolerant creature at a dairy festival. Goddamn, I'm an idiot!

"I'm not going to sit here, Bob, all high and mighty and pretend like I wasn't having fun, because honestly, I was having a ton of fucking fun. However, I was yearning for more. I didn't know how much longer I could exaggerate in this lifestyle. I needed to find my feet, my grounded intellect of realism. That was a commission that I found to be very hard, but I never stopped searching for it. In order for me to sit here and write out all of the stories that took place under the influence of Capsizing Bryan would take me a lifetime. Again, not bragging, just clarifying a very complicated predicament, but I do have a strange one to share. One that will forever echo in my mind as one of the most shocking, weird (and oddly, very erotically stimulating) situations I've ever been in. Humor me for a slight bit, and allow me to entertain and arouse you. And unfortunately, begin to shadow in the darkness to the masterpiece I was painting as day-by-day, I slowly let myself become... Capsizing Bryan."

"If that's not the greatest setup for a story, than I don't know what is. Please, enlighten me, Ryan . . ."

Young,
Behold life.
It's going to be beautiful,
Fun,
Loving,
Easy and pure.
Now, vaguely older,
Life is harder than I thought,
But still fun.
I will try to become something,
Do something,
Mean something.
Now, much older in life,
This shit sucks.
Life is a bitch,
And death is an option.
I want to be a Toys 'R' Us kid,
And never grow up.
Peter Pan was right.

It was a Wednesday night in my hometown, which meant one great thing, <u>DOLLAR BEER NIGHT</u> at a local pub. My roommate at this time was the bartender at this particular saloon, so my tab was always nonexistent, which is beautiful when I was practically working for peanuts for any shitty side job I could land. We take care of our own where I come from. I'm not sure what it is about dollar beer nights, but for some reason it always seems to attract the misfits, degenerates, drunks, sluts, and true partiers. Or my kind of people should I say. On the contrary, it always seems to draw an equally dominating crowd of douchebags with a large chip on their shoulders and something to prove. But fuck them types, bar fights are for those who can't get laid and highly lack a vivid imagination. I avoid them wisely. This Wednesday night was not far off from the normal of any other, same little group of punks' looking to brawl, sluts looking for cheap drinks and an even cheaper thrill, the local drunks patiently awaiting the ensuing inevitable chaos, and my buddy and me, just looking to get some action and free drinks. Ahhhhh . . . Dollar beer night . . . Gotta love it . . . As the hours began to drunkenly fall off the clock, and the tavern patrons started to get loud and fall down wasted, it was now hunting time.

My buddy, 'Chester,' and myself, struck up a conversation with two girls standing by the high-rise table that we were sitting at. I was talking with a five foot two, attractive, slender little Blondie named 'Alexis.' Weighing in at about ninety pounds and seductive as a sunset streetwalker. She was very convicted with herself, had nothing to hide and didn't miss a drop of her drink. A good trait, if I do say so myself. Chester was talking with her five foot nine friend, 'Trina.' She was a mocha-flavored girl (or black) with voluptuous lips and a tight ass to boot. Trina was skinny, intelligent and a very self-assured little woman. Likewise, she was very seductive and seemingly horny in public. When the conversation went silent for a brief couple of minutes, they would scan around the bar, evaluating the other men in the room, confirming or conflicting with their current decision.

But the moment for opportunity was about to come, someone had to make a move, a stand. Show or fold time. And that was when I saw two (at odds) heterosexuals get up from the bar to hit the bathroom together, which meant I had a short window to make something profound happen. I quickly got up from my seat, ran over to snag up the two unoccupied barstools that were left open and without resistance I jogged them back to our table, threw one chair next to me and the other next to Chester. Don't judge me—it's every man for himself in these types of situations (at least in my game) you snooze you lose.

"Would you like to sit down?" I asked Alexis and Trina.

They were a bit clashed at first, because my nice jester now established the fact that they must sit with us for at least one beer, just to be nice I assume. So, they comfortably took a seat and we all four began to drift away into our own world of dialogue.

I was deep in chat with Alexis, and honestly, after I got the attention from her, I really cut out of whatever the fuck Chester and Trina were talking about. I was lost in my own cosmos with Alexis and that was all I needed. We of course went through the rigorous process of exchanging the pleasantries. Where are you from? What's your name? What do you listen to? Blah, blah, blah, et cetera. We saw the two guys return from the bathroom, only to find their beers with coasters over the mouths and no chairs to sit on, we shared a relaxing laugh, all while going down the list of boring 'Get to Know You' subjects. But, after about forty minutes or so, the talk between Alexis and I began to loosen up and the bona fide and authentic babble was now here to stay. As I sat at the high-rise table by the entrance, people watching and chatting with Alexis, I felt her warm hand leisure slide over my leg and take a firm grasp of my cock. I was intrigued to say the least. I looked over to Alexis, with conspiracy in my expression and stiffness growing in my cock. I looked Alexis' right in her beautiful blue eyes and cocked a devious smirk.

"I can deepthroat a cock for a minute and a half without ever having a gag reflex." She nicely told me.

"Well, what says I give it up on the first night? I'm a good girl, haven't you heard?" I calmly replied with my penis thickening in strictness.

"You're a good girl, huh? I bet I could get into your panties." Alexis responded.

"And I bet I could wear your panties as a hat." I jokingly replied.

We both had a laugh at the existing conversational wind change.

"I get the feeling that you can fuck like an animal? Am I wrong?" She asked me.

"I would love to say you are wrong, but you couldn't get any closer to the truth without blowing it for a night." I retorted.

"Do you know how many times I've heard that from men?" Alexis questioned.

"If I answered that, then I might indirectly state my own opinion of your sexual whereabouts, and if I over shoot that number and possibly offend you, well then I'm looking at nothing but a night of dreary self-pleasure courtesy of my own hand. So, instead, why don't we just test each other out for a night and see how happy or disappointed we can be?" I rapidly countered.

"That sounds fair. I like your scheme. But there are a few problems?" She hit back.

"And what is that?" I fired back.

"Well, for starters, I like it rough." She said.

"Then we can agree on that. I'll play rough." I replied.

"I don't think you understand. I like it really rough, and to be honest, I'm not sure if you got it in you." Alexis insulted me with.

I had no choice but to let out a little evil chuckle of desire.

"What's so funny?" She asked.

"I think I'm up for the challenge to defile you." I coolly retorted.

"Ohhhh. Defile. Good word. Maybe you are up for it?" She cockily responded.

This talk was really beginning to turn me on, and with no hesitation from her, she now started to stroke my dick under the high-rise table and make me increase much more in heat.

"Are you sure you're up for the task at hand?" Alexis asked.

"What do you want me to do?" I stupidly asked the sultry woman.

"I want to be choked, slapped, spit on, fucked and beat. I want you to take advantage of me." She assertively replied without a second of self-control.

"If you come home with me, I promise you will never forget this night for as long as you live." I confidently spoke while thinking (maybe) I was starting to sound like a rapist.

"I want to see how hard you can go, little boy." Alexis spat in my face.
I cocked another wicked grin and let out an underhanded laugh.

"Little boy? That's cute . . . You are not going to fucking walk tomorrow." I spoke back, now with dominance glaring from my expression.

"Now we just have to make sure your friend can close the deal on Trina. We came here together, and we said we won't leave without each other." Alexis broadly mentioned.
GREAT!! I don't pray much, but on this dollar beer night occasion, in a small southern California city, on a Wednesday night, I don't think God has ever heard prayers so loud from a man of desperation and lust. They may've been Sinful prayers, but still prayers, nonetheless. I now had a hard cock being stroked under the table by a beautiful little nympho, whispering some of the dirtiest shit I've ever heard in my ear and hoping to feel this girl from the inside. And a buddy who was taking his sweet ass time to talk this innocent tartlet out of her pussy protection and deep into his lap; a question of faith, if you will. But God Dammed, my prayers were heard . . .

Just as normal to this local watering hole, some feral douchebag bumped into another undomesticated douche on the wilderness of the packed dance floor and a drink was spilled. Let the madness proceed. Wild haymakers were thrown around the packed boogie floor and six people all began to fold and collapse on top of each other. Blood started to run and the bouncers quickly dragged the fighting monkeys outside, not yet realizing that one of them was alone and the other five were friends. And through the window by the table that we sat, we saw a miniature, wannabe gangster of a white kid—take on five much older, and substantially much larger in size, grown ass men. And that poor kid took a pretty savage ass-whooping, but, from what I heard, he greatly deserved. It all started when he got his drink vaguely spilled from his hand, and his first reaction was to try and slap his glass upside the head of the fellow partier who spilt it. But, his drunken vision missed significantly, and his glass got smashed into the head of a blameless bystander, which just happened to be a helpless woman. Needless to say, all hell broke loose after that. And Chester, Trina, Alexis and I, watched this kid get hauled outside and get beat and kicked repeatedly till the guys saw his body go limp and ran off into the darkness. Probably not paying their tabs, I'm sure? Fucking cheap Bastards!

However, it was a perfect diversion for Chester and I. And if you learn anything from me here tonight—Poor . . . A word that is thrown around too often between the dependent and weak, begging and consuming powerless, stands for only one thing. 'Pass Over Opportunity Regularly.' I didn't make it up. I acquired the knowledge from someone much smarter than myself . . . And let me tell you this. I was not about to be pussy poor for the night. This was just the commotion we needed, and I jumped on this pithy moment of self-satisfying ecstasy as fast I could.

"This place always turns into a tampon factory around closing time. Would you and Trina like to come back with Chester and I to my house? I got some alcohol and pot, if anyone smokes?" I openly invited them on the spot of chaos.

They both looked at each other. You could see the answer before it was of speaking.

"Sure. But we have to pay our bill first." Alexis answered for their two-person entourage.

"Don't worry about it, I'll pay it. Chester, bring them to the truck before the cops show up so we can leave peacefully. I'll pay the bill and meet you at the truck." I energetically commanded.

It was dollar beer night, how expensive could their bill be?

With great haste, Chester led Alexis and Trina out the door and on the way to the truck around the corner. I headed for the bar to square up their check and tell my roommate that I would see her at home. Not much to my surprise, it was only a $29 dollar check, which I kindly cleared up and hit the door for the truck. In hindsight, it might've been much more dangerous for them to leave with us, than to just remain at the bar or head home. But fuck, that's simply semantics. Alexis and I piled into the back seat and Trina road shotgun while Chester drove (or should I say sped) us home. We made it about four street lights and my fingers were already deep inside of Alexis' wet pussy and her hand was bottomless in my underwear, rubbing and jacking off my cock. I took a short look upfront, only to see Chester with his hands gripped tight on the steering wheel while Trina had her face buried in his lap with a tight mouth grip around his penis.

"A good start, right, Bob?"

"—Sounds intense thus far. Let's just agree that this story ends in some form of deviant repulsive action and move on?"

"You only wish it was that fucking easy, don't you?"

"One could only hope, Ryan . . ."

Capsizing Bryan,
The immaculate creation,
The undeserved myth,
The novel legend,
The ultimate failure.

As we slide up sideways to my house, drunk, tainted and horny for more, it was time for the true excitement to really begin. The unadulterated sexual play promptly brought us out to the garage to blast some music, fashion a racket and spoil profoundly in the favors of party that we had at our disposable. With the Sailor Jerry Rum tastefully poured and shot down, beers opened and trampled quickly, bong hits perfectly lit, smoked and inhaled. Our cocks were rubbed and erotically stimulated by an interracial little Oreo cookie of girls, dancing around the garage getting faultlessly wasted. This was Sex, Drugs & Rock 'N Roll, at its very best. Alexis came to me and pulled out an available chair, had me take and seat and she began to straddle my lap, rubbing her jean covered pussy against my already hard jean protected cock and was teasing me even more. We began to make out once again, and the heat was steadily building. She pulled back from my wet lips and looked me in the eyes.

"Want to get wild?" Alexis asked.

"You bet your tight ass I do." I replied with eager in my voice.

"Would you like an Oxycontin?" Alexis kindly offered. 'Oh boy, this is gonna get wild.' I thought to myself. Without much thought or hesitation, I replied.

"Sure. Why not?"

She reached into the little pocket on the top of her jeans and pulled out four pills—asked me to 'open my mouth,' she put two pills on my tongue and two on hers. She then grabbed her drink off the end table, put it to my lips and I washed down the two pills with a plentiful sip of Sailor Jerry and coke. She then took the drink and sipped hers down with a vast gulp. She removed her drink and we started to make out some more, now with hands down each other's pants and common sense nowhere to be found, it was fucking party time. We stopped for a brief second and I saw her eyes wander to something behind me. I turned my head and what I saw was a climbing rope sitting on a self. I turned back to Alexis.

"What do you want to do with that?" I asked.

"You will see. Grab the rope and take me to your room." she ordered.

Then she jumped off my lap and started to walk away to the part of the house that my room was located. I stood from my chair, with my cock fully hard and pressed dense against my jeans, grabbed the rope and followed close behind. She was the first to enter my room and I was a mere step behind, I turned around to lockup my door and then whipped back around to her . . . And what I saw was remarkable . . . She was already standing butt fucking naked with her clothes thrown in the corner. She was a tiny little girl, and had a pretty, tight, shaved petite pussy with clean and beautiful teensy pink cunt lips. I quickly walked over to her and pushed her on the bed and started to ravage her petite body. I started kissing up and down her neck, around her lips, down to her tits, and then making it down to her sexy little pussy, licking and tasting her tight twat. Her pussy was soaking wet, dripping to her asshole, and I slurped up every last drop as I made her shift and jolt in her place. She was moaning, begging even, for more, asking me to suck her pussy, screaming demanding orders of cunnilingus. I did every last little act she wanted me to perform to get her so fucking wet she could no longer hold herself back. She put her hands on my shoulders and pushed me up so I was standing tall above her; she ripped my belt off, pulled my pants down, removed my shirt and got me just as delightfully naked as she. Then, she looked over to the rope that I threw on my desk.

"I want you to tie me up and rape me." Alexis commanded of me.

I was a bit taken aback from her request, but did find it rather hot. I've always enjoyed some rough sex, but her proclamation was downright filthy, and honestly, right in my fucking wheelhouse. She wanted some rough sex, and I was gonna give it to her. I pushed her back on to the bed and jumped my bare ass over her, now with my cock exposed and rock hard, I spit on my fingers and jammed three of them deep inside her. I slid my fingers in and out of her with extreme force, feeling the bottom of her incredibly drenched pussy and pushing for more. Faster, harder, deeper and stronger, I finger blasted her tight pussy till I saw her eyes start to roll back in her head and her moans grow in volume. She forcefully grabbed my cock and began to jack me off with reason. I started to groan in pleasure as the play started to enhance. I locked my elbow and would shove my fingers inside her. She was getting much more heated, and wanted it to get violent. I could see it in her eyes.

"Get rough with me!" She yelled with anger.

I progressively improved my firmness of push inside her pussy and was now reaching for the insides of her stomach. I began to get intensely rougher with her, carelessly smashing my fingers into her five foot two shallow pussy. The aggression was rising from both parties and control was becoming mine. Or so I thought . . . We were butt naked and slobbering all over one another as the force was overwhelming us both, and then, out of nowhere . . . She pushed me off of her and punched me right in the center of my chest.

"GET ROUGH WITH ME!" She screamed.

I'm not going to lie—it did slightly hurt, but not enough for me to stop. She wanted to be manhandled, and I'm pretty sure that's why she picked a guy of my size and strength.

So, I clutched her little arms, powerfully flipped her to her stomach and pushed her face down into the bed. I grabbed the rope, tied her legs to her hands so her pussy was wide open, and commandingly rammed my cock deep inside her dripping wet cunt. As deep and hard as I could get my dick down her vaginal canal, I fucked this miniature girl all while slapping her ass till it turned red and holding her head down solid to the bed. Smoothing her and making her my little bitch, she squirmed and screamed as I held her down and pounded her tight pussy.

"Fuck me harder!" Alexis begged.

And as asked, I grabbed her ass checks and spread them apart so I could get a full contact position to destroy her tiny hole, not to anger the crazy little nymphomaniac and get another punch to the chest. I began to absolutely ruin her cunt. I fucked her harder, faster, deeper, and with pure reckless intent to hurt and humiliate her. Viciously and crudely I held this helpless little bitch down and smashed her tight cunt till I felt the very bottom of her uterus. Pushing my cock so deep inside that I wanted to see that motherfucker pop out her mouth. She was screaming, yelling, begging and tearing up. I then took a firm grasp of her hair and picked her head up and began to explode it down countless times to the pillow like a wrestling beat down. As I kept her in this position for thirty minutes, I slammed my dick so hard inside her she could no longer hold back her satisfied delight and she squealed at the top of her lungs and let out a vibrated squirting cum of bliss.

I rolled off of her and took a well-needed deep breath and caught my wind. Alexis was still tied, and every couple of seconds twitching in cumtastic lust. She kindly asked me to untie her so she could breathe. So I popped off the bed, stood over her, let loose her small arms and she was now set free. Then, without a millisecond to think, she quickly rolled over and KICKED me in the fucking chin. Not a knockout kick, but enough to cause some authentic pain. I glared at her, now dizzy, confused, and highly upset.

"WHAT THE FUCK WAS THAT FOR, YOU STUPID BITCH?!" I shouted at her.

"There you go. Get angry and fuck the shit out of me. Rape me, you fucking pussy!" Alexis yelled back.

Holy Jesus Fuck!! It was then, at that very moment, that I thought to myself, "This chick is fucking batshit nuts." This was unlike any sex I've had before, and to be completely frank, pretty Goddamn stimulating. I grabbed this whore by her fragile little arms and tossed her down with tremendous might and pure obsession onto the bed, ripped her legs wide open and mercilessly fucked her brains out. Trying my damndest to make her cry and punish her like the streetwalker she wanted to be. I was thrusting my penis deep inside her gash and intensely tearing her pussy apart, into pieces even. She was now under my control, and I was going to collide myself inside her until I saw her eyes squint in pain. Her pussy ran wet rivers with desire. You could smell her cunt in the air. Alexis loved every second of this. I, at this point, was beginning to become woozy from the alcohol, the Oxy, the tough blow to the chin, and all the dynamic fucking, and my endurance was fading. She could see my energy getting weak, and Alexis then proceeded to openhanded slap the fuck out of me, five, maybe six times with rule and influence.

"Stop being a faggot and fuck me like a man!" She lustfully cried. "Do you have a knife?" She then asked.

I did, much to her surprise, actually have a long, very sharp, ten-inch blade that I keep under my bed for home protection. However, I've never been asked to bring it out for sexually play.

"I do in fact. Why do you ask?" I replied and questioned.

"Pull it out and hold it to my throat while you fuck me. I want to feel helpless. I want to feel raped." She said.

So . . . Well, I reached under my bed, pulled out the blade, removed it from its holster and pressed it tense against her throat, pushing it just under her chin and tight to her jugular. I was actually choking her with it, to be more precise.

"There you go, Ryan. Now fuck me like a victim." Alexis screamed.

I started back with the wild act of fucking her with bravado and muscle. I was pounding, slamming, smashing, fucking, and digging my cock deep inside her with every last bit of energy I could muster up. She was screaming even louder than before. She was begging for me to run the knife across her throat, down her chest, in between her tits and back up to her throat. I was obeying with every last perverted request and enjoying every second of ultimate control over this woman. As I slid the blade around her body, I could feel her pussy tighten with pleasure and satisfaction. She was yelling 'Gods' name out louder than I've ever made a girl howl before. She was kissing me, slapping me, thanking me, cursing at me, and spitting on me all at the same time. It was at this very moment in time, with my rock hard dick painfully plunging inside her damp slot, that I had an unpleasant and repugnant thought. I had a crossing thought of the Natalee Holloway murder case.

"I understand, this is a morbid and ghastly thought to have during sex. But let me explain, hear me out. This is sometimes how my mind can wander. Hang in there, I promise it will make sense in the end, Bob."

The scumbag that was arrested for her murder was bragging to his friends that he killed her and the cops would never find her body. However, when he was apprehended, he quickly changed his tune and told the cops, "We were having rough sex and things got out of control." was actually his recorded confession. Those words sat with me for many years after her case. I've had some rough and crazy sex, but no one ever ends up dead. But, he was obviously lying to help save his own ass and made some bullshit story to better suit his case of defense.

And now, as I was indulging in some causal, innocent, and in every reverence of the term, 'Excessively Rough Sex,' was the first time I worried about that authentic fact of reckoning. As I was drunkenly, franticly, and vigorously fucking Alexis' pussy hard, with a sharp knife pushed taut against her throat and my alcohol intoxicated, drug induced balance beginning to be questioned. I was overwhelmed with sorrow and guilt and had no choice but to stop. I quickly took the knife and put it away, hide it back under the bed and took a spot lying next to her. I was pale, sweating, overheating from the Oxy and sex, and DID NOT want to use the weapon anymore. Things got to be a little crazier than I think I was ready for at that time, and I had to find shelter. She laid down on my chest and asked 'what was wrong,' but I held in my inner thoughts of murder and shame in the hopes of not making her feel insecure or perverted in any way, and just relaxed with her in my arms for a bit.

A brief and well-needed moment of silence was in order, and that was exactly what we did.

After about twenty minutes, she asked if she should just suck me off to make me cum, a request that was both nice and caring. But cumming was not what was on my mind. I told her to just lay with me and pass out till the next coming morning, and that was purely what we decided to do.

— I told you Capsizing Bryan was crazy —

When I woke the next day, Alexis was gone and I would never (still to this day) see or hear from her again. Leading me to think, was this a dream, a nightmare, a bad joke or just a well played out expression of dark thoughts all colliding as the universe was apparently trying to tell me that it's never too late to start looking forward with positivity and hope. A message or sign from the other side, if you will.

... R.I.P. Natalee Holloway ...

"That story being told, Bob, if you have gathered a caliper for the way my mind works, and more importantly, my stance on justice, or should I say Vigilante Justice. I think that boy should be dragged out to the middle of the street by his dick and beaten with bats, glass bottles, sharp objects and anything else that family can get their hands on until he is killed slowly, painfully, brutally and absolutely justified. But that's just my opinion."

"I really have absolutely no words for this anecdote, Ryan. I think that little story was just a little more than I'm willing to stomach also."

"I just wanted to shed a little light inside the dark mind of a twisted young sex story between two (obviously) perverted youths."

"Do you think God will ever forgive you for what've you have done in your life, Ryan?"

"Great question . . . But, hang in there, Bob, it's still much, much too early to start begging for forgiveness!"

DRUNKEN INTERMISSION CHAPTER:

Who Is Capsizing Bryan?

"Longing to be loved, is asking to be forgotten."

"**I** am going to step off the finishing path of my story, Bob, just for a speedy minute to share a little bit of what I deem as humor and complete interest, in my dark and beautiful lost mind. An exposé of Sex, Drugs & Rock 'N Roll! I started 'Blogging,' much like every other struggling writer out there does, in the hopes of expressing my philosophical point of views and sharing my profoundly interesting stories of life. However, much of what I wrote was never worthy of gaining attention, publication or recognition. Most of it came out as either big-headed sexual conquests, irritated point of views, or sloppy words on a worthless page. Although, every once in awhile I wrote something that was either meaningful or just downright hilarious. This is one that I consider absolutely funny till the end of time. This is what I wrote. Hope you laugh."

This is a scatterbrain, unedited, complete synopsis of the last eleven months of my life. Well . . . The parts I can actually remember, through all the drunken times and also through the sober times. Enjoy . . .

Got drunk.
Woke up late for work and took a couple Vicodin.
Fucked a blond bimbo.
Threw up.
Drank myself silly.
Fell down some stairs.
Had sex with a hot brunette.
Don't remember her name but knew she had a great ass and a giant set of tits.
Really funny.
Lost some bets.
Won some bets.
Vomited.
Woke up late for work.
Went to the gym.
Wrote a lot.
Wrote a little.
Wrote a lot of mean stuff to my ex-girlfriend but never sent it.
Might still do that.
Met a girl in traffic.
Had dinner with her.
Fucked her that night.
She was crazy O.C.D.
Drank some more and took a couple more Vicodins.
Didn't want to feel anything.
Had sex with a flight attendant.
She was a little wild.
Drank absinth.
Didn't go well.
Threw up some more that morning.
Watched a funeral of someone I didn't know.
Went to the gym.
Drank myself stupid with my friends.
I got really close with them once again since my chick left me.

I think I like them more.
They're nice.
. . . . Shit my pants.
Took some ecstasy.
Wore daisy dukes to a cowboy bar for no good reason.
Got naked at a few parties.
Fucked a Milf.
She was kind.
Didn't feel anything for a couple of weeks.
Lost my mind.
Got sick.
Drank some more hard alcohol.
Had too many laughs.
Didn't work out for five weeks.
Lost a lot of weight.
Gained a lot of weight.
Hooked up with a girl form the UK.
Don't remember her name.
Just know she was a terrible kisser.
Slept two hours in three days.
Slept all weekend.
Popped some more Vicodin.
Never got mad.
Cried.
Jacked off and was a lot better.
Fucked a stripper.
Two of them actually.
Swore off women forever.
Got over that in an hour.
Thought about my ex.
Jerked off and didn't think about her for months.
Wrote some good stuff.
Wrote a lot of bad crap.
Drank until I was sober.
Smoked a lot of cigarettes.
Smoked a pound of grass.
Drank ridiculous amounts.
Fucked around with a married woman.
Felt badly so I stopped and left.

Got taken advantage of by a cougar.
She bought me way too many shots and took me home.
She walked inside my grandparent's house with a sheet on.
Yes. I live with my grandparent's.
Don't judge me!
They laughed.
She looked a lot better when I was hammered.
Took some weird pills and forgot my name.
Burned my arm with cigarettes.
Fucked a lesbian.
Yeah.
I don't know how that one worked out either.
Drank three bottles of wine in two hours.
Pulled my penis out at a party and put it on the bar.
People laughed . . . I think?
Smoked a cig.
Then some weed.
Slept.
Was late for work everyday for a month.
Got refocused.
Stopped drinking so much.
Worked out all the time.
Finished my screenplay.
Got bored.
Drank myself retarded.
Almost died in a car crash.
Fucking trippy!!
Forgot about a lot.
Took some more Vicodin.
. . . . Shit my pants again.
Went out with friends.
Took two girls home at once.
Went to Vegas.
Drank way too much and laid on the floor with fat girls.
My friends were ashamed of me.
Lost money.
Found money.
Bought a bunch of silly hats.

Watched two girls dance naked for a buddy and me.
Really fun.
Drank an entire bottle of Jack Daniels.
Wrote some more.
Went home with a chick and ate her pussy.
Got pink eye and never called her again.
Got the pink eye taken care of.
Laughed.
Loved.
Drank till my penis didn't work.
Had very interesting conversations.
Found out how good my life can be.
Got depressed.
Contemplated suicide.
Then realized it's expensive to get buried.
I think I made out with a whore.
It was dark and I was drunk.
Forgot my name.
Forgot her name.
Smoked weed with some weird chicks.
Went to the bar every night for three months straight.
Got old.
Did some sleeping.
Vomited.
Then some more.
Help build the worlds biggest Slip 'N Slide.
Really fun.
But really hurt.
Got ripped.
Lost it.
More silly hats.
Fucked a girl from Georgia.
Or maybe Tennessee . . . one or the other?
I can't remember.
She was very nice.
Almost cared what people thought.
Moved on.
Got really drunk and smashed a garage up with my
friends.

Pulled an all-nighter and went to the beach.
We all got sun burnt.
What a surprise?
Had sex with some girl named Tiffany? . . .
—Wait . . . Maybe Jennifer?
Couldn't really remember.
Hope I was good.
Hope she was good.
Drank till we all forgot our names.
Took some more Vicodin.
Hurt myself on purpose to see if I can still feel.
Didn't work.
Met some girl who could read right through me.
That was fun.
Had some really bad times.
But more good times.
Almost quit my job.
Made love to a housewife.
Drank all her wine.
Got lost.
Found my way.
Lost it again.
Took some Adderall.
Got Fucking AMPED!
Drank an entire 18 pack in front of the cops in Vegas
with my buddy.
Bought a coke and a purse for the cops.
Stole a little purse from a store and gave it to my mom.
My brother stole a toy tractor.
Again, don't judge us!
Watched some fireworks.
Fucked in my truck.
Fucked in a buddy's car.
Spit fire out of my mouth.
Listened to a lot of music.
Thought I was in love.
She was crazy.
She's now a prostitute.
. . . . More shit in my pants.

Drank for 36 hours straight.
Fucked a fat girl.
She nearly sucked my tongue out of my mouth.
Thought it was a pop sickle, I guess?
Almost got a D.U.I.
Stopped drinking and driving.
Good idea Number One!
Got really wasted and pissed my pants on a friends couch.
We laughed about it, kind of?
Got it cleaned.
Thought about my ex again.
Masturbated and forgot about her.
Saw a movie with my family.
Went to the beach.
Ate some weird plant and started hallucinating.
Drank more liquor and it went away.
Solved a math problem.
Don't know why?
Didn't clean my room.
Worked out.
Fell into a plant in my underwear.
We all laughed.
Slept with two girls in one day.
Four girls in one week.
Forgot about pussy and partied.
Took a vow never to get married.
Met some cool people.
Met some assholes.
Watched my friends get silly and destructive.
Thought I was smarter then I really was.
Gave up trying to be smart.
Fucked this woman who would have taken care of me.
I said no thanks.
Wrote some more then burned it for fun.
Took some more Vicodin.
Washed it down with shots.
Went to a club and danced like 'Saturday Night Fever.'

Became a Jersey Shore fist pumping son of a bitch for a little while.
Told three women I slept with that I was married.
I think they bought it.
Ate some vagina.
Drank.
Drank.
Drank.
And drank.
Slept.
Went to work.
I think?
Learned how to stay single.
Loved every minute of it.
Watched the most porn ever in one day.
Got walked in on during sex.
Took a town car to the strip club alone.
Spent $300 dollars but had the time of my life.
Gave my watch, some money, and anything of value I had on to a can collector at a USC football game.
Still don't know why I did that?
Learned to laugh at anything and everything.
Life is really not that hard.
Went through some shit.
Put some people through some shit.
Drank Vodka.
Rum.
Whiskey.
Beer.
And Wine.
Gave away a diamond ring to a girl in Vegas.
Gave a Tie away to another girl in Vegas.
Can't figure out why I give stuff away when I'm drunk?
Gave my phone to another girl in Vegas and told her to call me.
Got the phone back.
My buddy hooked up with her.
Found out life's a bitch sometimes.
So I fucked that bitch.

I won.
Made up new words.
Wrote some crap.
Took a crap.
Wrestled on the concrete.
Bad outcome.
Got chocked out.
I don't think I have ever won a drunken wrestling match?
I always vomit or go to sleep after.
Laughed till I cried.
Drank some more hard alcohol out the bottle.
. . . . Took a wet shit in my pants.
Found out that I am pretty smart.
Got in a fight with an Armenian in big bear over a $14 dollar sled.
Broke that sled in three runs.
Fuck him.
Became very aware of how great my friends and family are.
Got over my ex and loved every second of everyday.
    And this is only the past 11 months of my life that in reality . . . I can essentially remember . . .

CHAPTER TWENTY-THREE:
Venus, My Beautiful Goddess Of Pain.

"I love strippers."

My Dr. Jekyll and Mister Hyde person of 'Capsizing Bryan,' was now largely in control. He was now calling the shots, driving the car, and I was merely an innocent bystander on his road of ruin. It was now time to completely let go of the ropes of control I once held so tight, and succumb to the pressures of being the malignant asshole that I was starting to become so easily. Let the fantasy ride begin . . .

I had met an ex-stripper turned waitress, on a highly intoxicated Sunday afternoon, and she was anything but your normal breed of female. "Before we get too deep, Bob, let me describe her so you can see the picture perfectly."

"I am here for your listening pleasure, Ryan."

"Now that's a statement I like, Mayor Bob."

She was a soul searching, stargazing, and life loving young woman. Also, she was plagued with an alter ego of her own that shadowed her real existence. She was beautiful, witty, charming, funny, very strange, and an absolute delight to be around. Her outlook on life, surprisingly mirrored much of my own, and she was both consumed with heartbreak and thoughts of suicide from time-to-time. She went by the name of 'Venus,' and she was one of the most interesting characters I've ever had the pleasure to meet. Venus was spacey, obsessive, reckless and young. Much like me, Venus had the same downward spiraling mindset of drinking herself to death. She longed to be loved, but remained very distant. She was battling demons of her own, and desperately probing this earth to find herself, or her own place in life if you will. She was a slight alcoholic with a drug enthusiastic attitude, and loved the art of fuck and pleasure.

The Sunday that I met her, I had woken up in a friend's apartment out in Pasadena, dazed and confused from the long and extensively drunk night before. And with five other buddies in the same condition as I, we all hit the bottle and bong first thing in the A.M. . . And as we got the marijuana and liquor passed around bright and early, the next on our agenda was some food and beer. We headed back to Burbank, and went to our local Hooters for a Sunday-Funday. When we arrived, the quest to keep the party rolling all day and night was our only concern. We were the loud, obnoxious, and already drunk by noon group of guys that you see at a Sunday brunch.

Venus was our waitress, and she was both patient and understanding with our current state of perplexity and intoxication. She walked over to our table with her tight and tacky shirt pressed dense against her huge set of double-D tits. Standing about five foot six from the ground, with an equally plump ass, and long black hair, she was just what this group of drunken scumbags wanted to see, a fine piece of ass, to say the least. Venus was flirtatious, bubbly, amusing, and quickly drawn to a couple friends of mine. I was already slurring my words and falling in my chair, so she didn't pay too much attention to me. We ordered shots, beers, some wings, and more shots, followed by countless more pitchers of beer. Venus was rather good company to our table, flirting with the couple of guys she found attractive, all the while trying to stab off my many smashed and muddled pickup attempts. She was very inviting of herself, looking for attention, and this was just the group of guys to pay it to her. Without much actual conversation done, she walked over to one of the other guys at our table and slipped him a note with her number and the time she would be off. Just a mere short hour away, so we all decided to stay and keep pouring shots down our throats and more beers to wash the burn down. We waited around till she clocked out and we all walked out together. The plan was to head back to a friend's house and keep the party raging like it was Goddamn 1999, and Venus was onboard till the very end. Which, in hindsight, probably wasn't the best choice on her part? But, clear thoughts are not always made sometimes when it comes to partying.

Venus informed us that she would be driving herself to the party, so my drunk-ass and another friend decided to ride with her and give directions to limit any confusion. When we arrived, it was going to become an all night drunkfest. Pull out the booze, let's get wild, let's get crazy, and let's make some bad fucking decisions. With the alcohol and beers flowing with grace and ease down our gullets, the smoke from cigarettes and weed consuming our lungs, the party was quickly escalating. I was already unreachably fucked up, so I started to get a little frisky with Venus. I was distastefully groping at her boobs and ass, pulling on her hair, talking some sexual nonsense, and clearly not showing much concern. However, much to my surprise and the surprise of everyone else, she didn't seem to mind too much, and actually found it rather amusing. I was a frisky little fucker when I was younger . . .

After about four or five hours of this all night Binge-athon, another buddy of ours showed up with a party favor that goes by the name of 'Snuff.' If you are not familiar with it, allow me to explain. It is a broken down powder type of tobacco, which you essentially ingest, via the old snorting method. It is a light brown powder that tastes like shit, and it burns like hell. But if you snort enough of it, it actually gives you a pretty kickass brain rush. Once that shit was pulled out, it became a fucking party. We all were indulging in many lines of this garbage and having a fucking great time. The music was ear piercingly loud, the screams from the partygoers were much louder, and the fun from everyone involved was in abundance. Venus was trying to get with a buddy of mine, but he was in a dark place in his life, and a female was just not on his agenda, so that little fling quickly died that night. As the night wore into the morning hours, and the drunken slurs turned into passing out drunks, it was time to call it a night.

It's been a long time since I've seen your face,
But I can still remember just the way you taste.

About a month went by, and Venus never did hear back from the guy at the party that she was so fascinated with. He had no plans of dating due to his dark outlook on relationships or even the simple act of having an empty fuck. So one night in a drunken state of conversation I asked my friend if he had any intentions of pursuing her. I already knew the answer, but figured I would ask, and not much to my surprise, he said 'no.' So, I took it upon myself to give her a call and see if maybe I could stir up a little bit of trouble. I was very attracted to her, and found her big tits and bubble butt an absolute bonus, so what was the worse that could happen? I gave her a ring one night and invited her over to Levi's house to watch the Lakers game and enjoy some drinks. And believe it or not, she said 'yes.' Within a few short hours, Venus and her girlfriend had arrived over to Levi's house, and the cocktails were poured stiff and strong. We all watched the game, had some laughs, smoked some pot and enjoyed the company all around. It was relaxing, nice and drama free. After the game had rang its last buzzer, Venus' girlfriend wanted to head back home and crash out for the night, which was a rather cockblock move on her part if I do say so myself. But what was I to do? Venus said goodbye and drove off to deliver her friend back home. Levi and I sat outside in the beautiful night weather having some drinks and talking about life, love and the pursuit of happiness. And that was when my phone got a call. Shockingly . . . it was Venus.

"Hello." I answered.

"Hey, what are your plans for the rest of the night?" Venus asked.

"Just chill here and get comfortably numb. What about you, girly?" I replied.

"Do you mind if I come back?" She questioned.

"Not at all, come have some fun." I retorted.

"Cool. I'll see you in a couple minutes." She responded.

I hung up the phone and went back to talking with Levi.

"Who was that?" Levi asked.

"Venus. She wants to come back." I said.

"Sweet. I like chicks." Levi jokingly replied.

"Ha-ha-ha, good luck, buddy. This one is mine." I said back.

"We'll see, brother." He replied.

We both headed back into the house to take note on our current party supplies and get things kicked off right. We whipped up a vat of margaritas and got ready to do some more partying. A couple minutes later, Venus returned and we poured up the drinks and all got down to some interesting conversations ranging from sex, money, love, drugs, sex for money, her past stripper life, our fixation on strippers, and everything in between. It was very frank and free for three individuals to talk openly about such weird, outlandish and controversial subjects without the haze of judgment or clout above us. We talked about spirituality, religion (or the lack thereof) the different ways we three all lost our virginity, and even the many diverse sexcapades we've been a part of. Levi could clearly see that Venus and I had a vibe toward one another, and he decided to part ways and head off to bed. 'Lock up when you guys leave,' he told us as he headed off for the night.

Venus and I remained for a while, drinking tequila, smoking some pot and inching closer to each other as the conversation shifted from friendly and free, to dirty and pleasure seeking. We began to run down the list of favored sexual positions, role-playing, dirty talking, and assertiveness of fuck. We both had enormous sex drives, the proper tools in our pants to perform, and the wild ambition to carry out the beautiful act. Venus was comfortable with her sexy body, which was very clear to me. And I've never been a slouch in the bedroom either. As our intimate raise in conversation was making us both horny and willing, we kept getting closer and closer. It was almost impossible for me to not tackle her, rip her clothes off and fuck her right where she sat. Venus could see that I was a bit too intoxicated and wobbly on my own two feet to drive, and kindly offered me 'a ride home.'

"That would be great. Thank you." I replied.

"Don't mention it." She stated.

We got up from our seats, locked up Levi's door and made our way to Venus' car. As we made our way down the road to my house, we played to the fact that sex had been the only subject we've been talking about for the last two hours, joking and flirting. Then . . . we had arrived at my house. "What do I have to do to fucking ravage this girl wildly and passionately?" I asked myself.

She put her car in park, but left it running. However, I could clearly read her body language, and she was searching for something. She wanted something. Perhaps a kiss or an invite in, some tongue action? I wasn't really all too sure. I just felt she was longing for something. I leaned my head in her direction and waited for her to connect. And just as I predicted, she leaned in the rest of the way and we began to make out with one another. Venus had a soft tongue, luscious lips, and was a very good kisser. She didn't hold back and we started to profoundly swap spit and breath heavy, and as the intensity of this innocent scamming session was becoming something much greater. As both our hands started to wander, the level of pleasure was growing. The car began to steam up as the breathing was increasing. She rubbed her hands up and down my thighs and around my cock, above the pants at this moment, but she could sense that I was excited through my jeans. I slid my hand under her shirt and started to feel her big voluptuous tits. They were just as firm as I envisioned.

The sexual tension could no longer contain itself, and she jammed her hands down my pants and took a firm grip on my rock hard cock. Venus was showing me that she meant business, and it was time for me to retort. I took my hand and put it down her pants, quickly making my way inside her underwear and pushed my fingers inside her pussy, which was already saturated wet with craving. I moved around inside her for a little, making her shift and jolt in her seat. I heard her moan deeply as I pushed my fingers to the end of her pussy and back out. Her hand was now fixed to my cock, united and not leaving, up and down she stroked my shaft as I grew harder and harder. The little game of teasing each other was becoming way too overwhelming, and it was getting clear that we both wanted to fuck like wild animals. We decided to exit the little tin box that was holding us back from expressing our true emotions and headed into my room. We quickly locked the door, ripped our clothes off, getting beautifully butt naked, and started to make out once again . . .

As we stood in the center of the room, our hands were now viciously all over each other. Venus would pull and stroke at my hard cook, getting it ready for introduction to her soaking wet cunt. I walked her backwards to the bed as I bite at her lips and forcefully threw her down to her back on the bed and climbed over her. I saw her eyes light up with my assertive push and I could see she wanted a man in charge. I started to lick around her big and beautiful breasts, down her stomach, around her belly button and back up to her lips. Her body was magnificent, lovely, and just downright brilliant. The intense emotions were building and we were both ready to have some rough, firm, dirty fucking futile sex.

I took a firm hold of my cock and with primal instinct, slid my dick deep inside her tight and moist pussy, watching as her eyes rolled back in her head and she moaned in sheer amusement. We started off slow, back and fourth, in and out, kissing and rubbing our hands over each other's bodies . . . Then, the speed was quickly picking up, faster, harder, faster and harder, deeper and deeper. The moans were getting louder and the body heat was rising. I would slam my cock to the bottom of her pussy and watch her scream out in pure bliss. She was scratching my back with her sharp nails, and I was holding her body down taut. This was becoming a primitive event. We then decided to switch positions.

I flipped her on her hands and knees, took a rough grip of her waist, and threw my cock down inside her. She loved it, her elbows buckled, and she collapsed face first onto the pillow as she was begging and screaming for more. I was powerfully getting rougher with her, but not yet breaking her limit. I was thrusting inside her, deeper, stronger and firmer. I was vastly pushing with as much force as I could muster up to shove myself infinitely inside her sexy box and making her experience every vein in my rock hard cock. The shouting was getting louder, the pleasure was enhancing, and we were now full out fucking like zoo creatures. I would grab every expanse of her long, strong and vibrate brunette hair, rip her head back and make her stare into the mirror as I fucked her cunt passionately, violently, enthusiastically, and with elegant power and unadulterated authority. We started in with some blameless name calling at one another to enhance the satisfaction.

"Fuck me hard, you mother fucker!" Venus screamed at me.

I pushed my self harder down in her pussy, rougher, deeper and with intent to destroy and hopefully make her walk funny tomorrow.

"You like that, you fucking bitch?!" I yelled back.

"Yes. Yes. Yes, fuck me harder!" She begged of me.

I grabbed her hair and jammed her face down on the pillow and pounded away on her pussy. I was now standing with my knees bent, and her ass in the air as I fucked her down tight on to the bed. The sweat was dripping from my body and I was going to town on Venus. I was holding her down and essentially making her my bitch, and she loved every depraved fucking second of this escapade. I was overly excited to be having sex with her— so needless to say . . . I didn't last but more than twenty minutes till I felt my point of explosion on the horizon.

"I'm going to cum." I yelled.

Venus rapidly rolled over onto her back, opened her mouth and grabbed my cock. She placed my dick over her wide-open and awaiting mouth as I burst my load all over her mouth, face and hair all while letting out my animal roar! She had a satisfied smile on her face, and mine was just as big and grateful. We rolled over, wiped up the mess, and laid back. Both of us were now flatteringly incapacitated, fulfilled, and in utter paralyzed contentment. We shared a well-needed cigarette, talked of how great and rewarding our little endeavor was, and passed out drunk for the night . . .

> Give me your tears,
> For I desire your pain,
> Be a victim to my fears,
> For they're both one in the same.

"Now, Brother Bob, I would love nothing more than to sit here and stuff some bullshit down your throat, and tell you that every little sex session we shared from that night on was just as innocent and causal, fun and enjoyed, pleasurable and tantalizing. But, then I would be doing just that, bullshitting you, lying to you, fabricating some self-righteous story to come out as the overall hero. And if you've learned anything from me by now, lying just isn't my fucking style. This story is one of truth, honesty, and pure genuine relief. So I will tell you how it all actually went down, to help bring closure to Venus, because Lord knows she deserves it. And also so you clearly see that I am no Goddamn hero and have never claimed to be. But mostly, so you can see the downright piece of shit that I was becoming. The self-centered, evil little prick that was now taking over control of me, and overwhelmingly making me lose my sense of judgment, right or wrong, and just becoming something that I never wanted to be. Like 'Dexter' once said, my dark passenger had taken over, and there was no going back."

Over the span of almost two years, when Venus and I would decide to stumble into bed together, it was anything but nice, I'll be the first to admit it . . . It was abusive . . . I was becoming sexually abusive, mentally abusive, physically and emotionally abusive. I was domineering, aggressive, revolting, and terribly drunk, I was just an absolute misery to have sex with. The road to recovery requires complete honesty, so here it goes . . .

I would call Venus after a night of extensive splurge drinking, around two or three in the morning, make her come over, I wouldn't say but two words to her before I would forcefully rip her clothes off. Then I would proceed to fuck the living shit out of her. And not in a sexy way, trust me. I was an asshole. I would force her into positions she didn't want to do, in the hopes of truly hurting her and making her feel insignificant and worthless. I would slap her, spit on her, and hold her down and continue to mercilessly fuck her very hard even when she begged me to stop and sometimes would even cry. I called her every name under the sun as I did these heartless acts to her. I would call her names such as (but not limited to) whore, cunt, bitch, worthless cum bucket, fucktoy, slut, even a cheap sperm dumpster—anything and everything that my dark mind could drum up to make her feel irrelevant and replaceable in my selfish world. The sex was always extremely rough, pressured, one sided, and always all about me.

As a result of the nonstop drinking and drug abuse I was putting myself through, I was constantly numb, callous, insensitive and just plain black from the inside out. Poor Venus would come over to please me sexually, but literally found absolutely no joy in our fuck sessions whatsoever. And why should she? I was violent, hateful, ego-driven, and trying my damnedest to purposely inflict pain onto Venus to help cover the gaping wound that was left when Marilyn broke my heart. I can't necessarily call it rape, because she came over every time I would call, but it was most defiantly a self-absorbed enterprise. I call it a 'Silver Back Attack.' It's borderline rape, but instead with someone who willing submits to the cruel punishment rather than an unknown stranger. I knew she wasn't enjoying the way I would take advantage of her, slap her, spit on her, pull her hair out from her head, and even one time punch her in the head countless times. I was fully playing to the fact that she was insecure and was a victim to my twisted and depraved little game I was making her a slave to. I knew she desired attention, she wanted to be loved, she wanted to be treated right, but I didn't care. As far as I was concerned, she was nothing more than some whore off the street, a sex slave, an object, and a toy, nothing else. She was merely put here to do what she was told, take the abuse, get me off and then shut the fuck up. Most nights would end in me busting a load all over her, passing out drunk and waking the next day to get incomprehensibly drunk once more, and do it all over again. I never cared about her at this time in life, and both parties involved, knew it very well.

What I was so blind to see, was every night we did have sex, her nights always ended in her crying herself to sleep and praying that just once I gave a shit. Venus would attempt to tell me that she 'loved me,' that 'she could help me,' or even go as far as to say, 'save me.' But it went in one ear and out the other. When she told me she loved me, I would look her dead in the eye, and effortlessly and candidly repeat those three little words right back to her, just to keep us naked and fucking. But she and I knew damn well I was lying through my fucking drunken teeth. Many nights I forced Venus into having sex she never really wanted, and numerous times I desired her tears, her pain, shit . . . I wanted her to worship me, and bow to me like the dog that she was. I was drinking and fucking to wash away the memories of Marilyn, but was failing dramatically. Everyday I wished, prayed, begged for death, but for some reason always fell short. I am not sure why I was doing all these evil and degrading things to Venus, I just knew it felt fucking good. I am not proud of telling this story in the slightest, but that is guilt that I will forever have to live with. I just want the truth to be told . . .

With the risk of sounding devilishly possessed by a darker rule, or demonically overwhelmed by Satan's control. I was now becoming pure evil, and I was enjoying every Goddamn second of it. I will not cop out and try to say there was some stronger force that had taken over me, or was beyond my willpower or restraint to stop. I was well aware of the pain, suffering and destruction I was causing. The physical throbbing ache I was extorting, and the mental abuse I was putting Venus through, and unfortunately, at that particular time in my life, it made me feel alive and powerful. The wellbeing of Venus was not in my care, nor was the thought of my own life. I forcefully fucked her, time and time again, and between her tears of soreness and confusions of thoughts, she was growing tired of my constant cruelty and excruciating cock torture.

CHAPTER TWENTY-FOUR:
I Missed a Great Opportunity to Die.

"Right or wrong, this is the end."

I had quickly become a nonstop drunk. I was now strongly addicted to the party lifestyle. I was a pill popping, weed smoking, money stealing lowlife. I had no regard for the law, for my life, for the future, or for anything for that matter. I was becoming a great liar, and an even better worthless train wreck. I was getting close to hitting rock bottom, and honestly . . . I could not fucking wait! Bring it on!

Venus was growing increasingly tired of my many lies of sexual exclusiveness, my abusive approach on our so-called 'love life.' And she was mainly exhausted at the many nights I could so easily look her in the eyes and tell her that 'I loved her,' and then turn around and fuck her like I paid for it and then send her packing distraught and sore. She was sick of hearing the empty words fall from my tongue, sick of hearing stories about me hooking up with other women around town, and sick of me lying my way through all her attempts to try and make me a decent human being. In other words, she was just plain sick of me. And I don't blame her.

I was lying to the people I loved, stealing money from any outlet I could find it, using all the profits to support my drug and alcohol fueled lifestyle. And ultimately, trying to stay completely numb and hopefully repress the pain that I felt within from one day surely resurfacing. I was in all stresses of the term, an all around piece of shit. I cared entirely about nothing. I had no religious beliefs. Actually, I hated 'God' for what he was putting me through. I vowed to punch him in the face if we ever did meet. My health, future, longevity, financial or physical wellbeing was long forgotten and washed away. Fuck it all!! My love for the daylight had turned into extreme hate and repulsion. I longed for the nightfall, so I could once again become the emotion vampire that I loved being so much—merely traveling around this world and sucking the life and love out of any innocent, naive and vulnerable woman or girl that walked in front of my path of wrath.

Venus and I would see each other once or twice a week. However, it always ended in tears being shed on her part, and loss of semen on mine. Every time she saw me, I was stumbling, slurring, horny, careless and not willing to give her the time of day she desired. Not even willing to give her the slightest bit of respect, or even a vague sense of integrity. I just kept damaging her soul, her body, her mind, and wasn't going to stop to look back. After the nights that I would fuck her so sloppily, violently, mindlessly, I would pass out drunk and forget about everything. The effects of pouring alcohol down my valueless throat and ingesting mass amounts of drugs were beginning to show very lucidly. I would gasp for air as I slept . . . Or should I say, struggled for life at night. I was over consumed, addicted, painfully attached and longer for a better high. I felt like 'Nicolas Cage,' from the film 'Leaving Las Vegas.' Venus was sick and tired of my death wish, my drinking, my abusive outlook towards her, and had no more choices but to walk away; most likely for her own safety and welfare. There was no telling what I was capable of when I would get into my unreachable moments of being blacked out hammered and sadistic. I believe she feared for her life at times . . .

"I cannot stay and watch you drink yourself to death and hurt me in the end. I'm sorry, Ryan. I must go before things go any further." Venus said.

There was nothing, or no one that was going to stand in the way of me getting the end result that I sought after, longed for, FUCKING prayed for!

"So be it." I inconsiderately blew off her attempt to talk some common sense into me and kept on trucking.

Not she or anyone else was going to stop me from abusing my alcohol, my pills, my pot, my cigarettes, or even matter to me anymore. I was searching for an answer at the bottom of every empty liquor bottle, vacant fuck, morning vomit, booze shit or wasted night. This world was going to have to try harder than that if it wanted to kill me.

As I kept this freight train of substance abuse running full steam ahead, I made sure to always keep a bright and shinny smile on my face and laugh, not to arise any questions from the outside world or my inner circle. I was living out an elaborate act, a methodically thought out scheme to keep the pressuring questions off my back of my overall happiness, or care for life at that, which all vanished the day I lost Marilyn. So, let go of the breaks and allow this train to please finally crash so I can find the peace I desire. Rock bottom has never been so close.

As I let her down,
I rose above.
As I fell at her feet,
Her spit found my face.
And what I thought was truth,
Turned out to be . . .

My best friend, Levi, was having his twenty-fourth birthday out in the sand of Glamis, and the party was set and ready for explosion. Because of my work schedule, I ended up riding with a buddy of mine named 'Stan,' and two of his friends 'Jack and Melissa.' I had my bags packed, my alcohol, weed and pill supply loaded to carry me through this long and adventurous weekend, and we all piled into his new pickup truck and hit the road for voyage and fun. Stan was towing his twenty-six foot trailer with his expensive sandrail inside. For those of you whom may not be familiar what a sandrail is . . . Picture a drag car with no doors, no windows or carpet. Just a couple of seats, a roll cage skeleton around the outside and a high performance motor to push all them ponies down the sand drag, a fun and fast toy. Stan was a helluva a drinker and an even better weed smoker, so the trailer was packed with all kinds of goodies to keep us perfectly intoxicated and numb through this trip.

As we made our way down the road, we were all very enthusiastic to embark on this trip and the spirits were high. However, very short lived . . . we didn't make it but ten miles down the freeway until Stan noticed that the break lights on the truck and trailer were not working. A real snafu if you will. But, without much hesitation, Stan alerted us that he had an SUV back at his house that was perfectly capable of towing this beast of a trailer and break lights that were sure to work. We flipped a bitch and headed back to Burbank to change out rides and keep the party going. When we got to Stan's house, we changed tires from the truck to the SUV because they were brand new and set to tow, smoked a joint, slammed a beer and jumped into his whip so we could continue our journey.

Stan had the music bumping with some old school gangster rap, the air that was flowing in the windows was warm and the excursion was fucking pleasant. Everyone was having a great time as we traversed down the freeway, and not a negative thought was floating around the vehicle. The weed at this point was hitting me hard, my heart was racing, a little onset of paranoia was coming into play, but happy I still was. I was more thrilled to get out of my hometown and away from my heavy thoughts of Marilyn and my much hated 'so called' real life. Real life, which was filled with nothing but pain and misery, so onward and outward, let's keep the good times a rollin'! Stan had some classic jams playing, he was a great entertainer of his guests, and the ride was going just well. Now, every word I say from here on out is very crucial and vital, so read carefully and pay close attention. Melissa had removed her seat belt and was lying down on the lap of her boyfriend, Jack. I was sitting shotgun, or for you old folks, the passenger seat, and Stan was driving. The ride was smooth, cool, and calm. With the music loud and positive thoughts high, just like most cases in this unfair life of ours, anarchy ensued . . .

With the blink of an eye, the SUV lost its back right tire and the motherfucker came off all at once. Rim, tire, lug nuts, all of it, flew off the SUV like a torpedo from hell and we dropped to the ground like a drunken fat girl dancing on a table. The SUV violently kicked and quickly turned to the left, and was now deathly staring down the center median of the freeway. We were in the far right lane, and we had a long stretch of four lanes to cross before we were to hit the center median. Stan took a speedy and reflexive grip of the steering wheel, attempting to over correct our sideways SUV, and yelled two of the most judicious and astonishing words, I have ever had the pleasure to hear with my own two ears.

"HOLD ON!" Stan shouted to the company in the SUV.
Obviously holding on for dear life in such a quickly turning traumatic event is a no-brainer, but it was damn funny to hear.

Melissa was asleep on Jack's lap, and she was unaware of the trouble we were in. Jack was still awake and sitting upright, he grabbed on to his OH-SHIT Handle (which is the handle located on the ceiling of each seat) promptly braced for impact and was as ready as he ever could've been for chaos. I took my hand and grabbed my OH-SHIT Handle with the tightest clench my body could produce. We were now sliding sideways, across the four lanes of the freeway with a ten-thousand pound trailer pushing us forward and no control whatsoever of the outcome. We managed to make it across all four lanes miraculously without hitting another car, and were facing the center median head-on . . .

<u>SMASH</u>!!! We slammed the median and the SUV was turned sideways, the passenger side was pressed tightly against the median and we were being pushed down the freeway by the trailer. I looked out my right window and just saw the sparks flying and the swiftly passing median. That fucking trailer pushed us for a good two, maybe three hundred yards down that road . . . All while the weight of the trailer was tipping the SUV toward the sky. When we finally did slide to a dead stop, the SUV was on its side, hard-pressed against the median, and the trailer was smashed into the back end of the SUV, almost in the seat of Jack and Melissa. Gas was spewing out from the broken engine of the SUV, and the propane tanks on the trailer were spitting out propane. We were all in downright shock, daze, and complete confusion. We all looked at each other, speechless and lost. Nobody was saying a word. Everyone had these dumbfounded looks on their faces. Then, in a quick instant . . .

"Is everybody ok?" I yelled in panic.

"Yes. Yeah. I am." Was the shocked collective reply.

"Ok. Let's get the FUCK out of here!" I shouted out.

The only form of exit we had was the rear doors of the SUV, which were smashed and open, glass was everywhere and terror was thick in the air. Jack grabbed his girlfriend, who was now certainly awake and distraught, and she was the first to exit. Jack went second, I went third, and the captain of the ship, Stan, went last. Which was a true and real form of pure captain etiquette. We all piled out of the back of that SUV and ran to a safe distance. The gas was still soaking the freeway and the propane was running. There was carnage all over the freeway. All four lanes had something from the accident in them. The traffic was at a dead stop and we had to start doing what we needed to do to survive. Stan ordered me to stop cars and start collecting the items on the road, meanwhile, Stan and Jack ran to the tipped up SUV and shut off the propane tanks and removed them as fast as they could and ran them away from the truck. If the truck did blow, we didn't need it to have any more fuel for the blaze than it already did from the gallons of fuel on the freeway. I did as I was requested, and began to pick up our personal items from the freeway. Thankfully traffic was stopping, and letting me do my task at hand. I got what I could hold and ran it all back to the pile of ruble on the shoulder of the freeway, setting down the material I had composed and still in complete fucking shock. We were all standing there, not saying a word, eyes wide-open, hearts racing and stuck in chockfull distress. The traffic started to flow again, and we were taking up the left shoulder, most of the fast lane, and half into the next lane.

The cops showed up on scene and started to ask questions. Stan took care of the cops the best he could, and when they asked if anyone in the vehicle was drinking alcohol or under the influence of any questionable substances, of course we all said 'no.' The police asked to search the trailer (the trailer which to remind you) had my entire weed stash and some pills, tucked away in my backpack. Stan brought him to the door of the trailer, and gratefully, it was jammed and distorted shut from the accident. Because no one was hurt and we managed to make it across four lanes without hitting another vehicle, the cops had no grounds to stand on. He called us a tow truck and went about his business, leaving us there and waiting for our rescue to show. Fucking lucky I say. There was my backpack full of weed and some pills, Stan's huge supply of weed, tons of alcohol, a broken bong on the floor, which had came crashing out on the forcing impact, nothing but trouble and nonsense was inside this trailer. When the police finally left, Stan approached me and informed me that the trailer was not really, 'Legally Registered to His Name,' if you will. The details of that are not relevant, but somewhat funny. I won't tell them. However, Stan and I still to this day, share a laugh about that night. Let's just say more than the air was hot that night. Ha-ha-ha.

As we waited on the side of the freeway, for about an hour or so, the only thought I had was Marilyn. Granted no one was hurt or killed, which was a blessing, don't get me wrong there. I was still thinking that if I told her this story, my close call of death, maybe she would forgive me and give me another chance. It could have ended in a very bad manner (thankfully didn't) however, I hoped it would open her eyes to the attempt I was putting in just to be with her, love her and care for her. I gave her a swift phone call on the busy and noisy traffic-packed side of the freeway, although, my labors were nastily shot down by the good old-fashioned 'Fuck You Button,' which is the ignore button for those of you whom may not know. I gave her one more frantic phone call and got the same result. I concluded it was time to give up on this attention-seeking escapade and focus at the task at hand. The tow-truck showed up, stopped all four lanes, and for the next forty-minutes, pulled the wreckage apart and towed us to the nearest lot of safety. It was an all night affair, one I couldn't wish for to end so I could hopefully hear back from Marilyn. But, not to ruin your anticipation for a loving reconciliation . . . She never called back!

I did essentially hear back from Marilyn, about two weeks later and she was asking me what the late night calls were about in that past incident. By that time though, I was already angry and detached, thus I downplayed the story and quickly got off the phone. The depressing and thoughtless way I was looking at that fright-crammed occurrence was like this . . .

"I almost got my guiltless ticket out of this heartbreak, this pain and suffer-inducing world, with no consequences to my merciless actions or payments to the people I've hurt . . . And I FUCKING MISSED IT! Death slipped right through my fingertips and got away from me once again. FUCK MY LUCK RIGHT IN THE ASS!"

CHAPTER TWENTY-FIVE:
Marilyn's Doppelganger.

"The rampage will be televised."

As I sat in my dim lit apartment, watching Ryan Vinci drink rum and mumble off his intoxicating story (which had yet to be determined as anything but drunken nonsense) I watched as he took a sip of his strong rum and let off a sloppy laugh.

"What's so funny?" I asked him.

"Well, you see, Bob . . ." Ryan spoke back.

"Once again, my name is not Bob—"

"—Please don't interrupt me, Bob, I'm in the middle of a story here." Ryan replied. Then he takes a massive gulp of his poison and looks back to me. "I would be lying if I told you that I didn't have some fun within this downward spiral of heartbreak and bullshit. I would be watering down my desire for women if I sat here and acted as if I didn't find myself in a brief moment of happiness between the legs of a beauty." Ryan says.

"Please elaborate." I asked of him.

"Alright, but don't cum your pants." Ryan counters.

"You're a retched pig sometimes."

"Don't I already know, Bob, don't I already know."

A buddy of mine had started to date a young model and he found himself in a very time consuming, deviously twisted, and sexually epic style of false relationship. My friend, 'Slayter,' was twenty-seven years of age and his new girlfriend, 'Angel,' was standing tall at a ripe and rare eighteen years old. Slayter was a spontaneous, sometimes wild, outspoken dude that lived to be radical. Angel was a smoking hot model with blond hair. And a holy tight body and a massive set of blockbuster fake tits that could make even Liberace question the cock. Together they were complete madness, but she was a fresh-faced model with a libido of a jackrabbit, and he was looking to get laid, so perfect harmony is what they thought they had found. I was twenty-two at the time and longing for my Marilyn. As if you didn't already know that? I remember this day as if it was yesterday. Probably because of the sheer pleasure and downright joy I got from this story, or maybe because I'm just a horny fuck sometimes. But either way, it was utterly grand and I must share.

The day was a Wednesday and I had popped into Slayter's house after work to do some beer drinking and chain smoking out on his patio. Not an out of the ordinary occurrence for us, but on this fine Wednesday, we were certainly touched by a higher passionate power. Slayter got a phone call from his girlfriend alerting him that her friend 'Marilyn,' was going to be coming by her house and they were looking to drink. I know what you're thinking, what a coincident that she had the same name? And yes, you are correct. I found it rather odd also, but however, also very, very stimulating. As he hung up the phone, Slayter looked over to me.

"You want to go drink with these girls?" Slayter asked.

"Is there dicks in gay porn?" I said back. "Of course I do, fucker."

"Ok. But I can't guarantee anything. Marilyn just got out of a relationship I believe, so don't be upset if she doesn't fuck you." He discloses.

"It's all good, man. I just want to go and drink to get my mind off some shit." I said back to him.

"Alright! Well then let's do this. Let's drive separate. This way if she's not digging you, you can always bounce." Slayter says.

"Fucking works with me." I reply.

We stood from our chairs, jumped into our trucks and hit the road for Northridge. I did find it rather ironic that Slayter's chick lived in the same city as Marilyn, but I didn't dwell on that fact all too long. I was just merely happy to go hang with some pretty girls and forget about life and heartbreak for a while. As I followed Slayter down the freeway, more and more serendipitous events kept coming to light. The exit we got off from, was the same I took to go to Marilyn's apartment, and the next three turns were the exact same I would take to led me to her door. And with one left instead of a right, Angel's house was actually a short two blocks away from Marilyn's place, which was both weird and funny. It was located next to a grocery store that Marilyn and I would go mostly every time to get food or things of necessity. Once again, I didn't take too much time to really soak this entire chance occurrence in. I was along for the ride at this point . . .

As he walked me to the door of Angel's house, I was nervous yet ready to meet someone different, someone fun, and hopefully someone beautiful. As the door opened to Angel's house, what I was blessed with was fucking downright mind blowing. Angel's friend, Marilyn, was a five-foot-five hottie with an incredibly tight body, a face like a goddess and a set of double-D fake tits on her that stood tall like a couple of good soldiers trying to impress their superiors. She had jet-black hair, glowing blue eyes and a body that could kill a priest. She was absolutely astonishing, stunning, gorgeous, and fucking ripe. Goddamn she was a sight to behold. Marilyn had it all, from her head down to her toes, she was utterly perfect in every way, and she too was only eighteen years of age. I can't stress enough how breathtaking this lovely girl was. Words cannot contain her inclusive standard of exquisiteness. She was by far the sexiest girl I've ever had the pleasure to lay my two perverse eyes on. And did I mention she had the same name as Marilyn? Hahaha.

Slayter and I were greatly welcomed to the night with a flurry of Jack Daniels' shots as an opener and Bud Light to wash it all down. It was a very gracious welcoming if I do say so myself. And just like that, within a short hour, the alcohol had taken a fast effect to us all and the partying was really beginning. The girls had on swimsuits under very short, shorts, and tight tank tops pressed taut against their fake tits. Both girls' were looking sexy as a motherfucker, and starting to become wild and fun. Slayter and I sat on the couch as they both became very talkative and interactive. The music got turned up loud, the intoxication was setting in and the shenanigans were truly starting. The girls got up from the couch and started to dance around with each other as the music played loud in the background and the shots and beers kept flowing. Things were escalating fast, and honestly, it was fucking awesome.

Marilyn and Angel were young, beautiful, fun, and drop dead sexy, so watching these two girls dance around with each other was fucking dazzling. The way these two girls moved with one another was a sight in itself. They were dancing close on each other, moving up and down, rubbing and teasing. Slayter and I were, for the lack of a better word (grateful) to even be blessed with this divine and glorious event, so we didn't say much. We both just sat on the couch in sheer amazement and excitement, enjoying the show and sipping on beer. I think thirty minutes must've gone by before we even said a word to each other. That was when Slayter looked over to me.

"Are you happy you came?" Slayter asked.

"I am fucking thrilled I came. Thanks for the invite, man." I said back to him.

We tapped our beers together, shared a 'cheers' of joy and converted our eyes back to the heavenly dance demonstration.

These two young girls had been dancing with one another for almost an hour now, and the body heat was rising. Without much thought, Angel took off her shirt and quickly got down to her bikini top. Marilyn didn't hesitate and stripped down to the same look. Enormously fucking sexy they both were. They started to get closer to each other and rub up and down on their bodies as they danced the night away. It was utterly earth shaking. We watched as they got face-to-face, hands moving up and down each other's bodies, and they began to share a holy kiss of cock hardening righteousness. This was a spectacular sight to behold. One that two guys that were just sitting on a patio in Burbank doing jackshit, ever thought they would see. It wasn't much longer after they broke from that kiss that Angel looked over to Slayter.

"Do you mind if I take my top off?" She asked for her boyfriends consent.

"I don't mind. Do your thing, girl." Slayter said back.

And just like that, her bikini top hit the floor and out came her very perky, very sexy fake tits into the open air. She started to dance up against Marilyn, now with her striking breasts out and they started to touch each other up and down. Angel rubbed her hands over Marilyn's top, and with a quick and effortless motion, removed her bikini top and out came her tits. The show was getting much better and I had nothing but a hard-on and empty thoughts. After Slayter and I watched Angel and Marilyn grind and tease on one another, Marilyn went to the fridge to grab more beers and noticed that we had burned through the entire pack of brews.

"We're out of beer." Marilyn said.

"I'll buy some." I quickly threw in my two cents.

"There's a Ralph's right across the street. I'll go with you to get some." Marilyn answered back.

That's right! DING! DING! DING! LIGHTBULB! The Ralph's that I used to always attend with the 'old Marilyn' so many times. The Ralph's that I spent so many nights grazing the isles for food of nutrition with her before she so heartless left me in the cold of despair. And now, I was presented with this once in a lifetime chance to walk those same isles with a much younger, much more sexually charged girl and hopefully, fucking hopefully run into the 'old Marilyn,' to finally prove that I am doing alright, and get that moment of vindication that I so justly deserved.

"Alright, let's go get some beer. I'm buying." I replied. Marilyn put back on her bikini top, slipped on some sandals and we were out the door like two drunken skunks to re-up on our supply of booze.

As we made our way across the street, I thought to myself, "This was my time of redemption. My time to show that I've moved on to better and brighter (bigger titty) sunsets and roads paved in gold." But, then it hit me, "Who gives a fuck what the 'old Marilyn' thinks?" She didn't care about me when I called from the side of a noisy freeway, she didn't care about me when she so selfishly put another cock inside her. So why should I make her care now? This was my time to have fun, and Dammit, that's exactly what I was going to do. We walked into Ralph's intoxicated, happy, half naked and thrilled to keep going. I could see the heads of every guy in the place turn as we passed. Not for me of course, for the hot piece of young ass that was so nice to be associated with me. It really made me feel good about myself for a fleeting moment. We headed to the alcohol section, I grabbed a thirty pack of Bud Light, another bottle of Jack (hoping to not let this party ever end) and we made our way to the front for purchase. Marilyn walked through the store in nothing but a bikini top, a tiny pair of Daisy Dukes and sandals with such grace and ease. I walked behind her, checking out her flawless body the whole time and soaking up every fucking second I could. We got to the front, I paid for the liquor and beer and we were on our way back to the party to continue this escapade of tryst. Making our way through the parking lot, a group of college students pulled up next to us and were hollering and yelling at her absolutely sexy appeal. They asked me if they could kindly have a beer from my pack (and like the nice guy that I am) I gave them six and Marilyn and I kept on trekking back to the pad.

When we got back to Angel's apartment, Marilyn didn't skip a beat, her top hit the floor faster than you can say 'big black dildo' and her spry tits were out once again. She made her way back to Angel who was still dancing and jumped right back into the sexy show. I went and loaded up the beers in the fridge, cracked the bottle of Jack and poured up some more shots. After we all had about four or five more shots, and washed it down with countless beers, the real fun started to kick off. Angel took Slayter over to a chair in the living room, sat him down, straddled his lap and they started to make out heavily. With nothing left for Marilyn and I to do, I approached her, put my hand on her face and started to intensely kiss her in the kitchen. I ran my hands up and down her sound body as I held her face tight to mine and kissed her with intent to fuck. Her hands began to mosey and she found her self close to my cock, and need I say it, my cock was harder than trigonometry!

I unbuttoned her tiny shorts, slid them off, grabbed her by the ass and picked her little body into the air, wrapping her legs around my waist and wasn't letting loose of her lips. I held her in the air as I made love to her mouth. We were all over each other and it felt fucking amazing. I took a grip of her bikini bottom, slowly took it down as I held her in the air and started to finger her tight, young, shaved and pristine pussy. She was sincerely moaning as I got her pussy dripping wet with lust and desire. I then took her, laid her down on the floor of the kitchen and made my way from her lips to her neck, kissing, sucking, licking and teasing her to understand that I wanted nothing more than to make her cum. As I slid my tongue down her neck, around her giant tits, across her stomach and down south to her immaculate pussy, I could feel her legs get tight around my head. I slowly took my mouth and put my lips around her clit, licking and stimulating her every touch to make her move and shake. Getting wet and nasty so I could suck up her juices, I licked and spit all over her pussy as I moved from her pussy to her tight asshole. Tasting her elegant fluids and making her shift in place. She tasted, as I would image heaven feels.

Living in the moment had consumed us, and for a second I think we both forgot that we were not the only people in the room. I stopped for a rapid trice to look over at Slayter and Angel, and what I saw was even better. Angel had gotten butt naked and was sitting on the face of Slayter and he was going to town on her. So, without much thought, I jumped right back into the insides of Marilyn and continued to lick her perfect pussy and ass, making her feel every bit of my tongue and mouth. I wanted her to know that I was merely here to treat her pussy like the princess that it was. What was happening in this kitchen in Northridge was blatantly sacred in every sense of the word. Marilyn's young pussy was clenched tight against my face as she felt the suckling experience of my wanting tongue, and with much effort and a little luck, I heard her let out one of the most life changing moans as she came loudly and forcefully. Screaming and yearning, she was filling me with her sacrosanct nectar.

"I'M CUMMING . . . I'M CUMMING . . . FUCK! I'M CUMMING, RYAN!" Marilyn shrieked at her highest pitch.

I felt a rush of her fluid wildly pour into my open and accepting mouth as I felt her body tighten and her legs chock around my head, forcing me to gasp for my breath. It was a moment that made me feel like more of a man than finding my first pubic hair. It was then that I heard Slayter and Angel talk from the corner.

"Let's leave these two alone." Angel said as they both stood from the chair and exited the living room.

Now with the run of the entire living room to our own little game of touch and tease, it was time to play, fuck, lust and live. I took a grip of Marilyn's hips as she laid on the kitchen floor dripping in ecstasy, and with the flip of my strong arms, pulled her up from the ground and carried her to the living room couch. I lustfully threw her down on the couch to her back, grabbed her hands and put them to my jeans so she could unbutton me and see what was waiting for her on the other side. As she got me out of my jeans and reached her hands down my underwear, she could feel that I was ever so excited. I think excited is an understatement. I was about ready to blow my fucking pants. Hahaha. She slid off my underwear and was presented with my rock hard cock, every inch, every vein, and every bit of my manhood. And she was pleasantly surprised I believe.

"I like your dick." Marilyn said as she stroked it up and down in her hand.

"Why thank you. He apparently likes you also." I replied.

I think because of the massive amounts of beers and Jack Daniels' I consumed, she was worried I might go soft on this endeavor. But there was not enough whiskey in the world to make my dick not get rare stone hard for this pretty young thing. She was fucking mind blowing, and I was going to fuck the entire life out of her for a night.

Now with both of us completely butt naked, I took my large body and put it over hers, spit in my palm, rubbed my cock, and slide my dick inside her in the hopes of feeling her Goddamn soul. In and out, harder and harder, deeper and deeper I went, as I watched her pretty face groan in sheer craving passion. Her tight pussy around my cock felt like gold to a vagrant. Her clit was softer than the most luxurious fabric. I kissed her lips, sucked on her beautiful tits, and held her neck taught as I put my cock to her deepest core. With every thrust I could feel her emotions gaining, her juices flowing, her moans building. After just a few minutes, my utter excitement began to take over, and my animal was coming out. It was then that I realized, I didn't just want to have sex with this girl, I didn't want to just fuck this girl, make this girl cum and forget me forever. I wanted to fuck her like she's never had before. Cum harder than she ever knew she could. Or get a cock harder than she thought humanly possible. No. I wanted more. I NEEDED more. I wanted to make her never fucking forget the sex and lust I was going to put into this. I wanted her to remember me forever. For God sakes, I wanted to destroy her!

I quickly took over control, flipped her on to her knees and hands, lubed up my cock and made sure to jam it in as hard as I could muster up inside her young wet pussy until I felt her fucking body buckle. I was now fucking Marilyn like something out of a porn scene, as I made sure to shove, thrust, ram and fuck her cunt so wildly that she couldn't ever utter a word. Nothing but her moaning screams was what I beloved. I wanted to hear that beautiful voice of hers treble in obsession as my cock was violently thrown to her inner dwellings. I wrapped her hair tight in my hand and RIPPED her head back as I pushed down on her lower back and forced her ass to rise up in the air so I could fuck deeper then she knew her pussy went. Pounding and slamming, fucking and slapping, I was fully, completely, and absolutely fucking this girl like she was my slave. With every firm slap on her tight ass cheeks I could hear her screams building. I could feel her cunt getting wetter and she was on the collapse of cumming. I pulled her face to mine as I hit her from behind and went to her ear.

"Tell me who owns this fucking pussy?!" I said in her ear.

"Oh my God! Oh my God! You own this fucking pussy. You do, baby! You're fucking me so hard. Please, please don't stop!" Marilyn said as she struggled to speak.

"I'm going to fucking destroy your pussy and make you my bitch!" I ordered.

"Please take advantage of me!" She begged of me.

And then, without a second to lose, I took my hands, wrapped them around her face, put my fingers in her mouth and pulled her face back as I choked her with my fingers and slammed her tight cunt like it was nothing but a toy—a toy with no feelings, no emotions, an empty slot of nothingness. I was now going so hard on her pussy that the loud sound of our skin slapping together could be heard for miles. The sweat from our bodies could fill an ocean, and the greed in our genitals could cure cancer. This was truly the closest to God I think I've ever been. And as my cock went in and out, harder and harder, she was begging me to call her names.

"You are my fucking bitch! You're my little fuck toy and I'm going to use your cunt!" I shouted at her.

"Please hurt my pussy. Hurt it! Show me whose pussy this is?" Marilyn pleaded of me.

I then wrapped my arms under hers and grabbed her by the wrists so she was being held purely by my strength, and started to slowly slam in and out, from the very tip of my cock, to the base of my balls, my dick was now becoming part of her insides. Our dirty privates were becoming one, as she could feel the sheer hardening of my cock as it was so brutally rammed inside her. I was now getting much more sadistic with her cunt, and making sure that she wouldn't walk right after I was done. I put her face down on the floor, put one foot on her face and the other planted firm on the ground, and started to fuck her even harder as she now had nowhere to go, no way to move, and more importantly, no way to escape. For very long and extreme blood rushing minutes I was going so hard on Marilyn that she was going from eighteen to thirty after I was done with her. She was crying with pain and pleasure in her voice as I finally reached my limit.

"I'M GOING TO FUCKING CUM!" I yelled.

"CUM IN MY MOUTH!" Marilyn shouted back.

I grabbed her by her hair, ripped her head up so her mouth could entirely face my cock and profoundly exploded all over her mouth, face and tits. A complete shower of fucking cum was unloaded on her beautiful exterior as I roared to the Gods of lust above. With heavy breathing, satisfied private parts and hearts racing, we laid down on the floor next to one another and let our sweaty bodies slide together and both pass out of pure fucking exhaustion . . . Or exhaustion from fucking, you could say!

I am a 'Fucking God' amongst men!

Marilyn and I never did exchange numbers or any other form of commutation that night. She had to rise very early the next morning and left me dirty-ass naked on the living room floor like a cheap whore. But I did end up seeing her about six or seven months later. Angel brought her over to Slayter's one night to hangout and smoke some pot, and we did get to chat about that night. We found ourselves outside on the patio alone as Slayter and Angel slipped away for about an hour to fuck inside. And I of course had to ask her about that night, to which she replied.

"That was the hardest, hottest, most intense fuck of my entire life, and I will never forget that night for as long as I live." Marilyn so eloquently said.

And that was all I needed to hear. I didn't even try to pursue her that night, because I knew there was no way I could ever live up to the passion and lust that I put into the first time I ever had the pleasure to feel her from the inside. I wanted to just have that first memory . . . Ok. I did try, but she shot me down because Slayter and Angel returned from their quickie. Hahaha. You can't hate a brother from trying, right? . . .

CHAPTER TWENTY 666:
Suicidal Fantasies.

"Suicide is gutless. However, an accidental death is solely justified."

Cue the music. Eminem. Rock Bottom.

N ow twenty-two years of age, my health was well (adequately enough) I had a loving family that made it through some of the most tumultuous of times. I had a great group of comical friends, a gentle environment surrounding me, and honestly, all this was downright killing me. There was no earthly world I wanted to live in without Marilyn. No alternate universe I wanted to survive in without her angelic touch and her voice of complete rarity. She was all I was longing for, wanted, and fucking NEEDED!! If I couldn't have Marilyn, than I wanted the nothingness to overcome. I invited the black to invade my reality and battle the Trojan soldiers that were protecting my heart. My eternal flame had reached its last dying flicker. This is it, the end, the fat lady had sung, the race was over and I was staggering to reach my grave, my peace, my purpose.

I had been fired from more jobs than I had ever quit. Lost all hope in writing or the voice it gave me. I was relentlessly drinking heaps of booze and poison, abusing pills, abusing my body. Feeding off the emotions of all the women who ever gave me a chance and wishing for nothing but pain and suffering. I was on it all, alcohol, liquor, pot, grass, dank, pain pills, uppers, downers and in-between-ers. Abusing every last one of my vices, cigarettes, smokes, fags, a little Meth and Speed, Ecstasy, Mollies and even Special-K. Anything I could get my hands on, I was now willing to ingest. Shit! The only things I hadn't indulged in were Cocaine, Heroin or Crack. I had a desperate outlook on life, and finally said fuck it all! I was abandoned by my own piece of shit, cock sucking 'so called father.' I was left for dead by the make-believe 'God' you all call your savior. And I was deserted and neglected by the only woman I had ever loved. This Baboon had taken all he could take. Goodbye cruel world ... Goodbye ...

The wild Baboon cries alone
Lost
Confused
And mistaken.
He is no saint
Nor a sinner.
For the Baboon knows no pain
Because the Baboon never existed.

It was a cold Saturday night in February, and the boys and I had been out drinking for quite sometime now and with all us feeling perfectly numb and Super Bowl Sunday just around the corner, we had no real complaints. With every lasting sip of the beautiful venom I was getting closer and closer to my fate. Like usual, we shut the bar down, felt the sting of the last call lights and left the watering hole in no condition for anything. With no after party in sight, we all decided to call it a night and head home. I was dropped off to my grandparents' house where I was shacking up in their dingy garage rent free and broke. I absolutely hated my current placement in life; financial slump (or lack thereof any cash capital) my complete downfall from writing, and my wishing to hold Marilyn once more. Set the stage, turn up the lights so we all can see, and let us begin . . .

I had a brand new Costco size bottle of Jack Daniels', about seven Norcos, a full pack of menthol cigarettes and a death wish! It was the perfect cocktail for a dazzling and guiltless suicide of a very soiled and tarnished evil life. I got back to my room, locked the door, gathered my supplies of vice and set them down on my desk. I cracked open the bottle of liquor and threw the cap with no intent to stop. I lit a smoke, took a heavy hit, swallowed two Norcos and began to pace. I left my 'Murphy bed' up so I had plenty of room to take pleasure in this enterprise the best I could. Just as easy as my ABC's, I started to pace back and fourth, back and fourth, sip after lavishly overflowing sip I was downing this bottle as fast as I could while chain smoking and talking to myself. My silent screams filled the air as I made my way wall to wall in my tiny garage. The cloudy smoke was a haze to a worthless life, a useless life. An unwanted life!

I walked back to my desk in a frenzy and took Norco number three and washed it down with a fulsome guzzle. I lit another smoke and was back to my frantic and anxious pacing. The task was simple, drink, smoke, drink, smoke, drink, smoke . . . Repeat! I was shifting through a very deadly range of emotions. Changing from sad to angry, laughing to crying, hating and loving. Longing and wishing to feel the end, feel the pain, and just maybe finally fucking feel something for GOD SAKES! . . . I made my way back to my desk and dropped Norco number four, wolfed it down with some more of my brown toxin and was back to my walking. I moved effortless from standing and crying, laughing and shouting, to falling to my knees in shame and disappointment, with my screams for Marilyn as a background, the effects were kicking in. It was now time for everything I ever wanted, ever needed . . . <u>**AN AUDIENCE!**</u>

With my dark, murky and sadistic minds eye artistry. I painted Marilyn in the room so she could witness the decline, the fall . . . The fucking end! I felt she might get lonely, so I made sure to place her next to this fantasy 'God' of forgiveness and the cowardly 'Devil' we all must fear. All three spectators standing sidelined as I made my way back and fourth. They were all going to be viewers to the show, <u>my show</u> . . .

. . . The Murder Show! . . .

I wanted them to see every second, every minute, and every fucking hour of this magnificent occasion of perpetual love. I walked to my desk and looked over to my three new audience members.

"You guys enjoying the show?" I begged for their attention.

"I don't think you have the balls to pull it off." The Devil chimed in.

"Ryan, this won't bring me back." Marilyn selfishly spoke.

"I'm not trying to get you back. I'm trying to forget you forever." I calmly retorted.

I reached on to my desk and grabbed another Norco . . .

"—Why don't you prove you have the pluck and make this easy on yourself?" God threw down his two cents.

"Fine." I replied as I grabbed two more pills and tossed them down my hopeless throat.

With a brawny gulp and no chaser, I was now copiously contaminated with six funny pills. I was aware just how much booze my body could physically consume to get drunk or wasted. I knew the correct amount of fluid ounces to reach a blackedout, intoxicated level of recklessly. And exactly how much drank it would take to induce some violent vomiting. But what I didn't know was the lethal concoction of booze, painkillers, sorrow and heartbreak it would require to take my final breath. My last hurrah, if you will. This was a feat I was willing to try for, struggle to accomplish in, wish for, maybe even fucking 'pray' for. As I made my way from one hazy side of the room to the other, my vision was starting to blur, my legs were getting weak and my mind was racing. I wasn't aware of how much time had passed, nor did I fucking care. I just kept on drinking and smoking as I was awaiting the conclusion of doom.

"I bet you $100 bucks says he dies?" God served up a playground bet.

"Goddammit, I wanted that bet." The Devil responded.

"I'll give you 10-1 odds." The Almighty lured him in.

"You got yourself a deal." Satan quickly replied with greed in his eyes.

"WHY DON'T YOU ALL JUST SHUT THE FUCK UP?!" I shouted.

"Ryan, you don't have to do this." Marilyn gave her last request.

. . . I took a look at her, and she was just as beautiful as ever. With her long brunette hair, her silky smooth legs for all to see and the lovely face that only an Angel would wish for.

"I can't. I can't stop. This is what I deserve." I helplessly replied in a tragic tongue. "God may forgive me, but I must whip myself scorn." I ended in sheer sinister promise.

My condition was worsening as I turned away from my onlookers and back to my goal of reckoning. With a lit cigarette in one hand, an almost completely empty bottle of Jack in the other, this was truthfully the best moment of my black tar covered life. I took a seducing hit from my fag. A wash of pollutant down my gullet and it was then, at that very instant . . .

. . . I was finally separated . . .

I was removed from my imperfect and damaged soul, secluded from this world just as I had hoped and everything went completely . . .

BLACK!!

When I eventually woke, I was lying on the hard concrete floor cover merely by a thin blood and cum stained rug and was significantly choking on my own vomit. I turned my head to the side and puked up the spew that was drowning my airways and took a life-changing gasp of never ending breath. The sickening barf was everywhere. All over my chest, my arms, my hair, on my face, and even formed a nice piss pool puddle under my head. My mouth was severely dehydrated and my nose smelt as if someone had shit inside it. My head was throbbing of disbelief and my thoughts were running rapid in revulsion and utter loathing flavor. I felt a sopping touch around my cock and took a look down, only to learn that I had flooded my pants in my own bitter profound piss. Rock bottom has never felt so great!

I have an abnormal tolerance for substance effects, which is why this action was so vividly recollected and flamboyantly remembered. I hardly sleep most nights, so it was nothing out of the ordinary that I would surprisingly wake during this filthy feat of depression and disgust. There I laid, next to a spilt bottle of liquor, a burnt out cigarette and a splitting headache, sheltered in urine and chunder with nothing more but my charming thoughts to ease the pain. Wide-awake and shaken, my emptiness had never felt so empty, my loneliness had never left so lonely, and my life had never felt so meaningful. This must be what it feels like to survive in a world filled with greed and lust, sloth and wrath, envy, gluttony and pride. This must be what it feels like to be truly . . .

...ALIVE!!...

I took a second to gather my strength, gather my thoughts and gather my footing. Then, with every little bit of fight I had left in me, I forced myself up from my polluted pile of puke and piss. Walked over to my desk, took a seat at the chair and began to chug some well-needed water. Ironically, the desk chair where I was seated, sat face-to-face with a mirror, and the produced image I saw was downright dreadful. A grown man, covered in his own evacuated urine, wretched disgorge, and lost twinkle, this was exactly the graphic representation I needed to see at that moment to make it all fit into perspective. My valueless photograph of vulnerability was both welcomed and condemned. Sweaty, sloppy, stinky and slimy (for sex it's a great combination) but for this, it was an awakening. I stared upon myself for almost an hour as I sat in the silence and sipped on water. Asking why? Wondering why? Begging why? I asked myself many deep question of what I was trying to accomplish? What I stood for? What my legacy would have been if I had died? Just what the fuck I was doing in the first place?

And here's what I got. My vindication, my resolution, my ultimate justification . . . **"NOTHING!** Not a God-damn thing! I would stand for nothing at all. Mean nothing. Be nothing, because overall, I <u>FUCKING</u> was nothing!"

Empty thoughts of life
He thought he knew all there was to know . . .
Ladies and Gentlemen, welcome to the Ryan Vinci Show!

James Dean. Jimi Hendrix. Jim Morrison. Marilyn Monroe. Heath Ledger. Tupac. John Belushi and Kurt

Cobain. Martin Luther King, Jr. Jimmy 'The Rev' Sullivan. John F. Kennedy. Bob Marley. Elvis Presley. Janis Joplin. Pat Tillman. Amy Wineshouse. Adam 'MCA' Yauch and Robin Williams. River Phoenix. Bruce Lee. Anna Nicole Smith. Aaliyah. Vincent van Gogh and Whitney Huston all had something in common. They all brought something special and unique into this world, something beautiful that we all could lean on in times of need. They were Hero's, idols, inspirational beings and creative influences we all could look towards . . . And the question I had was? What had I brought to the table?

Honestly, I had nothing to bring to the table but pain and hurt, clothing covered in my own gag and body waste. A massively misplaced setting of foul words and dirty play was all I seemed to be capable of. In all reality, I had no inheritance to leave behind. No words of wisdom, no actions of selfless love, no great deeds that changed the life of even one person. All I had was a long list of women that felt used and abused by my self-centered ways, a broken heart, a tainted mouth and evil persona. If I were to have my funeral then, on that day, what would the people say that actually attended this shitty and wasteful event?

There would be a countless number of troubled and twisted women, who probably hate my guts (and for good reason) shouting how happy they are that such an evil, manipulative and negligent person finally found his grave, all awaiting their turn to spit on my casket and wish that the flames of hell devour my body and fry my carcass. My family would call me a coward, a weakling, a garbage human being who never took responsibility for his actions or words. Which to be truthful is entirely accurate. I would have a best friend (which) in all due respect to the homosexual existence out there—I would literally go gay for. Not that you wonderful faggots out in this beautiful world are not good enough for me, you're just no Levi, let's face it. He would be pissed off with the fact that I could do such a selfish operation of removal, and leave him behind, reasonless and without the ap-

propriate and suitable answer of respect he deserves as my best friend, my brother, and my inspiration. I would have a room full of friends (hopefully) who thought this was just another narcissistic dig for attention, much like many of my other acts for approval were. I would have no money to leave behind, no writings of great hope, and no found memories of love, nothing at all, absolutely
FUCKING NOTHING!
I would be more of a Ghost alive then I would be dead. And that thought really, really, really HURT! This was not how I was going to leave this world. It was time to find a positive lifestyle, a legacy of my own, one which my family and friends would be proud of when I go.

Rise Baboon
Rise
For it is not your time!
The pavement hurt
The words stung
And the thought was righteous.
But you missed something
You forgot something
You miscalculated and now
Well now . . .
Now you must obey.

ENDEARING INTERMISSION CHAPTER:
Love.

Go Fuck Yourself! . . .

CHAPTER TWENTY-SEVEN:
To Live Is To Suffer, To Survive Is To Find Some Meaning In The Suffering!

— Friedrich Nietzsche.

"If you fear God or the Devil, you will never speak your true words. Both of those figures cannot hurt you, posses you or blind you. It is purely up to you to make the choice between right and wrong. Trust your voice."

Walking a tight rope, holding a drawn out handstand, running a marathon and being in love, all require three very important key elements. Balance, strength and control—if those three grave components are not followed with strict precision, you fall, and when you hit the bottom, it hurts, it sings and it's hopefully (for the sake of your wellbeing) life changing. This was my comprehensive rock bottom. My nothing left to lose moment (and luckily) I saw the light. I did have something to live for, to pursue, to accomplish and enjoy. I didn't really want to die. Shit, I wasn't even twenty-three yet and it was my birthday month. Death was an option, but not truly what I wanted. I just knew I didn't want to live my life in any more heartbreak and pain, sadness and sorrow, longing and wishing. I wanted to be happy, I wanted to be true and I wanted to be complete, just like we all do. It was time to make a change and make it fast. Take charge of this life of mine and stop playing the 'Innocent Victim Card.' It was time to smile, laugh, feel something and finally be great. And not because I was pretending, because I was genuinely happy, but most importantly, move on from my past life with Marilyn. Forgive the actions of my long and painful history (which) ultimately pushed me over the edge—and take responsibility and blame for the damage and ache I was causing to others, in other words, it was time to be a FUCKING MAN!

For the first time in a very long time, I looked inside myself, did hours of self-evaluation and began to ask. "What is it that you want, Ryan?" A very simple question in theory, however, the answers are astronomically unlimited, especially to a very ill and complicated mind like mine. A question so easy, so pedestrian and so straightforward, yet it holds such limitless confusion and baffle to a sadistically complex mind like the one I wore. 'Heavy lies the crown,' so they say. Of course I wanted Marilyn, but it was time to face facts, that just wasn't going to happen. It was finally time to give up on that pipedream fantasy and move on with my life. My life that was almost so selfishly taken from me in a fit of rage and what I thought was control (or maybe lack thereof) I hadn't quite figured it out. It was time to go on with the rest of my life and appreciate the love I did have surrounding me in my lovely world.

I had a beautiful nephew that I loved with all my heart and wanted nothing but the best for. Another nephew on the way, a caring family, my wonderful mother, two fantastic brothers, the world's best 'best-friend' anyone could ever ask or hope for, and my passion to tell a damn good story. It was time to get back from where I fell from and seek another outlet for my pain (and optimistically) a safer and healthier outlet.

Cue the music: Hey Ya! Outkast.

Guess who got his swagger back? My confidence was building, the joy in my heart was found once again, and I was fully, entirely and charmingly, HAVE! I was drinking less (way less) and when I did drink, it was out of celebration to life, carnival to fun and contentment. I cut out any shape and form of pills from my savage diet (minus special occasions of course) found my way back to the gym, was exercising six days a week, running all the time, smoking fewer cigarettes and was back on track for a fulfilling life. I was back writing again, almost every night. I was working on poetry, screenplays, short stories, treatments and anything else that caught my fancy. "You will never have to return to that place of hate and pain ever again. You're not the victim. You make your own life, and remember—fate is for the lazy. If you want something in this world, work hard for it. Stop thinking you are owed anything, because you're not. You will only get what you put in. You act like a piece of shit then you will get treated like a piece of shit. It's really that simple."

I would say that phrase to myself everyday as my own little speech, and still do till this very day, and probably till the day I meet my end. I started to seek out women for more than just a meaningless fuck of vacant sentiment. I was actually holding conversations with the women I would talk to, and wasn't trying to be the loudest, drunkest douchebag in the room. I celebrated my twenty-third birthday in Big Bear Mountains and took more Adderall pills while doing so—then what is probably remotely healthy. Like I said, I (somewhat) cut the pills out of my savage diet. Ha-ha-ha . . .

I came back to my family and was talking with them again, spending well-needed quality time with them and no longer living a life of complete privacy, mystery and secrecy. I was honest, endearing and very careful with my words, and even more cautious and vigilant with my actions. I didn't want to be the reason for anybody's tears, not anymore. I was evolving and dare I say it . . . I was growing up . . . 'Dr. Drew Pinsky' would be so Goddamn proud! I was seriously, literally (and as many times as I can exhaust the word) HAPPY! My focus was purely on creating a successful life for myself and I stopped victimizing my ego. My self-loathing attitude was gone, I found truth in my work and it was time to make my own luck. I was doing all this while never telling a single soul about the truth from my almost unintentional suicide. I told some friends a simple story that I choked on my own vomit, but I changed the narrative around completely to look as if it was just an accidental hazard of drinking too much. It was just a casual slipup in the alcohol game if you will . . .

Well, I did tell one person the comprehensive and bona fide tale, my bestfriend Levi of course. Because, I knew he was the only person strong enough to process the information of such a worthless and self-absorbed act on my part and not slut shame me with disappointment and heavy judgment. And you know what he said? . . .

"I knew that story you told before was all bullshit, but, I had to let you work it out, brother."

You know that moment when people say something to you, about the real truth, as if they were conscious and aware the whole time and you think to yourself. "They are only saying that to agree with me and make themselves feel smarter?" Levi was not saying it like that at all, not even in the fucking slightest. His eyes said it all. He looked me dead in the eye, and retorted his comprehension on the incident. I could feel it from his look alone that he knew what the fuck was really going on, and like I said earlier, Levi and I could speak to each other through a look, a smirk, a wink or a glance. He was giving me a stare in my eye I've never felt from him before, and what I gathered was. He was telling me he knew I was lying about my story of innocently drinking too much and puking, and he was telling me with his eyes alone, with authority, love and concern. "You're a big boy and I had to let you work this shit out on your own. I knew you would pull through, you always do, brother." That's what he was really saying, not with his words, but through his eyes of sympathetic uneasiness. He was never pushing or pressuring me for an answer or reason, a purpose or thought. He has always known I wear my heart on my sleeve, and he was just respecting the fact that I told him the real truth in the first place. I thank him and I love him even more for giving me the space I needed to figure this shit out alone.

That's the type of people Levi and I are, we would rather go through ten years of pain and misery, silent and dealing with it alone, than ever put the heavy burden of our problems on another person for even a minuscule second. It's a good thing he did stay silent (if he would've stepped in) I would've got defensive, much like I always did at that time in existence, I probably would have drank more than enough to end my life, and not been sharing this story. So, if you want to thank anyone, thank him for this entertainment. Without Levi by my side, life would have turned out a lot different, and not for the better. Thanks, brother . . .

I love you, Levi! 'No-Homo.' Fuck it! . . . Full Homo! HA!

There I was, alive, well, healthy, happy and now cruising down the boulevard of twenty-three with elegance and simplicity. Life was beginning to feel amazing to me once more. My childlike wonder had returned and I found solace in some of the most overlooked of things in this world. I was buried in my writing. I had finished my first screenplay and was now working on my second. I was taking well-needed bike rides with my nephew. We had welcomed my second beautiful nephew into our little family. And he was one of the smartest, cutest and good-mannered little boys I've ever seen. I was finally at peace with myself, and it was time to repair some past relationships that I had wrongfully and thoughtlessly destroyed.

I gave Venus a call and asked if I could bring her to dinner. She was reluctant (as you would image) a little shocked and distant at first. And for good reason, the last time she saw me, I was heartlessly punching her in the back of the head while drunkenly fucking her pussy from behind like she was a cheap whore off the street. But, she had found a new calling in life under the grace of 'God' and she decided to forgive our chaotic past (mostly caused by me and my dumbfuck actions of ego-centricity and disregard) and agreed to hear me out. Time to be a man, Ryan! We went out and had ourselves a couple lovely nights of dinner and entertainment, and she sat quietly and listened to me apologize time and time again for my irresponsible manipulation, my force-ful acts of pain against every part of her wellbeing, my disrespecting ways of self-pleasing physical takeover and the many nights I abused her flesh in the hopes of cumming out the throbbing ache I held within.

We had very long and extremely interesting talks about the gloomy places we were in at the time. Conver-sations about how we both once shared a vicious and de-structive fling together. The dark corners of our minds that we never thought we would have the power to crawl out from, the true beauty in life, and what love really means. It was perfect in all aspects of the word. The truthful conversations we had with each other were thought evoking, balancing and real. After a nice dinner and movie, Venus looked me in the eye with a puzzled and attractive daze.

"What changed in you? What made you want to right this wrong?" Venus finally asked the question I was wishing she would ask.

"Well, to be perfectly honest, I couldn't go another day regretting the harsh way I treated you. I was thoughtless, careless and just all around wrong. I never meant to hurt you. I lost control of myself and my own emotions, and felt the only way to feel better about my-self was to cause pain to others." I honestly opened up to her.

A feeling she knew all too well from some of the many questionable things she had done in her life. It's always pleasant when a person can relate to you in a certain ex-tent, and not just stare at you with judgment and disbe-lief in your true words and intentions.

"Thank you, Ryan. It really does mean a lot to me that you can admit you were wrong and take responsibility for you hurtfulness. Most people never look back." Venus replied.

"We can't know where it is we are heading if we don't stop to look where it is we came from, even if that place is one of hate and pain." I replied.

"That's very true . . . Well, nevertheless, all profound sentiments aside. It means worlds to me that you can grow up and say you're sorry." Venus brilliantly responded.

I thank Venus everyday for taking my call and giving me a chance to say how sorry I am, and will forever be sorry for the selfish and degrading things I did to her body and soul. And all the meaningless words I said to her in the past just to get her naked and take advantage of her. We both remain very close until this day, and will stand by one another till the end of time. With her giving me the chance to be open and honest, I lost a great deal of resentment and hate I was carrying for this world. And for once, I felt vulnerable, exposed, bare and human, and that was just what I needed. To be put in a place of mortal form, trueness and tender embrace. Of course, the corrupting and demeaning nature of the things I sloppily did and said to her can never truly be forgotten and forgiven. However, I will try to repair the shatter feelings I caused her and tell her nothing but the meaningful truth till the day I die in the hopes that one day the sting will no longer linger from our twisted and wrapped precedent. Venus, please stay strong, let the healing power of 'God and Righteousness' lead you to happiness, salvation, recovery and deliverance. I love you, Venus.

CHAPTER TWENTY-EIGHT:
Scarlett, My Submissively Sexy Slut.

"Bow down to me, crawl if you have to, for I own you in every conceivable way . . . Because a real mans job is to make your panties wet. Not your eyes."

I was now clear headed, leveled, grounded, somewhat pleased with myself and as the world would sleep; I was working hard to achieve something great, lasting and hopefully, memorable . . . My thoughts of self-loathing suicide had taken a back seat (most of the times) and life, as I knew it, was grandly starting to improve and better itself. I was now ready to adventure, push the boundaries of sexual awareness, and indulge in something magical and kinky. I wanted to feel something out-of-this world with another person, something that could change me forever.

"Why you ask, Bob?"

"Nope, I didn't ask—"

"—Well, it was simple . . . I was no stranger when it came to sexual conquests, but I always had this thought that something was missing in my folder of pleasure and tryst. Regular sex had begun to bore me in most cases. One-nightstands were just as lacking in excitement and charm, and masturbation had lost all its intimacy and feel—but mostly, just because I wanted to try something fresh and write a new chapter in my book of sex and bliss. I wanted to experiment with something intensely different than what it was I have had before. More truthfully, I needed to try something poles apart. Like drug addicts say, I needed a fix . . ."

"And once again, Ryan, I didn't ask. I was just listening to your twisted little fairytale."

. . . And that was when I met Scarlett. Oh Scarlett, Scarlett, my cute little harlot. Scarlett was a five-foot-five blonde, with a wild and kinky side to say the least. She had the thirst for sweat and cum and the ache for pain and pleasure. Scarlett was erotic, she was risky, and she had a dynamite attitude and the ability to lose her shit at the drop of a hat. Scarlett possessed something carnal and free that I had never (and I mean NEVER) found in the many women before her. She was raw, she was filthy, she was lewd, and she was every fucking thing I was looking for and more. She was to say, all that and a bag of chips.

I had met Scarlett at my brothers' birthday party. She came with a friend of the group and had absolutely no connection or ties to the Los Angeles scene, which was even more appealing. When I saw Scarlett walk in, wearing a skintight silver dress that looked almost painted on and hugged her womanly curves ever so perfectly, I could sense that she had a side to her that I was longing to see. I followed her around the party most of the night, hoping to slip in a second of charm and attraction, and hopefully, just maybe, feel this woman from the inside and fuck her like an animal. We would chat it up when we got a chance, and I believe she could feel my lusting vibe towards her. As most of the partygoers had hit their sloppy level of intoxication, the night was quickly going to be coming to an end. It was somewhere south of four A.M. and Scarlett and I had finally found a connection. Luckily, she lived within a few miles of where my brothers' party was, so we jumped in her car and headed back to her house with the thought of strange and beautiful sex. Well . . . At least that was my thought.

"People, strap on your ball gags, tighten the handcuffs around your wrists, pull out your whips, chains and paddles. Bend over and get ready for a spanking as you slide a buttplug up your ass, put a cock ring on, get wet and hard, for this story is about to get kinky and down-right fucking stimulating . . ."

"I don't even know where to begin with some of the strange words you say, Ryan."

"Pull that old dick out, Bob, this shit is gonna turn you on."

Scarlett and I went on to have some rough and unin-hibited sex that night, which was both mind-blowing and very real. However, I'm not going to tell you that story. Not because I don't feel you're worth it, but because I want to bring you down the rabbit hole much deeper, to the true depths of our dark and degenerate lifestyle so you can truly see just how we evolved as lovers, as peo-ple, as fucking pornstar pros. Let's fast forward, jump ahead about a year and allow me to tell you some of the much more invigorating stories.

CUE THE MUSIC:
And crank that motherfucker up!
Rihanna. S&M.

It had been a month and a half since I had last seen Scarlett, this was not by choice, but because I had em-barked on a month long road trip and was on the com-plete other side of the United States. The road trip was finally set to end in Palm Springs, and Scarlett and I had a hotel room rented which we planned to ravage and de-stroy. We talked via text in the car as I was approaching Palm Springs, asking her if she was ready?

"I need to feel your cock inside me so bad, baby." Scarlett replied. "I have been a very bad little whore and I need you to punish me, Master."

"I am going to fuck you so hard that you will not be able to walk tomorrow, you little slut." I wrote back. "Did you bring the bag of toys?" I asked her.

"Of course, Master." She responded.

Over the course of a year and some change, her and I had built a sophisticated bag of fuck toys to fulfill our every fantasy and desire. The collection was ranging from a ball gag, anal beads, buttplugs, handcuffs, throat numbing spray for the purpose of deepthroat. Some leg restraints, a couple dildos, a few vibrators, a larger collar for her neck with a matching leash, and my personal favorite, a large paddle with the word 'slut' written into the leather stitching, solely for the purpose of leaving an imprint of the word 'slut' if the body is struck hard enough. And let me tell you, it really did work. All these toys, plus my very dominant force of rule and my dirt filthy imagination caused for some of the most thought-provoking sex I have ever had.

I created a rule system for Scarlett to follow and strict punishments to those very rules if any of them were ever broken. We had nicknames, safe words, fabricated fantasies and fetishes and always wanted more. I was her 'Master, Daddy, Ruler or Owner,' and she loved screaming each and every last one of them names. Scarlett loved to be under my control, my order, and my every last power thirsty HOWL! She had many names and was obedient with them all. We played mind games with each other, teasing and pushing one another to the edge of sheer aggression and anger to see just how lowdown and dirty the sex could get. We lived out many fantasies. Everything from rape, step dad and daughter taboos, stepbrother and sister, public fucks and anal adventures, and I've laid more cum on her face than I ever did kisses. And I slapped her around to the point that she would cry in a corner and beg me to stop yet be longing for more. Scarlett was a good little bitch who knew her place and loved to be put in that place. She was a twisted little whore with the mind of a fucked up pornstar and the body of a teenage schoolgirl. But, I am digressing, let me get back on track to that lovely night in Palm Springs when Scarlett, Scarlett, my perverted little harlot got the fucking of a lifetime.

As I was dropped off to the front of the hotel, I grabbed my bags, found Scarlett waiting in the casino and we made our way up to our room. As we stood and talked in the elevator, the sexual tension was so heavy I feared the elevator might plummet from the overwhelming weight. We exited the metal box of craving emotion and made our way to the hotel room, unlocked the door, entered the room and I quickly tossed my bags down on the floor. Earlier in the day I told her to wear an old dress that she didn't care about because I was going to rip the fucking thing off of her when I got her alone. And like a good little slut, she did just that. As the door slammed behind us and my bags hit the floor, I took a hold of her hair, pulling her head back so she could look up to me and we began to intensely kiss and slobber all over one another. It had been a month and some change since I had last fucked her, so needless to say foreplay was not in the cards for this first bang. I grabbed strong to her tight little yellow sundress and with one swift and bold strike, ripped the fucking thing completely off, stripping her down to her panties and bra. I then grabbed the sides of her panties and lifted her in the air by them as I tossed her down to the bed and ripped her panties off in the process. I climbed my large and horny body over hers and forcefully took hold of her face as I passionately kissed her with everything I had. Like I said, it had been a month and some time since our last fuck, so I was damn near ready to explode before my cock even entered her wet pussy. With her beautifully naked body under mine, she undid my belt, slid my pants and underwear off and took a hold of my already raging hard cock. The feel of her hand around my dick was almost crippling as I fought back the urge to blow my load all over her.

"I missed your big cock, Daddy." She seductively spoke.

"I can't wait to fuck your tight cunt, baby." I replied.
She spit in the palm of her hand, rubbed it on my cock and jammed my throbbing erection inside her dripped

wet cum hole. Let me reiterate, it had been a month and some change, so I'm sure you can image what happened next . . . I FUCKING BLEW LIKE A GODDAMN VOLCANO AFTER A FEW SHORT MINUTES OF FUCKING HER!!! But it's all right, have no fear, for this was just the beginning to our long weekend of tryst and play. And yes, I will tell you all about it . . .

Submit to me
For I am your Master.
Submit to me
For I am your Ruler.
Submit to me
For I now control you.
Submit and submit
For this is real.

After we cleaned up the mess from our very quick and extremely aggressive first fuck, we poured ourselves a stiff cocktail, smoked a joint and I took a couple of pain killers that Scarlett was kind enough to procure for me. Seeing as how I spent a month on the road, it wasn't as easy for me to get my hands on drugs, as it was when I was at home. Scarlett never really had a problem with any of my alcohol or drug abuse, in fact, at times I think she found it rather inviting. She was a complete pothead, to every definition of the term, so she didn't mind my out-of-control behavior. We drank about three or four cocktails, showered up together, dressed to impress and headed out for a night in the casinos. We made our way from blackjack table to bar, poker table to bar, slot machine to bar until both of us had blurry vision and mispronounced vernacular. It was time for the real fun to begin . . .

Scarlett knew I had a somewhat possessive and jealous demeanor to me, and she liked to use that to get me hard in the pants and even more belligerent in bed. She would dance around and flirt with other guys to get the hostile performance out of me that we both actually enjoyed very much. She would prance around, dressed in a skintight and fucking sexy little number, rubbing up to strange men and making sure to look me in the eyes as she did so. I admired her as she made her away around the very crowded bars full of horny men, talking to them all and making my protectiveness boil over. She would approach me from time to time only to ask:

"Am I making you jealous, Daddy?"

"I am going to destroy you when we get back to the room." I answered.

She would then dance away and continue her warpath of seductive invidious storm. And I hate to say it . . . I loved every Goddamn immoral second of it! Maybe she was a little FUCKED in the head, but so was I, and she knew just what to do in order for her to always get the best out of me. Oh Scarlett, Scarlett, my cockteasing little Harlot. With the level of complete intoxication at its highest, and the demonstration of her stage play mind games coming to an end, it was time for the real show to start. Stick a finger in your pussy and pull out your cock . . . The time for reckoning was finally here . . .

We left the packed bar and made our way back to the elevator. As the doors opened and the patrons inside exited, I pushed her little ass inside and threw her against the wall, grabbing her face and beginning to kiss her with intense pleasure. She could feel through my already pressed pants that my cock was profusely hard and ready for action. She ran her hand up and down the outside of my pants getting my breathing heavy and drooling all over her. I slipped up her dress and started to finger her dripping cum wet cunt with power and control. As the elevator made its way up the floors, I held her tight to the wall and mouth raped her face with my tongue like I would die tomorrow. We reached our floor and we quickly corrected our image before the doors opened and then exited, making our way down the long hallway she walked ahead of me and would pull her dress up showing off her beautiful taught ass and making me chase her even more. We got to our room, slipped the cardkey in, unlocked the door and I firmly kicked her little ass inside. With the sound of a slamming door as our background, the night was now about to get wild and primordial . . .

She brought me over to the bed, sat me down and told me to sit. I did just as she asked and then watched her make her way to the bathroom and close the door behind her. I ripped off my clothes and got butt naked as fast as I possibly could. After a few minutes she reappeared wearing nothing but a collar around her neck that had a leash attached and stretched to one hand, and in her other hand was a black duffel bag full of fuck toys. She walked over to me and threw the bag down on the bed and looked me in the eyes with the greatest sight of sexual ruin I have ever seen.

"Do what ever you want to me, Master!" Scarlett said and then handed me control of the leash.

It was now time for Daddy to show this little whore who was Boss! I took a firm grip of the leash and ordered her to get on her hands and knees. She did just as she was ordered and began to lick and suck on my feet and shins. Licking and kissing me up and down as she slowly made her way higher to my cock. She put her hand around my dick and looked up to me with submissive delight.

"I need you to punish me, Daddy." Scarlett seductively spoke.

And before she could think twice, I powerfully SLAPPED her across her little slut face.

"Tell me what you are, and what you're good for?" I destructively asked her.

"I am your little whore, and I am only good for fucking." She respectfully answered.

I then quickly SLAPPED her across the face three times more and spit on her.

"That's right, you little cunt. Don't you ever forget it! Now put my cock deep down your throat and choke like a good bitch." I controlled of her.

Slapping her ass red and making her tear up from the cruel smacks.

"OUCH!" She screamed as the hits to her ass began to get harder and harder.

I then walked her over like a dog to the black bag and told her to dump out all the toys. She did just as she was ruled and I was now looking at a hotel bed covered in sextoys, ready for me to use with my every perverted desire.

I pulled her face up to my cock by the leash and collar and put a ballgag around her face and strapped it on nice and tight. Then I bent her sexy ass over the bed, onto her stomach, with her already red ass up in the air, and strapped her feet to the bed. I walked to her hands, slapping a set of handcuffs around her wrists and tied it to the headboard. She was now fully and ultimately under my direct and govern. I reached over and grabbed my paddle, and with no hesitation at all, SLAPPED her ass so hard that the hotel staff could hear the sound of it penetrating her skin as she screamed in pain. SMACK, SLAP, HIT, SPANK, THUMP, BELT, WHACK, time and time again, beating her beautiful ass until the word 'Slut' was almost permanently imprinted all over her thighs and bottom. I spun the paddle in my hand, and for a moment, I felt the world go into slow motion. I felt like I was in the scene from 'Dazed and Confused,' when Ben Affleck's character was beating on that boy. Except, with a little less homoerotic touch. I had Scarlett completely restrained to the bed, with a ballgag in her mouth, a collar around her neck and a leash in my hand. And let me tell you . . . This was a sense of FUCKNG RAW POWER that you can't pay for . . . Well—I know you can, but you get the metaphor.

"How many more spankings do you want?" I asked.

"Please only three more." She let out a muffled beg from behind her ballgag.

SLAP, SLAP, SLAP, SMACK, SMACK, SMACK, THUMP, THUMP, THUMP! I gave her six extra confirmatory hits of discipline to make sure she knew I was in charge and heard her suppressed screams come from her ballgagged mouth.

I then took a hold of my rock hard cock and jammed it inside her pussy till I hit the very depths of her cunt. Slamming away on her pussy with force as she let out baffled squeals. Rough and hard I made Scarlett my absolute bitch and sex object. With each dynamic thrust and plunge I would slap her ass with the paddle and make the sound of her painful shrikes get louder and louder. I grabbed her fucking hair tight with my freehand and ripped her face back only so I could spit in her face and then slam her back down to the pillow. Now with her face buried in a hotel pillow, I started to fuck her even harder and with less care for her pussy. It was Goddamn invigorating and freeing as I turned her body into nothing more than a set of holes for my sheer amusement. Forcing my way down her cunt, she was crying out from the pillow and begging me to stop. I pulled her face up from the pillow by her long, flowing blond hair and looked her in the eye.

"WHAT DID YOU SAY, YOU LITTLE WHORE?!" I shouted.

"Please stop, it fucking hurts?" Scarlett begged of me.

Listening not to her weeping request, I SLAMMED her face back down to the bed and fucked her even harder than before, making sure that she felt every blood thirsty push of my intensely sadistic cock inside her little slut pussy. Making her eyes cry into the white pillow and her makeup smear the casing, she was turning the pillowcase into a fucking masterpiece painting of submissive art. I could no longer hear her screaming howl from the pillow and I pulled her face up to look her in the eyes and she was crying like a little teenage girl at a 'Hunger Games' screening.

"Please, Daddy, please stop." She begged once more.

"What are you, and what are you good for?" I asked Scarlett.

"I am your little fucking whore, and I am only good for you to fuck however you want!" She compliantly answered.

"So do you want me to stop?"

"No, Master. Use my body until you cum, that's what I'm here for." Scarlett replied.

"That's a good little slut."

I then got up from behind her and undid the ties around her feet and hands and took off the ballgag. Giving her a few minutes to catch her breath, re-gather her thoughts, and prepare for more abuse. I then laid down on the bed and ordered her to suck my cock and lick my asshole. She began to deepthraot my cock, getting her spit cascading down my balls and ass, as she then made her way from my cock to my asshole. She was a pro at tongue fucking my asshole and it was a feeling unlike anything I've ever felt. In and out, around and around, she would lick and suck on my asshole till I was near explosion. Up and down I let her venture from gagging on my dick and tasting my ass. She then grabbed my thighs and threw my legs up in the air and buried her face inside my ass for a good solid thirty minutes as she gave me the best asshole licking of all time. She used my ass as a hole and fucked it with her mouth and made me shake and vibrate in pure and unholy delight. Lick after beautifully sloppy lick, suck after choking suck, she turned my downstairs into a sopping mess of spit and gag. It was fucking amazing!

After she finished up her tour of deepthroat and ass licking, we took a well-needed break. We made ourselves an 80/20 mix of Sailor Jerry and coke and smoked a joint. I dropped three more painkillers and we took our butt naked bodies outside to the balcony to have a cigarette. I took a seat on one of the lounge chairs as we smoked and she sat down and put my still rock hard cock inside her pussy. Scarlett pulsated on my dick as we sat outside smoking and she made sure to not let me get soft.

"I want to burn you ass with my cigarette." I told her.

"Ok, Daddy. You can brand me so the world knows I belong to you." She properly answered . . .

. . . I then took my cherry red smoke and put it completely out on her ass cheek, burning it deep and leaving a brutal mark as she yelped in sharp pain and pleasure. It was Goddamn degrading and sadistic, but also made my villainous cock even harder than before.

I then stood her up from the chair and walked her over to the balcony's edge, leaning her over the edge face first so she could look down as I slide my cock deep inside her from behind. Her tits flopped over the edge and were out in the open air for all the bystanders below to see and enjoy as I pounded her pussy from behind and she was moaning and screaming in joy. Fuck after fuck, forceful push after push, and longing sigh after sigh I fucked her from behind as the people walking the late night streets looked up in amazement and disbelief. It was a sight to behold as we let ourselves become exhibitionists and unchained by the truly brutal world of laws and restraint. Free and naked the warm Palm Springs air consumed our bodies and our passionate moans filled the open air. The pure thrill of fucking for the world to see was something more than I can ever describe and brought us both to the point of fulfillment.

"I'M CUMMING, I'M CUMMING. DADDY, I'M FUCKING CUMMING!" Scarlett shouted over the edge as I slammed her pussy from behind.

And before I could comprehend the exact art of this beautiful and liberated experience, my cock was no longer able to hold in my load.

"Get on your fucking knees and take my cum!" I told Scarlett.

Faster than you can say 'cupcakes and blowjobs,' she dropped to her knees and opened her subservient mouth awaiting my jizz. I then unloaded a massive weight of cum all over her pretty little face and turned her into a beautiful little mess as I let out my WARRIOR CRY into the open air for all to hear. With her little face drenched in cum and her pussy satisfied. She never looked as gorgeous as she did in that very moment . . .

Between her legs,
I went searching for her soul.
Lost in the abyss of her taste,
I have never felt so alive.
Profound,
Unbound,
Crowned,
And kicked around.
She was the last of the great sickness.

"I know what you're thinking, Bob? You don't believe this story could have any more degeneracy and wickedness to it, without being anything less than a fable of one man's twisted, perverted and seriously lacking of proper sanity, distorted Imagination."

"You know, Ryan . . . As I sit here and write your tale, your sage, your deeply disturbing story of whatever it is you believe in. And only God knows where this narrative might end. I think I can finally say, truthfully . . . Maybe you should lay off the drugs."

"Drugs? No, no. For the drugs is not who I am, nor what defines me. Drugs don't blanket my pain, nor do they exaggerate my character. And as for what I believe in . . . I guess only the end of this romance will reveal."

After many long, drunken and completely wrapped nights of life changing rendezvous and fucks, Scarlett had ran up her L.A. bill and was forced to move about five hours up north. Which really changed the dynamic of our (so-called) sexually fueled relationship. Too many years of having this supremely heavy monkey riding on my back, reeking nothing but thoughts of being abandoned by so many. Her move only threw gas on my already blazing fire of insecurity and doubt. We went from seeing each other practically every night for almost two years, to seeing one another about every two or three weeks; giving me more than enough time to execute some more of my bad behavior. As I drank, I hurt, and as I hurt, I drank more to cope with the loss of my fuckbuddy. Sure . . . It wasn't the most logically sound plan in the world, But shit, I never really claimed to be a smart man, just a man. I needed a way to express my ache, my longing, and my animalistic lust. And one night the master plan came faster than a virgin on prom night.

It was late, probably south of three or four A.M. I made my way back home from a lengthy night of profuse drinking and even more sloppy flirtatious conduct, cussing and spitting at every poor female soul that crossed my broken path. I was intoxicated with horny fuel and blurry to sight, but masturbation sounded appealing. I flipped on the computer, pulled up some nameless porn to fill my sexual void and got to work. Stroke after stroke, my perfectly numb and limp cock felt no pleasure, no fulfillment or even lust, nothing but emptiness and bare calloused hands going up and down to create heat and chafe. So . . . much like the busted fool that I am, I dialed up Scarlett to hear her voice . . .

"Hello." She answered in a sleepy and half-baked tone.

"Hey. What are you doing?" I asked her.

"Sleeping. Why? What are you doing? You sound really drunk."

"I am extremely drunk. And I want to fuck."

"Baby, that sounds so good right now. I want to feel your cock." Scarlett pleasantly responded.

"Well, I have something to tell you . . ."
I could virtually hear her ears perk up like a fucking dog on the other end of the phone. She wasn't sure if I was going to say something sweet or drop a bombshell on her already shaky world.

"What do you need to tell me, Ryan?" She hesitantly asked.

"Well, I did something tonight. Something I'm not proud of, but it happened and I figured I would tell you." I replied without a single moment of thought or care.

". . . And what was that?" She fearfully asked with a crack in her voice.

Awaiting me to expose myself as the dog that I was, I could truly hear in her voice that she was worried. And being as I was still butt naked, this (for whatever reason) made me hard and very turned-on. So I began to stroke my cock . . .

"I fucked another girl tonight." I quickly word vomited to her via phone call.

Beat. Beat. Beat. Beat. Beat. Beat. Beat. Beat . . . My heart was racing as my cock was now throbbing . . . I waited for her reply . . . Beat. Beat. Beat . . .

"Did you hear me? I said I fucked a girl tonight." I said again.

I could hear her tighten up and cringe inside as I silently listened and stroked my man member.

"Are you fucking serious?" Scarlett answered.

And before I could blink, I could hear her starting to copiously cry on the other end of the phone.

"Ryan, why would you do that to me?" She asked in her now balling tone.

For whatever reason, this was exactly the thrill I needed. I pulled the porn back up to the screen and started to work my dick better than ever before as I punished her with every sentence of how I fucked another girl. I kept the details long, extensive and very, very descriptive. Telling her how I fucked her, where I fucked her, what she looked like and how I came. I explained with grave facet the positions, the sounds we made, everything from the feel of her pussy to the taste of her lips, all while she cried and whimpered on the other end. She begged and pleated, attempting her best to not believe this was true, but I could tell by her voice that she believed every last word that spewed from my worthless mouth. And as I made her cry for long over thirty minutes of punishment . . . I fired off a rocket of cum and screamed out into the phone.

"What was that?" She asked.

"Nothing. I was just doing something." I replied.

"Did you really fuck someone?" Scarlett begged with an expression of grief.

"No. I just wanted to fuck with you." I answered with a devilish laugh.

She let out a well-needed sigh of relief and we both talked for a little while longer on the phone before we hung-up and I hit the bed like a sack of rotten potatoes . . .

The most entertaining part of this little sinful prank, well (entertaining to my bent mindset) was that I never even touched another girl that night. And this little endeavor became a hobby of mine. Every once in awhile when I felt lonely and hurt, I would call her up and tell her stories about my indiscretions and depravity to make her cry while I would work my cock over and cum into the phone. And to be honest . . . I'm not really sure to this day if she ever knew I was jacking off on the other end. I guess we'll never know. But what I do know is . . . It was always a weird and strangely enthralling cum. Maybe I am a little FUCKED in the head? Who's to say?

Welcome to the World of Sex and Substances . . .
Don't let this land destroy you.

"Alright, Ryan . . . I think I finally have an answer to your question."

"Oh yeah, Bob. And just what question is that?"

"A little while back in your story, you had asked me if I thought Marilyn having intercourse with another woman behind your back was considered 'legitimate' cheating?"

"Yes! That is right. So now you have an answer. Well, Bob. Let's hear it."

"—In most cases, because of the different level of touch and penetration, intimacy and feeling, I would probably say no . . ."

"Ohhhh. Probably? This sounds like an interesting start."

"Shut up, Ryan. Let me talk please! I have listed to all your fucking bullshit for hours. It's my turn . . . I say probably, because it is not as bad in my book, as a male and female getting together for intercourse . . . However, in your case. I do consider it cheating! And you know what?"

"What's that, Bob?"

"I wish Marilyn did it more to you. I wish all these women cheated on you more! I wish they cheated with men, women, donkeys, fucking clowns, anything and everything, because you are a vile and evil human being!"

"Now we are talking, Bob! Justified cheating because in other words, you think I am an awful person?"

"Not in other words. Those are the fucking words!"

"So because I tell you my stories of immorality and expose to you my perverted mind, you think I deserve bad things to happen to me?"

"Exactly! I just wish all the women you have wronged and fucked over, have all done something behind closed doors to get back at you, because you are a fucking asshole! That's just my two cents."

"Well you know what, Bob . . . You're just an old, bitter dick." Ryan sarcastically answered as he giggles and takes a huge sip of his poisonous Sailor Jerry.

"And you're a fucking infant, Ryan!"

Ryan then lit another smoke as he just held up his middle finger like a goddamn child . . .

CHAPTER TWENTY-NINE:
The death of 'Mr. West.'

"Tell the people that are truly important to you, that you love them every single day. You may not get tomorrow."

"Before I share this dreadful and atrocious tale of losing one of the most unique, caring, downright humorous and honest friends I've known. I think we first must honor the real beauty of Mr. West, for you to truly appreciate and value the person he was. But also to understand the hole that was left in the hearts of all the people that were effected on this unspeakable day, Bob."

"I can appreciate that, Ryan. A moment of silence for the fallen . . ."

....

M̲r. West was an all-around great person. Some might even say, the best and dearest friend any one could ever have. He was fun loving, sincere, cared for his family and his large circle of friends. He had nothing but respect for the exquisiteness in life, he always wanted to make every one around him smile and feel special. Mr. West would stand by any one of his friends, help them out of the toughest situations, and it did not matter the hour of night or the problem at hand. If you called him at five in the A.M. he would come to your rescue. Mr. West never bad-mouthed anyone, always gave you the attention, warmth and affection you deserved. He loved animals, people, life and fun. He had a lot of friends, and he ran with many different groups, showing each and every person he came in contact with the time and respect they needed to feel a connection. He never had an awful thing to say about anyone. He cared, loved, laughed and enjoyed the company of his many friends (even some of the more dubious characters) it didn't matter, Mr. West was genuine and true, and always in great cheer and full of joy.

Mr. West never put the burden of his problems on anyone, always staying strong and smiling. He was the glue that held many people together. I watched him console some of the toughest and hardest men, making them know and feel that he was there for you, and will forever be there for you, myself being one of them. He helped me through many sad nights when I missed Marilyn. Mr. West was a special and extremely rare person. He was charming, an absolute delight to be around, and the most wonderful guy a friend could ever ask for. There was no issue too hard and straining, which you endured in your life, that Mr. West's appealing humor couldn't help you through, and bring a giant smile to your face while doing so. He was the loudest, entirely fun loving, and the most honest guy in the room. Never once did I see him cry. It's not every day you meet a person as world changing as Mr. West.

He understood the real essence of life and love. I never heard one person in my hometown have a bad thing to say about Mr. West. He was one of the most down to earth, breathtaking and loving individuals I've ever had the pleasure to meet. He was never scared to tell the people he loved, that he genuinely loved them, hug them, kiss them, and make sure they knew he was always there. He never wanted or had anything to do with drugs, meaningless violence or crime. He was pure, truthful and content. To sum up Mr. West in one word, he was 'Perfect!' Mr. West was a gentleman, a lover, a friend, an uncle and a downright extraordinary person.

I first met Mr. West when I was around nine or ten years old. He ran with my older brother and their age group of friends. I was a small fry growing up, and Mr. West was much bigger than I at the time. He always loved picking on me and trying to punk me around a bit—not in a harmful of vindictive manner, but sprinkled in a loving and caring manner, just friendly joking around and toughing me up for the real world. He was always playful and wonderful to me as a kid. He would show me attention in a room full of girls their age, and made sure I was having a good time as a young lad. Mr. West was different from all the other friends my brother had. He had a huge heart and selfless ambitions.

I went on to move to Florida, then some other cities after that, and when I finally did move back to my hometown of Burbank, I was around nineteen years old. I lived with a couple roommates, one of which was also very close friends with Mr. West. He came by the house one day, and we saw each other for the first time in many years, and Mr. West could not believe his eyes. I was now a towering six-foot-four and close to two hundred pounds. The first thing Mr. West did was run up to me and give me a strong and endearing hug, a kiss on the cheek and tell me he loved me, and, he meant it. That was the type of person Mr. West was. He wore his heart on his sleeve and always made sure to tell you how much he loved you, even if you saw him yesterday, it didn't matter, you got a hug and some caring and meaningful words of affection. He pulled me off his chest and held me tight by my shoulders, looking me in the eye.

"Holy shit, look at you! You're huge." He yelled in excitement.

"I've grown up a bit." I friendly joked.

"Man, I remember when you were at my waist and I used to punk you around." Mr. West jokingly laughed and replied.

"I remember those days. I'm not so little anymore." I confidently said as we both shared a laugh.

"Wow, so great to see you, brother! I'm so happy to see you're doing well." He genuinely said, then grabbed my body and pulled me in for another hug.

That is just one, of a giant list of meaningful, honest, caring and loving embraces I got the honor to share with Mr. West. He was a real man, never scared to be vulnerable and open with anyone. He never lied, hurt or tried in anyway to deceive you. Mr. West was never fearful of holding his tongue either, if you were acting like an idiot or dumbass, he would tell you right to your face. "Calm down, you're acting stupid. Pull it together." He would never say anything foul behind someone's back. If he had words to exchange, he waited until he saw you in person to inform you of his distaste over some questionable actions. A real gentleman, a charmer, he never disrespected or degraded any woman in any way. One of the best and cleanest souls to ever grace this earth with his uniqueness, love, care, sincerity, heartwarming behavior, smile, laugh and wholesome presence. You don't meet a person like Mr. West everyday. He was an exceptional individual, and extraordinary in every aspect of the word. It didn't matter if he knew you for only a year, or ten, he made you feel like his best friend, important and special. The most perfect human being in the world.

A warm soul
A kind heart
A smart mind
And a lost Angel.

It was six-thirty A.M. on a Monday, when my oldest brother called to tell me about the tragic and horrific news. Mr. West had fallen into some hard times and even harder decisions, he lost control of his thoughts and turned his gun on himself. My body instantly went completely numb, ghostly pale in color and freezing cold to the touch . . .

"No way! Mr. West would never do that." I yelled in shock and fright.

"I'm sorry, man, it's true." My brother replied with emptiness in his voice.

We hung up the phone and I, as well as the many sad and distraught people who knew him were forced to deal with this alarming and dreadful news of losing one of the best people this world has EVER seen, and will EVER see. I can't speak for the many effected people about this story, but I know to a certain extent, we all felt the same barren and hollow feeling in our hearts. The next week of everyone's lives was purely the saddest, most sorrow-ridden week to ever move off the calendar. All of Mr. West's friends and family would meet every day leading up to the funeral, to hug, cry, talk and cherish the many great memories and thoughts we all shared about him. We would all tell our best Mr. West story, crying, laughing, crying more and hugging each other even more. It was an unspeakable and sore-hearted week. We were all left missing a piece of our soul when Mr. West left us. People, who have not talked for years due to some disagreement in the past, found no choice but to call each other and repair those broken friendships, reunite, hug one another and voice their apologies and real concern for each other. There was nothing but love and care being past around my hometown that week. Nothing but wonderful conversations of the greatest and fondest memories we all shared about Mr. West, and expressed more vacant, heartbroken and distressing tears.

Speechless and wondering why, more than three-hundred people from all different groups and walks of life, came together to treasure, express and remember Mr. West for the grand and astonishing things he stood for. To justly understand the authentic and abundant pain that was in the town air is beyond explanation. And to be honest, I don't hold the proper wording skills to express that fact. I can't paint you a picture, tell you a story, or hug you long enough for you to really comprehend the heartache that was being past around that week. We were all left asking why? Sad, angry, upset, abandoned, heartbroken, numb, crying, missing his touch and praying for nothing but rest and peace for one of the most mind blowing and remarkable souls this earth has ever met . . .

Mr. West's funeral was on that following Saturday. And this day of mourning was going to be the hardest, saddest and one of the most unreal days all of these beautiful people affected by this tragedy were ever going to have to face. More than two-hundred-and-fifty people showed up to morn, grieve, cry, hug, talk and love the last memories we all had of Mr. West. There was a million different emotions floating around and bouncing off the walls of that church. Every one was crying, mourning, sweating, talking about the recent loss of this brilliant soul, wishing for an explanation, and screaming to 'God' why? A completely awful and horrifying event, one that nobody in that room was truly prepared for or could have ever been primed for, which also includes me. I am not going to make this about me in any vain or selfish fashion. However, I can't speak for the many sad people in that church. So, all I can do is tell you the best I can, the feelings and thoughts I went through on this dreadful and horrendous day.

I was numb, thoughtless, petrified and overwhelmingly sad as I sat in my church seat. I watched as many of his closest friends and loved ones took the stage to share a few words of the great loss they have suffered and the fondest and finest memories they all have and will forever remember about Mr. West. It was a very breathtaking and eye-opening experience, just a downright unfortunate event, and one that I solely hope never to undertake or endure again in my lifetime. I was choking back my tears and heartache the best I possibly could. I don't like to cry in the company of others, but it was getting harder and harder with every person that took the podium. It was truly the most gut-wrenching and stomach-turning situation I've ever seen. Everybody that went up on that stage and said some of the most profound, pure, loving, caring and meaningful words, all with tears pouring from their eyes and a giant hole in their hearts, was utterly sad and devastatingly grief-stricken.

When the service took its final words and we were all asked to walk outside, I was ready to let it out and cry. All I wanted to do was hug someone close to me, cry on someone's shoulder and express my concern. I got up from my seat, watching as the crying faces passed me, all making their way out the front of the church to head to the viewing. And I really was in complete shock, sorrow-amazement and a great deal of pain. I followed the line of heartbroken people out front, walked through the big, wooden, elegant church doors and looked around outside . . . Nearly three-hundred people, standing out front, all with tears soaking their eyes, holding each other, screaming to the 'Lord', hugging one another and talking about the tragic loss of the beautiful Mr. West . . . That was when I lost it . . .

I retreated to a far corner alone and my eyes starting to explode with tears and pain. I was handed a flyer on the way outside, it had the breakdown for the rest of the day, and a handsome, lovely and amazing picture of Mr. West on the cover. He was holding a new puppy with the most wonderful and loving smile on his face. The most ironic and paradoxical part about that photo in particular, was that the day that picture was taken; I also was at that house. There was a large group of us friends at that time in life, introducing a new puppy to the family of one of our dearest friends. I did not have the strength or sheer inner power to look at the picture for too long. I held it against my chest, pacing back and fourth, chain-smoking, crying and racking my brain for an answer why?

I would take the picture form my chest every couple of minutes and stare at the face of the most significant and important souls this earth ever had the pleasure to see. I could only look at the photo for a second or two, with my eyes waterlogged in tears and my heart empty, I put the picture back to my chest. I continued pacing

355

back and fourth, smoking, missing Mr. West with every fiber of my body and mind. And wishing to myself, that he is in the most wonderful, dazzling and pleasant 'Heavens,' which he truly and ultimately deserves for his genuine love, care and beauty. Nothing but the very best, for the most unbelievable, charming and one-of-a-kind individuals I've ever met. I love you, Mr. West, with all my heart.

I long for you,
I care for you,
I miss you.
Please come back Mr. West.

"With the risk of sounding self-righteous, smug, pompous or conceited, Bob, I must share this thought with you . . . Because, it was very insightful, profound, bountiful and a tremendously moving moment for me at this time in life. I had no choice but to think about my very desperate and hopeless night, when I almost carried out the same tactless act of behavior, and I said to myself. 'This could have been your funeral, you could've made just as many people who care about you feel this same lasting pain and heartache. Crying, and asking why?' I made sure to look around to all the crying faces to grasp the true reality of this heartbreaking situation. People don't realize the importance and impact they can have on the minds, hearts and souls of others. Sometimes in the heat of a frantic and angry moment, we feel we are in control (or so we believe) however—we're as far from control and reason than we could ever possibly be. In just one night, the lives of almost three hundred people were changed forever. Lost, speechless, sad and heartbroken. It was an immediate second of revelation for me, wondering to myself, what the story would have been told if I was found dead in my room, choked to death on my own vomit and piss in my pants. I never wanted to feel that way again, it was sad, leveling, and real. But, enough about me . . ."

This is about the magnificent and exceptional Mr. West. The loss of Mr. West will be one of the most dreadful, nauseating, unpromising, miserable, tear-filled, depressing and speechless times, all of the pour people who were forced to share with each other, had to go through. His death was more than an eye-opener. We all felt just how fragile, soft and fast life can move. And, we also felt just how important it is to be with the people you love as much as you humanly can, tell them how much you love them, care for them and need them. The death of Mr. West brought all of these people affected by this tragedy closer together, and for once in a long time, everybody in that crowd was in complete love and care for thy fellow human. Nothing else mattered, no issues of the past, present or future, were relevant. Just the catastrophic loss of the greatest friend, son, brother, uncle and person, this world ever got to see . . .

"May you find the most beautiful rest, absolute peace, pure love and nothing but entertaining company in Heaven. Mr. West, you will be forever missed, loved, thought about, talked about, and remembered for the best of qualities that you stood for. You are an angel, a wonderful individual, and the brightest person to ever grace this gloomy, dark world. I want to say to you, from the bottom of my heart, I love you and I miss you, buddy. Rest in Peace. I love you, Mr. West."

R.I.P. Mr. West

CHAPTER THIRTY:

September, My Teenage C*****e Dream!

"I can't really say I've lost myself, because after all . . . I was never really found."

I've lived through quite a life. Had some good times, endured some bad, and learned to smile when the rest of the world was crying. Not because I'm heartless. But because I finally understand the beauty and absolute power of the 'moment.' The old saying goes, "Smile and the world smiles with you. Cry, and you cry alone." If ever this were true . . . It would be now in my placement of life . . . I've never really asked for much out of life, or at least I never thought so. I have made mistakes (plenty of fucking mistakes) and like always, I land on my balanced feet. So follow me deeper into the mind of a misplaced youth as I show you that life is a journey, a mystery. A Goddamn rollercoaster for those who look the evildoers in the face and tell them to FUCK OFF!! Before we reach the end of my story where I tell you all about the lessons I've learned, the wisdom I have gained. All the intellect I have collected and cultured. How I have expanded on my insight and became a better person. And then serve you 'My Profound Fucking Ending.' I don't want to leave you with the taste of suicide in your mouth, so I feel the need to share something more uplifting (at least from my pov) to help raise the tone and bring you to the end of this story in a cheerful mood. Or at the very least . . . Try to!

I have grown up on the same street for a big portion of my life. I have lived other places, but this house, this street; this community if you will, has been my home base for many, many years. And as I was in the age of twenty-six and still learning, a beautiful, dazzlingly, fun loving and divine little thing had moved onto my street. I saw her from time-to-time, always admiring from a distance and hoping for an interaction, a connection or a simple introduction. She was a vibrant little woman, full of life and smiles. She walked around the street with her dog and I was always waiting for the right time to introduce myself. Not in a cheap as Charlie kinda way. But in a romantic, sweeping her off her feet style of 'Jerry Maguire' love shit. Say whatever you want, it's how I saw things. So fuck you if you don't like it. Deal with it—
. . . Anyways, the time had never came just yet, and I was always wondering and waiting for my moment to say hi. As weeks turned into months, I drew up very lengthy and descriptive stories of just who and what this girl did. I hardly caught her at the right times. Either I was coming and she was going, or she was arriving and I was leaving. The timing was just never in our favor. Until . . . The glorious moment had finally exposed itself.

I was sitting in the living room of my grandparents' house, babysitting my little nephew and playing trains, or cars, or some other fun game with the little boy. And then I took a look out the screen door and saw her walking her dog down to the end of the street in front of my house. She was looking as cute as ever, with her friend by her side and the dog on a leash. She was short, standing only about five-foot-three, wearing some cut off jean shorts, a tight fitting shirt with her big breasts squeezed inside it and a fitted hat to top it off. Her blonde hair was flowing out the back and her body was nice, taut and chic. She was a beautiful little thing, and I knew this was as good as any moment for me to say hi. I asked my little nephew if he would like to walk to the bridge and say hello to the puppy. Not much to my surprise (being as he was a child) he was more than excited to pet the dog. He answered with a loud 'Yes,' and we made our way out the front door and towards the dog.

My nephew was always a little shy at first, so as we got closer to the puppy, he started to realize that it had people connected to it, which then he started growing a little bit apprehensive. I assured him that he would be fine, but his little worried mind was much too overactive with the idea of talking to strangers that we had to take a detour on to the bridge before we could proceed. We played coy on the bridge for a few minutes as we all looked at each other. I was telling my nephew that we should go pet the puppy, and she was saying that he was safe and we should walk over. After a few minutes of cat and mouse, I finally convinced the little guy to take the plunge and we walked over to say hi. As I slowly began to approach her, I won't lie—I was now starting to sweat with a shy sense of nervousness. When we finally got to her and the puppy, it was now time for me to act and hopefully whip up something charming, funny, or at the very least, entertaining to get me into the mind of this sexy little thing from across the way. A real girl next-door story. Take that America . . .

"Is your dog friendly?" I opened with.

"Yeah. He's great with children." She replied.

I asked my little nephew if he would like to pet the dog, and he was a little reluctant at first, but after I began to pet the puppy to open the door, he saw that it was nothing more than a cute little animal and began to play with the doggie. After I knew the bond was growing between us all, I then decided to turn my attention back to this cute little girl and start my conversation.

"I'm Ryan, by the way. I've seen you around but I don't think we've formally met." I said while holding out my hand for a handshake.

"I'm September." She said as she shook my hand.

"Pleasure to meet you, September." I replied.

"How long have you lived here?" She asked.

"I've lived here off and on most of my life. My grand-parents have owned this house long before I was born so I've been on this street a very long time." I answered.

"That's cool. This is a very quite neighborhood." September retorted.

"Yeah. This is a very nice place to live." I replied. I then made sure my little nephew was doing all right and paid some attention to him and the dog, checking in and doing my 'uncle-like' duties. Then, I regained my composure and continued my conversation with September.

"When did you move in?" I asked . . . Even though I already knew the answer from admiring her from across the street.

"We've been here for about two months and some change." She answered.

"That's cool. Welcome to the neighborhood." I replied with a stupid cliché form of tongue.

"Thank you." September responded.

After a few minutes of the pleasantries coming to an end and my small nephew getting sidetracked with the arrival of my grandparents coming home from their walk down the street, it was time to say goodbye. My nephew took off in a full sprint to greet my grand folks and I was now forced with the awkward bye.

"Well, it was a great pleasure to meet you, September." I said.

"You also, Ryan." She replied.

"We should hang out sometime. If you're interested, that is?" I retorted.

"Sure. Take down my number." September said. I pulled out my phone and jotted down her number and ended my conversation with a silly joke "We should party sometime." Not the best of my conversational endings, but hey, at least I tried. With a friendly handshake and the words goodbye spoken, we walked away and went our different ways for the day . . .

Try to ignore
All the blood on the floor.
For I have never been right
But I can't resist a fight.
Lost in my numb mind
I have no more time to find.

"I can see by your face Bob, that you are not sure of the understanding to this sequence of events?"

"At this point Ryan, I am merely just a helpless victim along for your wild ride."

"Not a victim, but more an onlooker. Enjoy the ride. I hope it's unlike anything you've ever been through before."

"Once again . . . My name isn't, Bob! —"

"—Shut up, Bob. Listen close, for this moment will never happen again."

Armed with nothing but her phone number, it was now time for me to make my way and express my attraction. I didn't wait the allotted three days to make my approach, nor did I even wait a day. I don't follow the so-called 'Bro Code,' or 'Players Handbook,' or any other fucking guy rules when it comes to charming a woman of interest. I make my attack. Sorry . . . My connection, when I want, how I want, and I say fuck the rules right in the fucking face. Because after all, fate is for the goddamn lazy! And lazy is not what I am. I didn't even wait but an hour until I sent September a message to ensure she knew I was into her. SHIT! I was into everything about her. The beautiful lips that were so perfectly placed on her face, the sexy smooth legs that rested beneath her tight cut off jean shorts. The huge set of boobs that were pressed tight against the white shirt she wore with confidence and ease. Her soft voice, her shiny hair, her tiny frame and her wonderful smile, so, why waste time? I found my new poison, and her name was September . . .

She took a few hours to reply to my message, which did stir up a bit of anxiety in my little, tainted and constantly intoxicated heart. But I knew she would reply—Well, I wanted her to. I've never been that overly confident in my progress with a woman. I more live on hope and expect my charm (or profane placement of perfectly produced words) to do the job when all else fails. I'm a dreamer, and she was now my dream. So it was time to make dreams come true . . . And after a few staggering hours of anxious and eager worry, my phone finally chirped out with her reply. We began a long and drawn out conversation of all the 'get-to-know-you' kinda stuff, and it wasn't long until we knew quite much about each other. We slowly started our relationship with cigarette breaks on the community bridge, to talk and walk, which turned into personal hangouts and backyard chats. And not long after a few weeks, she told me that she was only at the lovely age of eighteen . . . We had an eight-year age gap, however, it didn't really seem to be that big of a deal. She was pretty familiar with some of the same stuff I was into, and to be completely honest, she didn't act eighteen. I was under the impression she was at least twenty-two. But who am I to judge? I didn't mind the age gap, and she didn't seem to care too much about it either, so down the fuzzy road of lust we drove.

"Now, Bob. I'm not going to go on and on with the many, and I mean fucking many, stories about our perverted and twisted nights of drunken sex and fantasy to stimulate your brain, raise your cock and possibly be the reason you die of a heart attack."

"—Thank god. —"

"—Don't interrupt me, Bob. But, I do have a funny story to tell you, because after all, we're friends now and I feel like I can trust you with my inner most deviant actions."

"What can I say, Ryan . . . Please do share."

"Alright, but only because you said please." Ryan replied while giggling.

September and I had both celebrated a birthday, and I was now standing at the age of twenty-seven, and she was elegantly bound to the age of nineteen. We have had more sex than Metallica on the road, and fulfilled more fantasies than a Disney dream cruise. We were more than involved in one of the most daily changing relationships I've ever been a part of, and the fights only led us to have some of the wildest makeup fucks this side of the Mississippi. After all was said and done, objects broken and bodies completely used in sexual conquest from both sides. It was a new high we decided to embark on, and embark we fucking did . . . what is it that I'm talking about, you ask? The dust of the devil . . . The ole' 70's dream . . . The actresses' confidence . . . The hookers' coffee . . . The salesmen's substance . . . The bullshitters powder . . . The whisper's voice . . . Yes. I think you know what I'm talking about . . . COCAINE! . . .

"Now, now, Bob! I know what you're thinking? THIS FUCKING GUY!! After all his overly opinionated rants and self-righteous chants of how disgusting and distasteful coke is, here this motherfucker is doing it, and with a teenager nonetheless! WHAT . . . A . . . GODDAMN HYPOCRITE! And you know what, you're right . . . I don't ever apologize, and this is not where I'm going to start. So if you don't like it, too bad, it's my story!"

"That is precisely what I was thinking! You're a real piece of work, you know that, Ryan?"

"Yes, I am fucking aware, BOB!"

At the age of twenty-seven, I decided to make my first shady cocaine deal and search it out with the intent to destroy. I purchased some from a friend of mine and had a grand plan drawn up with September to lock ourselves in my room with a huge bottle of vodka, a few grams of cocaine, two packs of cigarettes and our magnificently corrupted imaginations to be the guide for pleasurable entertainment and intense animation. Let the MOTHER FUCKIN' RIDE BEGIN!!!!

Cue the music.
Crazy in Love (Beyonce' cover)
Sung by Sofia Karlberg.

I had recently remodeled the garage in which I once attempted to kill myself in with the assistance of alcohol and narcotics, and not to toot my own horn . . . but toot fucking toot! I made one helluva a pad for myself to currently reside in. And this was now going to be the backdrop for a night of cocaine and alcohol abuse in a positive manner. Which does seem a little contradicting, I understand that. But nevertheless, it was going to be a positive night indeed. We showed up, both ready and more than excited, cut up the coke into about twenty proper lines of ecstasy and exhilaration, and it was time to start . . . We both made a wicked strong cocktail, had one final smoke before the event was to produce itself, and said our goodbyes to a good night sleep!

. . . . SNIIIIIIFFFFFFFFFFFFFF . . . .

And just like that, the cocaine tickle in the back of my throat was now finding its way down and my eyes widened in peace and love as I was now riding the wave of extreme momentary high. My jaw clenched, my words started to pour and my need for a cigarette was beyond measure. Welcome to the world of Cocaine. Don't let this land destroy you . . .

One line, two line, three line, four. I was now full-fledged cokedout of my fucking gourd. As September would make her way to the glass table for more, I was quickly behind. With every line snorted, removed another article of clothing until we were no longer dressed and stood before one another, fully naked, fucked out of our minds and drinking for the Gods above. This high was incredible, unexplainable, unimaginable, and just downright fucking good! We talked and talked as we walked around naked and pounded alcohol like it was water. Back and fourth we paced, line after line we snorted, drink after drink we slammed, and smoke after smoke we enjoyed. It was pretty damn wild to say the least, and this was just about half into the stash . . .

Being that I was severely inexperienced in the art of cocaine combat, I wasn't exactly certain in just how the quality of this product was, nor the intensity of it's high. I asked September of just how the newly purchased product was or how it stacked up to her times before, and she was more than pleased with the exhilarating high. This sack of coke was good, great—actually, it was fucking amazing! I felt the kick of it beginning to hit me harder and harder as the hours went on, and we were both now ready to really get down and dirty. A thought of mine (or should I more precisely say a fantasy) was to have cocaine snorted off my cock. I'm not sure why, or how this whimsy even became relevant in my head, I just know it was always lingering somewhere inside my multifaceted and twisted imagination.

September was young and full of life, and more importantly, she shared the same perverse sense of fun that was so ramped through my mind. So needless to say, she was ready and willing with every part of her beautiful and sinful soul. I walked over to the glass table, hard cock out and swinging, and loaded up a thick line of 'The White China' down my cock and brought it to her. Without even a second of hesitation, she ripped the line clear off my dick and we both let out a chatter of sheer amusement. A true warrior's yell! Things were really starting to heat up . . .

As more time passed and the fade of each line would drop, we longed for more cocaine, more excitement, and more fucking pleasure. And then just as quickly as our wonderfully wicked minds could draw up, we both came up with another amazing idea. Why don't I snort some lines off her body? Of course! FUCKING BRILLIANT! Where to start, where to start? My first thought was of course her tits. Being that she had plump, sexy and succulent tits, it was a given. So, I grabbed a line and laid it out on her chesty upstairs and threw my head in there like the last scene from 'Scarface.' And with an intense up-snort of 'Yayo,' I felt the sensation roar to my skull as my face went numb and my thoughts went bleak . . . FUUUUCCCCKKKK!!! I think I was falling in love with Cocaine . . .

"Hahaha . . . Sorry, Bob. I had to laugh at that one."

"I shake my head in your pure hypocritical way of life."

"Oh fuck off . . . Like you've never been guilty of the same thing."

After a harsh rip of coke off her tits, I was now searching for another body part to better entertain my perverted mind, and what better place than her young, tight, hairless and tasty pussy. I took out some more 'Colombian Marching Powder' and strung a plentiful line across her pubic area just above her lovely pussy and dove in there headfirst like I was rescuing her cherry pop from a shark attack. I snorted that line up with such force that it was thrown to the back of my throat and I was utterly fucked beyond belief.

"GODDAMN!" I yelled out.

"Do you like doing coke off my pussy, Daddy?" September asked me.

"It's fucking amazing, love." I replied.

"You should do a line off my ass now." She suggested. Why not? I was already three sheets to the wind, might as well keep this train wreck rolling. I rolled her over to her stomach, lined up a nice thick row of booger sugar on each one of her ass cheeks and was as ready as I could be. I grabbed the rolled up two-dollar bill—

"—Wait, wait. Hold up a second, Ryan. A two-dollar bill?"

"Yeah, Bob." Ryan answers with mocking recoil.

"You know I must ask, why a two-dollar bill?"

"I snort my coke with a two-dollar bill, Bob. Because after all, I'm not a fucking MONSTER!"

"I still see no sense in it."

"Can I please finish my story, Bob?" Ryan asked while throwing his hands up in sardonic deem.

"Please, continue."

"Like . . . I . . . Said . . ."

I grabbed the rolled up Two-Dollar Bill and started with a quick snort off just one cheek, letting it settle down my throat and exacerbate my high and keep me coming back for more. And before I let the full affect kick in, I jumped right into her other cheek and cleaned up the other line before I made off to the fridge to make some more cocktails and keep the cigarettes burning. This was a complete cocaine cocktail competition . . .

We were both blown out of our minds, comfortably drunk, peacefully perverted and it was about time for some good ole' fashioned pleasure. I laid September down on her back and softly started to kiss the inside of her legs as I made my way from her ankles to her pussy and back down to her ankles. I was licking, kissing, tasting and slobbering all over her legs to make her gyrate in concentrated bliss. Then when she was dripping wet, I moved my mouth over her tight pussy and began to taste every last drop of her young nectar. I slid my tongue inside her open hole to make sure she could feel the pushing force of my horny mouth as she screamed in downright disbelief. The body's sensation on cocaine is amplified, much like that of Ecstasy or any other drug for that matter, so as we gave each other pleasure and touch, our bodies were fucking melting with absolute felicity. I made sure to stay in between her legs until I felt the surge of her juices flow into my wide-open and accepting mouth as she shouted out loud with the most intense orgasm I've ever heard. It was fucking beautiful.

"Because you are a twisted old man. Here are some more gold-polished turds that I know you're going to enjoy about this story, Bob."

"Something tells me that I'm not going to, Ryan. Because to be completely honest, I haven't enjoyed any of this since I first met you in the park."

"Oh behave, Bob. I bring light into your miserable life, Old timer."

"Go on with it already, Ryan."

"Have you ever heard of Boofing?"

"I can't say that I have, Ryan."

"Well, allow me to explain . . ."

After September let loose a flowing gush of orgasmic bliss into my mouth from my cocaine-powered oral, it was time to step it up a bit and try something that I have always wanted to try.

"—Let me guess, Ryan . . . Boofing?"

"You are fucking correct, Bob! Boofing!"

September was very grateful for my attention to her beautifully unique downstairs, which made her eager to return the favor . . . However, I was in the mood for something just a little different.

"Do you want me to blow you, Daddy?" September asked me.

"Not yet, baby. I want to try something else." I replied.

"Anything for my Daddy." She seductively responded. I then grabbed the rolled up two-dollar bill and loaded the end of it, just at the very tip, with a good amount of cocaine. I handed the two-dollar bill over to September.

"I am going to get down on my hands and knees, and then I want you to stick the end of that in my ass and blow the coke in my asshole, love." I told September.

"What?" She answered with a puzzled surprise.

"I want you to blow the coke up my ass so I can see how it feels." I shot back.

She couldn't help but to laugh, which in turn made me giggle out.

"I am serious, baby. I want to see how it hits and how it feels."

"You got it, Daddy. Get down on the floor." September replied.

I then got down on my hands and knees, cock and balls out and ass pointed up into the air and spread my cheeks open to fulfill a fantasy of complete perverted amusement. I could feel September come in close as the breathing from both of us began to rise and she took a hold of my ass cheeks and slid the two-dollar bill into my asshole. It was slightly warm at first, and edgy, but I was in anticipated thrill awaiting the effects . . .

"Are you ready, Daddy?" September asked.

"Let it rip, skip." I replied.

I felt her slowly move into the other end of the two-dollar bill and the heat from her face was closing in on my ass. She put her lips to the other end of the two-dollar bill . . . And with a swift and heavy blow . . . She blew the coke deep into my ass and it hit me harder than a rhino fucking a hamster. It was searing hot, intensely strong and fucking exhilarating. I felt the rush go to my insides and the high was incredible. It is a significantly different flash from when you take it the old school method of snorting it. It is blown straight into your bloodstream so it hits faster, harder and much more in its purity. It is most certainly fun, and pretty ego changing when you really do think of the vulnerability of the act—but very fucking fun! It was flowing around inside my asshole and burning like a son-of-a-bitch and getting me higher than I ever knew possible.

"How did that feel, Daddy?" September asked.

"That was fucking amazing!" I replied.

I then got back up and shook my ass clean of any residue and we made another drink and joked about the Boofing experience . . .

"I am not one for too much ass play, Bob . . . But I really did enjoy this the first time I ever did it."

"You are by far the sickest individual I have ever met, Ryan."

"Ha! That was the kicker, huh." Ryan just laughed as he got up and made himself another Sailor Jerry cocktail.

. . . May The Rock Gods Above Bless This Cocaine . . .

Somewhere south of three or four in the morning, and about five lines left to snort, September and I have done everything we could come up with . . . Well, that was until I had another thought. I had bought a set of handcuffs for our many nights of sexual tryst, and what better time for some arousing restraint than when both of us were higher then Benjamin Franklin's kite in a lighting storm. I went to my closet and pulled out the set and propositioned an idea to handcuff her to the ceiling joists running across my room. She was not only eager, but also turned on more than a pornstar on her first shoot. I threw her sexy ass on the bed and ordered her to stand and put her hands above her head. The sheer dominant veracity in my voice made her dripping wet. She did just as she was told and I handcuffed her so she was locked in around the ceiling joist. Butt naked, young, wet, cokedup and drunk, this was one of the closest times I've ever felt like a true ruler than ever before.

I walked over to the computer and put on Marilyn Manson's "Dope Show" and then made my way back to the bed to watch my little chained up slave perform a show for Daddy that would change the world (at least my world) and got ready for some more perverted fun. I had fashioned a paddle out of an old piece of wood that I had lying around, and sanded it down smooth, painted it and threw a strap on it for better support and control—and that was now my weapon of choice to get September to do just as I wanted, desired, and pleased.

I told her to begin dancing for me as I stood with my paddle in hand and ready to punish her if she did not do as I said. She started slow, moving her tight ass in my face and making me beg to kiss her cheeks. Cock harder than a fucking rock I was standing in pure joy as she moved with such grace and beauty. I wanted to make sure she knew I was in charge, so I gave her a lineup of five very hard and firm SLAPS to her little ass so her numb and coke-intoxicated body knew it was mine and mine only!

"Ouch, Daddy." September shouted out.

"You're my little bitch, right?" I asked her.

"Of course, Daddy. I'll do whatever you want." She so properly responded.

"Good. I want you to tease me with your pussy." I told her.

She then started to dance back and fourth, walking towards my face and waving her tight cunt in front of my mouth so I could come just to the edge of licking it, and then quickly backing away before my tongue could make contact. Which was making my throbbing cock even more ready for eruption. I laughed with sharp pleasure as this diabolical dance of discipline was the most profound thing ever witnessed since the birth of Christ and more intense then the biblical words written in verses of the holy book. Watching her naked ass dance in such a restrained way was overpowering to my every good thought, and I just wanted to ravage her every body part.

I jumped on the bed, with paddle in hand and ready to rule my little slave however I pleased. I slapped her ass with a firm smack and grabbed on her big tits while she danced in my arms and made me want to do nothing but fuck her senselessly. I wanted to savagely fuck her like a beast, feel the inside depths of her soul and completely own her every action. SMACK, SLAP, WAP, CRACK, SLAM AND SPANK. I abused her ass with my paddle of control and owned her for this very godly time of innocent, intoxicated, and full on coke-fueled domination. I reached down to the glass table and recklessly grabbed the last huge handful of the 'Heavenly Zip Powder' and rubbed it on both of our faces with slapdash behavior and pure intense thrill as we snorted up the last of it and polished our bodies together with the intent to fuck! And fuck we did . . . For hours and hours . . .

Riddle me with desire and sin
I get with angels and I always win.
Lost in wonderland and looking for time to find
I'm scared to know I'm always on your mind.

"Before I get to the end and grace you with the pleasure of hearing 'My Profound Fucking Ending,' first we must see what will be the end to 'The Story of Kat and Drake.' I'm sure you're oddly curious to hear how it all unravels or connects?"

"Oddly enough, and I can't believe I'm even saying it, I am a slight bit curious of how you're little story inside a story comes to its final breath."

"Well then you are in luck, my good sir. Allow me to entertain you for just a little while longer."

"I am not sure if 'entertain' is really the right word I would use to describe this tale of disgust and devastation I've just subjected myself to listening to, but sure, why not? Hit me with the end, Ryan, let's hear their ending."

"I like you, Bob. I might even go as far as to say love. You always tell the truth in a world where only three things tell the truth."

"—Great. I'll bite. Now I have to fucking ask. And just what are these three things?"

"Children, drunk people, and yoga pants."

"Haha. Good one. Well . . . Let's hear the ending for Kat and Drake."

"Easy, Tiger, we're getting there. Take a chill pill. What's wrong Bob did your Viagra just kick in or something, what's the rush?"

"Just tell me the Goddamn ending, please?"

"As you wish, Mister Vulgar."

"Before you do finish, Ryan. I think I am ready to hear if you have an answer for my question that I asked you back when you described the saga of Venus?"

"Do I think 'God' will ever forgive me for what I have done? That question? Was it the cocaine being blown into my asshole that begs for the question of forgiveness?" Ryan asked while smirking and devilishly laughing.

"Actually . . . It is a sinful combination of all your toxically twisted tales that I believe begs the question of holy forgiveness."

"In a simple answer . . . No. No I don't believe 'God' will ever forgive me for what I have done."

"And you are okay with that?" I asked Ryan in anticipating doubt.

"Yes, I am. Because, like I said many times before, I do not believe that 'God' or the 'Devil' are real. The biggest lie we are force-fed growing up, is that no matter what we do in life, we will never be enough for the stand-ards of holiness. We will never be able to live up to the terms and conditions of 'God' and the righteous life. And to think that we are given such powerful brains and the ability to think, formulate and act on some of our most darkest desires, to only die and find out that our whole existence has been drawn out for us from the moment of birth, is just a crook of fucking bullshit. If that's the case, why even get out of bed everyday. Why strive to be great, or why even try anything for that matter. If all we are is a puppet on strings, then really we have no reason to think, talk, act, move or challenge anything in this world. Just sit back and let whatever happens, happen. The church tells you that we are just characters in 'Gods' play . . . If that's the case, then he must be fucked in the head to have come up with me."

"That is a valid point, Ryan. So what about for-giveness?"

"I forgive myself for all the wrong and hurt I have caused. And that is good enough for me. You want the truth, Bob. Here is the downright truth. Trinity, Marilyn, Venus, Scarlett and September. I loved them all in so many different and intriguing ways. They all brought something very unique and special into my dark-lit life and to be honest—I was always too fucking blind and drunkenly dumb to see that they loved me back. So If I regret anything . . . It's that I didn't tell each and every one of them, that I loved them when I had the chance. So fuck off, Bob! Can I finish my Goddamn story?"

"Sorry. The floor is all yours."

The Story of Kat and Drake: Part Four.

They now have seen the light of day

Tasted the glory and expressed as they may

Nothing was missing but a factor of time

Longing to be with each other as they stood in the line

They managed to run and escape the bad dream

Becoming one in the same famous bloodstream

Kat always knew that Drake was her melody

She would've done anything to erase his felony

In front of the world they had no more battle

We all listened and heard the loud rattle

Guns were drawn and shots were fired

Their blood pumped as their hearts were wired

She kissed him goodbye before they entered the grave

Eye to eye they finally forgave

Together they held their shared lucky charms

As the bullets ripped through, they both died in their arms.

The End...

"All I need is a sheet of paper and something to write with, and then I can turn the world upside down."

— Friedrich Nietzsche

CHAPTER THRITY-ONE:
"My Profound Fucking Ending."

"Love the most you can. Without love, ultimately—we have nothing at all."

W elcome, ladies and gentlemen, boys and girls. This is to the Fetish Freaks and 'Family Guy' geeks. To my Saints and Sinners. The beautiful women locked in sexual restraints and my little blonde spinners. This is to all my deliciously deviant Diva's and lavishly lusty ladies. To the prolifically proud and the desperately endowed. Spoken to the lost lairs who can survive the fires, and to my charming lover whom will always recover. As we turn the page, ride the wave, bath in sage and wildly rave, we have finally seen the end. Social media has taken over our youth, reality television is the reason for our generational ignorance, and yet every <u>FUCKING</u> person thinks they know <u>EVERYTHING!</u> We live in a world where it's more important to look beautiful than it is to possess intelligence. The plague of 'Kim K and Honey Boo-Boo' has swept our poor nation and destroyed us from the inside out.

Douchiness has become a way of life and tolerated, amplified by grocery bags full of dicks like the Jersey shore cunts and D-bags. We're comfortably lost in this abyss of persuading pretentious personas telling us what's considered 'cool,' and why they're better than us feeble others. We've allowed ourselves to be blinded by the stupid 'false idols' we have given such power to, and meanwhile, children starve and hopeless people who can't catch a break suffer and die. The world has lost its fucking mind. Bill Cosby is a rapist. Jared Fogle is a God-damn pedophile. Chris Brown is a woman beater, and my boy, Charlie Sheen, caught the Goddamn dreaded HIV, and we as a people line up to air out the dirty laundry of all these 'celebrity types' to escape our mindless reali-ties.

We consume ourselves with these deadly scandals of Tiger woods and Jesse James cheating, or Kanye West announcing he will run for president to distract us from our mundane and unsatisfying lives. We abundantly feed and thirst for the bad news and even worse behavior of these celebrities to help ease our angst and fear, causing us to act in such a manner to intensify our own shitty behavior. Schools, movie theaters and malls are being shot up as we watch innocent people die before our own eyes, and yet all we can talk about is which house one of these overpaid and talentless 'so-called reality celebri-ties' has built, or what's the latest car on the market is that 'Shitstick Bieber' is driving. It really is FUCKING PATHETIC! Let's put down our phones, logoff of Insta-gram, Facebook, Snapcaht and Tinder. It's time for us to reconnect as a people, in person, the way life was in-tended. I guess this is it . . . This is the moment we've all been waiting for . . . "My Profound Fucking Ending!"

This is where I go on a violent and daring rampage, slamming, bashing and slathering the entire social sys-tem, which has caused me such anger and hatefulness. This is where I find clever ways to project my current state of distaste and even more disturbed thoughts of all these overly prideful wannabes who have encouraged our youth with their own twisted set of values, and have manifested an entire nation of IPhone zombies, floating from one selfie to the next in the hopes of showing off how dazzlingly and great their 'Internet Life's' are, all while slowly dying inside with every post or swipe. But I'm not going to do that . . . Not because I hold myself accountable for my words and need I say it (MY HATE) towards the colossal collapse of human interaction thanks to the invention of social media and the vicious uprising of cell phones and useless Twitter conversations.

Or how the game of going out and getting laid, which I have enjoyed playing for so many years, is now reduced to sitting around in your living room, eating Cheetos in your pajamas with reruns of 'Friends' playing in the background as we swipe left or right to determine if we are a compatible match for genital intercourse. Tinder has gotten so out-of-hand, that when someone actually does approach you in public to tell you that they find you attractive, you are almost blown off your feet and instantly become anxious and uptight, asking yourself "What's wrong with them? Who just talks to a stranger? Gross . . ." We are a nation of people so excessively consumed with worrying about what the thousands of 'so-called acquaintances' on our Facebook page think about us, that we've lost sight of bothering ourselves with the thoughts of our own close friends and family.

We sit at dinner tables in large groups, with every single person glued to their phones and updates. Interesting conversation with another human being has been devoured and spit out, and replaced by checking the statuses of others and the unholy 'like' button. We speak in Hastags and abbreviations because we've become so unbelievably lazy that we can't even be bothered with the simple task of putting together an eloquent and expressive sentence to explain our train of thought or way of feeling. But honestly, enough about you . . . Let's get back to me . . .

You're Goddamn right this is
"My Profound Fucking Ending!"
Let's Make It Count!

"As the birds sing, five in the morning with a shimmer in his eye, this is where I found hope, this is where I found peace, this is where I finally found what I was looking for . . . A person to believe in when I was left with nothing to ever believe in again. Not a saint, nor a sinner. Not a loser, or a winner, but finally, a fucking real person . . ."

— Bob.

I can't exactly pinpoint the precise moment I started running from myself? Or even the initial reason why? I just know I have been running so damn long that I forgot what it was that I was running from. Was it the person I was, or perhaps the person I was becoming? Or maybe even the person I wanted to be? But then that wouldn't make any Godforsaken sense. So honestly, I can't even tell you the reason why I started to run in the first place. But on the run I have been, and finally, I am tired. I'm exhausted, I'm sick, I'm piss poor, with no fucks to give and even less of a fuck to gain. I'm giving up, I'm throwing in the towel, and at long last, I'm calling it a fucking day!

I'm addicted! I know that now. I have discovered that about myself. I have accepted that, and I am enlightened! I will say it again . . . I . . . AM . . . ADDICTED! But I am not addicted to the alcohol, the drugs, the women, or the staying up late and making a slew of bad decisions. It's not the Ecstasy, the Cocaine, the Painkillers, the Marijuana or the Rum cocktails. It's never been about the money, the cars, the houses and the bitches. It's not the Los Angeles facade I never wanted, nor the pompous arrogant character I wished to achieve. You know what I'm addicted to? IT'S THE FUCKING FIGHT! I love the Goddamn fight!

I love it so much, that the fight is all I ever wanted. The fight to be stronger, faster, smarter and better then I was yesterday. The fight to beat any horrific drug comedown, or to experience any mind-blowing drug high. I am addicted to the fight of a vast challenge. Any challenge, I just want to be in the **FIGHT!** I would watch everything I worked so hard to gain burn up in illustrious flames in order to be involved in the almighty fight. SHIT! Who am I kidding? — I would even light the match! And after all this fighting, fucking, writing and titty sucking . . . I had an episode where the fight came to a crashing end . . . And that was when I eventually felt my addiction in the fullest possible way.

Shattered and beaten,
He never let the world see him cry.

At twenty-six, I gave up a year of my life to watch my grandfather battle a hard case of cancer and help tend to him with my loving grandma. It was a battle he unfortunately didn't win, he passed away at eighty-three. And it was more than an eye-opening human dealing to say the least. At twenty-eight, I found out that my first girlfriend, Trinity, had suffered kidney failure after her diabetes had began to spiral out-of-control and she was forced to have a kidney transplant. Unfortunately, that was a fight in which she did not win and passed away at twenty-five. I guess sometimes the fight can be more than we are able to handle. May they both rest in absolute peace . . .

But yet, day-to-day, we tell ourselves the same lies . . . This will never be me, this will never happen to me. I will never feel like that. I will never fall like that. Nothing can stop me. I said, I preach, I fucking scream . . . NOTHING CAN STOP ME! And we believe this bullshit as it so confidently falls from our delicate tongues. Yes, we really do believe it. Not only believe, but practice, and actually, almost feel convicted certainty in these thoughts, these beliefs, these over zealous sincerities. And hey, I am probably the guiltiest of them all . . . I created this way of thinking; therefore, I must follow this way of life, be this way of life, and advocate this fucking way of FUCKING life. Yes, the profanity was necessary.

Why? Well . . . Because before you know it, after all the indestructible thoughts we live on in a daily manner, all come to a head when you are no longer as strong as you once thought, and you are looking to meet your maker. Or taker, what ever it is you decide to hold faith in?

When the day comes, it's strange just how quickly you learn your most desired, passionate and enviable addiction . . . Just two months into being twenty-eight years old, I, once and for all (with every stress of the term) got the MOTHER-FUCKING karma that was due to come my way! With forty-eight hours till the grave, I now understood what it was to fight. I learned what it was to hurt, to undergo some of the most immense pain conceivable. And for once, now I was the weak one . . .

48 HOURS TO THE GRAVE . . .

Written By

Ryan Vinci

As the countless beers flowed down my throat on a beautiful and sunny day on the beach of Huntington, California, no thought was ever imagined that life as I knew it could ever be broken, shaken or altered—For I was an animal, a beast, something out of a comic book. I've built my body on extreme hard work, hour after long hour securing my existence as a warrior, a fighter, nothing short of a modern day solider of the streets. Almost to say that I even felt indestructible from all my intense work on this bulletproof body that I've taken the utmost diligent time to create—For I was never going to be stopped. Or at least I so foolishly thought!

Sunday morning came from a long weekend drinking in the bright sun of the charming beach, and what better way to top off a weekend of substance abuse then with a brunch filled with alcohol and good vibes. And just as easy as the Bloody Marys and Screwdrivers were tossed back, the sun became the moon and night had fallen. With a few stops on some Main Street bars to better fuel my already intoxicating buzz, it was finally time to call it an end and head back to my true reality as a dirty construction worker quietly struggling to make a name as a writer. Or maybe just get a little recognition as a great creative mind to help ease the pain of this stinging sensation of wasted time and burning failure.

As I was dropped off back at home, back to my almost depressing life of hard labor and drunken times, I was anything but worried that life would ever be changed. I smoked one last cigarette and drank one more beer before calling it a night and passing out without a momentary care. 3:45 A.M. hit the clock and I was suddenly awaken by the ferocious force to vomit. I ran to the bathroom in a frantic hurry, barely making the toilet bowl as spew was violently thrown from my throat. "Maybe just a side effect of the alcohol consumed earlier in the day?" Was my rational thought, nothing more, nothing less... I lazily made the trip to my bed and went back to rest without a single care... Then... The day came, and what followed this ease into Monday morning was nothing short of a fucking horror film.

When I finally woke to the sound of my screaming alarm clock at 7:00 A.M. I was incredibly lost, dizzy, my body was unbelievably heavy, it felt weighted down by an army tank. My head was throbbing, I was saturated in sweat and hurting in every humanly way. The agonizing pain in my stomach was bringing me to my knees. I wasn't sure if it was food poising, stomach flu, or just a bad concoction of alcohol and cigarettes. I just knew whatever it was, was fucking horrific. My asshole began to swelter and I was blowing my insides out into the toilet bowl minute after minute. Plagued with fire burning diarrhea, my body was officially in some kind of flu-like shock.

Hot and cold, sweating and shaking, I was starting to become more and more uncomfortable with my current situation. Thinking that maybe some water would help to cleanse my gut, I forcefully drank bottle after bottle in the hopes of flushing my system and praying to get back to normal. However, the water had only the opposite effect and my body rejected the thoughtful endearment to help and shot the water back out threw my top hole and I started to puke red and black. Painful and unwanted, my body was rejecting any attempt to help ease the ache of vomit and searing hot shit... And this was only day one...

As the second day rolled around, the flu feeling had turned more into a death feeling. Or at least I was wishing for death. I couldn't lay on my left side due to some kinda sever pain in my jugular, and my fierce diarrhea and stomach wrenching vomit sessions had become much more violent and uncontrolled. I had shit leaking from my poop pipe and I was dry heaving in gut throbbing pain. The dry heaves felt as if my insides were being rearranged and my stomach was literally going to come flying out from my sore throat. As my ass now become an enemy not to be trusted, I was in sheer disbelief that this type of pain and suffering could be even remotely real. This had to be death, this had to be fate; this was purely karma coming to snatch what little life was left in me for all the wrong doings I've done. Welcome the darkness, for the light of day and the hope of life has now become an illusion.

As pride and self-righteous belief forcefully overtook any sense of reality about being sick, weak, helpless or plagued. I allowed myself to suffer and stagger through this pain, this misery, this disgusting position of life. I had some unreasonable idea, design, fucking idiotic creation that my body would naturally beat this agonizing assault on my wellbeing — that I literally had the power to (will) this sickness out of me through strong thinking and natural remedy. And that was when the seizures started...

About ten times a day my body would lockup in uncontrollable, excruciating, un-fucking-imaginable pain, and I would shake, jolt and shiver in some of the most intense pain I could never even formulate in my best of writing days. My body was locked, and my spine was sharp and set in place as the rest of my motor skills were stripped away and muscles would give up on any hope of control, and for the next thirty minutes I would lay in bed and seizure with nothing but death in mind...

Day two fell off the calendar, day three and four came and went with no food, no water, no sleep and more vomit and shit than I think my toilet could handle. I was now starting to really believe I was dying. This was nothing out of a Wikipedia description of the stomach flu, food poisoning, or some bug ever caught. I could not pinpoint my symptoms, and I was seriously longing for some medical attention. By day four, it was clear my warrior body had no chance of beating this venom that has properly fucked my body from the inside out. It was time to throw in the towel and admit defeat. I decided on the waking of day five that it was time to sack up and call it a game...

My girlfriend, September, had seen all she could witness and was no longer going to let my pride stop me from staying alive. She helped my weary and puny body into the car and we headed off to the hospital to hopefully discover a proper answer. On the short mile and half drive from my house to the ER, the intense sensation of being passenger in a moving vehicle was anything but normal. As we made it only two or three blocks from my house, my vision went completely white and I was thrown into some kind of dazed-&-confused-like state. One much more bloodcurdling then any bad high of drugs has ever shown me. This shit was real, and boy, oh boy, did I not enjoy this altered consciousness...

I could no longer see anything inches in front of me, my hearing was beginning to buzz and I was sweating in fear. It was a bit more overwhelmingly menacing than I think I was ready for. When we got to the entrance of the ER, September helped me out of the car and sat me down on a bench out front so she could go park the whip. My vision was still blazingly white and I, for a brief moment, think I slightly (as much as possible) understand what type of experience it would be for a blind person in this wild and crazy world. I could hear the voices of people around, and feel the vibrations of humanity, but I couldn't see a fucking thing. I was literally functioning off only four senses. Talk about a reality check... I don't think I want to cover this bill...

When September arrived back from parking, we went through the whole rigmarole of getting checked in at the ER, awaiting our service and struggling to stay focused. As I was admitted, they took a look over me, ran a few tests as I described the amount of pain I was suffering from, and all the lovely symptoms that were bringing me to my knees. Then, the next thing I knew an IV was put in my arm and in a hospital room I sat and waited. They pumped bag after bag of fluids hoping to get my extreme level of dehydration back up, and after bag number seven, they asked if 'I was feeling the urge to urinate?'

"No. Not at all I answered."
And I think that was when they knew something was much worse than they first predicated...

After the results came back from the many tests they ran, I was informed that my kidneys had failed due to some kind of cruel virus that decided to put my ass in my place. The talk of dialysis was thrown around the drawing board for a few minutes, and then the decision was made to move me into the Intensive Care Unit and run me threw the Goddamn ringer with tests, probes and everything else under the sun.

After about five days of fighting, and I must emphasize on the word FIGHTING to stay alive in the ICU. Between gut changing vomit, and the most toxic shits this side of the Mississippi, not to mention a few accidental shits in the bed and some unholy anal leakage, the diagnosis came back that I had gotten a very rare disease called 'Lemierre's Syndrome.' I was plagued with a blood clot in my jugular vein because of it, and also suffered one clot in my right arm. I had a mild case of pneumonia and sepsis, and the treatment began almost the second the analysis came back. Like I said... I'm addicted to 'The Fight!'

I spent a total of twelve days in the hospital, and was discharged with an IV in my arm and had to inject myself daily with antibiotics, eat Morphine like they were Ritz Crackers to help manage the massive amount of pain I was in (which in all reality) wasn't too much of a punishment, and also take blood thinners to help relieve the blood clot in my neck. The intravenous accordance went on for three weeks after I got out, and the thinners for my crap like blood is still up in the air with a final timeline.

The reason I wrote this little composition titled '48 Hours to The Grave,' is because once I did regain my composure (moderately, of course) the doctor asked, 'Why I waited five days to come into the hospital?' Which, not much to my poorly humorous character, I answered:

"Because my girlfriend made me. I was going to wait until Monday."

And that was when he told me that if I'd had waited those extra two days, there would have been no hope for me... Turns out having a decently high IQ, doesn't mean you're wise when it comes to knowing your health limitations... Another lesson learned the hard way, just the way I 'apparently' like it!

Roses are red
Violets are blue.
I gave you herpes
And now you itch too.

"What do you think about that, Bobby Boy?"

"I think that for a man I just met, and had the pleasure (I guess if I can use that word) to listen to . . . You have to be one of the most profane, perverted, preposterous and prolific people I've ever come in contact with. You should come with a fucking warning label."

"Why thank you, Bob."

"That was very south of a compliment, Ryan."

"Hey, one man's trash is another man's treasure. And one man's pain is another man's pleasure."

"However you chose to justify it."

"Fuck you, Bob."

"Very mature . . . So, I presume this is the point in the story where you tell me all about what you've learned through all these trials and tribulations?"

"You're absolutely fucking correct, Ole' Bob!"

For many long years now I've been battling the strong waves in the alcohol ocean, digging my way out from the avalanche of cocaine, drenched from the pouring rain of ecstasy and painkillers, parting the marijuana clouds, and lighting my way through the darkness of meaningless sex with just the tip of my burning cigarette . . . And I believe it is finally clear now. I've got a SERIOUS PROBLEM with self-control. However, that is not the lesson in which this life has bestowed upon me. The true moral to the story is that through it all, you have to remember to smile. If you're not having fun doing it, then it's just not worth it. And that little lecture can and should be applied to everything you do in life. Have fun with it all, even the horrible times, because in the end . . . None of this crap matters if you didn't have fun. Even your darkest hour is only sixty minutes . . .

I have begun to imagine a world where everyone is gifted, noble, respectful, slightly misunderstood and defined at the same time. I look around this world and I see fighters, better yet . . . I see WARRIORS! I see lovers, I see the heartbroken, the silent and careless youth that want to stand for something, believe in something. Young or old, we're all going to die at some point. So what is it going to all mean when we pass? Well . . . Who the fuck really cares right now? If you can't control the outcome of a set situation, then why attempt to attack the key holder? The higher power, the God, the Devil, the ultimate decider, whatever the fuck you want to call it? Make use of your time, be something, be anything for God sakes. Just don't be the victims. Hold tight to your convictions and stay strongly pursuing your dreams. Explore your desires, express your thoughts, venture the world and take part in some sexual exploits. We are all animals and a child at heart, the only question is—are you ready to acknowledge that fact? We can hurt and we can be hurt. BIG DEAL! We always heal and life as we know it . . . Moves the fuck on . . .

Sure, through this process I think I've recognized the truth that I am still madly in love with Marilyn. However, I'm not even quite sure whom the person is that I love anymore. It's been so long since we've spoken, or even seen each other for that matter. I think I am in love with a very well thought out illusion and trapped in a prison of my own pain. Creating a luminary and a voice for a person that no longer exists. All so I can feel closer to someone who was never mine in the beginning. However, just because the words sound so dire and empty, re- member this. I have hope, and Goddammit I have a little bit of luck. Sure the distance is long between us, but the space cannot remain black and hallow forever. I know one day our paths will cross. And who knows? It could be just the right timing? Or at the very least, she will tell me to fuck off? Both options are a great possibility, and would probably bring a slight sense of closure. And If Marilyn is reading? Which I know she is. I think I have earned the right to explain myself . . .

Dear, Marilyn.

Marilyn, I know I'm fucked up. I am aware. I am completely fucking aware. I am a particularly complicated human whose code is pretty tremendously flawed. I've accepted that fire-burning fact. However, I cannot resist making sure you truly understand just who I am. I comprehend that between the events of the past and all the makings of a cheap summer-of-love flick, that we are not right for each other. Maybe it was that we just shared the same outlandish libidos. Who really knows? This is no longer a moment of clarification. Or even a confession at that. Think of this as more of a look back at your darker days. I find it hard to believe that I was so terrible to you that your only option was to let it all go up in flames. But, I understand where you're coming from. Get out before the water rose too high and you witnessed a meaningless death. I get it. I was no easy pill to swallow. I will admit that. Nevertheless, that does not negate from the legitimacy that what we had was primal and fierce. I loved you then and I love you now. I just hope you can truthfully admit you hear the pain behind my words. Sure, I've moved on and found my chosen path, blah, blah, blah (or at least what I hope is a fucking path) and I'm living my own life. So don't get it twisted, sweetheart.

When I started this novel. I wanted to write something fascinating, entertaining, heartfelt, painful, erotic, charming, sad, ego jolting and inspiring. I wanted to write a book that would hold true to a generation, a time of fun and joy, a moment in someone's shoes. I wanted it to be beautiful, dark, unrivaled and also easily forgotten. Further more, I just wanted to make some money to buy lots of alcohol in the hopes of forgetting you forever. I did admit to some very obsessively crazy acts committed on behalf of missing and longing for you, which, lets face it; is just borderline insane. But what can I say? I really missed you there for a little while. I guess I always thought I would've died in some blaze of glory. But, I'm getting off track . . .

What I'm really trying to say is, despite all the things I was attempting to accomplish with this novel, I can now see its nothing like I wanted or even close to what I strived for. It's become just a lengthy back-and-fourth schizophrenic argument over how I lost the only woman that ever understood me. I let her walk away because my ego was too much to contain. As the words pour out of me, I can honestly say. I don't give a fuck what is to become of this novel, this book, this Goddamn confession of heartache and grief. I really just wanted you to know my story. Just in case we never get the chance again. I wanted you to see that I poured my heart and soul into something that I'm genuinely proud of, and it's all because I met you.

I don't really give a fuck about the chapters about my father. That piece-of-shit never deserved the family he was graced with. All the pain, the sorrow, the emptiness that was left after him; will never compare to the vacant feeling I was left with after losing you. I went through so many years just hoping to run into you and have one more conversation, one more hug, one more encounter. I'm not even sure what I would say if I did see you, I just wanted the fucking opportunity. I guess what my conclusion is; letting you go was the best inspiration I've ever had the bitter pleasure to experience. You gave me the creative influence to pursue my dreams and hopefully make something out of myself. For that, I wanted to say thank you. I wanted to speak true for a minute. And just tell a good-ole'-fashioned story of a boy that loves a girl.

I realize the fact that if anything ever does become of my words, any chance of winning you back is pretty much thrown out of the fucking ten-story window. Plus, I'm sure you've heard it all before. The weak and childlike attempts to win you back. The candid excuses of how the men you've dated have changed. How they can promise you the world, yada, yada, yada, and all the other bullshit that goes along with it. So, I will save you the pathetic tries. My only wish is for you find the happiness you crave and the love you deserve. Stay kind and stay young. You are the most beautiful 'Muse' this world has ever seen.

People see me smiling all the time and assume I'm always happy. Or they watch me get angry and assume I'm an easily aggravated person. Or just because I sleep around, that I'm trying to bed the world and be some selfish hustler and fulfill my need to inflate my overblown self-esteem. But you, you're the only woman who has actually seen me for who I really am. You took the time to find out and uncover the truth. That is why losing you will forever remain as one of the most heartbreaking times in this crazy little thing called life.

Well . . . That's my piece. This will hopefully be the last love letter I ever write for you (unless I get blackout drunk and email you) which, in that case—I should probably just say sorry now. If this book goes on to bomb and I fail dramatically. At least I got to tell you one last time that I deeply, deeply love you.

— Please don't ever forget me.

I love you, Marilyn.

I have found that a big portion of my life has been devoted to over thinking just what I will be after all the rage I hold inside is gone. And honestly, I still have not yet uncovered that answer. But day-by-day I keep searching, and I'm sure I will eventually get my answer. But, until then, I try to keep things simple these days. "Drink like a Rockstar. Fuck like a Pornstar. Live like a God. And die Immortalized." Just one of the many virtues I've created and live by. The reason being, is because now I finally recognize that I have been living behind these tall bricks, drinking in the pain of all the wrong, and in the end have had nothing but misery and suffering. Which, to be completely frank, has become very fucking boring! I'm over it. I'm breaking down these walls and allowing myself to feel once more. Why? Because fuck it, that's why . . . I may have been traveling in a mysterious and perverse fairytale, but at least it was my fairytale. And I have had fun in this fallen circus. It's been a villainous freakshow, but I wouldn't have it any other way. If I had to put a movie title to define my life, I think the most suiting one would be 'Flashbacks of A Fool.'

"I have a question for you, Ryan?"

"What's that, Bob?"

"Where do you go from here?"

"How so—?"

"—What's next on the list for you? What do you wish to feel again?"

"Are you asking me if now I will be pursuing some movie-like, deep and intimate love from another human to help save me from myself?"

"Those are your words, but ultimately—yes. That is what I'm asking?"

"You see, Bob . . . It's never been about finding someone to help save me from myself. I've always just wanted to be left alone so I can continue with my self-destructive lifestyle and kill myself with a little bit of pride left."

"Is that still how you feel?"

"Mostly on Monday's . . ." Ryan smirks as he answers.

"Then what is the main objective that demands your attention while you travel through life?"

Like I said, I'm keeping it simple. Live Fast, Die Young, and Leave a Good Looking Tattooed Corpse. And, with just a tiny bit of baleful hope and eternal reliance, live just long enough to see how "Ray Donavan" finally comes to a spectacular end. I fucking love that show, Bob."

"Do you feel you are achieving that, Ryan?"

"I think for the most part I am, Bob . . . I really think I am."

"So what now?"

"Well . . . With the song 'Backyard,' by 'Of Monsters And Men,' playing loud in the background, it is time for me to close these tired eyes and move on . . . Goodbye world, it has been fun. See ya on the other side, Bob . . ."

His bloodstream was running wicked with whiskey
His lost mind ran dirty with delicious dominance
His heart raced fast with fluttered fabrications
His cock was wrapped with wild women
He was the neglected nightmare
The longing and loathing loser
The tainted & teased tornado
He smoked simple solitude
Pissing polluted poison
Fantastically he fell
And never did
He return.
Fuck!

That's it ladies and gentlemen. That is the story of how I found this man in the park and listened to his entire story (while choking down vomit at some points) before I watched him die before me . . . With a dead man on my couch, I think I have earned the right to go have a drink. I am heading down to the local pub and will return to clean up this thorny mess. Before I make my way out of the door, I have one more piece of his to share. I found a poem tucked away inside Ryan's pocket, it was grubby in spilt liquor, snot stains and what looked possibly to be semen upon the note. The paper was ravaged in several cigarette burns and suffered from some major ripped edges, but I managed to salvage it for all to hear. And it reads like this:

RYAN VINCI

Dear, World.

Fake smiles to warm your heart
While I fuck your sister and make her smell my fart.
Most days I live in downright danger
It's probably because I was touched by a stranger.

I'll treat your daughter nice and give her a smoochie
But at the end of the night I'm gonna taste her coochie.
I'm at the community college looking for sexy coeds to raid their lockers
Just hoping to find a picture of their teenage knockers.

I know I'm sick, I know I'm twisted
I'm just a pervert who stays unlisted.
I want to fuck you on the bed and fuck on the floor
Knock, knock . . . Now I'm in your backdoor.

Curse my name as you insult my lifestyle of slum
Moments later I'll have you soaked in my cum.
Maybe I am a little fucking insane
Because I want to bend you over and spank you with a cane.

It's been a joy. It's been a gas
Now I want the whole world to kiss my broke ass.
Your overbearing approval has never been my desire
So I'll light a match and set this book on fire.

My words may have fallen short of being properly poetic
But you cannot deny I'm somewhat magnetic.
Once, twice, three times a beast
This is my touching confession, however I'm also the priest.

I'm playing leapfrog
On a jog
While I inhale the smog
And got my dick deep in a hog.

Kiss me goodbye for this is my grandiose farewell
I'll see all you rotten bastards in the depths of hell.

— Love, Ryan Anthony Michael Vinci.

As I sat amongst the drunks and deviants, I couldn't help but think about Ryan, and all the stories he confessed to me in absolute confidence just hoping that I would take the time to share his story—if we can call it that. There was no doubt that he was a lowlife, no question there . . . But I wasn't sure if the kid really knew what he wanted out of life, or if he just teetered on the edge of alcohol wasted and drug influenced reality, not truly understanding the potential of his dark mind. Was he always so hapless or did time bring him to such a cynical outlook? Was he even actually cynical or was it all a theatric play? Did he really believe in his downfall or merely kneel down for the raping like a powerless victim? Was he truly a victim or did he just suffer from jealousy about the circumstances of others? Did he ever think about others? Not so much saying he was a heartless narcissist, but just more of a person who doesn't really seem to hold much value of himself or anything that's essentially good in this world. Maybe he felt he didn't deserve happiness? Or wasn't in the right importance of life to justify happiness? Or maybe he was just so damn wildly blind that he didn't recognize happiness as it slapped him across his dumb face? Did I come across some devilish spawn, or perhaps a fallen angel? Who was this person, and why, why I ask you, did he cross paths with me?

Now I had questions and I began to feel almost engrossed in rage that he left this world so early without giving me the answers that I believe I so rightfully earned. If that SOB wasn't dead, well . . . Now, now I just wanted to ring him by his blood clotted neck and get my fucking answers! I found myself lost in deep thought over this boy, and could not seem to formulate an appropriate answer to what it was I just witnessed (or suffered through) while watching him drink himself into the grave. And then I was shaken out of my confusing daze by one of the local patrons at my pub named, 'Saint Sasha.' She was given that name in a joking platform for her almost uncanny ability to go on perplexing and sometimes belligerent rants over the most simple of conversations.

"What's wrong, _____? You look as if you've just seen a damn ghost." Saint Sasha asked.

"With all due respect, Sasha, I'm not really in the mood to go back—&—forth with you tonight."

"Suit yourself, _____. I was just wondering how you managed to let things slip away because of the influence of some stranger?" Sasha stabbed.

"What the fuck did you just say, Saint Sasha?"

"I find myself troubled in the idea that some boy you barely know, or even remotely care about for that matter, could take you away from the habitual injudicious monster you typically portray and accomplish?" The lackluster Saint asked.

"—Sorry, Sash, you're confusing me yet again . . . Is this going to be some overly complex story of some dull bullshit like another parking ticket or juice bars?"

"Have you ever heard the fable of 'The Patient bullet,' _____?" Sasha asked.

"I can't say that I have, but I'm almost fully certain you're going to tell me?" I replied with a snarky tone.

"In 1893, a man named Henry Ziegland left his lover for reasons unknown, and because of the breakup, his lover was left jolted by the traumatic incident and found no other form for her unholy pain but suicide. So, as legend has it, one lonely night she decided to take her own life by a gunshot to the head. Her brother could not cope with the unexpected death of his sister and became bloodthirsty-enraged with vengeance. He set off to take karmic justice into his own hands and hunted down Henry. Finding Ziegland, he shot at him and down to the earth's surface Henry fell. Thinking that he had achieved justice for his lonesome sister, the brother then left and went home, only to take his own life (ironically mind you) by a gunshot to the head. However, Henry did not die on that fateful day, but survived because the bullet had grazed his face and was then buried into the tree standing behind him. Some twenty years later, Henry

Ziegland, decided to chop down the enormous tree, and with axe in hand, he started to hack and slice in the hopes of removing this colossal creature from his property. Quickly becoming inpatient, Henry found himself making no progress with the simple task of removing the tree so he resorted to the effortless and unimaginative ease of friendly dynamite. Packing the base of the tree with enough dynamite to blowup 'Jack's beanstalk,' he was now ready for action. With the painless press of a button, the dynamite was ignited and the explosion went off without a hitch . . . BOOM!!! . . . However, when the tree exploded, it also set free the vindicated bullet that was lodged inside some twenty years back and sent it catapulting out like a rocket ship from the Angel of Death . . . And where did the bullet end up? Right between the eyes of Henry Ziegland himself, killing him on impact and correcting the scales of karmic honesty." Sasha so uninvitingly finished.

. . .Very confused, I had no choice but to get to the bottom of this phenomenal wormhole with Saint Sasha.

"So the moral to your story is that eventually everybody get's what they deserve?" I obviously answered Sasha.

"No. The moral to the story is that if you're not willing to put in all your sweat, all your tears and all your blood into altering something in your life, then you are not worthy of change in the first place. Without the hard work of fighting for something you truly want altered in life, then you are not only deserving of whatever the outcome may be, but you are also to blame for the savage misfortune which has been bestowed upon you." Saint Sasha replied.

I was now beyond confused with her recent gain in a 'somewhat understandable' wisdom (seeing as how most encounters with Sasha end in some drunken, ill-mannered, self-delusional vortex of anger and bitterness) and I thought to myself, "maybe this crazy old witch actually knows something complex and meaningful? Why not dig a little deeper into this rabbit hole," I asked myself.

"What exactly is it that you're trying to say here, Sasha?" I had no choice but to ask.

"Come on, _____ . . . You know just what I'm referring to. Don't you find it rather odd that on the day that marks the seventh year anniversary of your wife's death, the day that you claimed as your last breathing day on this earth, that you would save a man's life on the same day you sketch the drawing to end your own?" Saint Sasha convolutedly replied.

"What in God's Holy Fuck are really talking about? Is there a piece to this crazed puzzle I'm missing?" I answered with a harsh tone.

I saw Saint Sasha rub her face with an intensely baffling alcoholic scratch, almost scalping her hair off in the process as she so perplexingly found herself just about lost in her seat for a slight moment. And then, she looked back to me once more, but this time her eyes were glazed over and deathly white and that momentary and rare sense of remarkable knowledge was quickly stripped and detached.

"I don't know, man . . . I think I've had too much vodka. What were we talking about again?" Sasha dizzily asked.

"Never mind, just forget it." I replied.

In war, we found solitude.
Through peace, we sought destruction.
Why did we have to lose ourselves
To see each other?

Knowing that I have most certainly stayed up very, very late, and completely peaked out on my allotted amount of whiskey cocktails and ambiguous, self-manifested, hazy-holy lexis of Saint Sasha's failing mind, it was now time for me to head home and hopefully formulate a plan of attack to disposing of Ryan's body. As I drunkenly walked down the vast and empty streets on a late night, I wasn't sure if the lights that lit the road ahead were friend or foe. I couldn't understand that if the words spoken by Saint Sasha (maybe) came from a place of compelling insight, or if I just lived through yet another one of her pathetic and thoughtless rants of complete disconnected reason?

For once, it truly was hard to tell. I didn't keep my mind to tight on her easily forgotten interaction, because, after all . . . I had a much bigger problem at hand that was in desperate need of solving. As I came to my front door, I felt my heartbeat race as my blood began to pump with toxic elixir. The salivation in my mouth was thick and my mind was in full swing as I inserted the key, unlocked and opened the door. The floor creaked in a vaporous pitch as I slowly made my way inside and turned the corner to the couch where I knew Ryan was laying . . .

However, what I saw was nothing short of a 'Tarantino Miracle.' Ryan was sitting up on the couch. He was clean shaved, showered, and well-dressed (in some threads of mine) which he apparently helped himself to, and once again drinking Sailor Jerry Rum. He had the music playing thunderously in the room, and the song was 'Highway to Hell,' by ACDC.

"I . . . I . . . I . . ." I began to speak . . .

"—Welcome home, 'Memphis' . . ." Ryan promptly interrupted me.

I felt a sudden dash of some supernatural, ghostly terror wash over me as I was thrown back into my body with a fast and hardened haunting reality check, which felt as if it was launched from a mischievous sprite-like slingshot to my soul.

"—What . . . What . . . WHAT ARE YOU DOING ALIVE?" I asked with a dumbfounding gaze upon my surprised face.

"—Alive?" Ryan shook his head as he confusingly answered.

"Wait . . . Did you just call me Memphis?" I pointed at him.

"Well, that's your name, isn't it?"

"Yes. Yes, it is my name. You've been resorting to 'Bob' since I met you." I retorted.

"Now that's just dumb. That's not your name. Your name is Memphis. In Latin means beautiful and enduring."

"That is correct . . . Let's backseat the whole name debacle here for a minute—I don't understand what's going on here? Are you really alive or am I hallucinating from all the whiskey? This has to be just a strange and unusual dream."

"Memphis, I am very much alive, and boy, oh boy, do I feel fucking great!"

"But you were dead when I left you! I saw it with my own two eyes. You were most certainly fucking dead, Ryan! I would bet my life on it." I replied with a huge rise in volume.

"Maybe dead inside, Memphis, but far from Goddamn dead!"

"This is some kind of sick and twisted joke." I replied as I started to feel woozy and sick inside. "I think I have to sit down, I'm not feeling so well."

I slowly made my way over to the recliner chair in my living room and took a well-needed and loud plop down to my undercarriage to help reduce my queasiness. My world was spinning as I found myself in a heavily complicated shock and bewilderment . . .

Ryan then stood and made his way to the dining room table, fixed himself another Sailor Jerry cocktail, lit a cigarette and stood before me. However, as I stared up at him with a very (and I mean very) speechless gawk, or better yet, motionless astound . . . What I saw was extraordinarily different. What once before was a dark, unpromising, ominous and satanic aura that surrounded him, was now replaced with a vague light. Nothing close to a Godly light, it was far from that—but more of a now optimistic and almost glowing atmosphere of hopefulness, or an impulsive will to survive. He, for the first time since I met him, looked as if he actually stood an honest chance in this fucked up world. The boy looked dazzlingly to say the least. I couldn't believe my eyes. I started to think to myself, "Maybe I drank too much. Maybe this was all just a highly structured sham and I was imaging it."

"You're not imaging it, Memphis. What you're seeing is all too real, my friend." Ryan answered, throwing me into a telepathic standstill.

. . . I took both my hands and viciously rubbed my eyes in the hopes that when I removed them all this madness would magically disappear and I would find that this was merely a distorted vision from my lifelong-beaten mind. But, as I pulled my hands from my face . . . There he stood.

"How is this possible?" I openly asked with nothing but chaos fluttering around the inner makings of my psyche.

"Well, you see, Mister Memphis . . . I had lost all hope, and to be completely honest—wasn't going to find it again. So, I set out on a debaucherous course of devastation to meet my maker, so to speak. I somehow, in my senseless reason, thought that I had nothing more to look forward to in this assfucked world that surrounds us. And I truly did believe that . . . That was until I read this!" Ryan said as he threw down the suicide note that I had written just hours before I met him. "It was because I found this note, that I found I did have something to look forward to." He finished as I gazed upon him in the most utterly stunned mindset know to man.

"I'm sorry, but that doesn't make any fucking sense at all. That note is a pitiful and distressed cry for the end. I wrote that in sheer desperation for the longing of my dead wife. I wrote that because I'm not strong enough to face this world without her. So how could my lowest moment, be your moment of salvation and recovery?" I tore back with bitter fury and rage.

"Don't you see, Memphis? You wrote this note because you lost the one person that you truly loved. The one person you loved more than your material possessions, more than your social bronze, more than your stories and most importantly, more than yourself. You lost everything, Memphis." He replied with a tear in his eye.

"I may be out of line here, but how does my shattering demise even remotely constitute a positive upswing to your dark life?" I asked.

Ryan SLAMMED his hand down on the coffee table with some self-gained refuge, commanding my attention and rightfully earning it!

"Don't you fucking get it, Memphis?! You had everything you ever desired, and it was RIPPED away from you! And nobody can blame you for deciding to take your own way out. Nor do you fucking owe this world any kind of explanation for your pain and suffering. You don't owe these people A GODDAMN THING! I know now, that what I felt was nothing even slightly compared to what it is you're feeling. You saved my life, Memphis! You have opened my eyes, and now I finally can see. You devoted your life to this person, and from the note, this was no façade in the wind. You found me on what was to be my last day, but instead, it was really meant to be yours." Ryan spoke with a glorious rage.

In the past seven years that I have been without my loving wife, I for a quick moment, found another human being that justly understood my ever so misunderstood stance. I found connection . . . I found peace.

"What do you plan to do from here, Ryan?" I asked.

"Well, the diabolical plan has not yet been sketched out by the heavens above, but I will tell you this . . . I hope to find what it was that you had. Lord knows I could use it. I've done more than my fair share of a biblical giants handful of drugs, and been with some of the most enchanting of women. I've live through the party, and actually saw some light at the end of the tunnel. I guess now there's nothing more to do but find my own peace amongst the chaos."

"That's all we can do, right?" I asked.

"Indeed, my friend. Indeed."

For a shared silent moment, we both sat and stared at one another. I could see something different in Ryan's eyes. I could feel something different. This man was ready for change and willing to fight for it!

"So where do you begin in your new journey of control, Ryan?" I questioned.

"That's just it, Memphis. My whole life has been an exercise of control. Either I've been on the abusive receiving end of it, or I've been the one abusing it. Now I can ultimately see, control is nothing but an ill and perverse delusion for the weak and predatory types. You can't control the outcome, no matter how bad you wish, or trust, or practice or pray. Control is never ours to begin with. The universe has its design, and you just better hope you fit in. I say, may we give up control, may we stop trying to dilute the universes plan that was written many years ago. This life is a rollercoaster, a mythical journey through madness, sin, passion, pleasure and pain. Sit down, find your bliss, hold on tight, and enjoy the fucking ride . . . And as you finally give up the deception of control. Remember to have fun and take fucking notes."

"That is one very out-of-the-ordinary way to look at life, my friend." I replied. "Do you have a plan of action, or a beginning point to this pristine life of unanswered questions and moments of tough times lightly salted with good?" I finished with intrigue.

. . . Ryan then stood once more, headed back to the table for another cocktail and smoke. He lit his cigarette and meandered over to my record collection. I sat in silence, hanging on a toasty burnt thread as I awaited his response. I watched as he pulled a record from my extensive album assemblage and loaded it onto the turntable. As the needle hit the spinning record, I heard the music rain in heavily loud deed through the speakers. 'Stairway to Heaven,' performed live by none other than "Led Zeppelin" themselves. Ryan then turned to me with smoke in mouth and cocktail in hand, took a drag and removed the cigarette.

"I believe I finally do have a action plan to this grave life—and as far as the unanswered questions go? Now I can see why they went unanswered for so very long . . . That was because I was asking the wrong fucking ones. When my life fell on dark times, I always asked 'Why me?' but now, as I'm sure I will fall into darkness once again at some point, I just ask, 'Try me?' You see, Memphis, if you change the perspective, then much of the purpose also follows the change. When I used to ask, 'What do you drive?' I never got the answer I longed for. Now I ask, 'What are you driven by?' In this life of ours, we will all fall in absolute pain, we all experience heartbreak, and we will all become the broken souls that we never wanted to be. And before long, we let that same pain control us and make us see that only the evil and careless seem to have the most fun. Thus, we begin to follow in the same footsteps, and act with the same heartless manner. Forward we move as a shattered street of throbbing ache is left smoldering behind us. Then time begins to pass, and actions become more and more volatile as the level of evil we are willing to partake in becomes worse and worse. Degenerates and perverts we become as less of life seems to matter and pussy, drugs, alcohol and money overweighs anything profound, individual or realistic. And as that very time passes us, we once in a little while look in the mirror. However, what we see starts to make us sick to the core of our stomachs. So more distorted and perverted we live, and much more numb we have to make ourselves to help cope with this newfound sense of self-loathing, death wishing, worthless souls we now are. That same time becomes nothing but an enemy, until the day finally comes that we look our self in the mirror and we can't stand what the fuck it is we are. And with a hard and passionate punch to the glass which projects our meaningless image, the blood from our devastated knuckles is the only thing that reminds us that we are still on the path that ends the same as everyone else. That we bleed, we ache, and we die! Without purpose, Memphis, everything in life can be hallow and vein. The only question is, will you find a purpose before it is too late?" Ryan finished as he took a gulp of his drink.

I am not a smoker by any means, but after I sat in speechless gaze, I had no choice but to light up one of his smokes after his statement of overwhelming prospect to life. 'This kid might be onto something,' I thought to myself, and just then, the finishing Rock 'n' Roll solo kicked in to one of the greatest songs ever written, and Ryan set his drink down and walked towards the door. As he opened the door for exit, I felt I needed just one more answer ...

"—Wait," I said as I stood from my chair to catch him before he exited. "With all the dark, dirty and rotten times this life has served you, how can you possibly go back out there with such ease and peace of mind? What do you have to say to this world to get you through the day? I have to know just how you smile when all hope seems to violently crash down around you? Ryan, what do you have to tell this world?" I asked with sheer curiosity.

... Ryan turned to me with a happy smile on his face and what looked to be faith in his eye. And what I saw was just shy of something holistic in the most sinister sense. Was he wicked, or was he clean? All I knew was, the man I looked upon had more than enough bad happen to him to give up and call it quits, but yet he kept on pursuing. Why? Why did he keep on? I had to know ...

"Memphis, I wake up everyday, look this beautiful fucking world right in its pretty little face. This world, which has caused me more pain then I ever imagined, and caused me to become a person I never wanted to ever be ... And I ask it this ..."

IS THAT REALLY THE BEST YOU FUCKING GOT?!

To the one badass motherfucker that has stood by me through all the bullshit. We laughed together—we cried together . . . This one is for you, brother! I love you . . . Never let the animal inside die!

"Until the fucking wheels fall off!"